"Watts's dark, suspenseful, nightmarish vision of intelligent life in a hostile universe is remorseless in its outlook and unflinching in its conclusions."

—*SF Site* (Chosen as One of the 10 Best of 2006)

"Extremely thought-provoking, taking its premise to the ultimate conclusion, showing that the alien without might be closely related to the alien within."

—*Interzone*

"A first-contact novel notable for the utter remorselessness of its commitment to its central premise."

—*Vector*

"A fascinating first-contact tale. This is a provocative exploration of the nature of human consciousness and what it means to be human."

—*Romantic Times BOOKreviews*

"The genius of *Blindsight* is that its author has been clever enough to build a story that demonstrates [his] case. . . . Much of the narrative pleasure of *Blindsight* comes from a conjoined experience of doubled discovery: as we gradually get to understand the nature of the crew . . . we find ourselves simultaneously beginning to get some sense of the alien species orbiting Ben in something . . . that Watts describes in terms that evoked, for me, some great, granulated, anfractuous rat king of shrikes multiplied a thousandfold from the simple single shrike out of Dan Simmons's *Hyperion,* which so goosed my midbrain. . . . It is a sign of the pervasive toughness of *Blindsight* that its human readers can take pleasure in [the] message, because what the scramblers say to us in the end is, 'Shut up.'"

—*The New York Review of Science Fiction*

"Edgy, humorous, and heartbreaking by turns, *Blindsight* is jargon-rich and dense with information. At times it is difficult to keep up with the tightly packed ideas that pour from its every page. Once it has its reader hooked, however, this book becomes impossible to put down. . . . *Blindsight* is a real tour de force."
—*SF Weekly*

"Watts explores the nature of consciousness in this stimulating hard SF novel, which combines riveting action with a fascinating alien environment. . . . Watts puts a terrifying and original spin on the familiar alien-contact story."
—*Publishers Weekly* (starred review)

"The author's view of space travel is just as compelling as the pressure-haunted diseased landscape he painted earlier. Once again, the darkness is waiting: either as a hiding place, or as a threat."
—*Starlog*

"Watts continues to challenge readers with his imaginative plots and superb storytelling."
—*Library Journal*

"Watts packs in enough tantalizing ideas for a score of novels while spinning new twists on every cutting-edge genre motif from virtual reality to extraterrestrial biology. Watts' fifth, finest, most fascinating book."
—*Booklist*

"*Blindsight* is a terrific piece of new hard SF . . . a hard SF novel that won't let you go, and a bombardment of ideas that you won't be able to let go of once they've wormed their viral way into your meaty little brain."
—*SFRevu*

BLINDSIGHT

TOR BOOKS BY PETER WATTS

Starfish
Maelstrom
ßehemoth: ß-Max
ßehemoth: Seppuku
Blindsight

BLINDSIGHT

PETER WATTS

A TOM DOHERTY ASSOCIATES BOOK   TOR®   NEW YORK

This is a work of fiction. All of the characters, organizations, and events portrayed in this
novel are either products of the author's imagination or are used fictitiously.

BLINDSIGHT

Copyright © 2006 by Peter Watts

A Tor Book
Published by Tom Doherty Associates, LLC
175 Fifth Avenue
New York, NY 10010

www.tor.com

Tor® is a registered trademark of Tom Doherty Associates, LLC.

Library of Congress Cataloging-in-Publication Data

Watts, Peter, 1958–
    Blindsight / Peter Watts.
        p. cm.
    "A Tom Doherty Associates book."
    ISBN-13: 978-0-7653-1964-7
    ISBN-10: 0-7653-1964-0
    1. Life on other planets—Fiction. I. Title.

PR9199.3.W386B58 2006
813'.6—dc22

                                                        2006005917

Printed in the United States of America

0 9 8 7 6 5 4 3 2

FOR LISA

If we're not in pain, we're not alive.

THIS IS WHAT FASCINATES ME MOST IN EXISTENCE: THE
PECULIAR NECESSITY OF IMAGINING WHAT IS, IN FACT,
REAL.

—PHILIP GOUREVITCH

YOU WILL DIE LIKE A DOG FOR NO GOOD REASON.

—ERNEST HEMINGWAY

CONTENTS

BLINDSIGHT

PROLOGUE

TRY TO TOUCH THE PAST. TRY TO DEAL WITH THE PAST.
IT'S NOT REAL. IT'S JUST A DREAM.

—TED BUNDY

IT DIDN'T START out here. Not with the scramblers or *Rorschach,* not with Big Ben or *Theseus* or the vampires. Most people would say it started with the Fireflies, but they'd be wrong. It *ended* with all those things.

For me, it began with Robert Paglino.

At the age of eight, he was my best and only friend. We were fellow outcasts, bound by complementary misfortune. Mine was developmental. His was genetic: an uncontrolled genotype that left him predisposed to nearsightedness, acne, and (as it later turned out) a susceptibility to narcotics. His parents had never had him optimized. Those few TwenCen relics who still believed in God also held that one shouldn't try to improve upon His handiwork. So although both of us *could* have been repaired, only one of us *had* been.

I arrived at the playground to find Pag the center of attention for some half-dozen kids, those lucky few in front punching him in the head, the others making do with taunts of *mongrel* and *polly* while waiting their turn. I watched him raise his arms, almost hesitantly, to ward off the worst of the blows. I could see into his head better than my own; he was scared that his attackers might think those hands were coming up to hit *back,* that they'd read it as an act of defiance and hurt him even more. Even then, at the tender age of eight and with half my mind gone, I was becoming a superlative observer.

But I didn't know what to do.

I hadn't seen much of Pag lately. I was pretty sure he'd been avoiding me. Still, when your best friend's in trouble you help out, right? Even if the odds are impossible—and how many eight-year-olds would go up against six bigger kids for a sandbox buddy?—at least you call for backup. Flag a sentry. *Something.*

I just stood there. I didn't even especially *want* to help him.

That didn't make sense. Even if he hadn't been my best friend, I should at least have empathized. I'd suffered less than Pag in the way of overt violence; my seizures tended to keep the other kids at a distance, scared *them* even as they incapacitated *me.* Still. I was no stranger to the taunts and insults, or the foot that appears from nowhere to trip you up en route from A to B. I knew how that felt.

Or I had, once.

But that part of me had been cut out along with the bad wiring. I was still working up the algorithms to get it back, still learning by observation. Pack animals always tear apart the weaklings in their midst. Every child knows that much instinctively. Maybe I should just let that process unfold, maybe I shouldn't try to mess with nature. Then again, Pag's parents hadn't messed with nature, and look what it got them: a son curled up in the dirt while a bunch of engineered superboys kicked in his ribs.

In the end, propaganda worked where empathy failed. Back then I didn't so much think as observe, didn't deduce so much as *remember*—and what I remembered was a thousand inspirational stories lauding anyone who ever stuck up for the underdog.

So I picked up a rock the size of my fist and hit two of Pag's assailants across the backs of their heads before anyone even knew I was in the game.

A third, turning to face the new threat, took a blow to the face that audibly crunched the bones of his cheek. I remember wondering why I didn't take any satisfaction from that sound, why it meant nothing beyond the fact I had one less opponent to worry about.

The rest of them ran at the sight of blood. One of the braver promised me I was dead, shouted *"Fucking zombie!"* over his shoulder as he disappeared around the corner.

Three decades it took, to see the irony in that remark.

Two of the enemy twitched at my feet. I kicked one in the head until it stopped moving, turned to the other. Something grabbed my arm and I swung without thinking, without *looking* until Pag yelped and ducked out of reach.

"Oh," I said. "Sorry."

One thing lay motionless. The other moaned and held its head and curled up in a ball.

"Oh *shit*," Pag panted. Blood coursed unheeded from his nose and splattered down his shirt. His cheek was turning blue and yellow. "Oh *shit* oh shit oh *shit* . . ."

I thought of something to say. "You all right?"

"Oh *shit,* you— I mean, you *never* . . ." He wiped his mouth. Blood smeared the back of his hand. "Oh *man,* are we in trouble."

"They started it."

"Yeah, but you— I mean, *look* at them!"

The moaning thing was crawling away on all fours. I wondered how long it would be before it found reinforcements. I wondered if I should kill it before then.

"You'da *never* done that before," Pag said.

Before the operation, he meant.

I actually did feel something then—faint, distant, but unmistakable. I felt angry. "They *started*—"

Pag backed away, eyes wide. "What are you *doing*? Put that down!"

I'd raised my fists. I didn't remember doing that. I unclenched them. It took a while. I had to look at my hands very hard for a long, long time.

The rock dropped to the ground, blood-slick and glistening.

"I was trying to help." I didn't understand why he couldn't *see* that.

"You're, you're not the same," Pag said from a safe distance. "You're not even *Siri* anymore."

"I am too. Don't be a fuckwad."

"They cut out your brain!"

"Only half. For the ep—"

"I *know*, for the epilepsy! You think I don't know? But you were *in* that half—or, like, *part* of you was . . ." He struggled with the words, with the concept behind them. "And now you're *different*. It's like, your mom and dad *murdered* you—"

"My mom and dad," I said, suddenly quiet, "saved my life. I would have *died*."

"I think you *did* die," said my best and only friend. "I think Siri died, they scooped him out and threw him away and you're some whole other kid that just, just *grew back* out of what was left. You're not the *same*. Ever since. You're not the *same*."

I still don't know if Pag really knew what he was saying. Maybe his mother had just pulled the plug on whatever game he'd been wired into for the previous eighteen hours, forced him outside for some fresh air. Maybe, after fighting pod people in gamespace, he couldn't help but see them everywhere. Maybe.

But you could make a case for what he said. I do remember Helen telling me (and *telling* me) how difficult it was to adjust. *Like you had a whole new personality,* she said. And why not? There's a reason they call it *radical* hemispherectomy: half the brain thrown out with yesterday's krill, the remaining half press-ganged into double duty. Think of all the rewiring that one lonely hemisphere must have struggled with as it tried to take up the slack. It turned out okay, obviously. The brain's a very flexible piece of meat; it took some doing, but it adapted. *I* adapted. Still. Think of all that must have been squeezed out, deformed, *reshaped* by the time the renovations were through. You could argue that I'm a different person than the one who used to occupy this body.

The grown-ups showed up eventually, of course. Medicine was bestowed, ambulances called. Parents were outraged, diplomatic volleys exchanged, but it's tough to drum up neighborhood outrage on behalf of your injured baby when playground surveillance from three angles shows the little darling—and five of his buddies—kicking in the ribs of a disabled boy. My mother, for her part, recycled the usual complaints about problem children and absentee fathers—Dad was off again in some other hemisphere—but the dust settled pretty quickly. Pag and I even stayed friends, after a short hiatus that reminded us both of the limited social prospects open to schoolyard rejects who don't stick together.

So I survived that and a million other childhood experiences. I grew up and I got along. I learned to fit in. I observed, recorded, derived the algorithms and mimicked appropriate behaviors. Not much of it was . . . *heartfelt,* I guess the word is. I had friends and enemies, like everyone else. I chose them by running through checklists of behaviors and circumstances compiled from years of observation.

I may have grown up distant but I grew up *objective,* and I have Robert Paglino to thank for that. His seminal observation set everything in motion. It led me into Synthesis, fated me to our disastrous encounter with the scramblers, spared me the worse fate befalling Earth. Or the better one, I suppose, depending on your point of view. Point of view *matters*: I see that now, blind, talking to myself, trapped in a coffin falling past the edge of the solar system. I see it for the first time since some beaten bloody friend on a childhood battlefield convinced me to throw my own point of view away.

He may have been wrong. *I* may have been. But that, that *distance*—that chronic sense of being an alien among your own kind—it's not entirely a bad thing.

It came in especially handy when the real aliens came calling.

THESEUS

BLOOD MAKES NOISE.

—SUZANNE VEGA

IMAGINE YOU ARE Siri Keeton.

You wake in an agony of resurrection, gasping after a record-shattering bout of sleep apnea spanning one hundred forty days. You can feel your blood, syrupy with dobutamine and leuenkephalin, forcing its way through arteries shriveled by months on standby. The body inflates in painful increments: blood vessels dilate, flesh peels apart from flesh, ribs crack in your ears with sudden unaccustomed flexion. Your joints have seized up through disuse. You're a stick man, frozen in some perverse *rigor vitae*.

You'd scream if you had the breath.

Vampires did this all the time, you remember. It was *normal* for them, it was their own unique take on resource conservation. They could have taught your kind a few things about restraint, if that absurd aversion to right angles hadn't done them in at the dawn of civilization. Maybe they still can. They're back now, after all—raised from the grave with the voodoo of paleogenetics, stitched together from junk genes and fossil marrow steeped in the blood of sociopaths and high-functioning autistics. One of them commands this very mission. A handful of his genes live on in your own body so it too can rise from the dead, here at the edge of interstellar space. Nobody gets past Jupiter without becoming part vampire.

The pain begins, just slightly, to recede. You fire up your inlays and access your own vitals. It'll be long minutes before your body responds fully to motor commands, hours before it stops hurting. The pain's an unavoidable side effect. That's just what happens when you splice vampire subroutines into Human code. You asked about painkillers once, but nerve blocks of any kind *compromise metabolic reactivation*. Suck it up, soldier.

You wonder if this was how it felt for Chelsea, before the end. But that evokes a whole other kind of pain, so you block it out and concentrate on the life pushing its way back into your extremities. Suffering in silence, you check the logs for fresh telemetry.

You think: *That can't be right.*

Because if it is, you're in the wrong part of the universe. You're not in the Kuiper Belt where you belong: you're high above the ecliptic and deep into the Oort, the realm of long-period comets that only grace the sun every million years or so. You've gone *interstellar*, which means (you bring up the system clock) you've been undead for eighteen hundred days.

You've overslept by almost five years.

The lid of your coffin slides away. Your own cadaverous body reflects from the mirrored bulkhead opposite, a desiccated lungfish waiting for the rains. Bladders of isotonic saline cling to its limbs like engorged antiparasites, like the opposite of leeches. You remember the needles going in just before you shut down, way back when your veins were more than dry twisted filaments of beef jerky.

Szpindel's reflection stares back from his own pod to your immediate right. His face is as bloodless and skeletal as yours. His wide sunken eyes jiggle in their sockets as he reacquires his own links, sensory interfaces so massive that your own off-the-shelf inlays amount to shadow puppetry in comparison.

You hear coughing and the rustling of limbs just past line of sight, catch glimpses of reflected motion where the others stir at the edge of vision.

"Wha . . . " your voice is barely more than a hoarse whisper, ". . . happ . . . ?"

Szpindel works his jaw. Bone cracks audibly.

". . . Sssuckered," he hisses.

You haven't even met the aliens yet, and already they're running rings around you.

So we dragged ourselves back from the dead: five part-time ca-davers, naked, emaciated, barely able to move even in zero g. We emerged from our coffins like premature moths ripped from their cocoons, still half-grub. We were alone and off course and utterly helpless, and it took a conscious effort to remember: They would never have risked our lives if we hadn't been essential.

"Morning, commissar." Isaac Szpindel reached one trem-bling, insensate hand for the feedback gloves at the base of his pod. Just past him, Susan James was curled into a loose fetal ball, murmuring to herselves. Only Amanda Bates, already dressed and cycling through a sequence of bone-cracking isometrics, possessed anything approaching mobility. Every now and then she tried bouncing a rubber ball off the bulkhead; but not even she was up to catching it on the rebound yet.

The journey had melted us down to a common archetype. James's round cheeks and hips; Szpindel's high forehead and lumpy, lanky chassis—even the enhanced carboplatinum brick shit house that Bates used for a body—all had shriveled to the same desiccated collection of sticks and bones. Even our hair seemed to have become strangely discolored during the voyage, although I knew that was impossible. More likely it was just filtering the pallor of the skin beneath. Still. The pre-dead James had been dirty blond, Szpindel's hair had been almost dark enough to call black, but the stuff floating from their scalps looked the same dull kelpy brown to me now. Bates kept her head shaved, but even her eyebrows weren't as rusty as I remembered them.

We'd revert to our old selves soon enough. Just add water. For now, though, the old slur was freshly relevant: The Undead really did all look the same, if you didn't know how to look.

If you did, of course—if you forgot appearance and watched for motion, ignored meat and studied *topology*—you'd never mistake one for another. Every facial tic was a data point, every conversational pause spoke volumes more than the words to either side. I could see James's personae shatter and coalesce in the flutter of an eyelash. Szpindel's unspoken distrust of Amanda Bates shouted from the corner of his smile. Every twitch of the phenotype cried aloud to anyone who knew the language.

"Where's—" James croaked, coughed, waved one spindly arm at Sarasti's empty coffin gaping at the end of the row.

Szpindel's lips cracked in a small rictus. "Gone back to Fab, eh? Getting the ship to build some dirt to lie on."

"Probably communing with the Captain." Bates breathed louder than she spoke, a dry rustle from pipes still getting reacquainted with the idea of respiration.

James again: "Could do that up here."

"Could take a dump up here, too," Szpindel rasped. "Some things you do by yourself, eh?"

And some things you kept *to* yourself. Not many baselines felt comfortable locking stares with a vampire—Sarasti, ever courteous, tended to avoid eye contact for exactly that reason—but there were other surfaces to his topology, just as mammalian and just as readable. If he had withdrawn from public view, maybe I was the reason. Maybe he was keeping secrets.

After all, *Theseus* damn well was.

She'd taken us a good fifteen AUs toward our destination before something scared her off course. Then she'd skidded north like a startled cat and started climbing: a wild high three-g burn off the ecliptic, thirteen hundred tonnes of momentum bucking against Newton's first. She'd emptied her Penn tanks, bled dry her substrate mass, squandered a hundred forty days' of fuel in hours. Then a long cold coast through the abyss, years of stingy accounting, the thrust of every antiproton weighed against the drag of sieving it from the void. Teleportation isn't magic: the Icarus stream couldn't send us the actual antimatter it made, only the quantum specs. *Theseus* had to filterfeed the raw material from space, one ion at a time. For long dark years she'd made do on pure inertia, hording every swallowed atom. Then a flip; ionizing lasers strafing the space ahead; a ramscoop thrown wide in a hard brake. The weight of a trillion trillion protons slowed her down and refilled her gut and flattened us all over again. *Theseus* had burned relentlessly until almost the moment of our resurrection.

It was easy enough to retrace those steps; our course was there in ConSensus for anyone to see. Exactly why the ship had blazed that trail was another matter. Doubtless it would all come out during the post-rez briefing. We were hardly the first vessel to travel under the cloak of *sealed orders,* and if there'd been a pressing need to know by now we'd have known by now. Still, I wondered who had locked out the Comm logs. Mission Control, maybe. Or Sarasti. Or *Theseus* herself, for that matter. It was easy to forget the Quantical AI at the heart of our ship. It stayed so discreetly in the background, nurtured and carried us and permeated our existence like an unobtrusive god; but like God, it never took your calls.

Sarasti was the official intermediary. When the ship did speak, it spoke to him—and Sarasti called it *Captain*.

So did we all.

He'd given us four hours to come back. It took more than three just to get me out of the crypt. By then my brain was at least firing on most of its synapses, although my body—still sucking fluids like a thirsty sponge—continued to ache with every movement. I swapped out drained electrolyte bags for fresh ones and headed aft.

Fifteen minutes to spin-up. Fifty to the post-resurrection briefing. Just enough time for those who preferred gravity-bound sleep to haul their personal effects into the drum and stake out their allotted 4.4 square meters of floor space.

Gravity—or any centripetal facsimile thereof—did not appeal to me. I set up my own tent in zero g and as far to stern as possible, nuzzling the forward wall of the starboard shuttle tube. The tent inflated like an abscess on *Theseus*'s spine, a little climate-controlled bubble of atmosphere in the dark cavernous vacuum beneath the ship's carapace. My own effects were minimal; it took all of thirty seconds to stick them to the wall, and another thirty to program the tent's environment.

Afterward I went for a hike. After five years, I needed the exercise.

Stern was closest, so I started there, at the shielding that separated payload from propulsion. A single sealed hatch blistered the aft bulkhead dead center. Behind it, a service tunnel wormed back through machinery best left untouched by Human hands. The fat superconducting torus of the ramscoop ring; the antennae fan behind it, unwound now into an indestructible soap bubble big enough to shroud a city, its face turned sunward to catch the faint quantum sparkle of the Icarus antimatter stream. More shielding behind that; then the telematter reactor, where raw hydrogen and refined information conjured fire three hundred times hotter than the sun's. I knew the incantations, of course— antimatter cracking and deconstruction, the teleportation of quantum serial numbers—but it was still magic to me, how we'd come so far so fast. It would have been magic to anyone.

Except Sarasti, maybe.

Around me, the same magic worked at cooler temperatures and to less volatile ends: a small riot of chutes and dispensers crowded the bulkhead on all sides. A few of those openings would choke on my fist: one or two could swallow me whole. *Theseus*'s fabrication plant could build everything from cutlery to cockpits. Give it a big enough matter stockpile and it could have even built another *Theseus,* albeit in many small pieces and over a very long time. Some wondered if it could build another crew as well, although we'd all been assured that was impossible. Not even these machines had fine enough fingers to reconstruct a few trillion synapses in the space of a human skull. Not yet, anyway.

I believed it. They would never have shipped us out fully assembled if there'd been a cheaper alternative.

I faced forward. Putting the back of my head against that sealed hatch I could see almost to *Theseus*'s bow, an uninterrupted line of sight extending to a tiny dark bull's-eye thirty meters ahead. It was like staring at a great textured target in shades of white and gray: concentric circles, hatches centered within bulkheads one behind another, perfectly aligned. Every

one stood open, in nonchalant defiance of a previous generation's safety codes. We could keep them closed if we wanted
to, if it made us feel safer. That was all it would do, though;
it wouldn't improve our empirical odds one whit. In the event
of trouble those hatches would slam shut long milliseconds before Human senses could even make sense of an alarm. They
weren't even computer-controlled. *Theseus*'s body parts had
reflexes.

I pushed off against the stern plating—wincing at the tug and
stretch of disused tendons—and coasted forward, leaving Fab
behind. The shuttle-access hatches to *Scylla* and *Charybdis*
briefly constricted my passage to either side. Past them the spine
widened into a corrugated extensible cylinder two meters across
and—at the moment—maybe fifteen long. A pair of ladders ran
opposite each other along its length; raised portholes the size of
manhole covers stippled the bulkhead to either side. Most of
those just looked into the hold. A couple served as general-
purpose airlocks, should anyone want to take a stroll beneath the
carapace. One opened into my tent. Another, four meters farther
forward, opened into Bates's.

From a third, just short of the forward bulkhead, Jukka
Sarasti climbed into view like a long white spider.

If he'd been Human I'd have known instantly what I saw
there, I'd have smelled *murderer* all over his topology. And I
wouldn't have been able to even guess at the number of his victims, because his affect was so utterly without remorse. The
killing of a hundred would leave no more stain on Sarasti's surfaces than the swatting of an insect; guilt beaded and rolled off
this creature like water on wax.

But Sarasti wasn't Human. Sarasti was a whole different animal, and coming from him all those homicidal refractions meant
nothing more than *predator*. He had the inclination, was born to

it; whether he had ever acted on it was between him and Mission Control.

Maybe they cut you some slack, I didn't say to him. *Maybe it's just a cost of doing business. You're mission-critical, after all. For all I know you cut a deal. You're so very smart, you know we wouldn't have brought you back in the first place if we hadn't* needed *you. From the day they cracked the vat you knew you had leverage.*

Is that how it works, Jukka? You save the world, and the folks who hold your leash agree to look the other way?

As a child I'd read tales about jungle predators transfixing their prey with a stare. Only after I'd met Jukka Sarasti did I know how it felt. But he wasn't looking at me now. He was focused on installing his own tent, and even if he *had* looked me in the eye there'd have been nothing to see but the dark wraparound visor he wore in deference to Human skittishness. He ignored me as I grabbed a nearby rung and squeezed past.

I could have sworn I smelled raw meat on his breath.

Into the drum (*drums,* technically; the BioMed hoop at the back spun on its own bearings). I flew through the center of a cylinder sixteen meters across. *Theseus*'s spinal nerves ran along its axis, the exposed plexii and piping bundled against the ladders on either side. Past them, Szpindel's and James's freshly erected tents rose from nooks on opposite sides of the world. Szpindel himself floated off my shoulder, still naked but for his gloves, and I could tell from the way his fingers moved that his favorite color was green. He anchored himself to one of three stairways to nowhere arrayed around the drum: steep narrow steps rising five vertical meters from the deck into empty air.

The next hatch gaped dead-center of the drum's forward wall; pipes and conduits plunged into the bulkhead on each side. I grabbed a convenient rung to slow myself—biting down once more on the pain—and floated through.

T-junction. The spinal corridor continued forward, a smaller diverticulum branched off to an EVA cubby and the forward airlock. I stayed the course and found myself back in the crypt, mirror-bright and less than two meters deep. Empty pods gaped to the left; sealed ones huddled to the right. We were so irreplaceable we'd come with replacements. They slept on, oblivious. I'd met three of them back in training. Hopefully none of us would be getting reacquainted any time soon.

Only four pods to starboard, though. No backup for Sarasti.

Another hatchway. Smaller this time. I squeezed through into the bridge. Dim light there, a silent shifting mosaic of icons and alphanumerics iterating across dark glassy surfaces. Not so much bridge as cockpit, and a cramped one at that. I'd emerged between two acceleration couches, each surrounded by a horseshoe array of controls and readouts. Nobody expected to ever *use* this compartment. *Theseus* was perfectly capable of running herself, and if she wasn't we were capable of running her from our inlays, and if we weren't the odds were overwhelming that we were all dead anyway. Still, against that astronomically off-the-wall chance, this was where one or two intrepid survivors could pilot the ship home again after everything else had failed.

Between the footwells the engineers had crammed one last hatch and one last passageway: to the observation blister on *Theseus*'s prow. I hunched my shoulders (tendons cracked and complained) and pushed through—

—into darkness. Clamshell shielding covered the outside of the dome like a pair of eyelids squeezed tight. A single icon glowed softly from a touchpad to my left; faint stray light followed me through from the spine, brushed dim fingers across the concave enclosure. The dome resolved in faint shades of blue and gray as my eyes adjusted. A stale draft stirred the webbing floating from the rear bulkhead, mixed oil and machinery at the back of my throat. Buckles clicked faintly in the breeze like impoverished wind chimes.

I reached out and touched the crystal: the innermost layer of two, warm air piped through the gap between to cut the cold. Not completely, though. My fingertips chilled instantly.

Space out there.

Perhaps, en route to our original destination, *Theseus* had seen something that scared her clear out of the solar system. More likely she hadn't been running away from anything but *to* something else, something that hadn't been discovered until we'd already died and gone from Heaven. In which case . . .

I reached back and tapped the touchpad. I half-expected nothing to happen; *Theseus*'s windows could be as easily locked as her Comm logs. But the dome split instantly before me, a crack then a crescent then a wide-eyed lidless stare as the shielding slid smoothly back into the hull. My fingers clenched reflexively into a fistful of webbing. The sudden void stretched empty and unforgiving in all directions, and there was nothing to cling to but a metal disk barely four meters across.

Stars, everywhere. So many stars that I could not for the life of me understand how the sky could contain them all yet be so black. Stars, and—

—nothing else.

What did you expect? I chided myself. *An alien mothership hanging off the starboard bow?*

Well, why not? We were out here for *something*.

The others were, anyway. They'd be essential no matter where we'd ended up. But my own situation was a bit different, I realized. *My* usefulness degraded with distance.

And we were over half a light-year from home.

WHEN IT IS DARK ENOUGH, YOU CAN SEE THE STARS.
—RALPH WALDO EMERSON

WHERE WAS I when the lights came down?

I was emerging from the gates of Heaven, mourning a father who was—to his own mind, at least—still alive.

It had been scarcely two months since Helen had disappeared under the cowl. Two months by our reckoning, at least. From her perspective it could have been a day or a decade; the Virtually Omnipotent set their subjective clocks along with everything else.

She wasn't coming back. She would only deign to see her husband under conditions that amounted to a slap in the face. He didn't complain. He visited as often as she would allow: twice a week, then once. Then every two. Their marriage decayed with the exponential determinism of a radioactive isotope and still he sought her out, and accepted her conditions.

On the day the lights came down, I had joined him at my mother's side. It was a special occasion, the last time we would ever see her in the flesh. For two months her body had lain in state along with five hundred other new Ascendants on the ward, open for viewing by the next of kin. The interface was no more real than it would ever be, of course; the body could not talk to us. But at least it was *there,* its flesh warm, the sheets clean and straight. Helen's lower face was still visible below the cowl, though eyes and ears were helmeted. We could touch her. My father often did. Perhaps some distant part of her still felt it.

But eventually someone has to close the casket and dispose of the remains. Room must be made for the new arrival; and so we came to this last day at my mother's side. Jim took her hand one more time. She would still be available in her world, on her terms, but later this day the body would be packed into storage facilities crowded far too efficiently for flesh-and-blood visitors. We had been assured that the body would remain intact—the muscles electrically exercised, the body flexed and fed, the corpus kept ready to return to active duty should Heaven experience some inconceivable and catastrophic meltdown. Everything was reversible, we were told. And yet—there were so many who had Ascended, and not even the deepest catacombs go on forever. There were rumors of dismemberment, of nonessential body parts hewn away over time according to some optimum-packing algorithm. Perhaps Helen would be a torso this time next year, a disembodied head the year after. Perhaps her chassis would be stripped down to the brain before we'd even left the building, awaiting only that final technological breakthrough that would herald the arrival of the Great Digital Upload.

Rumors, as I say. I personally didn't know of anyone who'd come back after Ascending, but then why would anyone want to? Not even Lucifer left Heaven until he was pushed.

Dad might have known for sure—Dad knew more than most people, about the things most people weren't supposed to know—but he never told tales out of turn. Whatever he knew, he'd obviously decided its disclosure wouldn't have changed Helen's mind. That would have been enough for him.

We donned the hoods that served as day passes for the Unwired, and we met my mother in the spartan visiting room she imagined for these visits. She'd built no windows into the world she occupied, no hint of whatever utopian environment she'd constructed for herself. She hadn't even opted for one of the prefab visiting environments designed to minimize dissonance among visitors. We found ourselves in a featureless beige sphere five meters across. There was nothing in there but her.

Maybe not so far removed from her vision of utopia after all, I thought.

My father smiled. "Helen."

"Jim." She was twenty years younger than the thing on the bed, and still she made my skin crawl. "Siri! You came!"

She always used my name. I don't think she ever called me *son*.

"You're still happy here?" my father asked.

"Wonderful. I do wish you could join us."

Jim smiled. "Someone has to keep the lights on."

"Now you *know* this isn't good-bye," she said. "You can visit whenever you like."

"Only if you do something about the scenery." Not just a joke, but a lie; Jim would have come at her call even if the gauntlet involved bare feet and broken glass.

"And Chelsea, too," Helen continued. "It would be so nice to finally meet her after all this time."

"Chelsea's *gone,* Helen," I said.

"Oh yes, but I know you stay in touch. I know she was special to you. Just because you're not *together* anymore doesn't mean she can't—"

"You know she—"

A startling possibility stopped me in mid-sentence: Maybe I hadn't actually told them.

"Son," Jim said quietly. "Maybe you could give us a moment."

I would have given them a fucking lifetime. I unplugged myself back to the ward, looked from the corpse on the bed to my blind and catatonic father in his couch, murmuring sweet nothings into the datastream. Let them perform for each other. Let them formalize and finalize their so-called relationship in whatever way they saw fit. Maybe, just once, they could even bring themselves to be honest, there in that other world where everything else was a lie. Maybe.

I felt no desire to bear witness either way.

But of course I had to go back in for my own formalities. I adopted my role in the familial set piece one last time, partook of the usual lies. We all agreed that this wasn't going to change anything, and nobody deviated enough from the script to call anyone else a liar on that account. And finally—careful to say *until next time* rather than *good-bye*—we took our leave of my mother.

I even suppressed my gag reflex long enough to give her a hug.

Jim had his inhaler in hand as we emerged from the darkness. I hoped, without much hope, that he'd throw it into the garbage receptacle as we passed through the lobby. But he raised it to his mouth and took another hit of vasopressin, that he would never be tempted.

Fidelity in an aerosol. "You don't need that anymore," I said.

"Probably not," he agreed.

"It won't work anyway. You can't imprint on someone who isn't even there, no matter how many hormones you snort. It just—"

Jim said nothing. We passed beneath the muzzles of sentries panning for infiltrating Realists.

"She's *gone*," I blurted. "She doesn't care if you find someone else. She'd be happy if you did." *It would let her pretend the books had been balanced.*

"She's my wife," he told me.

"That doesn't mean what it used to. It never did."

He smiled a bit at that. "It's my life, son. I'm comfortable with it."

"Dad—"

"I don't blame her," he said. "And neither should you."

Easy for him to say. Easy even to accept the hurt she'd inflicted on him all these years. This cheerful façade here at the end hardly made up for the endless bitter complaints my father had endured throughout living memory. *Do you think it's easy when you disappear for months on end? Do you think it's easy always wondering who you're with and what you're doing and if you're even alive? Do you think it's easy raising a child like that on your own?*

She'd blamed him for everything, but he bore it gracefully because he knew it was all a lie. He knew he was only the pretense. She wasn't leaving because he was AWOL, or unfaithful. Her departure had nothing to do with him at all. It was me. Helen had left the world because she couldn't stand to look at the thing who'd replaced her son.

I would have pursued it—would have tried yet again to make my father *see*—but by now we'd left the gates of Heaven for the streets of Purgatory, where pedestrians on all sides murmured in astonishment and stared open-mouthed at the sky. I followed their gaze to a strip of raw twilight between the towers, and gasped—

The stars were falling.

The Zodiac had rearranged itself into a precise grid of bright points with luminous tails. It was as though the whole planet had been caught in some great closing net, the knots of its mesh aglow with St. Elmo's fire. It was beautiful. It was terrifying.

I looked away to recalibrate my distance vision, to give this ill-behaved hallucination a chance to vanish gracefully before I set my empirical gaze to high beam. I saw a vampire in that moment, a female, walking among us like the archetypal wolf in sheep's clothing. Vampires were uncommon creatures at street level. I'd never seen one in the flesh before.

She had just stepped onto the street from the building across the way. She stood a head taller than the rest of us, her eyes shining yellow and bright as a cat's in the deepening dark. She realized, as I watched, that something was amiss. She looked around, glanced at the sky—and continued on her way, totally indifferent to the cattle on all sides, to the heavenly portent that had transfixed them. Totally indifferent to the fact that the world had just turned inside-out.

It was 1035 Greenwich Mean Time, February 13, 2082.

They clenched around the world like a fist, each black as the inside of an event horizon until those last bright moments when they all burned together. They screamed as they died. Every radio up to geostat groaned in unison, every infrared telescope went briefly snowblind. Ashes stained the sky for weeks afterward; mesospheric clouds, high above the jet stream, turned to glowing rust with every sunrise. The objects, apparently, consisted largely of iron. Nobody ever knew what to make of that.

For perhaps the first time in history, the world *knew* before being *told*: If you'd seen the sky, you had the scoop. The usual arbiters of newsworthiness, stripped of their accustomed role in filtering reality, had to be content with merely labeling it. It took them ninety minutes to agree on *Fireflies*. A half hour after that, the first Fourier transforms appeared in the noosphere; to no one's great surprise, the Fireflies had not wasted their dying breaths on static. There was pattern embedded in that terminal chorus, some cryptic intelligence that resisted all earthly analysis. The experts, rigorously empirical, refused to speculate: They only admitted that the Fireflies had said *something*. They didn't know what.

Everyone else did. How else would you explain 65,536 probes evenly dispersed along a lat-long grid that barely left any square meter of planetary surface unexposed? Obviously the Flies had taken our picture. The whole world had been caught with its pants down in panoramic composite freeze-frame. We'd been *surveyed*—whether as a prelude to formal introductions or outright invasion was anyone's guess.

My father might have known someone who might have known. But by then he'd long since disappeared, as he always did during times of hemispheric crisis. Whatever he knew or didn't, he left me to find my own answers with everyone else.

There was no shortage of perspectives. The noosphere seethed with scenarios ranging from utopian to apocalyptic. The Fireflies had seeded lethal germs through the jet stream. The Fireflies had been on a nature safari. The Icarus Array was being retooled to power a doomsday weapon against the aliens. The Icarus Array had already been destroyed. We had decades to react; anything from another solar system would have to obey the light-speed limit like everyone else. We had days to live; organic warships had just crossed the asteroid belt and would be fumigating the planet within a week.

Like everyone else, I bore witness to lurid speculations and talking heads. I visited blathernodes, soaked myself in other people's opinions. That was nothing new, as far as it went; I'd spent my whole life as a sort of alien ethologist in my own right, watching the world behave, gleaning patterns and protocols, learning the rules that allowed me to infiltrate human society. It had always worked before. Somehow, though, the presence of *real* aliens had changed the dynamics of the equation. Mere observation didn't satisfy anymore. It was as though the presence of this new outgroup had forced me back into the clade whether I liked it or not; the distance between myself and the world suddenly seemed forced and faintly ridiculous.

Yet I couldn't, for my life, figure out how to let it go.

Chelsea had always said that telepresence emptied the Humanity from Human interaction. "They say it's indistinguishable," she told me once, "just like having your family right there, snuggled up so you can see them and feel them and smell them next to you. But it's not. It's just shadows on the cave wall. I mean, sure, the shadows come in three-D color with force-feedback tactile interactivity. They're good enough to fool the civilized brain. But your gut knows those aren't *people,* even if it can't put its finger on *how* it knows. They just don't *feel* real. Know what I mean?"

I didn't. Back then I'd had no clue what she was talking about. But now we were all cavemen again, huddling beneath some overhang while lightning split the heavens and vast formless monsters, barely glimpsed in bright strobe-frozen instants, roared and clashed in the darkness on all sides. There was no comfort in solitude. You couldn't get it from interactive shadows. You needed someone *real* at your side, someone to hold on to, someone to share your airspace along with your fear and hope and uncertainty.

I imagined the presence of companions who wouldn't vanish the moment I unplugged. But Chelsea was gone, and Pag in her wake. The few others I could have called—peers and former clients with whom my impersonations of rapport had been especially convincing—didn't seem worth the effort. Flesh and blood had its own relationship to reality: necessary, but not sufficient.

Watching the world from a distance, it occurred to me at last: I knew exactly what Chelsea had meant, with her Luddite ramblings about desaturated Humanity and the colorless interactions of virtual space. I'd known all along.

I'd just never been able to see how it was any different from real life.

. . .

Imagine you are a machine.

Yes, I know. But imagine you're a different *kind* of machine, one built from metal and plastic and designed not by blind, haphazard natural selection but by engineers and astrophysicists with their eyes fixed firmly on specific goals. Imagine that your purpose is not to replicate, or even to survive, but to gather information.

I can imagine that easily. It is in fact a much simpler impersonation than the kind I'm usually called on to perform.

I coast through the abyss on the colder side of Neptune's orbit. Most of the time I exist only as an absence, to any observer on the visible spectrum: a moving, asymmetrical silhouette blocking the stars. But occasionally, during my slow endless spin, I glint with dim hints of reflected starlight. If you catch me in those moments you might infer something of my true nature: a segmented creature with foil skin, bristling with joints and dishes and spindly antennae. Here and there a whisper of accumulated frost clings to a joint or seam, some frozen wisp of gas encountered in Jupiter space perhaps. Elsewhere I carry the microscopic corpses of Earthly bacteria who thrived with carefree abandon on the skins of space stations or the benign lunar surface, but who had gone to crystal at only half my present distance from the sun. Now, a breath away from absolute zero, they might shatter at a photon's touch.

My heart is warm, at least. A tiny nuclear fire burns in my thorax, leaves me indifferent to the cold outside. It won't go out for a thousand years, barring some catastrophic accident; for a thousand years, I will listen for faint voices from Mission Control and do everything they tell me to. So far they have told me to study comets. Every instruction I have ever received has been a precise and unambiguous elaboration on that one overriding reason for my existence.

Which is why these latest instructions are so puzzling, for they make no sense at all. The frequency is wrong. The signal strength is wrong. I cannot even understand the handshaking protocols. I request clarification.

The response arrives almost a thousand minutes later, and it is an unprecedented mix of orders and requests for information. I answer as best I can: Yes, this is the bearing at which signal strength was greatest. No, it is not the usual bearing for Mission Control. Yes, I can retransmit: Here it is, all over again. Yes, I will go into standby mode.

I await further instructions. They arrive 839 minutes later, and they tell me to stop studying comets immediately.

I am to commence a controlled precessive tumble that sweeps my antennae through consecutive five-degree arc increments along all three axes, with a period of ninety-four seconds. Upon encountering any transmission resembling the one that confused me, I am to fix upon the bearing of maximal signal strength and derive a series of parameter values. I am also instructed to retransmit the signal to Mission Control.

I do as I'm told. For a long time I hear nothing, but I am infinitely patient and incapable of boredom. Eventually a fleeting, familiar signal brushes against my afferent array. I reacquire and track it to its source, which I am well-equipped to describe: a trans-Neptunian comet in the Kuiper Belt, approximately two hundred kilometers in diameter. It is sweeping a twenty-one-cm tightbeam radio wave across the heavens with a periodicity of 4.57 seconds. This beam does not intersect Mission Control's coordinates at any point. It appears to be directed at a different target entirely.

It takes much longer than usual for Mission Control to respond to this information. When it does, it tells me to change course. Mission Control informs me that henceforth my new destination is to be referred to as *Burns-Caulfield*. Given current fuel and inertial constraints I will not reach it in less than thirty-nine years.

I am to watch nothing else in the meantime.

I'd been liaising for a team at the Kurzweil Institute, a fractured group of cutting-edge savants convinced they were on the verge of solving the quantum-glial paradox. That particular logjam had stalled AI for decades; once broken, the experts promised we'd be eighteen months away from the first personality upload and only two years from reliable Human-consciousness emulation in a software environment. It would spell the end of corporeal history, usher in a Singularity that had been waiting impatiently in the wings for nigh on fifty years.

Two months after Firefall, the institute canceled my contract.

I was actually surprised it had taken them so long. It had cost us so much, this overnight inversion of global priorities, these breakneck measures making up for lost initiative. Not even our shiny new post-scarcity economy could withstand such a seismic shift without lurching toward bankruptcy. Installations in deep space, long imagined secure by virtue of their remoteness, were suddenly vulnerable for exactly the same reason. Lagrange habitats had to be refitted for defense against an unknown enemy. Commercial ships on the Martian Loop were conscripted, weaponized, and reassigned; some secured the high ground over Mars while others fell sunward to guard the Icarus Array.

It didn't matter that the Fireflies hadn't fired a shot at any of these targets. We simply couldn't afford the risk.

We were all in it together, of course, desperate to regain some hypothetical upper hand by any means necessary. Kings and corporations scribbled IOUs on the backs of napkins and promised to sort everything out once the heat was off. In the meantime, the prospect of Utopia in two years took a back seat to the shadow of Armageddon reaching back from next Tuesday. The Kurzweil Institute, like everyone else, suddenly had other things to worry about.

So I returned to my apartment, split a bulb of Glenfiddich, and arrayed virtual windows like daisy petals in my head. Everyone Icons debated on all sides, serving up leftovers two weeks past their expiry date:

Disgraceful breakdown of global security.

No harm done.

Comsats annihilated.
Thousands dead.

Random collisions. *Accidental* deaths.

(Who sent them?)

We should have seen them coming. Why didn't we—

Deep space. Inverse square. Do the math.

They were stealthed!

(What do they *want*?)

We were raped!

Jesus Christ. They just took our *picture*.

Why the silence?

Moon's fine. Mars's fine.

(Where are they?)

Why haven't they made contact?

Nothing's touched the O'Neills.

Technology Implies
Belligerence!

(Are they coming back?)

Nothing attacked us.   *Yet.*

Nothing *invaded*.   *So far.*

(But where *are* they?)

(Are they coming *back*?)

(Anyone?)

JIM MOORE VOICE ONLY
ENCRYPTED
ACCEPT?

The text window blossomed directly in my line of sight, eclipsing the debate. I read it twice. I tried to remember the last time he'd called from the field, and couldn't.

I muted the other windows. "Dad?"

"Son," he replied after a moment. "Are you well?"

"Like everyone else. Still wondering whether we should be celebrating or crapping our pants."

He didn't answer immediately. "It's a big question, all right," he said at last.

"I don't suppose you could give me any advice? They're not telling us anything at ground level."

It was a rhetorical request. His silence was hardly necessary to make the point. "I know," I added after a moment. "Sorry. It's just, they're saying the Icarus Array went down, and—"

"You know I can't— Oh." My father paused. "That's ridiculous. Icarus's fine."

"It is?"

He seemed to be weighing his words. "The Fireflies probably didn't even notice it. There's no particle trail as long as it stays offstream, and it would be buried in solar glare unless someone knew where to search."

It was my turn to fall silent. This conversation felt suddenly *wrong*.

Because when my father went on the job, he went dark. He *never* called his family.

Because even when my father came *off* the job, he never talked about it. It wouldn't matter whether the Icarus Array was still online or whether it had been shredded and thrown into the sun like a thousand kilometers of torn origami; he wouldn't tell either tale unless an official announcement had been made. Which—I refreshed an index window just to be sure—it hadn't.

Because while my father was a man of few words, he was *not* a man of frequent, indecisive pauses, and he had hesitated before each and every line he'd spoken in this exchange.

I tugged ever-so-gently on the line—"But they've sent ships"—and started counting.

One one-thousand, two one-thousand—

"Just a precaution. Icarus was overdue for a visit anyway. You don't swap out your whole grid without at least dropping in and kicking the new tires first."

Nearly three seconds to respond.

"You're on the moon," I said.

Pause. "Close enough."

"What are you— Dad, why are you telling me this? Isn't this a security breach?"

"You're going to get a call," he told me.

"From who? Why?"

"They're assembling a team. The kind of . . . people you deal with." My father was too rational to dispute the contributions of the recons and hybrids in our midst, but he'd never been able to hide his mistrust of them.

"They need a Synthesist," he said.

"Isn't it lucky you've got one in the family."

Radio bounced back and forth. "This isn't nepotism, Siri. I wanted very much for them to pick someone else."

"Thanks for the vote of conf—"

But he'd seen it coming, and preempted me before my words could cross the distance: "It's not a slap at your abilities and you know it. You're simply the most qualified, and the work is vital."

"So why—" I began, and stopped. He wouldn't want to keep me away from some theoretical gig in a WestHem lab.

"What's this about, Dad?"

"The Fireflies. They found something."

"What?"

"A radio signal. From the Kuiper. We traced the bearing."

"They're *talking*?"

"Not to us." He cleared his throat. "It was something of a fluke that we even intercepted the transmission."

"Who are they talking to?"

"We don't know."

"Friendly? Hostile?"

"Son, we don't *know*. The encryption seems similar, but we can't even be sure of that. All we have is the location."

"So you're sending a team." *You're sending* me. We'd never gone to the Kuiper before. It had been decades since we'd even sent robots. Not that we lacked the capacity; we just hadn't bothered because everything we needed was so much closer to home. The Interplanetary Age had stagnated at the asteroids.

But now something lurked at the farthest edge of our backyard, calling into the void. Maybe it was talking to some other solar system. Maybe it was talking to something closer, something en route.

"It's not the kind of situation we can safely ignore," my father said.

"What about probes?"

"Of course. But we can't wait for them to report back. The follow-up's been fast-tracked; updates can be sent en route."

He gave me a few extra seconds to digest that. When I still didn't speak, he said, "You have to understand. Our only edge is that as far as we know, *Burns-Caulfield* doesn't know we're onto it. We have to get as much as we can in whatever window of opportunity that grants us."

But *Burns-Caulfield* had hidden itself. *Burns-Caulfield* might not welcome a forced introduction.

"What if I refuse?"

The time lag seemed to say *Mars*.

"I know you, son. You won't."

"But if I *did*. If I'm the best qualified, if the job's so vital . . ."

He didn't have to answer. I didn't have to ask. At these kind of stakes, mission-critical elements didn't get the luxury of choice. I wouldn't even have the childish satisfaction of holding my breath and refusing to play—the will to resist is no less mechanical than the urge to breathe. Both can be subverted with the right neurochemical keys.

"You killed my Kurzweil contract," I realized.

"That's the least of what we did."

We let the vacuum between us speak for a while.

"If I could go back and undo the—the thing that made you what you are," Dad said finally, "I would. In a second."

"Yeah."

"I have to go. I just wanted to give you the heads-up."

"Yeah. Thanks."

"I love you, son."

Where are you? Are you coming back?
"Thanks," I said again. "That's good to know."

This is what my father could not unmake. This is what I am:

I am the bridge between the bleeding edge and the dead center. I stand between the Wizard of Oz and the man behind the curtain.

I *am* the curtain.

I am not an entirely new breed. My roots reach back to the dawn of civilization but those precursors served a different function, a less honorable one. They only greased the wheels of social stability; they would sugarcoat unpleasant truths, or inflate imaginary bogeymen for political expedience. They were vital enough in their way. Not even the most heavily-armed police state can exert brute force on all of its citizens all of the time. Meme management is so much subtler; the rose-tinted refraction of perceived reality, the contagious fear of threatening alternatives. There have always been those tasked with the rotation of informational topologies, but throughout most of history they had little to do with increasing its *clarity*.

The new millennium changed all that. We've surpassed ourselves now, we're exploring terrain beyond the limits of merely human understanding. Sometimes its contours, even in conventional space, are just too intricate for our brains to track; other times its very axes extend into dimensions inconceivable to minds built for fucking and fighting on some prehistoric grassland. So many things constrain us, from so many directions. The most altruistic and sustainable philosophies fail before the brute brain stem imperative of self-interest. Subtle and elegant equations *predict* the behavior of the quantum world, but none can *explain* it. After four thousand years we can't even prove that reality exists beyond the mind of the first-person dreamer. We have such need of intellects greater than our own.

But we're not very good at building them. The forced matings of minds and electrons succeed and fail with equal spectacle. Our hybrids become as brilliant as savants, and as autistic. We graft people to prosthetics, make their overloaded motor strips juggle meat and machinery, and shake our heads when their fingers twitch and their tongues stutter. Computers bootstrap their own offspring, grow so wise and incomprehensible that their communiqués assume the hallmarks of dementia: unfocused and irrelevant to the barely-intelligent creatures left behind.

And when your surpassing creations find the answers you asked for, you can't understand their analysis and you can't verify their answers. You have to take their word on faith—

—or you use information theory to *flatten* it for you, to squash the tesseract into two dimensions and the Klein bottle into three, to simplify reality and pray to whatever Gods survived the millennium that your honorable twisting of the truth hasn't ruptured any of its load-bearing pylons. You hire people like me; the crossbred progeny of profilers and proof assistants and information theorists.

In formal settings you'd call me *Synthesist*. On the street you'd call me *jargonaut* or *poppy*. If you're one of those savants whose hard-won truths are being bastardized and lobotomized for powerful know-nothings interested only in market share, you might call me a *mole* or a *chaperone*.

If you were Isaac Szpindel you'd call me *commissar*, and while the jibe would be a friendly one, it would also be more than that.

I've never convinced myself that we made the right choice. I can cite the usual justifications in my sleep, talk endlessly about the rotational topology of information and the irrelevance of semantic comprehension. But after all the words, I'm still not sure.

I don't know if anyone else is, either. Maybe it's just some grand consensual con, marks and players all in league. We won't admit that our creations are beyond us; they may speak in tongues, but our priests can read those signs. Gods leave their algorithms carved into the mountainside but it's just li'l ol' me bringing the tablets down to the masses, and I don't threaten anyone.

Maybe the Singularity happened years ago. We just don't want to admit we were left behind.

> ALL KINDS OF ANIMALS COMING HERE. OCCASIONAL
> DEMONS TOO.
>
> —IAN ANDERSON, *CATFISH RISING*

THE THIRD WAVE, they called us. All in the same boat, driving into the long dark courtesy of a bleeding-edge prototype crash-graduated from the simulators a full eighteen months ahead of schedule. In a less fearful economy, such violence to the timetable would have bankrupted four countries and fifteen multicorps.

The first two waves came out of the gate in even more of a hurry. I didn't find out what had happened to them until thirty minutes before the briefing, when Sarasti released the telemetry into ConSensus. Then I opened wide; experience flooded up my inlays and spilled across my parietal cortex in glorious high-density fast-forward. Even now I can bring those data back, fresh as the day they were recorded. I'm *there*.

I'm *them*.

I am unmanned. I am disposable. I am souped-up and stripped-down, a telematter drive with a couple of cameras bolted to the front end, pushing g's that would turn meat to jelly. I sprint joyously toward the darkness, my twin brother a stereoscopic hundred klicks to starboard, dual streams of backspat pions boosting us to relativity before poor old Theseus had even crawled past Mars.

But now, six billion kilometers to stern, Mission Control turns off the tap and leaves us coasting. The comet swells in our sights, a frozen enigma sweeping its signal across the sky like a lighthouse beam. We bring rudimentary senses to bear and stare it down on a thousand wavelengths.

We've lived for this moment.

We see an erratic wobble that speaks of recent collisions. We see scars—smooth icy expanses where once-acned skin has liquefied and refrozen, far too recently for the insignificant sun at our backs to be any kind of suspect.

We see an astronomical impossibility: a comet with a heart of refined iron.

Burns-Caufield sings as we glide past. Not to us; it ignores our passage as it ignored our approach. It sings to someone else entirely. Perhaps we'll meet that audience some day. Perhaps they're waiting in the desolate wastelands ahead of us. Mission Control flips us onto our backs, keeps us fixed on target past any realistic hope of acquisition. They send last-ditch instructions, squeeze our fading signals for every last bit among the static. I can sense their frustration, their reluctance to let us go; once or twice, we're even asked if some judicious mix of thrust and gravity might let us linger here a bit longer.

But deceleration is for pansies. We're headed for the stars.

Bye, Burnsie. Bye, Mission Control. Bye, Sol.

See you at heat death.

Warily, we close on target.

There are three of us in the Second Wave—slower than our

predecessors, yes, but still so much faster than anything flesh-constrained. We are weighed down by payloads which make us virtually omniscient. We see on every wavelength, from radio to string. Our autonomous microprobes measure everything our masters anticipated; tiny onboard assembly lines can build tools from the atoms up, to assess the things they did not. Atoms, scavenged from where we are, join with ions beamed from where we were: thrust and materiel accumulate in our bellies.

This extra mass has slowed us, but midpoint braking maneuvers have slowed us even more. The last half of this journey has been a constant fight against momentum from the first. It is not an efficient way to travel. In less-hurried times we would have built early to some optimal speed, perhaps slung around a convenient planet for a little extra oomph, coasted most of the way. But time is pressing, so we burn at both ends. We must reach our destination; we cannot afford to pass it by, cannot afford the kamikaze exuberance of the First Wave. They merely glimpsed the lay of the land. We must map it down to the motes.

We must be more responsible.

Now, slowing toward orbit, we see everything they saw and more. We see the scabs, and the impossible iron core. We hear the singing. And there, just beneath the comet's frozen surface, we see structure: an infiltration of architecture into geology. We are not yet close enough to squint, and radar is too long in the tooth for fine detail. But we are smart, and there are three of us, widely separated in space. The wavelengths of three radar sources can be calibrated to interfere at some predetermined point of convergence—and those tripartite echoes, hologramatically remixed, will increase resolution by a factor of twenty-seven.

Burns-Caulfield stops singing the moment we put our plan into action. In the next instant I go blind.

It's a temporary aberration, a reflexive amping of filters to *compensate for the overload. My arrays are back online in seconds, diagnostics green within and without. I reach out to the others, confirm identical experiences, identical recoveries. We are all still fully functional, unless the sudden increase in ambient ion density is some kind of sensory artifact. We are ready to continue our investigation of Burns-Caulfield.*

The only real problem is that Burns-Caulfield seems to have disappeared. . . .

Theseus carried no regular crew—no navigators or engineers, no one to swab the decks, no meat wasted on tasks that machinery orders of mag smaller could perform orders of mag better. Let superfluous deckhands weigh down other ships, if the non-Ascendant hordes needed to attach some pretense of usefulness to their lives. Let them infest vessels driven only by commercial priorities. The only reason *we* were here was because nobody had yet optimized software for First Contact. Bound past the edge of the solar system, already freighted with the fate of the world, *Theseus* wasted no mass on self-esteem.

So here we were, rehydrated and squeaky clean: Isaac Szpindel, to study the aliens. The Gang of Four—Susan James and her secondary personae—to talk to them. Major Amanda Bates was here to fight, if necessary. And Jukka Sarasti to command us all, to move us like chess pieces on some multidimensional game board that only vampires could see.

He'd arrayed us around a conference table that warped gently through the Commons, keeping a discreet and constant distance from the curved deck beneath. The whole drum was furnished in Early Concave, tricked unwary and hungover brains into thinking they were looking at the world through fish-eye lenses. In deference to the creakiness of the *nouveaux undead* it spun at a mere fifth of a g, but it was just warming up. We'd be at half-grav in six hours, stuck there for eighteen out of every twenty-four until the ship decided we were fully recovered. For the next few days, free fall would be a rare and blessed thing.

Light sculptures appeared on the tabletop. Sarasti could have fed the information directly to our inlays—the whole briefing could have gone through ConSensus, without the need to assemble physically in the same place—but if you want to be sure everyone's paying attention, you bring them together.

Szpindel leaned in conspiratorially at my side. "Or maybe the bloodsucker just gets off seeing all this meat in close quarters, eh?"

If Sarasti heard he didn't show it, not even to me. He pointed to a dark heart at the center of the display, his eyes lost behind black glass. "Oasa object. Infrared emitter, methane class."

On the display it was—nothing. Our apparent destination was a black disk, a round absence of stars. In real life it weighed in at over ten Jupiters and measured 20 percent wider at the belly. It was directly in our path: too small to burn, too remote for the reflection of distant sunlight, too heavy for a gas giant, too light for a brown dwarf.

"When did *that* show up?" Bates squeezed her rubber ball in one hand, the knuckles whitening.

"X-ray spike appears during the 'seventy-six microwave survey." Six years before Firefall. "Never confirmed, never reacquired. Like a torsion flare from an L-class dwarf, but we should see anything big enough to generate that kind of effect and the sky's dark on that bearing. IAU calls it a statistical artifact."

Szpindel's eyebrows drew together like courting caterpillars. "What changed?"

Sarasti smiled faintly, keeping his mouth closed. "The metabase gets—*crowded,* after Firefall. Everyone *skittish,* looking for clues. After Burns-Caulfield explodes—" He clicked at the back of his throat. "Turns out the spike might arise from a sub-dwarf object after all, if the magnetosphere's torqued enough."

Bates: "Torqued by what?"

"Don't know."

Layers of statistical inference piled up on the table while Sarasti sketched background: Even with a solid bearing and half the world's attention, the object had hidden from all but the most intensive search. A thousand telescopic snapshots had been stacked one on another and squeezed through a dozen filters before something emerged from the static, just below the three-meter band and the threshold of certainty. For the longest time it hadn't even been real: just a probabilistic ghost until *Theseus* got close enough to collapse the waveform. A quantum particle, heavy as ten Jupiters.

Earthbound cartographers were calling it *Big Ben. Theseus* had barely passed Saturn's orbit when it showed up in the residuals. That discovery would have been moot for anyone else; no other ship caught en route could have packed enough fuel for anything but the long dejected loop back home. But *Theseus*'s thin, infinitely attenuate fuel line reached all the way back to the sun; she could turn on the proverbial dime. We'd changed course in our sleep and the Icarus stream tracked our moves like a cat after prey, feeding us at light speed.

And here we were.

"Talk about long shots," Szpindel grumbled.

Across the table, Bates flicked her wrist. Her ball sailed over my head; I heard it bounce off the deck (*not the deck,* something in me amended: *handrail*). "We're assuming the comet was a deliberate decoy, then."

Sarasti nodded. The ball riccocheted back into my line of sight high overhead and disappeared briefly behind the spinal bundle, looping through some eccentric, counterintuitive parabola in the drum's feeble grav.

"So they want to be left alone."

Sarasti steepled his fingers and turned his face in her direction. "That your recommendation?"

She wished it was. "No, sir. I'm just saying that Burns-Caulfield took a lot of resources and effort to set up. Whoever built it obviously values their anonymity and has the technology to protect it."

The ball bounced one last time and wobbled back toward the Commons. Bates half-hopped from her seat (she floated briefly), barely catching it on its way past. There remained a newborn-animal awkwardness to her movements, half Coriolis, half residual rigor. Still: a big improvement in four hours. The rest of the Humans were barely past the walking stage.

"Maybe it wasn't much trouble for *them* at all, eh?" Szpindel was musing. "Maybe it was dead easy."

"In which case they might or might not be as xenophobic, but they're even more advanced. We don't want to rush into this."

Sarasti turned back to the simmering graphics. "So?"

Bates kneaded the recovered ball with her fingertips. "The second mouse gets the cheese. We may have blown our top-of-the-line recon in the Kuiper, but we don't have to go in blind. Send in our own drones along separate vectors. Hold off on a close approach until we at least know whether we're dealing with friendlies or hostiles."

James shook her head. "If they were hostile, they could have packed the Fireflies with antimatter. Or sent one big object instead of sixty thousand little ones, let the impact take us out."

"The Fireflies only imply an initial curiosity," Bates said. "Who knows if they liked what they saw?"

"What if this whole *diversion* theory's just so much shit?"

I turned, briefly startled. James's mouth had made the words; *Sascha* had spoken them.

"You wanna stay hidden, you don't light up the sky with fucking *fireworks*," she continued. "You don't need a diversion if nobody's looking for you, and nobody's looking for you if you lie low. If they were so *curious,* they could've just snuck in a spycam."

"Risks detection," the vampire said mildly.

"Hate to break it, Jukka, but the *Fireflies* didn't exactly slip under the rad—"

Sarasti opened his mouth, closed it again. Filed teeth, briefly visible, clicked audibly behind his face. Tabletop graphics reflected off his visor, a band of writhing polychrome distortions where eyes should be.

Sascha shut up.

Sarasti continued. "They trade stealth for speed. By the time you react, they already have what they want." He spoke quietly, patiently, a well-fed predator explaining the rules of the game to prey that really should know better: *The longer it takes me to track you down, the more hope you have of escaping.*

But Sascha had already fled. Her surfaces had scattered like a flock of panicked starlings, and the next time Susan James's mouth opened, it was Susan James who spoke through it. "Sascha's aware of the current paradigm, Jukka. She's simply worried that it might be wrong."

"Got another we could trade it on?" Szpindel wondered. "More options? Longer warranty?"

"I don't know." James sighed. "I guess not. It's just . . . *odd,* that they'd want to actively mislead us. I'd hoped they were merely— Well." She spread her hands. "Probably no big deal. I'm sure they'll still be willing to talk, if we handle the introductions right. We just need to be a little more cautious, perhaps . . ."

Sarasti unfolded himself from his chair and loomed over us. "We go in. What we know weighs against further delay."

Bates frowned and pitched her ball back into orbit. "Sir, all we actually *know* is that an Oasa emitter's in our path. We don't even know if there's anyone *there*."

"There is," Sarasti said. "They expect us."

Nobody spoke for a few seconds. Someone's joints cracked in the silence.

"Er . . . ," Szpindel began.

Without looking, Sarasti flicked out his arm and snatched Bates's returning ball from the air. "Ladar pings *Theseus* four hours forty-eight minutes ago. We respond with an identical signal. Nothing. Probe launches half hour before we wake up. We don't go in blind, but we don't wait. They *see* us already. Longer we wait, greater risk of countermeasures."

I looked at the dark featureless placeholder on the table: bigger than Jupiter and we couldn't even see it yet. Something in the shadow of that mass had just reached out with casual, unimaginable precision and tapped us on the nose with a laser beam.

This was not going to be an even match.

Szpindel spoke for all of us: "You knew that all along? You're telling us *now*?"

This time Sarasti's smile was wide and toothy. It was as though a gash had opened in the lower half of his face.

Maybe it was a predator thing. He just couldn't help playing with his food.

It wasn't so much the way they looked. The elongate limbs, the pale skin, the canines and the extended mandible—noticeable, yes, even alien, but not disturbing, not *frightening*. Not even the eyes, really. The eyes of dogs and cats shine in the darkness; we don't shiver at the sight.

Not the way they looked. The way they *moved*.

Something in the reflexes, maybe. The way they held their limbs: like mantis limbs, long jointed things you just *knew* could reach out and snatch you from right across the room, any time they felt like it. When Sarasti looked at me—really *looked,* naked-eyed, unfiltered by the visor—a half-million years just melted away. The fact that he was extinct meant nothing. The fact that we'd come so far, grown strong enough to resurrect our own nightmares to serve us . . . meant nothing. The genes aren't fooled. They know what to fear.

Of course, you had to experience it in person. Robert Paglini knew the theory of vampires down to the molecules, but even with all those technical specs in his head he never really *got* it.

He called me, before we left. I hadn't been expecting it; ever since the roster had been announced our watches had blocked calls from anyone not explicitly contact-listed. I'd forgotten that Pag had been. We hadn't spoken since Chelsea. I'd given up on ever hearing from him again.

But there he was. "Pod-man." He smiled, a tentative overture.

"It's good to see you," I said, because that's what people said in similar situations.

"Yeah, well I saw your name in the noose. You've made it big, for a baseline."

"Not so big."

"Crap. You're the vanguard of the Human race. You're our first, last, and only hope against the unknown. Man, you *showed* them." He held his fist up and shook it, vicariously triumphant.

Showing them had become a cornerstone of Robert Paglino's life. He'd really made it work for him, too, overcome the handicap of a natural birth with retrofits and enhancements and sheer bloody-mindedness. In a world in which Humanity had become redundant in unprecedented numbers, we'd both retained the status of another age: *working professional.*

"So you're taking orders from a vamp," he said now. "Talk about fighting fire with fire."

"I guess it's practice. Until we run up against the real thing."

He laughed. I couldn't imagine why, but I smiled back anyway. It *was* good to see him.

"So, what are they like?" Pag asked.

"Vampires? I don't know. Just met my first one yesterday."

"And?"

"Hard to read. Didn't even seem to be aware of his surroundings sometimes, he seemed to be . . . off in his own little world."

"He's aware, all right. Those things are so fast it's scary. You know they can hold both aspects of a Necker cube in their heads at the same time?"

The term rang a bell. I subtitled, and saw the thumbnail of a familiar wire-frame box:

Now I remembered; classic ambiguous illusion. Sometimes the shaded panel seemed to be in front, sometimes behind. The perspective flipped back and forth as you watched.

"You or I, we can only see it one way or the other," Pag said. "Vamps see it both ways *at once.* Do you have any *idea* what kind of an edge that gives 'em?"

"Not enough of one."

"*Touché*. But hey, not their fault neutral traits get fixed in small populations."

"I don't know if I'd call the Crucifix glitch *neutral*."

"It was at first. How many intersecting right angles do you see in nature?" He waved one dismissive hand. "Anyway, that's not the point. The point is they can do something that's neurologically impossible for us Humans. They can hold *simultaneous multiple worldviews,* Pod-man. They just *see* things we have to work out step-by-step, they don't have to *think* about it. You know, there isn't a single baseline human who could just tell you, just off the top of their heads, every prime number between one and a billion? In the old days, only a few autistics could do shit like that."

"He never uses the past tense," I murmered.

"Huh? Oh, that." Pag nodded. "They never *experience* the past tense. It's just another thread to them. They don't remember stuff, they *relive* it."

"What, like a post-traumatic flashback?"

"Not so traumatic." He grimaced. "Not for *them,* at least."

"So this is obviously your current hot spot? Vampires?"

"Pod, vampires are the capital *H* hot spot for *anyone* with a 'neuro' in their CV. I'm just doing a couple of histology papers. Pattern-matching receptors, Mexican-hat arrays, reward/irrelevance filters. The eyes, basically."

"Right." I hesitated. "Those kind of throw you."

"No *shit*." Pag nodded knowingly. "That tap lucidum of theirs, that *shine*. Scary." He shook his head, impressed all over again at the recollection.

"You've never met one," I surmised.

"What, in the flesh? I'd give my left ball. Why?"

"It's not the shine. It's the"—I groped for a word that fit "—the *attitude,* maybe."

"Yeah," he said after a bit. "I guess sometimes you've just gotta be there, huh? Which is why I envy you, Pod-man."

"You shouldn't."

"I should. Even if you never meet whoever sent the 'Flies, you're in for one Christly research opportunity with that—Sarasti, is it?"

"Wasted on me. The only *neuro* in *my* file's under medical history."

He laughed. "Anyway, like I said, I just saw your name in the headlines and I figured, hey, the man's leaving in a couple of months, I should probably stop waiting around for *him* to call."

It had been over two years. "I didn't think I'd get through. I thought you'd shitlisted me."

"Nah. Never." He looked down, though, and fell silent.

"But you should have called her," he said at last.

"I know."

"She was *dying*. You should've—"

"There wasn't time."

He let the lie sit there for a while.

"Anyway," he said at last, "I just wanted to wish you luck." Which wasn't exactly true, either.

"Thanks. I appreciate that."

"Kick their alien asses. If aliens have asses."

"There's five of us, Pag. Nine if you count the backups. We're not exactly an army."

"Just an expression, fellow mammal. Bury the hatchet. Damn the torpedoes. Soothe the serpent."

Raise the white flag, I thought.

"I guess you're busy," he said. "I'll—"

"Look, you want to get together? In airspace? I haven't been to QuBit's in a while."

"Love to, Pod. Unfortunately I'm in Mankoya. Splice 'n' dice workshop."

"What, you mean *physically?*"

"Cutting-edge research. Old-school habits."

"Too bad."

"Anyway, I'll let you go. Just wanted, you know—"

"Thanks," I said again.

"So, you know. Bye," Robert Paglino told me. Which was, when you got down to it, the reason he'd called.

He wasn't expecting another chance.

Pag blamed me for the way it had ended with Chelsea. Fair enough. I blamed him for the way it began.

He'd gone into neuroeconomics at least partly because his childhood buddy had turned into a pod person before his eyes. I'd ended up in Synthesis for roughly the same reason. Our paths had diverged, and we didn't see each other in the flesh all that often; but two decades after I'd brutalized a handful of children on his behalf, Robert Paglino was still my best and only friend.

"You need to seriously thaw out," he told me, "and I know just the lady to handle the oven mitts."

"That is perhaps the worst use of metaphor in the history of human language," I said.

"Seriously, Pod. She'll be good for you. A, a *counterbalance—* ease you a bit closer to the comfy mean, you know?"

"No, Pag, I don't. What is she, another neuroeconomist?"

"Neuroaestheticist," he said.

"There's still a market for those?" I couldn't imagine how; why pay to tweak your compatibility with some significant other, when significant others themselves were so out of fashion?

"Not much of one," Pag admitted. "Fact is, she's pretty much retired. But she's still got the tools, my man. Very thigmotactic. Likes all her relationships face-to-face and in the flesh."

"I dunno, Pag. Sounds like work."

"Not like *your* work. She's got to be easier than the bleeding composites you front for. She's smart, she's sexy, and she's nicely inside the standard deev except for the personal contact thing. Which is not so much outright perversion as charming fetish. In your case it could even be therapeutic."

"If I wanted therapy I'd see a therapist."

"She does a bit of that too, actually."

"Yeah?" And then, despite myself, "Any good?"

He looked me up and down. "No one's *that* good. That's not what this is. I just figured you two would click. Chelse is one of the few who might not be completely put off by your intimacy issues."

"*Everyone's* got intimacy issues these days, in case you hadn't noticed." He must have; the population had been dropping for decades.

"I was being euphemistic. I meant your aversion to general Human contact."

"Making it euphemistic to call you Human?"

He grinned. "Different deal. We got history."

"No thanks."

"Too late. She's already en route to the appointed place."

"Appoin— You're an asshole, Pag."

"The tightest."

Which was how I found myself intrusively face-to-face in an airspace lounge south of Beth and Bear. The lighting was low and indirect, creeping from under seats and the edges of tables; the chromatics, this afternoon at least, were defiantly longwave. It was a place where baselines could pretend to see in infrared.

So I pretended for a moment, assessing the woman in the corner booth: gangly and glorious, a half-dozen ethnicities coexisting

peacefully with no single voice dominant. Something glowed on
her cheek, a faint emerald staccato against the ambient red shift.
Her hair floated in a diffuse ebony cloud about her head. As I
neared I caught occasional glints of metal within that nimbus, the
threads of a static generator purveying the illusion of weightless-
ness. In normal light her blood-red skin would doubtless shift
down to the fashionable butterscotch of the unrepentant mongrel.

She *was* attractive, but so was everyone in this kind of light;
the longer the wavelength, the softer the focus. There's a reason
fuckcubbies don't come with fluorescent lights.

You will not fall for this, I told myself.

"Chelsea," she said. Her little finger rested on one of the
table's inset trickle-chargers. "Former neuroaestheticist, presently
a parasite on the Body Economic thanks to genes and machines
on the cutting edge."

The glow on her cheek flapped bright lazy wings: a tattoo, a
bioluminescent butterfly.

"Siri," I said. "Freelance Synthesist, indentured servant to the
genes and machines that turned you into a parasite."

She waved at the empty seat. I took it, assessing the system before me, sizing up the best approach for a fast yet diplomatic dis-
connect. The set of her shoulders told me she enjoyed lightscapes,
and was embarrassed to admit it. Monahan was her favorite
artist. She thought herself a natural girl because she'd stayed on
chemical libidinals all these years, even though a synaptic edit
would have been simpler. She reveled in her own inconsistency: a
woman whose professional machinery edited thought itself, yet
mistrustful of the dehumanizing impact of telephones. Innately
affectionate, and innately afraid of unreturned affection, and in-
domitably unwilling to let any of that stop her.

She liked what she saw when looked at me. She was a little
afraid of that, too.

Chelsea gestured at my side of the table. The touchpads there glowed a soft, dissonant sapphire in the bloody light, like a set of splayed fingerprints. "Good dope here. Extra hydroxyl on the ring, or something."

Assembly-line neuropharm doesn't do much for me; it's optimized for people with more meat in their heads. I fingered one of the pads for appearances, and barely felt the tingle.

"So. A Synthesist. Explaining the Incomprehensible to the Indifferent."

I smiled on cue. "More like bridging the gap between the people who make the breakthroughs and the people who take the credit for them."

She smiled back. "So how do you do it? All those optimized frontal lobes and refits—I mean, if they're incomprehensible, how do you comprehend them?"

"It helps to find pretty much everyone else incomprehensible, too. Provides experience." There. That should force a bit of distance.

It didn't. She thought I was joking. I could see her lining up to push for more details, to ask questions about what I did, which would lead to questions about *me,* which would lead—

"Tell me what it's like," I said smoothly, "rewiring people's heads for a living."

Chelsea grimaced; the butterfly on her cheek fluttered nervously at the motion, wings brightening. "God, you make it sound like we turn them into zombies or something. They're just tweaks, mainly. Changing taste in music or cuisine, you know, optimizing mate compatibility. It's all completely reversible."

"There aren't drugs for that?"

"Nah. Too much developmental variation between brains; our targeting is *really* fine-scale. But it's not all microsurgery and fried synapses, you know. You'd be surprised how much rewiring can be done noninvasively. You can start all sorts of cascades just by playing certain sounds in the right order, or showing images with the right balance of geometry and emotion."

"I assume those are new techniques."

"Not really. Rhythm and music hang their hats on the same basic principle. We just turned art into science."

"Yeah, but when?" The recent past, certainly. Sometime within the past twenty years or so.

Her voice grew suddenly quiet. "Robert told me about your operation. Some kind of viral epilepsy, right? Back when you were just a tyke."

I'd never explicitly asked him to keep it a secret. What was the difference anyway? I'd made a full recovery.

Besides, Pag still thought that had happened to someone *else*.

"I don't know your specifics," Chelsea continued gently, "but from the sound of it, noninvasive techniques wouldn't have helped. I'm sure they only did what they had to."

I tried to suppress the thought, and couldn't: *I like this woman.*

I felt something then, a strange, unfamiliar sensation that somehow loosened my vertebrae. The chair felt subtly, indefinably more comfortable at my back.

"Anyway." My silence had thrown her off-stride. "Haven't done it much since the bottom dropped out of the market. But it *did* leave me with a fondness for face-to-face encounters, if you know what I mean."

"Yeah. Pag said you took your sex in the first person."

She nodded. "I'm very old school. You okay with that?"

I wasn't certain. I was a virgin in the real world, one of the few things I still had in common with the rest of civilized society. "In principle, I guess. It just seems . . . a lot of effort for not as much payoff, you know?"

"Don't I." She smiled. "Real fuckbuddies aren't airbrushed.

Got all these *needs* and *demands* that you can't edit out. How can you blame anyone for saying *no thanks* to all that, now there's a choice? You gotta wonder how our parents ever stayed together sometimes."

You gotta wonder why *they did*. I felt myself sinking deeper into the chair, wondered again at this strange new sensation. Chelsea had said the dopamine was tweaked. That was probably it.

She leaned forward, not coy, not coquettish, not breaking eye contact for an instant in the longwave gloom. I could smell the lemony tang of pheromones and synthetics mingling on her skin. "But there are advantages, too, once you learn the moves," she said. "The body's got a long memory. And you *do* realize that there's no trickler under your right finger there, don't you, Siri?"

I looked. My left arm was slightly extended, index finger touching one of the trickle pads; and my right had mirrored the motion while I wasn't watching, its own finger tapping uselessly on blank tabletop.

I pulled it back. "Bit of a bilateral twitch," I admitted. "The body creeps into symmetrical poses when I'm not looking."

I waited for a joke, or at least a raised eyebrow. Chelsea just nodded and resumed her thread. "So if you're game for this, so am I. I've never been entangled with a Synthesist before."

"Jargonaut's fine. I'm not proud."

"Don't you just always know just exactly what to say." She cocked her head at me. "So, your name. What's it mean?"

Relaxed. That was it. I felt *relaxed*.

"I don't know. It's just a name."

"Well, it's not good enough. If we're gonna to be swapping spit for any length of time you've gotta get a name that *means* something."

And we were, I realized. Chelsea had decided while I wasn't looking. I could have stopped her right there, told her what a bad idea this was, apologized for any misunderstanding. But then there'd be wounded looks and hurt feelings and guilt because after all, if I wasn't interested why the hell had I even shown up?

She seemed nice. I didn't want to hurt her.

Just for a while, I told myself. *It'll be an experience.*

"I think I'll call you Cygnus," Chelsea said.

"The swan?" I said. A bit precious, but it could have been worse. She shook her head. "Black hole. Cygnus X-1."

Ah. A dark, dense object that sucks up the light and destroys everything in its path. "Thanks a whole fucking lot. Why?"

"I'm not sure. Something dark about you." She shrugged, and gave me a great toothy grin. "But it's not unattractive. And let me give you a tweak or two, I bet you'd grow right out of it."

Pag admitted afterward, a bit sheepishly, that maybe I should have read that as a warning sign. Live and learn.

LEADERS ARE VISIONARIES WITH A POORLY DEVEL-
OPED SENSE OF FEAR AND NO CONCEPT OF THE ODDS
AGAINST THEM.

—ROBERT JARVIK

OUR SCOUT FELL toward orbit, watching Ben. We fell days behind, watching the scout. And that was *all* we did: sit in *Theseus*'s belly while the system streamed telemetry to our inlays. Essential, irreplaceable, mission-critical—we might as well have been ballast during that first approach.

We passed Ben's Rayleigh limit. *Theseus* squinted at a meager emission spectrum and saw a rogue halo element from Canis

Major—a dismembered remnant of some long-lost galaxy that had drifted into ours and ended up as roadkill, uncounted billions of years ago. We were closing on something from outside the Milky Way.

The probe arced down and in, drew close enough for false-color enhance. Ben's surface brightened to a seething parfait of high-contrast bands against a diamond-hard starscape. Something twinkled there, faint sparkles on endless overcast.

"Lightning?" James wondered.

Szpindel shook his head. "Meteorites. Must be a lot of rock in the neighborhood."

"Wrong color," Sarasti said. He was not physically among us—he was back in his tent, hardlined into the Captain—but ConSensus put him anywhere on board he wanted to be.

Morphometrics scrolled across my inlays: mass, diameter, mean density. Ben's day lasted seven hours, twelve minutes. Diffuse but massive accretion belt circling the equator, more torus than ring, extending almost a half-million kilometers from the cloud tops: the pulverized corpses of moons perhaps, ground down to leftovers.

"Meteorites." Szpindel grinned. "Told ya."

He seemed to be right; increasing proximity smeared many of those pinpoint sparkles into bright ephemeral hyphens, scratching the atmosphere. Closer to the poles, cloud bands flickered with dim, intermittent flashes of electricity.

Weak radio emission peaks at 31 and 400 m. Outer atmosphere heavy with methane and ammonia; lithium, water, carbon monoxide in abundance. Ammonia hydrogen sulfide, alkali halide mixing locally in those torn swirling clouds. Neutral alkalis in the upper layers. By now even *Theseus* could pick those things out from a distance, but our scout was close enough to see filigree. It no longer saw a disk. It gazed down at a dark convex wall in seething layers of red and brown, saw faint stains of anthracene and pyrene.

One of a myriad meteorite contrails scorched Ben's face directly ahead; for a moment I thought I could even see the tiny dark speck at its core, but sudden static scratched the feed. Bates cursed softly. The image blurred, then steadied as the probe pitched its voice higher up the spectrum. Unable to make itself heard above the longwave din, now it spoke down a laser. And still it stuttered. Keeping it aligned across a million fluctuating kilometers should have posed no problem at all; our respective trajectories were known parabolas, our relative positions infinitely predictable at any time t. But the meteorite's contrail jumped and skittered on the feed, as if the beam were being repeatedly, infinitesimally knocked out of alignment. Incandescent gas blurred its details; I doubted that even a rock-steady image would have offered any sharp edges for a Human eye to hold on to. Still. There was something *wrong* about it somehow, something about the tiny black dot at the core of that fading brightness. Something that some primitive part of my mind refused to accept as *natural*—

The image lurched again, and flashed to black, and didn't return.

"Probe's fried," Bates reported. "Spike there at the end. Like it hit a Parker spiral, but with a *really* tight wind."

I didn't need to call up subtitles. It was obvious in the set of her face, the sudden creases between her eyebrows: She was talking about a magnetic field.

"It's—" she began, and stopped as a number popped up in ConSensus: *11.2 Tesla*.

"*Holy shit,*" Szpindel whispered. "Is that right?"

Sarasti clicked from the back of his throat and the back of the ship. A moment later he served up an instant replay, those last few seconds of telemetry zoomed and smoothed and contrast-enhanced from visible light down to deep infrared. There was that same dark shard cauled in flame, there was the contrail burning in its wake. Now it dimmed as the object skipped off the denser atmosphere beneath and regained altitude. Within moments the heat trace had faded entirely. The thing that had burned at its center rose back into space, a fading ember. A great conic scoop at its front end gaped like a mouth. Stubby fins disfigured an ovoid abdomen.

Ben lurched and went out all over again.

"Meteorites," Bates said dryly.

The thing had left me with no sense of scale. It could have been an insect or an asteroid. "How big?" I whispered, a split second before the answer appeared on my inlays:

Four hundred meters along the major axis.

Ben was safely distant in our sights once more, a dark dim disk centered in *Theseus*'s forward viewfinder. But I remembered the close-up: a twinkling orb of black-hearted fires, a face gashed and pockmarked, endlessly wounded, endlessly healing.

There'd been *thousands* of the things.

Theseus shivered along her length. It was just a pulse of decelerating thrust, but for that one moment, I imagined I knew how she felt.

We headed in and hedged our bets.

Theseus weaned herself with a ninety-eight-second burn, edged us into some vast arc that might, with a little effort, turn into an orbit—or into a quick discreet flyby if the neighborhood turned out to be a little too rough. The Icarus stream fell invisibly to port, its unswerving energy lost to space-time. Our city-size, molecule-thick parasol wound down and packed itself away until the next time the ship got thirsty. Antimatter stock-piles began dropping immediately; this time we were alive to watch it happen. The dip was infinitesimal, but there was some-thing disquieting about the sudden appearance of that minus sign on the display.

We could have retained the apron strings, left a buoy behind in the telematter stream to bounce energy down the well after us. Susan James wondered why we hadn't.

"Too risky," Sarasti said, without elaboration.

Szpindel leaned in James's direction. "Why give 'em some-thing *else* to shoot at, eh?"

We sent more probes ahead, though, spat them out hard and fast and too fuel-constrained for anything but flyby and self-destruct. They couldn't take their eyes off the machines swing-ing around Big Ben. *Theseus* stared her own unblinking stare, more distant though more acute. But if those high divers even knew we were out there, they ignored us completely. We tracked them across the closing distance, watched them swoop and loop though a million parabolas at a million angles. We never saw them collide—not with each other, not with the cauldron of rock tumbling around Ben's equator. Every perigee dipped briefly into atmosphere; there they burned, and slowed, and ac-celerated back into space, their anterior scoops glowing with residual heat.

Bates grabbed a ConSensus image, drew highlights and a conclusion around the front end: "Scramjet."

We tracked nearly four hundred thousand in less than two days. That appeared to be most of them; new sightings leveled off afterward, the cumulative curve flattening toward some the-oretical asymptote. Most of the orbits were close and fast, but Sarasti projected a frequency distribution extending almost back to Pluto. We might stay out here for years, and still catch the occasional new shovelnose returning from its extended foray into the void.

"The faster ones are pulling over fifty g's on the hairpin turn," Szpindel pointed out. "Meat couldn't handle that. I say they're unmanned."

"Meat's reinforceable," Sarasti said.

"If it's got *that* much scaffolding you might as well stop splitting hairs and call it a machine anyway."

Surface morphometrics were absolutely uniform. Four hundred thousand divers, every one identical. If there was an alpha male calling the shots among the herd, it couldn't be distinguished on sight.

One night—as such things were measured on board—I followed a soft squeal of tortured electronics up to the observation blister. Szpindel floated there, watching the skimmers. He'd closed the clamshells, blocked off the stars and built a little analytical nest in their place. Graphs and windows spilled across the inside of the dome as though the virtual space in Szpindel's head was insufficient to contain them. Tactical graphics lit him from all sides, turned his body into a bright patchwork of flickering tattoos.

The Illustrated Man. "Mind if I come in?" I asked.

He grunted: *Yeah, but not enough to push it.*

Inside the dome, the sound of heavy rainfall hissed and spat behind the screeching that had led me here. "What *is* that?"

"Ben's magnetosphere." He didn't look back. "Nice, eh?"

Synthesists don't have opinions on the job; it keeps observer effects to a minimum. This time I permitted myself a small breach. "The static's nice. I could do without the screeching."

"Are you kidding? That's the music of the spheres, commissar. It's *beautiful*. Like old jazz."

"I never got the hang of that, either."

He shrugged and squelched the upper register, left the rain pattering around us. His jiggling eyes fixed on some arcane graphic. "Want a scoop for your notes?"

"Sure."

"There you go." Light reflected off his feedback glove, iridescing like the wing of a dragonfly as he pointed: an absorption spectrum, a looped time series. Bright peaks surged and subsided, surged and subsided across a fifteen-second time frame.

Subtitles only gave me wavelengths and Angstroms. "What is it?"

"Diver farts. Those bastards are dumping complex organics into the atmosphere."

"How complex?"

"Hard to tell, so far. Faint traces, and they dissipate like *that*. But sugars and aminos at least. Maybe proteins. Maybe more."

"Maybe life? Microbes?" An alien terraforming project . . .

"Depends on how you define *life*, eh?" Szpindel said. "Not even *Deinococcus* would last long down there. But it's a big atmosphere. They better not be in any hurry if they're reworking the whole thing by direct inoculation."

If they were, the job would go a lot faster with self-replicating inoculates. "Sounds like life to me."

"Sounds like agricultural aerosols, is what it sounds like. Those fuckers are turning the whole damn gas ball into a rice paddy bigger than Jupiter." He gave me a scary grin. "Something's got a *beeeg* appetite, hmm? You gotta wonder if we aren't gonna be a teeny bit outnumbered."

Szpindel's findings were front and center at our next get-together.

The vampire summed it up for us, visual aids dancing on the table: "Von Neumann self-replicating r-selector. Seed washes up and sprouts skimmers, skimmers harvest raw materials from the accretion belt. Some perturbations in those orbits; belt's still unsettled."

"Haven't seen any of the herd giving birth," Szpindel remarked. "Any sign of a factory?"

Sarasti shook his head. "Discarded, maybe. Decompiled. Or the herd stops breeding at optimal N."

"These are only the bulldozers," Bates pointed out. "There'll be tenants."

"A *lot* of 'em, eh?" Szpindel added. "Outnumber us by orders of mag."

James: "But they might not show up for centuries."

Sarasti clicked. "Do these skimmers build Fireflies? Burns-Caulfield?"

It was a rhetorical question. Szpindel answered anyway: "Don't see how."

"Something else does, then. Something already local."

Nobody spoke for a moment. James's topology shifted and shuffled in the silence; when she opened her mouth again, someone indefinably *younger* was on top.

"Their habitat isn't anything like ours, if they're building a home way out here. That's hopeful."

Michelle. The synesthete.

"Proteins." Sarasti's eyes were unreadable behind the visor. *Comparable biochemistries. They might eat us.*

"Whoever these beings are, they don't even live in *sunlight*. No territorial overlap, no resource overlap, no basis for conflict. There's no reason we shouldn't get along just fine."

"On the other hand," Szpindel said, "technology implies belligerence."

Michelle snorted softly. "According to a coterie of theoretical historians who've never actually met an alien, yes. Maybe now we get to prove them wrong." And in the next instant she was just *gone,* her affect scattered like leaves in a dust devil, and Susan James was back in her place saying:

"Why don't we just *ask* them?"

"Ask?" Bates said.

"There are four hundred thousand machines out there. How do we know they can't talk?"

"We'd have heard," Szpindel said. "They're drones."

"Can't hurt to ping them, just to make sure."

"There's no reason they should talk even if they *are* smart. Language and intelligence aren't all that strongly correlated even on Ear—"

"Why not *try,* at least?" James rolled her eyes. "It's what we're here for. It's what *I'm* here for. Just *send a bloody signal.*"

After a moment Bates picked up the ball. "Bad game theory, Suze."

"Game theory." She made it sound like a curse.

"Tit for tat's the best strategy. They pinged us, we pinged back. Ball's in their court now; we send another signal, we may give away too much."

"I know the rules, Amanda. They say if the other party never takes the initiative again, we ignore each other for the rest of the mission because game theory says you don't want to look *needy.*"

"The rule only applies when you're going up against an unknown player," the Major explained. "We'll have more options the more we learn."

James sighed. "It's just . . . you all seem to be going into this *assuming* they'll be hostile. As if a simple hailing signal is going to bring them down on us."

Bates shrugged. "It only makes sense to be cautious. I may be a jarhead but I'm not eager to piss off *anything* that hops between stars and terraforms superJovians for a living. I don't have to remind anyone here that *Theseus* is no warship."

She'd said *anyone*; she'd meant *Sarasti*. And Sarasti, focused on his own horizon, didn't answer. Not out loud, at least; but his surfaces spoke in a different tongue entirely.

Not yet, they said.

Bates was right, by the way. *Theseus* was officially tricked out for exploration, not combat. No doubt our masters would have preferred to load her up with nukes and particle cannons as well as her scientific payload, but not even a telemattered fuel stream can change the laws of inertia. A weaponized prototype would have taken longer to build; a more massive one, laden with heavy artillery, would take longer to accelerate. Time, our masters had decided, was of greater essence than armament. In a pinch our fabrication facilities could build most anything we needed, given time. It might take a while to build a particle-beam cannon from scratch, and we might have to scavenge a local asteroid for the raw material, but we could do it. Assuming our enemies would be willing to wait, in the interests of fair play.

But what were the odds that even our best weapons would prove effective against the intelligence that had pulled off the Firefall? If the unknown was hostile, we were probably doomed no matter what we did. The unknown *was* technologically advanced—and there were some who claimed that that made them hostile by definition. *Technology implies belligerence,* they said.

I suppose I should explain that, now that it's completely irrelevant. You've probably forgotten after all this time.

Once there were three tribes. The Optimists, whose patron saints were Drake and Sagan, believed in a universe crawling with gentle intelligence—spiritual brethren vaster and more enlightened than we, a great galactic siblinghood into whose ranks we would someday ascend. *Surely,* said the Optimists, *space travel implies enlightenment, for it requires the control of great destructive energies. Any race that can't rise above its own brutal instincts will wipe itself out long before it learns to bridge the interstellar gulf.*

Across from the Optimists sat the Pessimists, who genuflected before graven images of St. Fermi and a host of lesser lightweights. The Pessimists envisioned a lonely universe full of dead rocks and prokaryotic slime. *The odds are just too low,* they insisted. *Too many rogues, too much radiation, too much eccentricity in too many orbits. It is a surpassing miracle that even* one *Earth exists; to hope for* many *is to abandon reason and embrace religious mania. After all, the universe is fourteen billion years old: If the galaxy were alive with intelligence, wouldn't it be here by now?*

Equidistant to the other two tribes sat the Historians. They didn't have too many thoughts on the probable prevalence of intelligent, spacefaring extraterrestrials, *but if there* are *any,* they said, *they're not just going to be smart. They're going to be* mean.

It might seem almost too obvious a conclusion. What is Human history, if not an ongoing succession of greater technologies grinding lesser ones beneath their boots? But the subject wasn't merely *Human* history, or the unfair advantage that tools gave to any given side; the oppressed snatch up advanced weaponry as readily as the oppressor, given half a chance. No, the real issue was how those tools got there in the first place. The real issue was what tools are *for.*

To the Historians, tools existed for only one reason: to force the universe into unnatural shapes. They treated nature as an enemy, they were by definition a rebellion against the way things were. Technology is a stunted thing in benign environments, it never thrived in any culture gripped by belief in natural harmony. Why invent fusion reactors if your climate is comfortable, if your food is abundant? Why build fortresses if you have no enemies? Why force change upon a world that poses no threat?

Human civilization had a lot of branches, not so long ago. Even into the twenty-first century, a few isolated tribes had barely developed stone tools. Some settled down with agriculture. Others weren't content until they had ended nature itself, still others until they'd built cities in space.

We all rested eventually, though. Each new technology trampled lesser ones, climbed to some complacent asymptote, and stopped—until my own mother packed herself away like a larva in honeycomb, softened by machinery, robbed of incentive by her own contentment.

But history never said that everyone had to stop where we did. It only suggested that those who *had* stopped no longer struggled for existence. There could be other, more hellish worlds where the best Human technology would crumble, where the environment was still the enemy, where the only survivors were those who fought back with sharper tools and stronger empires. The threats contained in those environments would not be simple ones. Harsh weather and natural disasters either kill you or they don't, and once conquered—or adapted to—they lose their relevance. No, the only environmental factors that continued to matter were those that fought back, that countered new strategies with newer ones, that forced their enemies to scale ever-greater heights just to stay alive. Ultimately, the only enemy that mattered was an *intelligent* one.

And if the best toys do end up in the hands of those who've never forgotten that life itself is an act of war against intelligent opponents, what does that say about a race whose machines travel between the stars?

The argument was straightforward enough. It might even

have been enough to carry the Historians to victory—if such debates were ever settled on the basis of logic, and if a bored population hadn't already awarded the game to Fermi on points. But the Historian paradigm was just too ugly, too *Darwinian,* for most people, and besides, no one really cared anymore. Not even the Cassidy Survey's late-breaking discoveries changed much. So what if some dirtball at Ursae Majoris Eridani had an oxygen atmosphere? It was forty-three light-years away, and it wasn't talking; and if you wanted flying chandeliers and alien messiahs, you could build them to order in Heaven. If you wanted testosterone and target practice you could choose an afterlife chock-full of nasty alien monsters with really bad aim. If the mere thought of an alien intelligence threatened your worldview, you could explore a virtual galaxy of empty real estate, ripe and waiting for any God-fearing Earthly pilgrims who chanced by.

It was all there, just the other side of a fifteen-minute splice job and a cervical socket. Why endure the cramped and smelly confines of real-life space travel to go visit pond scum on Europa?

And so, inevitably, a fourth tribe arose, a Heavenly host that triumphed over all: the Tribe That Just Didn't Give a Shit. They didn't know *what* to do when the Fireflies showed up.

So they sent us, and—in belated honor of the Historian mantra—they sent along a warrior, just in case. It was doubtful in the extreme that any child of Earth would be a match for a race with interstellar technology, should they prove unfriendly. Still, I could tell that Bates's presence was a comfort, to the Human members of the crew at least. If you have to go up unarmed against an angry T rex with a four-digit IQ, it can't hurt to have a trained combat specialist at your side.

At the very least, she might be able to fashion a pointy stick from the branch of some convenient tree.

•   •   •

"I swear, if the aliens end up eating the lot of us, we'll have the Church of Game Theory to thank for it," Sascha said.

She was grabbing a brick of couscous from the galley. I was there for the caffeine. We were more or less alone; the rest of the crew was strewn from dome to Fab.

"Linguists don't use it?" I knew some that did.

"*We* don't." *And the others are hacks.* "Thing about game theory is, it assumes rational self-interest among the players. And people just aren't *rational.*"

"It used to assume that," I allowed. "These days they factor in the social neurology."

"*Human* social neurology." She bit a corner off her brick, spoke around a mouthful of semolina. "That's what game theory's good for. Rational players, or Human ones. And let me take a wild stab here and wonder if either of those is gonna apply to *that.*" She waved her hand at some archetypal alien lurking past the bulkhead.

"It's got its limitations," I admitted. "I guess you use the tools you can lay your hands on."

Sascha snorted. "So if you couldn't get your hands on a proper set of blueprints, you'd base your dream home on a book of dirty limericks."

"Maybe not." And then, a bit defensive in spite of myself, I added, "I've found it useful, though. In areas you might not expect it to be."

"Yeah? Name one."

"Birthdays," I said, and immediately wished I hadn't.

Sascha stopped chewing. Something behind her eyes flickered, almost *strobed,* as if her other selves were pricking up their ears.

"Go on," she said, and I could feel the whole Gang listening in.

"It's nothing, really. Just an example."

"So. Tell us." Sascha cocked James's head at me.

I shrugged. No point making a big thing out of it. "Well, according to game theory, you should never tell anyone when your
birthday is."

"I don't follow."

"It's a lose-lose proposition. There's no winning strategy."

"What do you mean, strategy? It's a *birthday*."

Chelsea had said exactly the same thing when I'd tried to explain it to her. *Look, I'd said, say you tell everyone when it is and
nothing happens. It's kind of a slap in the face.*

Or suppose they throw you a party, Chelsea had replied.

*Then you don't know whether they're doing it sincerely, or if
your earlier interaction just guilted them into observing an occasion
they'd rather have ignored. But if you* don't *tell anyone, and nobody
commemorates the event, there's no reason to feel badly because after all, nobody* knew. *And if someone* does *buy you a drink then
you know it's sincere because nobody would go to all the trouble of
finding out when your birthday is—and then celebrating it—if they
didn't honestly like you.*

Of course, the Gang was more up to speed on such things. I
didn't have to explain it verbally: I could just grab a piece of
ConSensus and plot out the payoff matrix, *Tell/Don't Tell* along
the columns, *Celebrated/Not Celebrated* along the rows, the
unassailable black-and-white logic of cost and benefit in the
squares themselves. The math was irrefutable: The one winning strategy was concealment. Only fools revealed their birthdays.

Sascha looked at me. "You ever show this to anyone else?"

"Sure. My girlfriend."

Her eyebrows lifted. "*You* had a girlfriend? A real one?"

I nodded. "Once."

"I mean *after* you showed this to her."

"Well, yes."

"Uh-huh." Her eyes wandered back to the payoff matrix. "Just curious, Siri. How did she react?"

"She didn't, really. Not at first. Then—well, she laughed."

"Better woman than me." Sascha shook her head. "I'd have dumped you on the spot."

My nightly constitutional up the spine: glorious dreamy flight along a single degree of freedom. I sailed through hatches and corridors, threw my arms wide and spun in the gentle cyclonic breezes of the drum. Bates ran circles around me, bouncing her ball against bins and bulkheads, stretching to field each curving rebound in the torqued pseudograv. The toy ricocheted off a stairwell and out of reach as I passed; the Major's curses followed me through the needle's eye from crypt to bridge.

I braked just short of the dome, stopped by the sound of quiet voices from ahead.

"Of *course* they're beautiful," Szpindel murmured. "They're *stars*."

"And I'm guessing I'm not your first choice to share the view," James said.

"You're a close second. But I've got a date with Meesh."

"She never mentioned it."

"She doesn't tell you everything. Ask her."

"Hey, *this* body's taking its antilibs. Even if yours isn't."

"Mind out of the gutter, Suze. Eros is only one kind of love, eh? Ancient Greeks recognized four."

"Riiight." Definitely not Susan, not anymore. "Figures you'd take your lead from a bunch of sodomites."

"*Fuck,* Sascha. All I'm asking is a few minutes alone with Meesh before the whip starts cracking again . . ."

"My body too, Ike. You wanna pull your eyes over *my* wool?"

"I just want to talk, eh? *Alone*. That too much to ask?"

I heard Sascha take a breath.

I heard Michelle let it out.

"Sorry, kid. You know the Gang."

"Thank *God*. It's like some group inspection whenever I come looking for face time."

"I guess you're lucky they like you, then."

"I still say you ought to stage a coup."

"You could always move in with us."

I heard the rustle of bodies in gentle contact. "How are you?" Szpindel asked. "You okay?"

"Pretty good. I think I'm finally used to being alive again. You?"

"Hey, I'm a spaz no matter how long I've been dead."

"You get the job done."

"Why, *merci*. I try."

A small silence. *Theseus* hummed quietly to herself.

"Mom was right," Michelle said. "They *are* beautiful."

"What do you see, when you look at them?" And then, catching himself: "I mean—"

"They're . . . prickly," Michelle told him. "When I turn my head it's like bands of very fine needles rolling across my skin in waves. But it doesn't hurt at all. It just tingles. It's almost electric. It's nice."

"Wish I could feel it that way."

"You've got the interface. Just patch a camera into your parietal lobe instead of your visual cortex."

"That'd just tell me how a *machine* feels vision, eh? Still wouldn't know how *you* do."

"Isaac Szpindel. You're a romantic."

"Nah."

"You don't *want* to know. You want to keep it mysterious."

"Already got more than enough *mystery* to deal with out here, in case you hadn't noticed."

"Yeah, but we can't *do* anything about that."

"That'll change. We'll be working our asses off in no time."

"You think?"

"Count on it," Szpindel said. "So far we've just been peeking from a distance, eh? Bet all kinds of interesting stuff happens when we get in there and start poking with a stick."

"Maybe for you. There's got to be a biological *somewhere* in the mix, with all those organics."

"Damn right. And you'll be talking to 'em while I'm giving them their physicals."

"Maybe not. I mean, Mom would never admit it in a million years but you had a point about language. When you get right down to it, it's a work-around. Like trying to describe dreams with smoke signals. It's noble, it's maybe the most noble thing a body can do but you can't turn a sunset into a string of grunts without losing something. It's *limiting*. Maybe whatever's out here doesn't even use it."

"Bet they do, though."

"Since when? You're the one who's always pointing out how *inefficient* language is."

"Only when I'm trying to get under your skin. Your pants—whole other thing." He laughed at his own joke. "Seriously, what are they gonna use instead, telepathy? I say you'll be up to your elbows in hieroglyphics before you know it. And what's more, you'll decode 'em in record time."

"You're sweet, but I wonder. Half the time I can't even decode *Jukka*." Michelle fell silent a moment. "He actually kind of throws me sometimes."

"You and seven billion others."

"Yeah. I know it's silly, but when he's not around there's a part of me that can't stop wondering where he's hiding. And when he's right there in front of me, I feel like *I* should be hiding."

"Not his fault he creeps us out."

"I know. But it's hardly a big morale booster. What genius came up with the idea of putting a vampire in charge?"

"Where else you going to put them, eh? You want to be the one giving orders to *him*?"

"And it's not just the way he moves. It's the way he *talks*. It's just *wrong*."

"You know he—"

"I'm not talking about the present-tense thing, or all the glottals. He—well, you know how he talks. He's *terse*."

"It's efficient."

"It's *artificial*, Isaac. He's smarter than all of us put together, but sometimes he talks like he's got a fifty-word vocabulary." A soft snort. "It's not like it'd kill him to use an adverb once in a while."

"Ah. But you say that because you're a linguist, and you can't see why anyone wouldn't want to wallow in the sheer beauty of *language*." Szpindel harrumphed with mock pomposity. "Now me, I'm a biologist, so it makes perfect sense."

"Really. Then explain it to me, oh wise and powerful mutilator of frogs."

"Simple. Bloodsucker's a transient, not a resident."

"What are— Oh, those are killer whales, right? Whistle dialects."

"I said forget the *language*. Think about the lifestyle. Residents are fish-eaters, eh? They hang out in big groups, don't move around much, talk all the time." I heard a whisper of motion, imagined Szpindel leaning in and laying a hand on Michelle's arm. I imagined the sensors in his gloves telling him what she felt like. "Transients, now—they eat *mammals*. Seals, sea lions, *smart* prey. Smart enough to take cover when they hear a fluke slap or a click train. So transients are *sneaky,* eh? Hunt in small groups, range all over the place, keep their mouths shut so nobody hears 'em coming."

"And Jukka's a transient."

"Man's instincts tell him to keep quiet around prey. Every time he opens his mouth, every time he lets us *see* him, he's fighting his own brain stem. Maybe we shouldn't be too harsh on the ol' guy just because he's not the world's best motivational speaker, eh?"

"He's fighting the urge to eat us every time we have a briefing? That's reassuring."

Szpindel chuckled. "It's probably not that bad. I guess even killer whales let their guard down after making a kill. Why sneak around on a full stomach, eh?"

"So he's *not* fighting his brain stem. He just isn't hungry."

"Probably a little of both. Brain stem never really *goes away,* you know. But I'll tell you one thing." Some of the playfulness ebbed from Szpindel's voice. "I've got no problem if Sarasti wants to run the occasional briefing from his quarters. But the moment we stop seeing him altogether? That's when you start watching your back."

Looking back, I can finally admit it: I envied Szpindel his way with the ladies. Spliced and diced, a gangly mass of tics and jitters that could barely feel his own skin, somehow he managed to be—

—charming. That's the word. Charming.

As a social necessity it was all but obsolete, fading into irrelevance along with two-party nonvirtual sex pairing. But even I'd tried one of those; and it would have been nice to have had Szpindel's self-deprecating skill set to call on.

Especially when everything with Chelsea started falling apart. I had my own style, of course. I tried to be charming in my own peculiar way. Once, after one too many fights about *honesty* and *emotional manipulation,* I'd started to think maybe a touch of whimsy might smooth things over. I had come to suspect that Chelsea just didn't understand sexual politics. Sure she'd edited brains for a living, but maybe she'd just memorized all that circuitry without giving any thought to how it had arisen in the first place, to the ultimate rules of natural selection that had shaped it. Maybe she honestly didn't know that we were evolutionary enemies, that *all* relationships were doomed to failure. If I could slip that insight into her head—if I could *charm* my way past her defenses—maybe we'd be able to hold things together.

So I thought about it, and I came up with the perfect way to raise her awareness. I wrote her a bedtime story, a disarming blend of humor and affection, and I called it:

The Book of Oogenesis

In the beginning were the gametes. And though there was sex, lo, there was no gender, and life was in balance.

And God said, "Let there be Sperm": and some seeds did shrivel in size and grow cheap to make, and they did flood the market.

And God said, "Let there be Eggs": and other seeds were afflicted by a plague of Sperm. And yea, few of them bore fruit, for Sperm brought no food for the zygote, and only the largest Eggs could make up the shortfall. And these grew yet larger in the fullness of time.

And God put the Eggs into a womb, and said, "Wait here: for thy bulk has made thee unwieldy, and Sperm must seek thee out in thy chambers. Henceforth shalt thou be fertilized internally." And it was so.

And God said to the gametes, "The fruit of thy fusion may abide in any place and take any shape. It may breathe air or water or the sulphurous muck of hydrothermal vents. But do not forget my one commandment unto you, which has not changed from the beginning of time: spread thy genes."

And thus did Sperm and Egg go into the world. And Sperm said, "I am cheap and plentiful, and if sowed abundantly I will surely fulfill God's plan. I shall forever seek out new mates and then abandon them when they are with child, for there are many wombs and little time."

But Egg said, "Lo, the burden of procreation weighs heavily upon me. I must carry flesh that is but half mine, gestate and feed it even when it leaves my chamber," for by now many of Egg's bodies were warm of blood, and furry besides. "I can have but few children, and must devote myself to those, and protect them at every turn. And I will make Sperm help me, for he got me into this. And though he doth struggle at my side, I shall not let him stray, nor lie with my competitors."

And Sperm liked this not.

And God smiled, for Its commandment had put Sperm and Egg at war with each other, even unto the day they made themselves obsolete.

I brought her flowers one dusky Tuesday evening when the light was perfect. I pointed out the irony of that romantic old tradition—the severed genitalia of another species, offered as a precopulatory bribe—and then I recited my story just as we were about to fuck.

To this day, I still don't know what went wrong.

THE GLASS CEILING IS IN *YOU.* THE GLASS CEILING IS
CONSCIENCE.

  —JACOB HOLTZBRINCK, *THE KEYS TO THE PLANET*

THERE WERE STORIES, before we left Earth, of a Fourth
Wave: a fleet of deep-space dreadnoughts running silent in our
wake, should the cannon fodder up front run into something
nasty. Or, if the aliens were friendly, an ambassadorial frigate
full of politicians and CEOs ready to elbow their way to the
front of the line. Never mind that Earth had no deep-space
dreadnoughts or ambassadorial spaceships; *Theseus* hadn't existed either, before Firefall. Nobody had told us of any such con-
tingent, but you never show the Big Picture to your front line.
The less they know, the less they can betray.

  I still don't know if the fourth wave ever existed. I never saw
any evidence of one, for whatever that's worth. We might have
left them floundering back at Burns-Caulfield. Or maybe they
followed us all the way to Big Ben, crept just close enough to
see what we were up against, and turned tail before things got
ugly.

  I wonder if that's what happened. I wonder if they made it
back home.

  I look back now, and hope not.

A giant marshmallow kicked *Theseus* in the side. *Down* swung
like a pendulum. Across the drum Szpindel yelped as if scalded;
in the galley, cracking a bulb of hot coffee, I nearly *was.*

  This is it, I thought. *We got too close. They're hitting back.*

  "What the—"

A flicker on the party line as Bates linked from the bridge. "Main drive just kicked in. We're changing course."

"To what? Where? Whose orders?"

"Mine," Sarasti said, appearing above us.

Nobody spoke. Drifting into the drum through the stern hatchway: the sound of something *grinding*. I pinged *Theseus*'s resource-allocation stack. Fabrication was retooling itself for the mass production of doped ceramics.

Radiation shielding. Solid stuff, bulky and primitive, not the controlled magnetic fields we usually relied on.

The Gang emerged sleepy-eyed from their tent, Sascha grumbling, "What the *fuck?*"

"Watch." Sarasti took hold of ConSensus and shook it.

It was a blizzard, not a briefing: gravity wells and orbital trajectories, shear stress simulations in thunderheads of ammonium and hydrogen, stereoscopic planetscapes buried under filters ranging from gamma to radio. I saw breakpoints and saddlepoints and unstable equilibria. I saw fold catastrophes plotted in five dimensions. My augments strained to rotate the information; my meaty half-brain struggled to understand the bottom line.

Something was hiding down there, in plain sight.

Ben's accretion belt still wasn't behaving. Its delinquency wasn't obvious; Sarasti hadn't had to plot every pebble and mountain and planetesimal to find the pattern, but he'd come close. And neither he nor the conjoined intelligence he shared with the Captain had been able to explain those trajectories as the mere aftermath of some past disturbance. The dust wasn't just *settling*; some of it marched downhill to the beat of something that even now reached out from the cloud tops and pulled debris from orbit.

Not all that debris seemed to hit. Ben's equatorial regions flickered constantly with the light of meteorite impacts—much fainter than the bright wakes of the skimmers, and gone in the wink of an eye—but those frequency distributions didn't quite account for all the rocks that had fallen. It was almost as though, every now and then, some piece of incoming detritus simply vanished into a parallel universe.

Or got caught by something in *this* one. Something that circled Ben's equator every forty hours, almost low enough to graze the atmosphere. Something that didn't show up in visible light, or infrared, or radar. Something that might have remained pure hypothesis if a skimmer hadn't burned an incandescent trail across the atmosphere *behind* it when *Theseus* happened to be watching.

Sarasti threw that one dead center: a bright contrail streaking diagonally across Ben's perpetual nightscape, stuttering partway a degree or two to the left, stuttering back just before it passed from sight. Freeze-frame showed a beam of light frozen solid, a segment snapped from its midsection and jiggled just a hair out of alignment.

A segment nine kilometers long.

"It's *cloaked*," Sascha said, impressed.

"Not very well." Bates emerged from the forward hatch and sailed spinward. "Pretty obvious refractory artifact." She caught stairs halfway to the deck, used the torque of spin-against-spam to flip upright and plant her feet on the steps. "Why didn't we catch that before?"

"No backlight," Szpindel suggested.

"It's not just the contrail. Look at the clouds." Sure enough, Ben's cloudy backdrop showed the same subtle dislocation. Bates stepped onto the deck and headed for the conference table. "We should've seen this earlier."

"The other probes see no such artifact," Sarasti said. "*This* probe approaches from a wider angle. Twenty-seven degrees."

"Wider angle to what?" Sascha said.

"To the line," Bates murmured. "Between us and them."

It was all there on tactical: *Theseus* fell inward along an obvious arc, but the probes we'd dispatched hadn't dicked around with Hohmann transfers; they'd burned straight down, their courses barely bending, all within a few degrees of the theoretical line connecting Ben to *Theseus*.

Except this one. This one had come in wide, and seen the trickery.

"The farther from our bearing, the more obvious the discontinuity," Sarasti intoned. "Think it's clearly visible on any approach perpendicular to ours."

"So we're in a blind spot? We see it if we change course?"

Bates shook her head. "The blind spot's *moving,* Sascha. It's—"

"*Tracking* us." Sascha sucked breath between her teeth. *"Motherfucker."*

Szpindel twitched. "So what is it? Our skimmer factory?"

The freeze-frame's pixels began to *crawl*. Something emerged, granular and indistinct, from the turbulent swirls and curlicues of Ben's atmosphere. There were curves, and spikes, and no smooth edges; I couldn't tell how much of the shape was real, and how much a fractal intrusion of underlying cloudscape. But the overall outline was that of a torus, or perhaps a collection of smaller jagged things piled together in a rough ring; and it was *big*. Those nine klicks of displaced contrail had merely grazed the perimeter, cut across an arc of forty or fifty degrees. This thing hiding in the shadow of ten Jupiters was almost thirty kilometers from side to side.

Sometime during Sarasti's executive summary we'd stopped accelerating. *Down* was back where it belonged. We weren't, though. Our hesitant maybe-maybe-not approach was a thing of the past: We vectored straight in now, and damn the torpedoes.

"Er, that's thirty klicks across," Sascha pointed out. "And it's *invisible*. Shouldn't we maybe be a little *more* cautious now?"

Szpindel shrugged. "If we could second-guess vampires, we wouldn't *need* vampires, eh?"

A new facet bloomed on the feed. Frequency histograms and harmonic spectra erupted from flatline into shifting mountain-scapes, a chorus of visible light.

"Modulated laser," Bates reported.

Szpindel looked up. "From *that*?"

Bates nodded. "Right after we blow its cover. Interesting timing."

"*Scary* timing," Szpindel said. "How'd it *know*?"

"We changed course. We're heading right for it."

The lightscape played on, knocking at the window.

"Whatever it is," Bates said, "it's talking to us."

"Well then," remarked a welcome voice. "By all means let's say hello."

Susan James was back in the driver's seat.

I was the only pure spectator.

They all performed what duties they could. Szpindel ran Sarasti's sketchy silhouette through a series of filters, perchance to squeeze a bit of biology from engineering. Bates compared morphometrics between the cloaked artifact and the skimmers. Sarasti watched us all from overhead and thought vampire thoughts deeper than anything we could aspire to. But it was all just make-work. The Gang of Four was on center stage, under the capable direction of Susan James.

She grabbed the nearest chair, sat, raised her hands as if cue-ing an orchestra. Her fingers trembled in midair as she played virtual icons; her lips and jaw twitched with subvocal com-mands. I tapped her feed and saw text accreting around the alien signal:

RORSCHACH TO VESSEL APPROACHING 116°AZ −23°DEC REL. HELLO THESEUS. RORSCHACH TO VESSEL APPROACHING 116°AZ −23°DEC REL. HELLO THESEUS. RORSCHACH TO VESSEL APPROACHI . . .

She'd decoded the damn thing. Already. She was even answering it:

Theseus to Rorschach. Hello Rorschach.

HELLO THESEUS. WELCOME TO THE NEIGHBORHOOD.

She'd had less than three minutes. Or rather, *they'd* had less than three minutes: four fully-conscious hub personalities and a few dozen unconscious semiotic modules, all working in parallel, all exquisitely carved from the same lump of gray matter. I could almost see why someone would do such deliberate violence to their own minds, if it resulted in this kind of performance.

Up to now I had never fully convinced myself that even survival was sufficient cause.

Request permission to approach, the Gang sent. Simple and straightforward: just facts and data, thank you, with as little room as possible for ambiguity and misunderstanding. Fancy sentiments like *we come in peace* could wait. A handshake was not the time for cultural exchange.

YOU SHOULD STAY AWAY. SERIOUSLY. THIS PLACE IS DANGEROUS.

That got some attention. Bates and Szpindel hesitated momentarily in their own headspaces and glanced into James's.

Request information on danger, the Gang sent back. Still keeping it concrete.

TOO CLOSE AND DANGEROUS TO YOU. LOW ORBIT
COMPLICATIONS.

Request information on low orbit complications.

LETHAL ENVIRONMENT. ROCKS AND RADS. YOU'RE
WELCOME. I CAN TAKE IT BUT WE'RE LIKE THAT.

*We are aware of the rocks in low orbit. We are equipped to deal
with radiation. Request information on other hazards.*

I dug under the transcript to the channel it fed from. *Theseus*
had turned part of the incoming beam into a sound wave, according to the color code. Vocal communication, then. They *spoke*.
Waiting behind that icon were the raw sounds of an alien language.
Of course I couldn't resist.

"Anytime between friends, right? Are you here for the celebration?"

English. The voice was human, male. *Old*.

"We are here to explore," replied the Gang, although *their*
voice was pure *Theseus*. "Request dialogue with agents who sent
objects into near-solar space."

"First contact. Sounds like something to celebrate."

I double-checked the source. No, this wasn't a translation; this
was the actual unprocessed signal coming from—*Rorschach*, it
had called itself. Part of the signal, anyway; there were other elements, nonacoustic ones, encoded in the beam.

I browsed them while James said, "Request information about
your celebration"—standard ship-to-ship handshaking protocols.

"You're interested." The voice was stronger now, younger.

"Yes."

"You are?"

"Yes," the Gang repeated patiently.

"You are?"

The slightest hesitation. "This is *Theseus*."

"I know that, baseline." In Mandarin, now. "Who are *you*?"

No obvious change in the harmonics. Somehow, though, the voice seemed to have acquired an edge.

"This is Susan James. I am a—"

"You wouldn't be happy here, Susan. Fetishistic religious beliefs involved. There are dangerous observances."

James chewed her lip.

"Request clarification. Are we in danger from these observances?"

"You certainly could be."

"Request clarification. Is it the observances that are dangerous, or the low-orbit environment?"

"The environment *of* the disturbances. You should pay attention, Susan. Inattention connotes indifference," *Rorschach* said.

"Or disrespect," it added after a moment.

We had four hours before Ben got in the way. Four hours of uninterrupted nonstop communication made vastly easier than anyone had expected. It spoke our language, after all. Repeatedly it expressed polite concern for our welfare. And yet, for all its facility with Human speech it told us very little. For four hours it managed to avoid giving a straight answer on any subject beyond the extreme inadvisability of closer contact, and by the time it fell into eclipse we still didn't know why.

Sarasti dropped onto the deck halfway through the exchange,

his feet never touching the stairs. He reached out and grabbed a railing to steady himself on landing, and staggered only briefly. If I'd tried that I'd have ended up bouncing along the deck like a pebble in a cement mixer.

He stood still as stone for the rest of the session, face motionless, eyes hidden behind his onyx visor. When *Rorschach*'s signal faded in mid-sentence he assembled us around the Commons table with a gesture.

"It talks," he said.

James nodded. "It doesn't say much, except for asking us to keep our distance. So far the voice has manifested as adult male, although the apparent age changed a few times."

He'd heard all that. "Structure?"

"The ship-to-ship protocols are perfect. Its vocabulary is far greater than you could derive from standard nav chatter between a few ships, so they've been listening to all our insystem traffic— I'd say for several years at least. On the other hand, the vocabulary *doesn't* have anywhere near the range you'd get by monitoring entertainment multimede, so they probably arrived after the Broadcast Age."

"How well do they use the vocabulary they have?"

"They're using phrase-structure grammar, long-distance dependencies. FLN recursion, at least four levels deep and I see no reason why it won't go deeper with continued contact. They're not parrots, Jukka. They know the rules. That name, for example—"

"*Rorschach,*" Bates murmured, knuckles cracking as she squeezed her pet ball. "Interesting choice."

"I checked the registry. There's an I-CAN freighter called *Rorschach* on the Martian Loop. Whoever we're talking to must regard their own platform the way we'd regard a ship, and picked one of our names to fit."

Szpindel dropped into the chair beside me, fresh from a galley run. A bulb of coffee glistened like gelatin in his hand. "*That* name, out of all the ships in the innersys? Seems way too symbolic for a random choice."

"I don't think it was random. Unusual ship names provoke comment; *Rorschach*'s pilot goes ship-to-ship with some other vessel, the other vessel comes back with *Oh Grandma, what an unusual name you have, Rorschach* replies with some off-the-cuff comment about nomenclatural origins and it all goes out in the EM. Someone listening to all that chatter not only figures out the name and the thing it applies to, but can get some sense of meaning from the context. Our alien friends probably eavesdropped on half the registry and deduced that *Rorschach* would be a better tag for something unfamiliar than, say, the SS *Jaymie Matthews*."

"Territorial *and* smart." Szpindel grimaced, conjuring a mug from beneath his chair. "Wonderful."

Bates shrugged. "Territorial, maybe. Not necessarily aggressive. In fact, I wonder if they could hurt us even if they wanted to."

"I don't," Szpindel said. "Those skimmers—"

The Major waved a dismissive hand. "Big ships turn slowly. If they were setting up to snooker us we'd see it well in advance." She looked around the table. "Look, am I the only one who finds this odd? An interstellar technology that redecorates superJovians and lines up meteoroids like elephants on parade, and they were *hiding*? From *us*?"

"Unless there's someone else out here," James suggested uneasily.

Bates shook her head. "The cloak was directional. It was aimed at us and no one else."

"And even we saw through it," Szpindel added.

"Exactly. So they go to plan B, which so far amounts to nothing but bluster and vague warnings. I'm just saying, they're not *acting* like giants. *Rorschach*'s behavior feels—improvised. I don't think they expected us."

" 'Course not. Burns-Caulfield was—"

"I don't think they expected us *yet*."

"Um," Szpindel said, digesting it.

The Major ran one hand over her naked scalp. "Why would they expect us to just *give up* after we learned we'd been sniped? Of course we'd look elsewhere. Burns-Caulfield could only have been intended as a delaying action; if I was them, I'd plan on us getting out here eventually. But I think they miscalculated somehow. We got out here sooner than they expected and caught them with their pants down."

Szpindel split the bulb and emptied it into his mug. "Pretty large miscalculation for something so smart, eh?" A hologram bloomed on contact with the steaming liquid, glowing in soft commemoration of the Gaza Glasslands. The scent of plasticized coffee flooded the Commons. "Especially after they'd surveilled us down to the square meter," he added.

"And what did they see? I-CANs. Solar sails. Ships that take years to reach the Kuiper, and don't have the reserves to go anywhere else afterwards. Telematter didn't exist beyond Boeing's simulators and a half-dozen protypes back then. Easy to miss. They must've figured one decoy would buy them all the time they needed."

"To do what?" James wondered.

"Whatever it is," Bates said. "We're ringside."

Szpindel raised his mug with an infirm hand and sipped. The coffee trembled in its prison, the surface wobbling and blobbing in the drum's half-hearted gravity. James pursed her lips in faint disapproval. Open-topped containers for liquids were technically verboten in variable-gravity environments, even for people without Szpindel's dexterity issues.

"So they're bluffing," Szpindel said at last.

Bates nodded. "That's my guess. *Rorschach*'s still under construction. We could be dealing with an automated system of some kind."

"So we can ignore the keep-off-the-grass signs, eh? Walk right in."

"We can afford to bide our time. We can afford to not push it."

"Ah. So even though we could maybe handle it now, you want to wait until it graduates from *covert* to *invulnerable*." Szpindel shuddered, set down his coffee. "Where'd you get your military training again? Sporting Chance Academy?"

Bates ignored the jibe. "The fact that *Rorschach*'s still growing may be the best reason to leave it alone for a while. We don't have any idea what the—mature, I guess—what the mature form of this artifact might be. Sure, it hid. Lots of animals take cover from predators without *being* predators, especially young ones. Sure, it's . . . evasive. Doesn't give us the answers we want. But maybe it doesn't *know* them, did you consider that? How much luck would you have interrogating a Human embryo? Adult could be a whole different animal."

"Adult could put our asses through a meat grinder."

"So could the *embryo* for all we know." Bates rolled her eyes. "Jesus, Isaac, *you're* the biologist. I shouldn't have to tell you how many shy reclusive critters pack a punch when they're cornered. Porcupine doesn't want any trouble, but he'll still give you a faceful of quills if you ignore the warning."

Szpindel said nothing. He slid his coffee sideways along the concave tabletop, to the very limit of his reach. The liquid sat there in its mug, a dark circle perfectly parallel to the rim but canted slightly toward us. I even thought I could make out the merest convexity in the surface itself.

Szpindel smiled faintly at the effect.

James cleared her throat. "Not to downplay your concerns, Isaac, but we've hardly exhausted the diplomatic route. And at least it's willing to talk, even if it's not as forthcoming as we'd like."

"Sure it talks," Szpindel said, eyes still on the leaning mug. "Not like us."

"Well, no. There's some—"

"It's not just slippery, it's downright *dyslexic* sometimes, you noticed? And it mixes up its pronouns."

"Given that it picked up the language entirely via passive eavesdropping, it's remarkably fluent. In fact, from what I can tell they're more efficient at processing speech than we are."

"Gotta be efficient at a language if you're going to be so *evasive* in it, eh?"

"If they were human I might agree with you," James replied. "But what appears to us as evasion or deceit could just as easily be explained by a reliance on smaller conceptual units."

"Conceptual units?" Bates, I was beginning to realize, never pulled up a subtitle if she could help it.

James nodded. "Like processing a line of text word by word, instead of looking at complete phrases. The smaller the units, the faster they can be reconfigured; it gives you very fast semantic reflexes. The down side is that it's difficult to maintain the same level of logical consistency, since the patterns within the larger structure are more likely to get shuffled."

"*Whoa.*" Szpindel straightened, all thoughts of liquids and centipetal force forgotten.

"All I'm saying is, we aren't necessarily dealing with deliberate deception here. An entity who parses information at one scale might not be aware of inconsistencies on another; it might not even have conscious access to that level."

"That's not all you're saying."

"Isaac, you can't apply Human norms to a—"

"I *wondered* what you were up to." Szpindel dove into the transcripts. A moment later he dredged up an excerpt:

Request information on environments you consider lethal.
Request information on your response to the prospect of
imminent exposure to lethal environments.

GLAD TO COMPLY. BUT YOUR LETHAL IS DIFFERENT FROM
US. THERE ARE MANY MIGRATING CIRCUMSTANCES.

"You were *testing* it!" Szpindel crowed. He smacked his lips; his jaw ticced. "You were looking for an emotional response!"

"It was just a thought. It didn't prove anything."

"Was there a difference? In the response time?"

James hesitated, then shook her head. "But it was a stupid idea. There are so many variables, we have no idea how they— I mean, they're *alien* . . ."

"The pathology's classic."

"What pathology?" I asked.

"It doesn't mean anything except that they're different from the Human baseline," James insisted. "Which is not something *anyone* here can look down their nose about."

I tried again: "What pathology?"

James shook her head. Szpindel filled me in: "There's a syndrome you might have heard about, eh? Fast-talkers, no conscience, tend to malapropism and self-contradiction. No emotional affect."

"We're not talking about Human beings here," James said again, softly.

"But if we were," Szpindel added, "we might call *Rorschach* a clinical sociopath."

Sarasti had said nothing during this entire exchange. Now, with the word hanging out in the open, I noticed that nobody else would look at him.

We all knew that Jukka Sarasti was a sociopath, of course. Most of us just didn't mention it in polite company.

Szpindel was never that polite. Or maybe it was just that he seemed to almost *understand* Sarasti; he could look behind the monster and regard the *organism,* no less a product of natural selection for all the human flesh it had devoured in aeons past. That perspective calmed him, somehow. He could watch Sarasti watching him, and not flinch.

"I feel sorry for the poor son of a bitch," he said once, back in training.

Some would have thought that absurd. This man, so massively interfaced with machinery that his own motor skills had degraded for want of proper care and feeding; this man who heard X-rays and saw in shades of ultrasound, so corrupted by retrofits he could no longer even feel his own fingertips without assistance—this man could pity *anyone* else, let alone an infra-eyed predator built to murder without the slightest twitch of remorse?

"Empathy for sociopaths isn't common," I remarked.

"Maybe it should be. We, at least"—he waved an arm; some remote-linked sensor cluster across the simulator whirred and torqued reflexively—"*chose* the add-ons. Vampires *had* to be sociopaths. They're too much like their own prey—a lot of taxonomists don't even consider them a subspecies, you know that? Never diverged far enough for reproductive isolation. So maybe they're more syndrome than race. Just a bunch of obligate cannibals with a consistent set of deformities."

"And how does that make—"

"If the only thing you can eat is your own kind, empathy is gonna be the *first* thing that goes. Psychopathy's no disorder in *those* shoes, eh? Just a survival strategy. But they still make our skin crawl, so we—chain 'em up."

"You think we should've repaired the Crucifix glitch?" Everyone knew why we hadn't. Only a fool would resurrect a monster without safeguards in place. Vampires came with theirs built in: without his anti-Euclideans Sarasti would go *grand mal* the first time he caught close sight of a four-panel window frame.

But Szpindel was shaking his head. "We couldn't have fixed it. Or we *could* have," he amended, "but the glitch is in the visual cortex, eh? Linked to their omnisavantism. You fix it, you disable their pattern-matching skills, and then what's the point in even bringing them back?"

"I didn't know that."

"Well, that's the official story." He fell silent a moment, cracked a crooked grin. "Then again, we didn't have any trouble fixing the protocadherin pathways when it suited us."

I subtitled. Context-sensitive, ConSensus served up *protocadherin* γ-Y: the magical hominid brain protein that vampires had never been able to synthesize. The reason they hadn't just switched to zebras or warthogs once denied Human prey, why our discovery of the terrible secret of the right angle had spelled their doom.

"Anyway, I just think he's . . . cut off." A nervous tic tugged at the corner of Szpindel's mouth. "Lone wolf, nothing but sheep for company. Wouldn't you feel lonely?"

"They don't *like* company," I reminded him. You didn't put vampires of the same sex together, not unless you were taking bets on a bloodbath. They were solitary hunters and *very* territorial. With a minimum viable pred–prey ratio of one to ten—and human prey spread so sparsely across the Pleistocene landscape—the biggest threat to their survival had been competition from their own kind. Natural selection had never taught them to play nicely together.

That didn't cut any ice with Szpindel, though. "Doesn't mean he can't be lonely," he insisted. "Just means he can't fix it."

THEY KNOW THE WORDS BUT NOT THE MUSIC.

—ROBERT HARE, *WITHOUT CONSCIENCE*

WE DID IT with mirrors, great round parabolic things, each impossibly thin and three times as high as a man. *Theseus* rolled them up and bolted them to firecrackers stuffed with precious antimatter from our dwindling stockpiles. With twelve hours to spare she flung them like confetti along precise ballistic trajectories, and when they were safely distant she set them alight. They pinwheeled off every which way, gamma sleeting in their wake until they burned dry. Then they coasted, unfurling mercurial insect wings across the void.

In the greater distance, four hundred thousand alien machines looped and burned and took no obvious notice.

Rorschach fell around Ben barely fifteen hundred kilometers from atmosphere, a fast endless circle that took just under forty hours to complete. By the time it didn't return to our sight, the mirrors were all outside the zone of total blindness. A close-up of Ben's equatorial edge floated in ConSensus. Mirror icons sparkled around it like an exploding schematic, like the disconnected facets of some great expanding compound eye. None had brakes. Whatever high ground the mirrors held, they wouldn't hold it for long.

"There," Bates said.

A mirage wavered stage left, a tiny spot of swirling chaos perhaps half the size of a fingernail held at arm's-length. It told us nothing, it was pure heat shimmer, but light bounced toward us from dozens of distant relayers, and while each saw scarcely more than our last probe had—a patch of dark clouds set slightly awry by some invisible prism—each of those views refracted *differently*. The Captain sieved flashes from the heavens and stitched them into a composite view.

Details emerged.

First a faint sliver of shadow, a tiny dimple all but lost in the seething equatorial cloud bands. It had just barely rotated into view around the edge of the disk—a rock in the stream perhaps, an invisible finger stuck in the clouds, turbulence and shear stress shredding the boundary layers to either side.

Szpindel squinted. "Plage effect." Subtitles said he was talking about a kind of sunspot, a knot in Ben's magnetic field.

"Higher," James said.

Something floated above that dimple in the clouds, the way a ground-effect ocean liner floats above the depression it pushes into the water's surface. I zoomed: Next to an Oasa subdwarf with ten times the mass of Jupiter, *Rorschach* was tiny.

Next to *Theseus,* it was a colossus.

Not just a torus but a *tangle,* a city-size chaos of spun glass, loops and bridges and attenuate spires. The surface texture was pure artifice, of course; ConSensus merely giftwrapped the enigma in refracted background. Still. In some dark, haunting way, it was almost beautiful. A nest of obsidian snakes and smoky crystal spines.

"It's talking again," James reported.

"Talk back," Sarasti said, and abandoned us.

· · ·

So she did. And while the Gang spoke with the artifact, the others spied upon it. Their vision failed over time—mirrors fell away along their respective vectors, lines of sight degraded with each passing second—but ConSensus filled with things learned in the meantime. *Rorschach* massed $1.8 \cdot 10^{10}$ kilograms within a total volume of $2.3 \cdot 10^8$ cubic meters. Its magnetic field, judging by radio squeals and its Plage effect, was thousands of times stronger than the sun's. Astonishingly, parts of the composite image were clear enough to discern fine spiral grooves twined around the structure. ("Fibonacci sequence," Szpindel reported, one jiggling eye fixing me for a moment. "At least they're not *completely* alien.") Spheroid protuberances disfigured the tips of at least three of *Rorschach*'s innumerable spines; the grooves were more widely spaced in those areas, like skin grown tight and swollen with infection. Just before one vital mirror sailed out of range it glimpsed another spine, split a third of the way along its length. Torn material floated flaccid and unmoving in vacuum.

"Please," Bates said softly. "Tell me that's not what it looks like."

Szpindel grinned. "Sporangium? Seedpod? Why not?"

Rorschach may have been reproducing but beyond a doubt it was *growing,* fed by a steady trickle of infalling debris from Ben's accretion belt. We were close enough now to get a clear view of that procession: rocks and mountains and pebbles fell like sediment swirling around a drain. Particles that collided with the artifact simply *stuck*; *Rorschach* engulfed prey like some vast metastatic amoeba. The acquired mass was apparently processed internally and shunted to apical growth zones; judging by infinitesimal changes in the artifact's allometry, it grew from the tips of its branches.

The procession never stopped. *Rorschach* was insatiable.

It was a strange attractor in the interstellar gulf; the paths along which the rocks fell were precisely and utterly chaotic. It was as though some Keplerian black belt had set up the whole system like an astronomical windup toy, kicked everything into motion, and let inertia do the rest.

"Didn't think that was possible," Bates said.

Szpindel shrugged. "Hey, chaotic trajectories are just as deterministic as any other kind."

"That doesn't mean you can even *predict* them, let along set them up like that." Luminous intel reflected off the Major's bald head. "You'd have to know the starting conditions of a million different variables to ten decimal places. Literally."

"Yup."

"*Vampires* can't even do that. Quantical computers can't do that."

Szpindel shrugged like a marionette.

All the while the Gang had been slipping in and out of character, dancing with some unseen partner that—despite their best efforts—told us little, beyond endless permutations of *You really wouldn't like it here*. Any interrogative it answered with another— yet somehow it always left the sense of questions answered.

"Did you send the Fireflies?" Sascha asked.

"We send many things many places," *Rorschach* replied. "What do their specs show?"

"We do not know their specifications. The Fireflies burned up over Earth."

"Then shouldn't you be looking there? When our kids fly, they're on their own."

Sascha muted the channel. "You know who we're talking to? Jesus of fucking *Nazareth,* that's who."

Szpindel looked at Bates. Bates shrugged, palms up.

"You didn't get it?" Sascha shook her head. "That last exchange was the informational equivalent of *Should we render taxes unto Caesar*. Beat for beat."

"Thanks for casting us as the Pharisees," Szpindel grumbled.

"Hey, if the Jew fits . . ."

Szpindel rolled his eyes.

That was when I first noticed it: a tiny imperfection on Sascha's topology, a flyspeck of doubt marring one of her facets. "We're not getting anywhere," she said. "Let's try a side door." She winked out; Michelle reopened the outgoing line. "*Theseus* to *Rorschach*. Open to requests for information."

"Cultural exchange," *Rorschach* said. "That works for me."

Bates's brow furrowed. "Is that wise?"

"If it's not inclined to give information, maybe it would rather get some. And we could learn a great deal from the kind of questions it asks."

"But—"

"Tell us about home," *Rorschach* said.

Sascha resurfaced just long enough to say "Relax, Major. Nobody said we had to give it the right answers."

The stain on the Gang's topology had flickered when Michelle took over, but it hadn't disappeared. It grew slightly as Michelle described some hypothetical hometown in careful terms that mentioned no object smaller than a meter across. (ConSensus confirmed my guess: the hypothetical limit of Firefly eyesight.) When Cruncher took a rare turn at the helm—

"We don't all of us have parents or cousins. Some never did. Some come from vats."

"I see. That's sad. Vats sounds so dehumanizing."

—the stain darkened and spread across his surface like an oil slick.

"Takes too much on faith," Susan said a few moments later.

By the time Sascha had cycled back into Michelle it was more than doubt, stronger than suspicion; it had become an *insight,* a dark little meme infecting each of that body's minds in turn. The Gang was on the trail of something. They still weren't sure what.

I was.

"Tell me more about your cousins," *Rorschach* sent.

"Our cousins lie about the family tree," Sascha replied, "with nieces and nephews and Neanderthals. We do not like annoying cousins."

"We'd like to know about this tree."

Sascha muted the channel and gave us a look that said *Could it* be *any more obvious?* "It *couldn't* have parsed that. There were three linguistic ambiguities in there. It just ignored them."

"Well, it asked for clarification," Bates pointed out.

"It asked a follow-up question. Different thing entirely."

Bates was still out of the loop. Szpindel was starting to get it, though.

Subtle motion drew my eye. Sarasti was back, floating above the bright topography on the table. The light show squirmed across his visor as he moved his head. I could feel his eyes behind it.

And something else, behind *him.*

I couldn't tell what it was. I could point to nothing but a vague sense of something *out of place,* somewhere in the background. Something over on the far side of the drum wasn't quite right. No, that wasn't it; something *nearer,* something amiss somewhere along the drum's axis. But there was nothing there, nothing I could see—just the naked pipes and conduits of the spinal bundle, threading through empty space, and—

And suddenly, whatever had been wrong was right again. That was what finally locked my focus: the evaporation of some anomaly, a reversion to normalcy that caught my eye like a flicker of motion. I could see the exact spot along the bundle where the change had occured. There was nothing out of place there now—but there *had* been. It was in my head, barely sub-liminal, an *itch* so close to the surface that I knew I could bring it back if I just *concentrated*.

Sascha was talking to some alien artifact at the end of a laser beam. She was going on about familial relationships, both evolutionary and domestic: Neanderthal and Cro-Magnon and mother's cousins twice removed. She'd been doing it for hours now and she had hours yet to go but right now her chatter was distracting me. I tried to block her out and concentrate on the half-perceived image teasing my memory. I'd *seen* something there, just a moment ago. One of the conduits had had—yes, too many joints on one of the pipes. Something that should have been straight and smooth but was somehow articulated instead. But not *one* of the pipes, I remembered: an *extra* pipe, an extra *something* anyway, something—

Boney.

That was crazy. There was nothing there. We were half a light-year from home, talking to unseen aliens about family re-unions, and my eyes were playing tricks on me.

Have to talk to Szpindel about that, if it happened again.

A lull in the background chatter brought me back. Sascha had stopped talking. Darkened facets hung around her like a thun-dercloud. I pulled back the last thing she had sent: "We usually find our nephews with telescopes. They are hard as Hobblinites."

More calculated ambiguity. And *Hobblinites* wasn't even a *word*.

Imminent decisions reflected in her eyes. Sascha was poised at the edge of a precipice, gauging the depth of dark waters below.

"You haven't mentioned your father at all," *Rorschach* re-marked.

"That's true, *Rorschach*," Sascha admitted softly, taking a breath—

—and stepping forward.

"So why don't you just *suck my big fat hairy dick*?"

The drum fell instantly silent. Bates and Szpindel stared, open-mouthed. Sascha killed the channel and turned to face us, grinning so widely I thought the top of her head would fall off.

"Sascha," Bates breathed. "Are you *crazy*?"

"So what if I am? Doesn't matter to that thing. It doesn't have a *clue* what I'm saying."

"What?"

"It doesn't even have a clue what it's saying *back*," she added.

"Wait a minute. You said—*Susan* said they weren't parrots. They knew the rules."

And there Susan was, melting to the fore: "I did, and they do. But pattern-matching doesn't equal comprehension."

Bates shook her head. "You're saying whatever we're talking to—it's not even intelligent?"

"Oh, it could be intelligent, certainly. But we're not *talking* to it in any meaningful sense."

"So what is it? Voice mail?"

"Actually," Szpindel said slowly, "I think they call it a *Chinese Room* . . ."

About bloody time, I thought.

I knew all about Chinese Rooms. I was one. I didn't even keep it a secret, I told anyone who was interested enough to ask.

In hindsight, sometimes that was a mistake.

"How can you possibly tell the rest of us what your bleeding edge is up to if you don't understand it yourself?" Chelsea demanded back when things were good between us. Before she got to know me.

I shrugged. "It's not my *job* to understand them. If I could, they wouldn't be very bleeding edge in the first place. I'm just a, you know, a conduit."

"Yeah, but how can you translate something if you *don't* understand it?"

A common cry, outside the field. People simply can't accept that patterns carry their own intelligence, quite apart from the semantic content that clings to their surfaces; if you manipulate the topology correctly, that content just comes along for the ride.

"You ever hear of the Chinese Room?" I asked.

She shook her head. "Only vaguely. Really old, right?"

"Hundred years at least. It's a fallacy really, it's an argument that supposedly puts the lie to Turing tests. You stick some guy in a closed room. Sheets with strange squiggles come in through a slot in the wall. He's got access to this huge database of squiggles just like it, and a bunch of rules to tell him how to put those squiggles together."

"Grammar," Chelsea said. "Syntax."

I nodded. "The point is, though, he doesn't have any idea what the squiggles *are,* or what information they might contain. He only knows that when he encounters squiggle *delta,* say, he's supposed to extract the fifth and sixth squiggles from file *theta* and put them together with another squiggle from *gamma*. So he builds this response string, puts it on the sheet, slides it back out the slot and takes a nap until the next iteration. Repeat until the remains of the horse are well and thoroughly beaten."

"So he's carrying on a conversation," Chelsea said. "In Chinese, I assume, or they would have called it the Spanish Inquisition."

"Exactly. Point being you can use basic pattern-matching

algorithms to participate in a conversation *without having any idea what you're saying*. Depending on how good your rules are, you can pass a Turing test. You can be a wit and raconteur in a language you don't even speak."

"That's Synthesis?"

"Only the part that involves downscaling semiotic protocols. And only in principle. And I'm actually getting my input in Cantonese and replying in German, because I'm more of a conduit than a conversant. But you get the idea."

"How do you keep all the rules and protocols straight? There must be millions of them."

"It's like anything else. Once you learn the rules, you do it unconsciously. Like riding a bike, or pinging the noosphere. You don't actively think about the protocols at all, you just—*imagine* how your targets behave."

"Mmm." A subtle half-smile played at the corner of her mouth. "But—the argument's not really a fallacy then, is it? It's spot-on: You really *don't* understand Cantonese or German."

"The *system* understands. The whole Room, with all its parts. The guy who does the scribbling is just one component. You wouldn't expect a single neuron in your head to understand English, would you?"

"Sometimes one's all I can spare." Chelsea shook her head. She wasn't going to let it go. I could see her sorting questions in order of priority; I could see them getting increasingly . . . personal . . .

"To get back to the matter at hand," I said, preempting them all, "you were going to show me how to do that thing with the fingers . . ."

A wicked grin wiped the questions right off her face. "Oooh, that's *right* . . ."

It's risky, getting involved. Too many confounds. Every tool in the shed goes dull and rusty the moment you get entangled with the system you're observing.

Still serviceable in a pinch, though.

"It hides now," Sarasti said. "It's vulnerable now.

"Now we go in."

It wasn't news so much as review: We'd been straight-lining toward Ben for days now. But perhaps the Chinese Room hypothesis had strengthened his resolve. At any rate, with *Rorschach* in eclipse once more, we prepared to take intrusiveness to the next level.

Theseus was perpetually gravid; a generic probe incubated in her fabrication plant, its development arrested just short of birth in anticipation of unforeseen mission requirements. Sometime between briefings the Captain had brought it to parturition, customized for close contact and ground work. It burned down the well at high g a good ten hours before *Rorschach*'s next scheduled appearance, inserted itself into the rock stream, and went to sleep. If our calculations were in order, it would not be smashed by some errant piece of debris before it woke up again. If all went well, an intelligence that had precisely orchestrated a cast of millions would not notice one extra dancer on the floor. If we were just plain lucky, the myriad high-divers that happened to be line of sight at the time were not programmed as tattletales.

Acceptable risks. If we hadn't been up for them, we might as well have stayed home.

And so we waited: four optimized hybrids somewhere past the threshold of mere humanity, one extinct predator who'd opted to command us instead of eating us alive. We waited for *Rorschach* to come back around the bend. The probe fell smoothly around the well, an ambassador to the unwilling—or, if the Gang was right, maybe just a backdoor artist set to B and E an empty condo. Szpindel had named it *Jack-in-the-box,* after some antique child's toy that didn't even rate a listing in Con-Sensus. We fell in its wake, nearly ballistic now, momentum and inertia carefully precalculated to thread us through the chaotic minefield of Ben's accretion belt.

Kepler couldn't do it all, though; *Theseus* grumbled briefly now and then, the intermittent firing of her attitude jets rumbling softly up the spine as the Captain tweaked our descent into the maelstrom.

No plan ever survives contact with the enemy I remembered, but I didn't know from where.

"Got it," Bates said. A speck appeared at Ben's edge; the display zoomed instantly to close-up. "Proximity boot."

Rorschach remained invisible to *Theseus,* close as we were, close as we were coming. But parallax stripped at least some of the scales from the probe's eyes; it woke to spikes and spirals of smoky glass flickering in and out of view, Ben's flat endless horizon semivisible through the intervening translucence. The view trembled; waveforms rippled across ConSensus.

"Quite the magnetic field," Szpindel remarked.

"Braking," Bates reported. Jack turned smoothly retrograde and fired its torch. On Tactical, delta-v swung to red.

Sascha was driving the Gang's body this shift. "Incoming signal," she reported. "Same format."

Sarasti clicked. "Pipe it."

"*Rorschach* to *Theseus.* Hello again, *Theseus.*" The voice was female this time, and middle-aged.

Sascha grinned "See? She's not offended at all. Big hairy dick notwithstanding."

"Don't answer," Sarasti said.

"Burn complete," Bates reported.

Coasting now, Jack—*sneezed*. Silver chaff shot into the void toward the target: millions of compass needles, brilliantly reflective, fast enough to make *Theseus* seem slow. They were gone in an instant. The probe watched them flee, swept laser eyes across every degree of arc, scanned its sky twice a second and took careful note of each and every reflective flash. Only at first did those needles shoot along anything approaching a straight line: then they swept abruptly into Lorentz spirals, twisted into sudden arcs and corkscrews, shot away along new and intricate trajectories bordering on the relativistic. The contours of *Rorschach*'s magnetic field resolved in ConSensus, at first glance like the nested layers of a glass onion.

"*Sproinnnng*," Szpindel said.

At second glance the onion grew wormy. Invaginations appeared, long snaking tunnels of energy proliferating fractally at every scale.

"*Rorschach* to *Theseus*. Hello, *Theseus*. You there?"

A holographic inset beside the main display plotted the points of a triangle in flux: *Theseus* at the apex, *Rorschach* and Jack defining the narrow base.

"*Rorschach* to *Theseus*. I *seeee* you . . ."

"She's got a more casual affect than *he* ever did." Sascha glanced up at Sarasti, and did not add *You sure about this?* She was starting to wonder herself, though. Starting to dwell on the potential consequences of being *wrong,* now that we were committed. As far as sober second thought was concerned it was too little too late; but for Sascha, that was progress.

Besides, it had been Sarasti's decision.

Great hoops were resolving in *Rorschach*'s magnetosphere. Invisible to human eyes, their outlines were vanishingly faint even on

Tactical; the chaff had scattered so thinly across the sky that even the Captain was resorting to guesswork. The new macrostructures hovered in the magnetosphere like the nested gimbals of some great phantom gyroscope.

"I see you haven't changed your vector," *Rorschach* remarked. "We really wouldn't advise continuing your approach. Seriously. For your own safety."

Szpindel shook his head. "Hey, Mandy. *Rorschach* talking to Jack at all?"

"If it is, I'm not seeing it. No incident light, no directed EM of any kind." She smiled grimly. "Seems to have snuck in under the radar. And don't call me Mandy."

Theseus groaned, twisting. I staggered in the low pseudograv, reached out to steady myself. "Course correction," Bates reported. "Unplotted rock."

"*Rorschach* to *Theseus*. Please respond. Your current heading is unacceptable, repeat, your current heading is *unacceptable*. *Strongly* advise you change course."

By now the probe coasted just a few kilometers off *Rorschach*'s leading edge. That close it served up way more than magnetic fields: It presented *Rorschach* itself in bright, tactical color codes. Invisible curves and spikes iridesced in ConSensus across any number of on-demand pigment schemes: gravity, reflectivity, blackbody emissions. Massive electrical bolts erupting from the tips of thorns rendered in lemon pastels. User-friendly graphics had turned *Rorschach* into a cartoon.

"*Rorschach* to *Theseus*. Please respond."

Theseus growled to stern, fishtailing. On tactical, another just-plotted piece of debris swept by a discreet six thousand meters to port.

"*Rorschach* to *Theseus*. If you are unable to respond, please—*Holy shit!*"

The cartoon flickered and died.

I'd seen what had happened in that last instant, though: Jack passing near one of those great phantom hoops; a tongue of energy flicking out, quick as a frog's; a dead feed.

"I see what you're up to *now*, you *cocksuckers*. Do you think we're fucking *blind* down here?"

Sascha clenched her teeth. "We—"

"No," Sarasti said.

"But it *fi*—"

Sarasti *hissed,* from somewhere in the back of his throat. I had never heard a mammal make a noise quite like that before. Sascha fell immediately silent.

Bates negotiated with her controls. "I've still got—just a sec—"

"You pull that thing back *right fucking now,* you hear us? *Right fucking now.*"

"*Got it.*" Bates gritted as the feed came back up. "Just had to reacquire the laser." The probe had been kicked wildly off-course—as if someone fording a river had been caught in sudden undertow and thrown over a waterfall—but it was still talking, and still mobile.

Barely. Bates struggled to stay the course. Jack staggered and wobbled uncontrollably though the tightly-wound folds of *Rorschach*'s magnetosphere. The artifact loomed huge in its eye. The feed strobed.

"Maintain approach," Sarasti said calmly.

"Love to," Bates bit out. "Trying."

Theseus skidded again, corkscrewing. I could have sworn I heard the bearings in the drum *grind* for a moment. Another rock sailed past on Tactical.

"I thought you'd *plotted* those things," Szpindel grumbled.

"*You want to start a war,* Theseus? Is that what you're trying to do? You think you're up for it?"

"It doesn't attack," Sarasti said.

"Maybe it does." Bates kept her voice low; I could see the effort it took. "If *Rorschach* can control the trajectories of these—"

"Normal distribution. Insignificant corrections." He must have meant statistically: The torque and grind of the ship's hull felt pretty significant to the others.

"Oh, right," *Rorschach* said suddenly. "We get it *now*. You don't think there's anyone here, do you? You've got some high-priced consultant telling you there's nothing to worry about."

Jack was deep in the forest. We'd lost most of the tactical overlays to reduced baud. In dim visible light *Rorschach*'s great ridged spines, each the size of a skyscraper, hashed a nightmare view on all sides. The feed stuttered as Bates struggled to keep the beam aligned. ConSensus painted walls and airspace with arcane telemetry. I had no idea what any of it meant.

"You think we're nothing but a *Chinese Room*," *Rorschach* sneered.

Jack stumbled toward collision, grasping for something to hang on to.

"Your mistake, *Theseus*."

It hit something. It stuck.

And suddenly *Rorschach* snapped into view—no refractory composites, no profiles or simulations in false color. There it was at last, naked even to Human eyes.

Imagine a crown of thorns, twisted, dark and unreflective, grown too thickly tangled to ever rest on any Human head. Put it in orbit around a failed star whose own reflected half-light does little more than throw its satellites into silhouette. Occasional bloody highlights glinted like dim embers from its twists and crannies; they only emphasized the darkness everywhere else.

Imagine an artifact that embodies the very notion of torture, something so wrenched and disfigured that even across uncounted light-years and unimaginable differences in biology and outlook, you can't help but feel that somehow, the structure itself is in pain.

Now make it the size of a city.

It flickered as we watched. Lightning arced from recurved spines a thousand meters long. ConSensus showed us a strobe-lit hellscape, huge and dark and twisted. The composites had lied. It was not the least bit beautiful.

"Now it's too late," something said from deep inside. "Now every last one of you is dead. And Susan? You there, Susan?

"We're taking you *first*."

LIFE'S TOO SHORT FOR CHESS.

—LORD BYRON

THEY NEVER SEALED the hatch behind them. It was too easy to get lost up there in the dome, naked infinite space stretching a hundred eighty degrees on every axis. They needed all that emptiness but they needed an anchor in its midst: soft stray light from astern, a gentle draft from the drum, the sounds of people and machinery close by. They needed to have it both ways.

I lay in wait. Reading a dozen blatant cues in their behavior, I was already squirreled away in the forward airlock when they passed. I gave them a few minutes and crept forward to the darkened bridge.

"Of course they called her by name," Szpindel was saying.

"That was the only name they had. She *told* them, remember?"

"Yes." Michelle didn't seem reassured.

"Hey, it was *you* guys said we were talking to a Chinese Room. You saying you were wrong?"

"We—no. Of course not."

"Then it wasn't really threatening Suze at all, was it? It wasn't threatening any of us. It had no idea what it was saying."

"It's *rule-based,* Isaac. It was following some kind of flow-chart it drew up by observing Human languages in action. And somehow those rules told it to respond with threats of violence."

"But if it doesn't even know what it was saying—"

"It doesn't. It can't. We parsed the phrasing nineteen different ways, tried out conceptual units of every different length . . ." A long, deep breath. "But it attacked the probe, Isaac."

"Jack just got too close to one of those electrode thingies is all. It just arced."

"So you don't think *Rorschach* is hostile?"

Long silence—long enough to make me wonder if I'd been detected.

"Hostile," Szpindel said at last. *"Friendly.* We learned those words for life on Earth, eh? I don't know if they even apply out here." His lips smacked faintly. "But I think it might be something *like* hostile."

Michelle sighed. "Isaac, there's no *reason* for— I mean, it just doesn't make *sense* that it would be. We can't have anything it wants."

"It says it wants to be left alone," Szpindel said. "Even if it doesn't mean it."

They floated quietly for a while, up there past the bulkhead.

"At least the shielding held," Szpindel said finally. "That's something." He wasn't just talking about Jack; our own cara-pace was coated with the same stuff now. It had depleted our substrate stockpiles by two thirds, but no one wanted to rely on the ship's usual magnetics in the face of anything that could play so easily with the electromagnetic spectrum.

"If they attack us, what do we do?" Michelle said.

"Learn what we can, while we can. Fight back. While we can."

"*If* we can. Look out there, Isaac. I don't care how *embryonic* that thing is. Tell me we're not hopelessly outmatched."

"Outmatched, for sure. *Hopelessly,* never."

"That's not what you said before."

"Still. There's always a way to win."

"If I said that, you'd call it wishful thinking."

"If you said that, it would be. But I'm saying it, so it's game theory."

"Game theory again. Jesus, Isaac."

"No, listen. You're thinking about the aliens like they were some kind of mammal. Something that *cares,* something that looks after its investments."

"How do you know they aren't?"

"Because you can't protect your kids when they're light-years away. They're on their own, and it's a big cold dangerous universe so most of them aren't going to make it, eh? The most you can do is crank out *millions* of kids, take cold comfort in knowing that a few always luck out through random chance. It's not a mammal mind-set, Meesh. You want an earthbound simile, think of dandelion seeds. Or, or herring."

A soft sigh. "So they're interstellar herring. That hardly means they can't crush us."

"But they don't know about *us,* not in advance. Dandelion seed doesn't know what it's up against before it sprouts. Maybe nothing. Maybe some spastic weed that goes over like straw in the wind. Or maybe something that kicks its ass halfway to the Magellanic Clouds. It doesn't *know,* and there's no such thing as a one-size-fits-all survival strategy. Something that aces against one player blows goats against a different one. So the best you can do is mix up your strategies based on the odds. It's a weighted dice roll and it gives you the best mean payoff over the whole game, but you're bound to crap out and choose the wrong strategy at least some of the time. Price of doing business. And that means— *that* means—that weak players not only *can* win against stronger ones, but they're statistically *bound* to in some cases."

Michelle snorted. "*That's* your game theory? Rock Paper Scissors with statistics?"

Maybe Szpindel didn't know the reference. He didn't speak, long enough to call up a subtitle; then he brayed like a horse. "*Rock Paper Scissors!* Yes!"

Michelle digested that for a moment. "You're sweet for trying, but that only works if the other side is just blindly playing the odds, and they don't have to *do* that if they know who they're going up against in advance. And my dear, they have so very much information about *us* . . ."

They'd threatened Susan. By name.

"They don't know everything," Szpindel insisted. "And the principle works for *any* scenario involving incomplete information, not just the ignorant extreme."

"Not as well."

"But *some,* and that gives us a chance. Doesn't matter how good you are at poker when it comes to the deal, eh? Cards still deal out with the same odds."

"So that's what we're playing. Poker."

"Be thankful it's not chess. We wouldn't have a hope in hell."

"Hey. *I'm* supposed to be the optimist in this relationship."

"You are. I'm just fatalistically cheerful. We all come into the story halfway through, we all catch up as best we can, and we're all gonna die before it ends."

"That's my Isaac. Master of the no-win scenario."

"You can win. Winner's the guy who makes the best guess on how it all comes out."

"So you *are* just guessing."

"Yup. And you can't make an informed guess without data, eh? And we could be the very first to find out what's gonna happen to the whole Human race. I'd say that puts us into the semi-finals, easy."

Michelle didn't answer for a very long time. When she did, I couldn't hear her words.

Neither could Szpindel: "Sorry?"

"*Covert* to *invulnerable,* you said. Remember?"

"Uh-huh. *Rorschach*'s graduation day."

"How soon, do you think?"

"No idea. But I don't think it's the kind of thing that's gonna slip by unnoticed. And that's why I don't think it attacked us."

She must have looked a question.

"Because when it does, it won't be some debatable candy-ass bitch slap," he told her. "When that fucker rises up, we're gonna *know*."

A sudden flicker from behind. I spun in the cramped passageway and bit down on a cry: something squirmed out of sight around the corner, something with *arms,* barely glimpsed, gone in an instant.

Never there. Couldn't be there. Impossible.

"Did you hear that?" Szpindel asked, but I'd fled to stern before Michelle could answer him.

We'd fallen so far that the naked eye didn't see a disk, barely even saw curvature anymore. We were falling towards a *wall,* a vast roiling expanse of dark thunderclouds that extended in all directions to some new, infinitely-distant horizon. Ben filled half the universe.

And still we fell.

Far below, Jack clung to *Rorschach*'s ridged surface with bristly gecko-feet fenders and set up camp. It sent X-rays and ultrasound into the ground, tapped inquiring fingers and listened to the echos, planted tiny explosive charges and measured the resonance of their detonations. It shed seeds like pollen: tiny probes and sensors by the thousands, self-powered, near-sighted, stupid, and expendable. The vast majority were sacrificial offerings to random chance; only one in a hundred lasted long enough to return usable telemetry.

While our advance scout took measure of its local neighborhood, *Theseus* drew larger-scale bird's-eye maps from the closing sky. It spat out thousands of its own disposable probes, spread them across the heavens and collected stereoscopic data from a thousand simultaneous perspectives.

Patchwork insights assembled in the drum. *Rorschach*'s skin was 60 percent superconducting carbon nanotube. *Rorschach*'s guts were largely hollow; at least some of those hollows appeared to contain an atmosphere. No Earthly form of life would have lasted a second in there, though; intricate topographies of radiation and electromagnetic force seethed around the structure, seethed within it. In some places the radiation was intense enough to turn unshielded flesh to ash in an instant; calmer backwaters would merely kill in the same span of time. Charged particles raced around invisible racetracks at relativistic speeds, erupting from jagged openings, hugging curves of magnetic force strong enough for neutron stars, arcing through open space and plunging back into black mass. Occasional protuberances swelled and burst and released clouds of microparticulates, seeding the radiation belts like spores. *Rorschach* resembled nothing so much as a nest of half-naked cyclotrons, tangled one with another.

Neither Jack below nor *Theseus* above could find any points of entry, beyond those impassable gaps that spat out streams of charged particles or swallowed them back down. No airlocks or hatches or viewports resolved with increasing proximity. The fact that we'd been threatened via laser beam implied some kind of optical antennae or tightcast array; we weren't even able to find that much.

A central hallmark of von Neumann machines was self-replication. Whether *Rorschach* would meet that criterion—whether it would germinate, or divide, or give birth when it passed some critical threshold, whether it had done so already—remained an open question.

One of a thousand. At the end of it all—after all the measurements, the theorizing and deduction and outright guesswork—we settled into orbit with a million trivial details and no answers. In terms of the big questions, there was only one thing we knew for sure.

So far, *Rorschach* was holding its fire.

"It sounded to *me* like it knew what it was saying," I remarked.

"I guess that's the whole point," Bates said. She had no one to confide in, partook of no intimate dialogues that could be overheard. With her, I used the direct approach.

Theseus was birthing a litter, two by two. They were nasty-looking things, armored, squashed egg-shapes, twice the size of a human torso and studded with gardening implements: antennae, optical ports, retractable threadsaws. Weapons muzzles.

Bates was summoning her troops. We floated before the primary Fab port at the base of *Theseus*'s spine. The plant could just as easily have disgorged the grunts directly into the hold beneath the carapace—that was where they'd be stored anyway, until called upon—but Bates was giving each a visual inspection before sending it through one of the airlocks a few meters up the passageway. Ritual, perhaps. Military tradition. Certainly there was nothing she could see with her eyes that wouldn't be glaringly obvious to the most basic diagnostic.

"Would it be a problem?" I asked. "Running them without your interface?"

"Run themselves just fine. Response time actually improves without spam in the network. I'm more of a safety precaution."

Theseus growled, giving us more attitude. The plating trembled to stern; another piece of local debris, no longer in our path. We were angling toward an equatorial orbit just a few miniscule kilometers above the artifact; insanely, the approach curved right through the accretion belt.

It didn't bother the others. "Like surviving traffic in a high speed lane," Sascha had said, disdainful of my misgivings. "Try creeping across and you're roadkill. Gotta speed up, go with the flow." But the flow was turbulent; we hadn't gone five minutes without a course correction since *Rorschach* had stopped talking to us.

"So, do you buy it?" I asked. "Pattern-matching, empty threats? Nothing to worry about?"

"Nobody's fired on us yet," she said. Meaning: *Not for a second*.

"What's your take on Susan's argument? Different niches, no reason for conflict?"

"Makes sense, I guess." *Utter bullshit*.

"Can you think of any reason why something with such different needs *would* attack us?"

"That depends," she said, "on whether the fact that we *are* different is reason enough."

I saw playground battlefields reflected in her topology. I remembered my own, and wondered if there were any other kind.

Then again, that only proved the point. Humans didn't *really* fight over skin tone or ideology; those were just handy cues for kin-selection purposes. Ultimately it always came down to bloodlines and limited resources.

"I think Isaac would say this is different," I said.

"I guess." Bates sent one grunt humming off to the hold; two more emerged in formation, spinelight glinting off their armor.

"How many of these are you making, anyway?"

"We're breaking and entering, Siri. Not wise to leave our own house unguarded."

I inspected her surfaces as she inspected theirs. Doubt and resentment simmered just beneath.

"You're in a tough spot," I remarked.

"We all are."

"But you're responsible for defending us, against something we don't know anything about. We're only guessing that—"

"Sarasti doesn't *guess*," Bates said. "The man's in charge for a reason. Doesn't make much sense to question his orders, given we're all about a hundred IQ points short of understanding the answer anyway."

"And yet he's also got that whole predatory side nobody talks about," I remarked. "It must be difficult for him, all that intellect coexisting with so much instinctive aggression. Making sure the right part wins."

She wondered in that instant whether Sarasti might be listening in. She decided in the next that it didn't matter: Why should he care what the cattle thought, as long as they did what they were told?

All she said was, "I thought you jargonauts weren't supposed to have opinions."

"That wasn't mine."

Bates paused. Returned to her inspection.

"You do know what I do," I said.

"Uh-huh." The first of the current pair passed muster and hummed off up the spine. She turned to the second. "You simplify things. So the folks back home can understand what the specialists are up to."

"That's part of it."

"I don't need a translator, Siri. I'm just a consultant, assuming things go well. A bodyguard if they don't."

"You're an officer and a military expert. I'd say that makes you more than qualified when it comes to assessing *Rorschach*'s threat potential."

"I'm muscle. Shouldn't you be *simplifying* Jukka or Isaac?"

"That's exactly what I'm doing."

She looked at me.

"You *interact*," I said. "Every component of the system affects every other. Processing Sarasti without factoring you in would be like trying to calculate acceleration while ignoring mass."

She turned back to her brood. Another robot passed muster.

She didn't hate *me*. What she hated was what my presence implied.

They don't trust us to speak for ourselves, she wouldn't say. *No matter how qualified we are, no matter how far ahead of the pack. Maybe even because of that. We're contaminated. We're subjective. So they send Siri Keeton to tell them what we* really *mean.*

"I get it," I said after a moment.

"Do you."

"It's not about trust, Major. It's about *location*. Nobody gets a good view of a system from the inside, no matter who they are. The view's distorted."

"And yours isn't."

"I'm outside the system."

"You're interacting with me now."

"As an observer only. Perfection's unattainable but it isn't *unapproachable,* you know? I don't play a role in decision-making or research, I don't interfere in any aspect of the mission that I'm assigned to study. But of course I ask questions. The more information I have, the better my analysis."

"I thought you didn't have to *ask*. I thought you guys could just, read the signs or something."

"Every bit helps. It all goes into the mix."

"You doing it now? *Synthesizing?*"

I nodded.

"And you do this without any specialized knowledge at all."

"I'm as much of a specialist as you. I specialize in processing informational topologies."

"Without understanding their content."

"Understanding the shapes is enough."

Bates seemed to find some small imperfection in the battlebot under scrutiny, scratched at its shell with a fingernail. "Software couldn't do that without your help?"

"Software can do a lot of things. We've chosen to do some for ourselves." I nodded at the grunt. "Your visual inspections, for example."

She smiled faintly, conceding the point.

"So I'd encourage you to speak freely. You know I'm sworn to confidentiality."

"Thanks," she said, meaning, *On this ship, there's no such thing.*

Theseus chimed. Sarasti spoke in its wake: "Orbital insertion in fifteen minutes. Everyone to the drum in five."

"Well," Bates said, sending one last grunt on its way. "Here we go." She pushed off and sailed up the spine.

The newborn killing machines clicked at me. They smelled like new cars.

"By the way," Bates called over her shoulder, "you missed the obvious one."

"Sorry?"

She spun a hundred-eighty degrees at the end of the passageway, landed like an acrobat beside the drum hatch. "The reason. Why something would attack us even if we didn't have anything it wanted."

I read it off her: "If it wasn't attacking at all. If it was defending itself."

"You asked about Sarasti. Smart man. Strong leader. Maybe could spend a little more time with the troops."

Vampire doesn't respect his command. Doesn't listen to advice. Hides away half the time.

I remembered transient killer whales. "Maybe he's being considerate." *He knows he makes us nervous.*

"I'm sure that's it," Bates said.

Vampire doesn't trust himself.

It wasn't just Sarasti. They *all* hid from us, even when they had the upper hand. They always stayed just the other side of myth.

It started pretty much the same way it did for anything else; vampires were far from the first to learn the virtues of energy conservation. Shrews and hummingbirds, saddled with tiny bodies and overclocked metabolic engines, would have starved to death overnight if not for the torpor that overtook them at sundown. Comatose elephant seals lurked breathless at the bottom of the sea, rousing only for passing prey or redline lactate levels. Bears and chipmunks cut costs by sleeping away the impoverished winter months, and lungfish—Devonian black belts in the art of estivation—could curl up and die for years, waiting for the rains.

With vampires it was a little different. It wasn't shortness of breath, or metabolic overdrive, or some blanket of snow that locked the pantry every winter. The problem wasn't so much a lack of prey as a lack of *difference* from it; vampires were such a recent split from the ancestral baseline that the reproductive rates hadn't diverged. This was no woodland-variety lynx-hare dynamic, where prey outnumbered predators a hundred to one. Vampires fed on things that bred barely faster than they did. They would have wiped out their own food supply in no time if they hadn't learned how to ease off on the throttle.

By the time they went extinct they'd learned to shut down for *decades*.

It made two kinds of sense. It not only slashed their metabolic needs while prey bred itself back to harvestable levels, it gave us time to forget that we *were* prey. We were so smart by the Pleistocene, smart enough for easy skepticism; if you haven't seen any night-stalking demons in all your years on the savannah, why should you believe some senile campfire ramblings passed down by your mother's mother?

It was murder on our ancestors, even if those same enemy genes—co-opted now—served us so well when we left the sun a half-million years later. But it was almost—heartening, I guess—to think that maybe Sarasti felt the tug of other genes, some aversion to prolonged visibility shaped by generations of natural selection. Maybe he spent every moment in our company fighting voices that urged him to *Hide, hide, let them forget*. Maybe he retreated when they got too loud, maybe we made him as uneasy as he made us.

We could always hope.

Our final orbit combined discretion and valor in equal measure. *Rorschach* described a perfect equatorial circle 87,900 kilometers from Big Ben's center of gravity. Sarasti was unwilling to let it out of sight, and you didn't have to be a vampire to mistrust relay sats when swinging through a radiation-soaked blizzard of rock and machinery. The obvious alternative was to match orbits.

At the same time, all the debate over whether or not *Rorschach* had meant—or even understood—the threats it had made was a bit beside the point. Counterintrusion measures were a distinct possibility either way, and ongoing proximity only increased the risk. So Sarasti had derived some optimum compromise, a mildly eccentric orbit that nearly brushed the artifact at perigee but kept a discreet distance the rest of the time. It was a longer trajectory than *Rorschach*'s, and higher—we had to burn on the descending arc to keep in sync—but the end result was continuously line-of-sight, and only brought us within striking distance for three hours either side of bottoming out.

Our striking distance, that is. For all we knew *Rorschach* could have reached out and swatted us from the sky before we'd even left the solar system.

Sarasti gave the command from his tent. ConSensus carried his voice into the drum as *Theseus* coasted to apogee: "Now."

Jack had erected a tent about itself, a blister glued to *Rorschach*'s hull and blown semi-taut against vacuum with the merest whiff of nitrogen. Now it brought lasers to bear and started digging; if we'd read the vibrations right, the ground should be only thirty-four centimeters deep beneath its feet. The beams stuttered as they cut, despite six millimeters of doped shielding.

"Son of a bitch," Szpindel murmured. "It's *working*."

We burned through tough fibrous epidermis. We burned through veins of insulation that might have been some sort of programmable asbestos. We burned through alternating layers

of superconducting mesh, and the strata of flaking carbon sepa-
rating them.

We burned *through*.

The lasers shut down instantly. Within seconds *Rorschach*'s
intestinal gases had blown taut the skin of the tent. Black carbon
smoke swirled and danced in sudden thick atmosphere.

Nothing shot back at us. Nothing reacted. Partial pressures
piled up on ConSensus: methane, ammonia, hydrogen. Lots of
water vapor, freezing as fast as it registered.

Szpindel grunted. "Reducing atmosphere. Pre-snowball." He
sounded disappointed.

"Maybe it's a work in progress," James suggested. "Like the
structure itself."

"Maybe."

Jack stuck out its tongue, a giant mechanical sperm with a
myo-optical tail. Its head was a thick-skinned lozenge, at least
half ceramic shielding by cross-section; the tiny payload of sensors at its core was rudimentary, but small enough for the whole
assembly to thread through the pencil-thin hole the laser had
cut. It unspooled down the hole, rimming *Rorschach*'s newly-
torn orifice.

"Dark down there," James observed.

Bates: "But warm." 281° K. Above freezing.

The endoscope emerged into darkness. Infrared served up a
grainy grayscale of a—a tunnel, it looked like, replete with mist
and exotic rock formations. The walls curved like honeycomb,
like the insides of fossilized intestine. Cul-de-sacs and branches
proliferated down the passage. The basic substrate appeared to
be a dense pastry of carbon-fiber leaves. Some of the gaps between those layers were barely thick as fingernails; others looked
wide enough to stack bodies.

"Ladies and gentlemen," Szpindel said softly, "the Devil's Baklava."

I could have sworn I saw something move. I could have sworn it looked familiar.

The camera died.

RORSCHACH

MOTHERS ARE FONDER THAN FATHERS OF THEIR CHIL-
DREN BECAUSE THEY ARE MORE CERTAIN THEY ARE
THEIR OWN.

—ARISTOTLE

I COULDN'T SAY good-bye to Dad. I didn't even know
where he was.

I didn't *want* to say good-bye to Helen. I didn't want to go back
there. That was the problem: I didn't have to. There was nowhere
left in the world where the mountain couldn't simply pick up and
move to Mohammed. Heaven was merely a suburb of the global
village, and the global village left me no excuse.

I linked from my own apartment. My new inlays—mission-
specific, slid into my head just the week before—shook hands
with the noosphere and knocked upon the Pearly Gates. Some
tame spirit, more plausible than St. Peter if no less ethereal, took
a message and disappeared.

And I was *inside*.

This was no antechamber, no visiting room. Heaven was not
intended for the casual visitor; any paradise in which the flesh-
constrained would feel at home would have been intolerably
pedestrian to the disembodied souls who lived there. Of course,
there was no reason why visitor and resident had to share the
same view. I could have pulled any conventional worldview off
the shelf if I'd wanted, seen this place rendered in any style I
chose. Except for the Ascended themselves, of course. That was

one of the perks of the Afterlife: only *they* got to choose the face we saw.

But the thing my mother had become *had* no face, and I was damned if she was going to see me hide behind some mask.

"Hello, Helen."

"Siri! What a wonderful surprise!"

She was an abstraction in an abstraction: an impossible intersection of dozens of bright panes, as if the disassembled tiles of a stained-glass window had each been set aglow and animated. She swirled before me like a school of fish. Her world echoed her body: lights and angles and three-dimensional Escher impossibilities, piled like bright thunderheads. And yet, somehow I would have recognized her anywhere. Heaven was a dream; only upon waking do you realize that the characters you encountered looked nothing like they do in real life.

There was only one familiar landmark anywhere in the whole sensorium. My mother's heaven smelled of cinnamon.

I beheld her luminous avatar and imagined the corpus soaking in a tank of nutrients, deep underground. "How are you doing?"

"Very well. *Very* well. Of course, it takes a little getting used to, knowing your mind isn't quite *yours* anymore." Heaven didn't just feed the brains of its residents; it fed *off* them, used the surplus power of idle synapses to run its own infrastructure. "You *have* to move in here, sooner better than later. You'll never leave."

"Actually, I *am* leaving," I said. "We're shipping out tomorrow."

"Shipping out?"

"The Kuiper. You know. The Fireflies?"

"Oh yes. I think I heard something about that. We don't get much news from the outside world, you know."

"Anyway, just thought I'd call in and say good-bye."

"I'm glad you did. I've been hoping to see you without, you know."

"Without what?"

"You know. Without your father listening in."

Not again.

"Dad's in the field, Helen. Interplanetary crisis. You might have heard something."

"I certainly have. You know, I haven't always been happy about your father's . . . extended assignments, but maybe it was really a blessing in disguise. The less he was around, the less he could do."

"Do?"

"To you." The apparition stilled for a few moments, feigning hesitation. "I've never told you this before, but—no. I shouldn't."

"Shouldn't what?"

"Bring up, well, old hurts."

"What old hurts?" Right on cue. I couldn't help myself, the training went too deep. I always barked on command.

"Well," she began, "sometimes you'd come back—you were so very young—and your face would be so set and hard, and I'd wonder why are you so *angry,* little boy? What can someone so young have to be so angry about?"

"Helen, what are you talking about? Back from where?"

"Just from the places he'd take you." Something like a shiver passed across her facets. "He was still around back then. He wasn't so *important,* he was just an accountant with a karate fetish, going on about forensics and game theory and astronomy until he put everyone to sleep."

I tried to imagine it: my father, the chatterbox. "That doesn't sound like Dad."

"Well of course not. You were too young to remember, but he was just a little man, then. He still is, really, under all the secret missions and classified briefings. I've never understood why people never saw that. But even back then he liked to— Well, it wasn't his fault, I suppose. He had a very difficult childhood, and he never learned to deal with problems like an adult. He, well, he'd throw his weight around, I guess you'd say. Of course I didn't know that before we married. If I had, I— But I made a commitment. I made a commitment, and I never broke it."

"What, are you saying you were abused?" *Back from the places he'd take you.* "Are—are you saying *I* was?"

"There are all kinds of abuse, Siri. Words can hurt more than bullets, sometimes. And child abandonment—"

"He didn't abandon me." *He left me with* you.

"He abandoned *us,* Siri. Sometimes for months at a time, and I—and *we* never knew if he was coming back And he *chose* to do that to us, Siri. He didn't *need* that job, there were so many other things he was qualified to do. Things that had been redundant for years."

I shook my head, incredulous, unable to say it aloud: She hated him because he hadn't had the good grace to grow *unnecessary?*

"It's not Dad's fault that planetary security is still an essential service," I said.

She continued as if she hadn't heard. "Now there was a time when it was unavoidable, when people our age *had* to work just to make ends meet. But even back then people *wanted* to spend time with their families. Even if they couldn't afford to. To, to *choose* to stay working when it isn't even *necessary,* that's—" She shattered and reassembled at my shoulder. "Yes, Siri. I believe that's a kind of abuse. And if your father had been half as loyal to me as I've been to him all these years . . ."

I remembered Jim, the last time I'd seen him: snorting vasopressin under the restless eyes of robot sentries. "I don't think Dad's been disloyal to either of us."

Helen sighed. "I don't really expect you to understand. I'm not completely stupid, I've seen how it played out. I pretty much had to raise you myself all these years. I always had to play the heavy, always had to be the one to hand out the discipline because your father was off on some *secret assignment*. And then he'd come home for a week or two and he was the golden-haired boy just because he'd seen fit to drop in. I don't really blame you for that any more than I blame him. Blame doesn't solve anything at this stage. I just thought—well, really, I thought you ought to know. Take it for what it's worth."

A memory, unbidden: called into Helen's bed when I was nine, her hand stroking my scar, her stale sweet breath stirring against my cheek. *You're the man of the house now Siri. We can't count on your father anymore. It's just you and me. . . .*

I didn't say anything for a while. Finally: "Didn't it help at all?"

"What do you mean?"

I glanced around at all that customized abstraction: internal feedback, lucidly dreamed. "You're omnipotent in here. Desire anything, imagine anything; there it is. I'd thought it would have *changed* you more."

Rainbow tiles danced, and forced a laugh. "This isn't enough of a *change* for you?"

Not nearly.

Because Heaven had a catch. No matter how many constructs and avatars Helen built in there, no matter how many empty vessels sang her praises or commiserated over the injustices she'd suffered, when it came right down to it she was only talking to herself. There were other realities over which she had no control, other people who didn't play by her rules—and if they thought of Helen at all, they thought as they damn well pleased.

She could go the rest of her life without ever meeting any of them. But she knew they were out there, and it drove her crazy. Taking my leave of Heaven, it occurred to me that omnipotent though she was, there was only one way my mother would ever be truly happy in her own personal creation.

The rest of creation would have to go.

"This shouldn't keep happening," Bates said. "The shielding was good."

The Gang was up across the drum, squaring away something in their tent. Sarasti lurked offstage today, monitoring the proceedings from his quarters. That left me with Bates and Szpindel in the Commons.

"Maybe against direct EM." Szpindel stretched, stifled a yawn. "Ultrasound boots up magnetic fields through shielding sometimes, in living tissue at least. Any chance something like that could be happening with your electronics?"

Bates spread her hands. "Who knows? Might as well be black magic and elves down there."

"Well, it's not a total wash. We can make a few smart guesses, eh?"

"Such as?"

Szpindel raised one finger. "The layers we cut through couldn't result from any metabolic process *I* know about. So it's not 'alive,' not in the biological sense. Not that that means anything these days," he added, glancing around the belly of our beast.

"What about life *inside* the structure?"

"Anoxic atmosphere. Probably rules out complex multicellular life. Microbes, maybe, although if so I wish to hell they'd show up in the samples. But anything complex enough to think, let alone build something like *that*"—a wave at the image in ConSensus—"is gonna need a high-energy metabolism, and that means oxygen."

"So you think it's empty?"

"Didn't say that, did I? I know aliens are supposed to be all mysterious and everything, but I still don't see why *anyone* would build a city-sized wildlife refuge for anaerobic microbes."

"It's got to be a habitat for *something*. Why any atmosphere at all, if it's just some kind of terraforming machine?"

Szpindel pointed up at the Gang's tent. "What Susan said. Atmosphere's still under construction and we get a free ride until the owners show up."

"Free?"

"Free*ish*. And I know we've only seen a fraction of a fraction of what's inside. But something obviously saw us coming. It yelled at us, as I recall. If they're smart and they're hostile, why aren't they shooting?"

"Maybe they are."

"If something's hiding down the hall wrecking your robots, it's not frying them any faster than the baseline environment would do anyway."

"What you call a *baseline environment* might be an active counterintrusion measure. Why else would a *habitat* be so uninhabitable?"

Szpindel rolled his eyes. "Okay, I was wrong. We *don't* know enough to make a few smart guesses."

Not that we hadn't tried. Once Jack's sensor head had been irreparably fried, we'd relegated it to surface excavation; it had widened the bore in infinitesimal increments, patiently burning back the edges of our initial peephole until it measured almost a meter across. Meanwhile we'd customized Bates's grunts—shielded them against nuclear reactors and the insides of cyclotrons—and come perigee we'd thrown them at *Rorschach* like stones chucked into a haunted forest. Each had gone through Jack's portal, unspooling whisker-thin fiberop behind them to pass intelligence through the charged atmosphere.

They'd sent glimpses, mostly. A few extended vignettes. We'd seen *Rorschach*'s walls move, slow lazy waves of peristalsis rippling along its gut. We'd seen treacly invaginations in progress, painstaking constrictions that would presumably, given time, seal off a passageway. Our grunts had sailed through some quarters, staggered through others where the magnetic ambience threw them off balance. They'd passed through strange throats lined with razor-thin teeth, thousands of triangular blades in parallel rows, helically twisted. They'd edged cautiously around clouds of mist sculpted into abstract fractal shapes, shifting and endlessly recursive, their charged droplets strung along a myriad converging lines of electromagnetic force.

Ultimately, every one of them had died or disappeared.

"Any way to increase the shielding?" I wondered.

Szpindel gave me a look.

"We've shielded everything except the sensor heads," Bates explained. "If we shield *those* we're blind."

"But visible light's harmless enough. What about purely optical li—"

"We're *using* optical links, commissar," Szpindel snapped. "And you may have noticed the shit's getting through anyway."

"But aren't there, you know"—I groped for the word—"bandpass filters? Something that lets visible wavelengths through, cuts out the lethal stuff on both sides?"

He snorted. "Sure. It's called an atmosphere, and if we'd brought one with us—about fifty times deeper than Earth's—it *might* block some of that soup down there. 'Course, Earth also gets a lot of help from its magnetic field, but I'm not betting my life on any EM we set up in *that* place."

"If we didn't keep running into these *spikes,*" Bates said. "That's the real problem."

"Are they random?" I wondered.

Szpindel's shrug was half shiver. "I don't think anything about that place is random. But who knows? We need more data."

"Which we're not likely to get," James said, walking around the ceiling to join us, "if our drones keep shorting out."

The conditional was pure formality. We'd tried playing the odds, sacrificing drone after drone in the hope that one of them would get lucky; survival rates tailed exponentially to zero with distance from base camp. We'd tried shielding the fiberop to reduce aperture leakage; the resulting tethers were stiff and unwieldy, wrapped in so many layers of ferroceramic that we were virtually waving the bots around on the end of a stick. We'd tried cutting the tethers entirely, sending the machines out to explore on their own, squinting against the radiant blizzard and storing their findings for later download; none had returned. We'd tried everything.

"We can go in ourselves," James said.

Almost everything.

"Right," Szpindel replied in a voice that couldn't mean anything but *wrong*.

"It's the only way to learn anything useful."

"Yeah. Like how many seconds it would take your brain to turn into synchrotron soup."

"Our suits can be shielded."

"Oh, you mean like Mandy's drones?"

"I'd really rather you didn't call me that," Bates remarked.

"The point is, *Rorschach* kills you whether you're meat or mechanical."

"*My* point is that it kills meat *differently*," James replied. "It takes longer."

Szpindel shook his head. "You'd be good as dead in fifty minutes. Even shielded. Even in the so-called cool zones."

"And completely asymptomatic for three hours or more. And

even after that it would take days for us to actually die *and we'd be back here long before then,* and the ship could patch us up just like that. *We* even know that much, Isaac, it's right there in Con-Sensus. And if we know it, you know it. So we shouldn't even be having this argument."

"That's your solution? We saturate ourselves with radiation every thirty hours and then I get to cut out the tumors and stitch everyone's cells back together?"

"The pods are automatic. You wouldn't have to lift a finger."

"Not to mention the number those magnetic fields would do on your *brain.* We'd be hallucinating from the moment we—"

"Faraday the suits."

"Ah, so we go in deaf, dumb, and blind. Good idea."

"We can let light pass. Infrared—"

"It's all *EM,* Suze. Even if we blacked out our helmets completely and used a camera feed, we'd get leakage where the wire went through."

"Some, yes. But it'd be better than—"

"Jesus." A tremor sent spittle sailing from the corner of Szpindel's mouth. "Let me talk to Mi—"

"I've discussed it with the rest of the gang, Isaac. We're all agreed."

"*All* agreed? You don't have a working majority in there, Suze. Just because you cut your brain into pieces doesn't mean they each get a vote."

"I don't see why not. We're each at least as sentient as you are."

"They're all *you.* Just partitioned."

"You don't seem to have any trouble treating Michelle as a separate individual."

"Michelle's— I mean, yes, you're all very different *facets,* but there's only one original. Your alters—"

"Don't call us that." Sascha erupted with a voice cold as LOX. *"Ever."*

Szpindel tried to pull back. "I didn't mean—you know I didn't—"

But Sascha was gone. "What are you saying?" said the softer voice in her wake. "Do you think I'm just, I'm just *Mom,* play-acting? You think when we're together you're alone with *her?*"

"Michelle," Szpindel said miserably. "No. What I think—"

"Doesn't matter," Sarasti said. "We don't *vote* here."

He floated above us, visored and unreadable in the center of the drum. None of us had seen him arrive. He turned slowly on his axis, keeping us in view as we rotated around him.

"Prepping *Scylla.* Amanda needs two untethered grunts with precautionary armament. Cams from one to a million Angstroms, shielded tympanics, no autonomous circuitry. Platelet boosters, dimenhydrinate and potassium iodide for everyone by thirteen fifty."

"Everyone?" Bates asked.

Sarasti nodded. "Window opens four hours twenty-three." He turned back down the spine.

"Not me," I said.

Sarasti paused.

"I don't participate in field ops," I reminded him.

"Now you do."

"I'm a *Synthesist.*" He knew that. Of course he knew, everyone did: You can't observe the system unless you stay *outside* the system.

"On Earth you're a Synthesist," he said. "In the Kuiper you're a Synthesist. Here you're mass. Do what you're told."

He disappeared.

"Welcome to the big picture," Bates said softly.

I looked at her as the rest of the group broke up. "You know I—"

"We're a long way out, Siri. Can't wait fourteen months for feedback from your bosses, and you know it."

She leapt from a standing start, arced smoothly through holograms into the weightless core of the drum. But then she stopped herself, as if distracted by some sudden insight. She grabbed a spinal conduit and swung back to face me.

"You shouldn't sell yourself short," she said. "Or Sarasti, either. You're an observer, right? It's a safe bet there's going to be a lot down there worth observing."

"Thanks," I said. But I already knew why Sarasti was sending me into *Rorschach,* and there was more to it than *observation*.

Three valuable agents in harm's way. A decoy bought one-in-four odds that an enemy would aim somewhere else.

THE LORD WILL TAKE CONTROL OF YOU. YOU WILL DANCE
AND SHOUT AND BECOME A DIFFERENT PERSON.
—1 SAMUEL 10:6

"WE WERE PROBABLY fractured during most of our evolution," James once told me, back when we were all still getting acquainted. She tapped her temple. "There's a lot of room up here; a modern brain can run dozens of sentient cores without getting too crowded. And parallel multitasking has obvious survival advantages."

I nodded. "Ten heads are better than one."

"Our integration may have actually occurred quite recently.

Some experts think we can still revert to multiples under the right circumstances."

"Well, of course. You're living proof."

She shook their head. "I'm not talking about *physical* partitioning. We're the state of the art, certainly, but theoretically surgery isn't even necessary. Simple stress could do something like it, if it was strong enough. If it happened early in childhood."

"No kidding."

"Well, in theory," James admitted, and changed into Sascha who said, "Bull*shit in theory*. There's documented cases as recently as fifty years ago."

"Really." I resisted the temptation to look it up on my inlays; the unfocused eyes can be a giveaway. "I didn't know."

"Well it's not like anyone talks about it *now*. People were fucking *barbarians* about multicores back then—called it a *disorder,* treated it like some kind of disease. And their idea of a cure was to keep one of the cores and murder all the others. Not that they called it *murder,* of course. They called it *integration* or some shit. That's what people did back then: created other people to suck up all the abuse and torture, then got rid of them when they weren't needed anymore."

It hadn't been the tone most of us were looking for at an ice-breaking party. James had gently eased back into the driver's seat and the conversation had steered closer to community standards.

But I hadn't heard any of the Gang use *alter* to describe each other, then or since. It had seemed innocuous enough when Szpindel had said it. I wondered why they'd taken such offense—and now, floating alone in my tent with a few pre-op minutes to kill, there was no one to see my eyes glaze.

Alter carried baggage over a century old, ConSensus told me. Sascha was right; there'd been a time when MCC was MPD, a *disorder* rather than a *complex,* and it had *never* been induced deliberately. According to the experts of that time, multiple personalities arose spontaneously from unimaginable cauldrons of abuse—fragmentary personae offered up to suffer rapes and beatings while the child behind took to some unknowable sanctuary in the folds of the brain. It was both survival strategy and ritual self-sacrifice: powerless souls hacking themselves to pieces, offering up quivering chunks of self in the desperate hope that the vengeful gods called *Mom* or *Dad* might not be insatiable.

None of it had been real, as it turned out. Or at least, none of it had been confirmed. The experts of the day had been little more than witch doctors dancing through improvised rituals: meandering free-form interviews full of leading questions and nonverbal cues, scavenger hunts through regurgitated childhoods. Sometimes a shot of lithium or haloperidol when the beads and rattles didn't work. The technology to map minds was barely off the ground; the technology to edit them was years away. So the *therapists* and *psychiatrists* poked at their victims and invented names for things they didn't understand, and argued over the shrines of Freud and Klein and the old Astrologers, doing their very best to sound like practitioners of Science.

Inevitably, it was Science that turned them all into roadkill; MPD was a half-forgotten fad even before the advent of synaptic rewiring. But *alter* was a word from that time, and its resonance had persisted. Among those who remembered the tale, *alter* was codespeak for *betrayal* and *human sacrifice*. *Alter* meant *cannon fodder*.

Imagining the topology of the Gang's coexisting souls, I could see why Sascha embraced the mythology. I could see why Susan let her. After all, there was nothing implausible about the concept; the Gang's very existence proved that much. And when you've been peeled off from a pre-existing entity, sculpted from nonexistence straight into adulthood—a mere fragment of

personhood, without even a full-time body to call your own—
you can be forgiven a certain amount of anger. Sure you're all
equal, all in it together. Sure, no persona is better than any other.
Susan's still the only one with a surname.

Better to direct that resentment at old grudges, real or imagined; less problematic, at least, than taking it out on someone
who shares the same flesh.

I realized something else, too. Surrounded by displays docu-
menting the relentless growth of the leviathan beneath us, I could
not only see why Sascha had objected to the word; I could also
see why Isaac Szpindel, no doubt unconsciously, had spoken it in
the first place.

As far as Earth was concerned, everyone on *Theseus* was an
alter.

Sarasti stayed behind. He hadn't come with a backup.

There were the rest of us, though, crammed into the shuttle,
embedded in custom spacesuits so padded with shielding we
might have been deep-sea divers from a previous century. It was
a fine balance; too much shielding would have been worse than
none at all, would split primary particles into secondary ones,
just as lethal and twice as numerous. Sometimes you had to live
with moderate exposure; the only alternative was to embed
yourself like a bug in lead.

We launched six hours from perigee. *Scylla* raced on ahead
like an eager child, leaving its parent behind. There was no ea-
gerness in the systems around me, though. Except for one: the
Gang of Four almost *shimmered* behind her faceplate.

"Excited?" I asked.

Sascha answered: "Fuckin' *right*. *Field* work, Keeton. First
contact."

"What if there's nobody there?" *What if there is, and they don't like us?*

"Even better. We get a crack at their signs and cereal boxes without their traffic cops leaning over our shoulders."

I wondered if she spoke for the others. I was pretty sure she didn't speak for Michelle.

Scylla's ports had all been sealed. There was no outside view, nothing to see inside but bots and bodies and the tangled silhouette swelling on my helmet HUD. But I could feel the radiation slicing through our armor as if it were tissue paper. I could feel the knotted crests and troughs of *Rorschach's* magnetic field. I could feel *Rorschach* itself, drawing nearer: the charred canopy of some firestormed alien forest, more landscape than artifact. I imagined titanic bolts of electricity arcing between its branches. I imagined getting in the way.

What kind of creatures would choose to live in such a place?

"You really think we'll get along," I said.

James's shrug was all but lost under the armor. "Maybe not at first. We may have gotten off on the wrong foot, we might have to sort through all kinds of misunderstandings. But we'll figure each other out eventually."

Evidently she thought that had answered my question.

The shuttle slewed; we bumped against each other like tenpins. Thirty seconds of micromaneuvers brought us to a solid stop. A cheery animation played across the HUD in greens and blues: the shuttle's docking seal, easing through the membrane that served as our entrance into *Rorschach's* inflatable vestibule. Even as a cartoon it looked vaguely pornographic.

Bates had been prepacked next to the airlock. She slid back the inner door. "Everybody duck."

Not an easy maneuver, swaddled in life-support and ferroceramic. Helmets tilted and bumped. The grunts, flattened overhead like great lethal cockroaches, hummed to life and disengaged from the ceiling. They scraped past in the narrow headroom, bobbed cryptically to their mistress, and exited stage left.

Bates closed the inner hatch. The lock cycled, opened again on an empty chamber.

Everything nominal, according to the board. The drones waited patiently in the vestibule. Nothing had jumped out at them.

Bates followed them through.

We had to wait forever for the image. The baud rate was less than a trickle. Words moved back and forth easily enough—"No surprises so far," Bates reported in distorted Jews-harp vibrato—but any picture was worth a million of them, and—

—there: Through the eyes of the grunt behind we saw the grunt ahead in motionless, grainy monochrome. It was a postcard from the past: sight turned to sound, thick clumsy vibrations of methane bumping against the hull. It took long seconds for each static-ridden image to accrete on the HUD: grunts descending into the pit; grunts emerging into *Rorschach*'s duodenum; a cryptic, hostile cavescape in systematic increments. Down in the lower left-hand corner of each image, time stamps and Teslas ran down the clock.

You give up a lot when you don't trust the EM spectrum.

"Looks good," Bates reported. "Going in."

In a friendlier universe machines would have cruised the boulevard, sending perfect images in crystal resolution. Szpindel and the Gang would be sipping coffee back in the drum, telling the grunts to take a sample of this or get a close-up of that. In a friendlier universe, I wouldn't even be here.

Bates appeared in the next postcard, emerging from the fistula. In the next her back was to the camera, apparently panning the perimeter.

In the one after that she was looking right at us.

"Oh . . . okay," she said. "Come on . . . down . . ."

"Not so fast," Szpindel said. "How are you feeling?"

"Fine. A bit—odd, but . . ."

"Odd how?" Radiation sickness announced itself with nausea, but unless we'd seriously erred in our calculations that wouldn't happen for another hour or two. Not until well after we'd all been lethally cooked.

"Mild disorientation," Bates reported. "It's a bit spooky in here, but . . . must be Grey syndrome. It's tolerable."

I looked at the Gang. The Gang looked at Szpindel. Szpindel shrugged.

"It's not gonna get any better," Bates said from afar. "The clock is . . . clock is ticking, people. Get down here."

We got.

Not living, not by a long shot.

Haunted.

Even when the walls didn't move, they did: always at the corner of the eye, that sense of crawling motion. Always at the back of the mind the sense of being *watched,* the dread certainty of malign and alien observers just out of sight. More than once I turned, expecting to catch one of those phantoms in the open. All I ever saw was a half-blind grunt floating down the passageway, or a wide-eyed and jittery crewmate returning my stare. And the walls of some glistening black lava tube with a hundred embedded eyes, all snapped shut just the instant before. Our lights pushed the darkness back perhaps twenty meters in either direction; beyond, mist and shadows seethed. And the *sounds—Rorschach* creaked around us like some ancient wooden hull trapped in pack ice. Electricity hissed like rattlesnakes.

You tell yourself it's mostly in your head. You remind yourself it's well-documented, an inevitable consequence of meat and magnetism brought too close together. High-energy fields release the ghosts and the grays from your temporal lobe, dredge up paralyzing dread from the midbrain to saturate the conscious mind. They fuck with your motor nerves and make even dormant inlays sing like fine fragile crystal.

Energy artifacts. That's all they are. You repeat that to yourself, you repeat it so often it loses any pretense of rationality and devolves into rote incantation, a spell to ward off evil spirits. They're not real, these whispering voices just outside your helmet, those half-seen creatures flickering at the edge of vision. They're tricks of the mind, the same neurological smoke-and-mirrors that convinced people throughout the ages that they were being haunted by ghosts, abducted by aliens, hunted by—

—vampires—

—and you wonder whether Sarasti really stayed behind or if he was here all along, waiting for you . . .

"Another spike," Bates warned as *tesla* and *sieverts* surged on my HUD. "Hang on."

I was installing the faraday bell. Trying to. It should have been simple enough; I'd already run the main anchor line down from the vestibule to the flaccid sack floating in the middle of the passageway. I was—that's right, something about a spring line. To, to keep the bell centered. The wall glistened in my headlamp like wet clay. Satanic runes sparkled in my imagination.

I jammed the spring line's pad against the wall. I could have sworn the substrate *flinched*. I fired my thrust pistol, retreated back to the center of the passage.

"They're here," James whispered.

Something was. I could feel it always behind me, no matter where I turned. I could feel some great roaring darkness swirling just out of sight, a ravenous *mouth* as wide as the tunnel itself.

Any moment now it would lunge forward at impossible speed and engulf us all.

"They're *beautiful* . . ." James said. There was no fear in her voice at all. She sounded awestruck.

"What? Where?" Bates never stopped turning, kept trying to keep the whole three-sixty in sight at once. The drones under her command wobbled restlessly to either side, armored parentheses pointing down the passageway in opposite directions. "What do you see?"

"Not out *there*. In *here*. *Everywhere*. Can't you see it?"

"I can't see anything," Szpindel said, his voice shaking.

"It's in the EM fields," James said. "*That's* how they communicate. The whole structure is full of *language*, it's—"

"I can't see *anything*," Szpindel repeated. His breath echoed loud and fast over the link. "I'm *blind*."

"*Shit*." Bates swung on Szpindel. "How can that—the radiation—"

"I d-don't think that's it . . ."

Nine Tesla, and the ghosts were everywhere. I smelled asphalt and honeysuckle.

"Keeton!" Bates called. "You with us?"

"Y-yeah." Barely. I was back at the bell, my hand on the ripcord. Trying to ignore whatever kept tapping me on the shoulder.

"Leave that! Get him outside!"

"No!" Szpindel floated helplessly in the passage, his pistol bouncing against its wrist tether. "No, throw me something."

"What?"

It's all in your head. It's all in your—

"Throw something! Anything!"

Bates hesitated. "You said you were bli—"

"*Just do it!*"

Bates pulled a spare suit battery off her belt and lobbed it. Szpindel reached, fumbled. The battery slipped from his grasp and bounced off the wall.

"I'll be okay," he gasped. "Just get me into the tent."

I yanked the cord. The bell inflated like a great gunmetal marshmallow.

"Everyone inside!" Bates ran her pistol with one hand, grabbed Szpindel with the other. She handed him off to me and slapped a sensor pod onto the skin of the tent. I pulled back the shielded entrance flap as though pulling a scab from a wound. The single molecule beneath, infinitely long, endlessly folded against itself, swirled and glistened like a soap bubble.

"Get him in. James! Get down here!"

I pushed Szpindel through the membrane. It split around him with airtight intimacy, hugged each tiny crack and contour as he passed through.

"*James!* Are you—"

"*Get it off me!*" Harsh voice, raw and scared and scary, as male as female could sound. Cruncher in control. "*Get it off!*"

I looked back. Susan James's body tumbled slowly in the tunnel, grasping its right leg with both hands.

"*James!*" Bates sailed over to the other woman. "Keeton! Help out!" She took the Gang by the arm. "Cruncher? What's the problem?"

"*That!* You *blind*?" He wasn't just *grasping* at the limb, I realized as I joined them. He was *tugging* at it. *He was trying to pull it off.*

Something laughed hysterically, right inside my helmet.

"Take his arm," Bates told me, taking his right one, trying to pry the fingers from their death grip on the Gang's leg. "Cruncher, *let go. Now.*"

"Get it off me!"

"It's your leg, Cruncher." We wrestled our way toward the diving bell.

"It's *not* my leg! Just *look* at it, how could it—it's *dead*. It's *stuck* to me . . ."

Almost there. "Cruncher, *listen,*" Bates snapped. "Are you with m—"

"Get it off!"

We stuffed the Gang into the tent. Bates moved aside as I dove in after them. Amazing, the way she held it together. Somehow she kept the demons at bay, herded us to shelter like a border collie in a thunderstorm. She was—

She wasn't following us in. She wasn't even *there*. I turned to see her body floating outside the tent, one gloved hand grasping the edge of the flap; but even under all those layers of Kapton and Chromel and polycarbonate, even behind the distorted half-reflections on her faceplate, I could tell that something was missing. All her surfaces had just *disappeared*.

This couldn't be Amanda Bates. The thing before me had no more topology than a mannequin.

"Amanda?" The Gang gibbered at my back, softly hysteric.

Szpindel: "What's happening?"

"I'll stay out here," Bates said. She had no affect whatsoever. "I'm dead anyway."

"Wha—" Szpindel had lots. "You *will* be, if you don't—"

"You leave me here," Bates said. "That's an order."

She sealed us in.

It wasn't the first time, not for me. I'd had invisible fingers poking through my brain before, stirring up the muck, ripping open the scabs. It was far more intense when *Rorschach* did it to me, but Chelsea was more—

—precise, I guess you'd say.

Macramé, she called it: glial jumpstarts, cascade effects, the splice and dice of critical ganglia. While I trafficked in the reading of Human architecture, Chelsea *changed* it—finding the critical nodes and nudging them just so, dropping a pebble into some trickle at the headwaters of memory and watching the ripples build to a great rolling cascade deep in the downstream psyche. She could hotwire happiness in the time it took to fix a sandwich, reconcile you with your whole childhood in the course of a lunch hour or three.

Like so many other domains of human invention, this one had learned to run without her. Human nature was becoming an assembly-line edit, Humanity itself increasingly relegated from production to product. Still. For me, Chelsea's skill set recast a strange old world in an entirely new light: the cut-and-paste of minds not for the greater good of some abstract society, but for the simple selfish wants of the individual.

"Let me give you the gift of happiness," she said.

"I'm already pretty happy."

"I'll make you happier. A TAT, on me."

"Tat?"

"Transient Attitudinal Tweak. I've still got privileges at Sax."

"I've been tweaked plenty. Change one more synapse and I might turn into someone else."

"That's ridiculous and you know it. Or every experience you had would turn you into a different person."

I thought about that. "Maybe it does."

But she wouldn't let it go, and even the strongest anti-happiness argument was bound to be an uphill proposition; so one afternoon Chelsea fished around in her cupboards and dredged up a hairnet studded with greasy gray washers. The net was a superconducting spiderweb, fine as mist, that mapped the fields of merest thought. The washers were ceramic magnets that bathed the brain in fields of their own. Chelsea's inlays linked to a base station that played with the interference patterns between the two.

"They used to need a machine the size of a bathroom just to house the magnets." She laid me back on the couch and stretched the mesh across my skull. "That's the only outright miracle you get with a portable setup like this. We can find hot spots, and we can even zap 'em if they need zapping, but TMS effects fade after a while. We'll have to go to a clinic for anything permanent."

"So we're fishing for what, exactly? Repressed memories?"

"No such thing." She grinned in toothy reassurance. "There are only memories we choose to ignore, or kinda think *around,* if you know what I mean."

"I thought this was the gift of happiness. Why—"

She laid a fingertip across my lips. "Believe it or not, Cyggers, people sometimes choose to ignore even *good* memories. Like, say, if they enjoyed something they didn't think they should. Or"—she kissed my forehead—"if they don't think they *deserve* to be happy."

"So we're going for—"

"Potluck. You can never tell till you get a bite. Close your eyes."

A soft hum started up somewhere between my ears. Chelsea's voice led me on through the darkness. "Now keep in mind, memories aren't historical archives. They're—improvisations, really. A lot of the stuff you associate with a particular event might be factually wrong, no matter how clearly you remember it. The brain has a funny habit of building composites. Inserting details after the fact. But that's not to say your memories aren't *true,* okay? They're an honest reflection of how you saw the world, and every one of them went into shaping how you *see* it. But they're not photographs. More like impressionist paintings. Okay?"

"Okay."

"Ah," she said. "There's something."

"What?"

"Functional cluster. Getting a lot of low-level use but not enough to intrude into conscious awareness. Let's just see what happens when we—"

And I was ten years old, and I was home early and I'd just let myself into the kitchen and the smell of burned butter and garlic hung in the air. Dad and Helen were fighting in the next room. The flip-top on our kitchen-catcher had been left up, which was sometimes enough to get Helen going all by itself. But they were fighting about something else; Helen *only wanted what was best for all of us* but Dad said *there were limits* and *this was not the way to go about it.* And Helen said *you don't know what it's like you hardly ever even* see *him* and then I knew they were fighting about me. Which in and of itself was nothing unusual.

What really scared me was that for the first time ever, Dad was fighting *back.*

"You do not *force* something like that onto someone. Especially without their knowledge." My father never shouted—his voice was as low and level as ever—but it was colder than I'd ever heard, and hard as iron.

"That's just *garbage,*" Helen said. "Parents *always* make decisions for their children, in their best interests, especially when it comes to medical iss—"

"This is not a medical issue." This time my father's voice *did* rise. "It's—"

"Not a medical issue! That's a new height of denial even for you! They cut out half his *brain* in case you missed it! Do you think he can recover from that without help? Is that more of your father's *tough love* shining through? Why not just deny him food and water while you're at it!"

"If mu-ops were called for they'd have been prescribed."

I felt my face scrunching at the unfamiliar word. Something small and white beckoned from the open garbage pail.

"Jim, be *reasonable.* He's so *distant,* he barely even *talks* to me."

"They said it would take time."

"But two years! There's nothing wrong with helping nature along a little, we're not even talking black market. It's over-the-counter, for God's sake!"

"That's not the point."

An empty pill bottle. That's what one of them had thrown out, before forgetting to close the lid. I salvaged it from the kitchen discards and sounded out the label in my head.

"Maybe the *point* should be that someone who's barely home three months of the year has got a bloody nerve passing judgment on *my* parenting skills. If you want a say in how he's raised, then you can damn well pay some dues first. Until then, just fuck right off."

"You will not put that shit into my son *ever again,*" my father said.

Bondfast™ Formula IV
μ-Opioid Receptor Promoters/Maternal Response Stimulant
"Strengthening ties between Mother and Child since 2042."

"Yeah? And how are you going to stop me, you little geek? You can't even make the time to find out what's going on in your own family; you think you can control me all the way from fucking orbit? You think—"

Suddenly, nothing came from the living room but soft choking sounds. I peeked around the corner.

My father had Helen by the throat.

"I think," he growled, "that I can stop you from doing anything to Siri ever again, if I have to. And I think you know that."

And then she saw me. And then he did. And my father took his hand from around my mother's neck, and his face was utterly unreadable.

But there was no mistaking the triumph on hers.

I was up off the couch, the skullcap clenched in one hand. Chelsea stood wide-eyed before me, the butterfly still as death on her cheekbone.

She took my hand. "Oh, God. I'm so sorry."

"You—you saw that?"

"No, of course not. It can't read minds. But that obviously . . . wasn't a happy memory."

"It wasn't all that bad."

I felt sharp, disembodied pain from somewhere nearby, like an ink spot on a white tablecloth. After a moment I fixed it: teeth in my lip.

She ran her hand up my arm. "It really stressed you out. Your vitals were— Are you okay?"

"Yeah, of course. No big deal." Tasting salt. "I am curious about something, though."

"Ask me."

"Why would you do this to me?"

"Because we can make it go *away*, Cygnus. That's the whole point. Whatever that was, whatever you didn't like about it, we know where it is now. We can go back in and damp it out just like *that*. And then we've got *days* to get it removed permanently, if that's what you want. Just put the cap back on and—"

She put her arms around me, drew me close. She smelled like sand, and sweat. I loved the way she smelled. For a while, I could feel a little bit safe. For a while I could feel like the bottom wasn't going to drop out at any moment. Somehow, when I was with Chelsea, I *mattered*.

I wanted her to hold me forever.

"I don't think so," I said.

"No?" She blinked, looked up at me. "Why ever *not*?"

I shrugged. "You know what they say about people who don't remember the past."

PREDATORS RUN FOR THEIR DINNER. PREY RUN FOR THEIR LIVES.

—OLD ECOLOGIST'S PROVERB

WE WERE BLIND and helpless, jammed into a fragile bubble behind enemy lines. But finally the whisperers were silent. The monsters had stayed beyond the covers.

And Amanda Bates was out there with them.

"What the fuck." Szpindel breathed.

The eyes behind his faceplate were active and searching. "You can see?" I asked.

He nodded. "What happened to Bates? Her suit breach?"

"I don't think so."

"Then why'd she say she was dead? What—"

"She meant it *literally*," I told him. "Not *I'm as good as dead* or

I'm going to die. She meant dead *now*. Like she was a talking corpse."

"How do—" *you know?* Stupid question. His face ticced and trembled in the helmet. "That's crazy, eh?"

"Define *crazy*."

The Gang floated quietly, cheek-to-jowl behind Szpindel in the cramped enclosure. Cruncher had stopped obsessing about the leg as soon as we'd sealed up. Or maybe he'd simply been overridden; I thought I saw facets of Susan in the twitching of those thick gloved fingers.

Szpindel's breath echoed secondhand over the link. "If Bates is dead, then so are we."

"Maybe not. We wait out the spike, we get out of here. Besides," I added, "she wasn't dead. She only said she was."

"Fuck." Szpindel reached out and pressed his gloved palm against the skin of the tent. He felt back and forth along the fabric. "Someone *did* put out a transducer—"

"Eight o'clock," I said. "About a meter." Szpindel's hand came to rest across the wall from the pod. My HUD flooded with secondhand numbers, vibrated down his arm and relayed to our suits.

Still five tesla out there. Falling, though. The tent expanded around us as if breathing, shrank back in the next second as some transient low-pressure front moved past.

"When did your sight come back?" I wondered.

"Soon as we came inside."

"Sooner. You saw the battery."

"Fumbled it." He grunted. "Not that I'm much less of a spaz even when I'm *not* blind, eh? Bates! You out there?"

"You reached for it. You almost caught it. That wasn't blind chance."

"Not blind chance. Blind*sight*. Amanda? Respond, please."

"Blindsight?"

"Nothing wrong with the receptors," he said distractedly. "Brain processes the image but it can't access it. Brain stem takes over."

"Your brain stem can see but you *can't*?"

"Something like that. Shut up and let me— Amanda, can you hear me?"

"...no..."

Not from anyone in the tent, that voice. It had shivered down Szpindel's arm, barely audible, with the rest of the data. From *outside*.

"Major Mandy!" Szpindel exclaimed. "You're alive!"

"...no..." A whisper like white noise.

"Well you're talking to us, so you sure as shit ain't *dead*."

"No..."

Szpindel and I exchanged looks. "What's the problem, Major?"

Silence. The Gang bumped gently against the wall behind us, all facets opaque.

"Major Bates? Can you hear me?"

"No." It was a dead voice—sedated, trapped in a fishbowl, transmitted through limbs and lead at a three-digit baud rate. But it was definitely Bates's voice.

"Major, you've got to get in here," Szpindel said. "Can you come inside?"

"...no..."

"Are you injured? Are you pinned by something?"

"...n—no."

Maybe not her voice, after all. Maybe just her vocal cords.

"Look. Amanda, it's dangerous. It's too damn hot out there, do you understand? You—"

"I'm not out here," said the voice.

"Where are you?"

". . . nowhere."

I looked at Szpindel. Szpindel looked at me. Neither of us spoke.

James did. At long last, and softly: "And *what* are you, Amanda?"

No answer.

"Are you *Rorschach*?"

Here in the belly of the beast, it was so easy to believe.

"No . . ."

"Then what?"

"N . . . nothing." The voice was flat and mechanical. "I'm nothing."

"You're saying you don't exist?" Szpindel said slowly.

"Yes."

The tent breathed around us.

"Then how can you speak?" Susan asked the voice. "If you don't exist, what are we talking to?"

"Something . . . else." A sigh. A breath of static. "Not me."

"Shit," Szpindel muttered. His surfaces brightened with resolve and sudden insight. He pulled his hand from the wall; my HUD thinned instantly. "Her brain's frying. We gotta get her inside." He reached for the release.

I put out my own hand. "The spike—"

"Crested already, commissar. We're past the worst of it."

"Are you saying it's safe?"

"It's lethal. It's *always* lethal, and she's *out there* in it, and she could do some serious damage to herself in her pres—"

Something bumped the tent from the outside. Something grabbed the outer catch and *pulled*.

Our shelter opened like an eye. Amanda Bates looked in at us through the exposed membrane. "I'm reading three point eight," she said. "That's tolerable, right?"

Nobody moved.

"Come *on,* people. Break's over."

"Ama—" Szpindel stared. "Are you okay?"

"In here? Not likely. But we've got a job to do."

"Do you—exist?" I asked.

"What kind of stupid question is that? Szpindel, how's this field strength? Can we work in it?"

"Uh . . ." He swallowed audibly. "Maybe we should abort, Major. That spike was—"

"According to my readings, the spike is pretty much over. And we've got less than two hours to finish setting up, run our ground truths, and get out of here. Can we do that without hallucinating?"

"I don't think we'll shake the heebie-jeebies," Szpindel admitted. "But we shouldn't have to worry about—extreme effects— until another spike hits."

"Good."

"Which could be any time."

"We weren't hallucinating," James said quietly.

"We can discuss it later," Bates said. "Now—"

"There was a pattern there," James insisted. "In the fields. In my head. *Rorschach* was talking. Maybe not to us, but it was talking."

"Good." Bates pushed herself back to let us pass. "Maybe now we can finally learn to talk back."

"Maybe we can learn to *listen,*" James said.

We fled like frightened children with brave faces. We left a base camp behind: Jack, still miraculously functional in its vestibule; a tunnel into the haunted mansion; forlorn magnetometers left to die in the faint hope they might not. Crude pyronometers and thermographs, antique radiation-proof devices that measured the world through the flex and stretch of metal tabs and etched their findings on rolls of plastic. Glow-globes and diving bells and guide ropes strung one to another. We left it all behind, and promised to return in thirty-six hours if we lived so long.

Inside each of us, infinitesimal lacerations were turning our cells to mush. Plasma membranes sprang countless leaks. Overwhelmed repair enzymes clung desperately to shredded genes and barely delayed the inevitable. Anxious to avoid the rush, patches of my intestinal lining began flaking away before the rest of the body had a chance to die.

By the time we docked with *Theseus* both Michelle and I were feeling nauseous. (The rest of the Gang, oddly, was not; I had no idea how that was possible.) The others would be presenting the same symptoms within minutes. Without intervention we would all be vomiting our guts out for the following two days. Then the body would pretend to recover; for perhaps a week we would feel no pain and have no future. We would walk and talk and move like any living thing, and perhaps convince ourselves that we were immortal after all.

Then we would collapse into ourselves, rotted from the inside out. We would bleed from our eyes and mouths and assholes, and if any God was merciful we would die before splitting open like rotten fruit.

But of course *Theseus,* our redeemer, would save us from such a fate. We filed from the shuttle into a great balloon that Sarasti had erected to capture our personal effects; we shed our contaminated space suits and clothing and emerged naked into the spine. We passed single-file through the drum, the Flying Dead in formation. Jukka Sarasti—discreetly distant on the turning floor—leapt up in our wake and disappeared aft, to feed our radioactive cast-offs into the decompiler.

Into the crypt. Our coffins lay open across the rear bulkhead.

We sank gratefully and wordlessly into their embrace. Bates coughed blood as the lids came down.

My bones hummed as the Captain began to shut me off. I went to sleep a dead man. I had only theory and the assurances of fellow machinery that I would ever be born again.

Keeton, come forth.

I woke up ravenous. Faint voices drifted forward from the drum. I floated in my pod for a few moments, eyes closed, savoring absences: no pain, no nausea. No terrifying subliminal sense of one's own body sloughing incrementally to mush. Weakness, and hunger; otherwise I felt fine.

I opened my eyes.

Something like an arm. Gray and glistening, far too—too *attenuate* to be human. No hand at its tip. Too many joints, a limb broken in a dozen places. It extended from a body barely visible over the lip of the pod, a suggestion of dark bulk and other limbs in disjoint motion. It hovered motionless before me, as if startled in the midst of some shameful act.

By the time I had breath enough to cry out, it had whipped back out of sight.

I erupted from the pod, eyes everywhere. Now they saw nothing: an empty crypt, a naked note-taker. The mirrored bulkhead reflected vacant pods to either side. I called up ConSensus: all systems nominal.

It didn't reflect, I remembered. *The mirror didn't show it.*

I headed aft, heart still pounding. The drum opened around me, Szpindel and the Gang conversing in low tones below. Szpindel glanced up and waved a trembling hand in greeting.

"You need to check me out," I called. My voice wasn't nearly so steady as I'd hoped.

"Admitting you have a problem is the first step," Szpindel called back. "Just don't expect miracles." He turned back to the Gang; James on top, they sat in a diagnostic couch staring at some test pattern shimmering on the rear bulkhead.

I grabbed the tip of a stairway and pulled myself down. Coriolis pushed me sideways like a flag in the breeze. "I'm either hallucinating or there's something on board."

"You're hallucinating."

"I'm *serious*."

"So am I. Take a number. Wait your turn."

He *was* serious. Once I forced myself to calm down and read the signs, I could see he wasn't even surprised.

"Guess you're pretty hungry after all that exhausting lying around, eh?" Szpindel waved at the galley. "Eat something. Be with you in a few minutes."

I forced myself to work up my latest synopsis while I ate, but that only took half a mind; the other half still shivered in residual thrall to fight-flight. I tried to distract it by tapping the BioMed feed.

"It was *real*," James was saying. "We all saw it."

No. Couldn't have been.

Szpindel cleared his throat. "Try this one."

The feed showed what she saw: a small black triangle on a white background. In the next instant it shattered into a dozen identical copies, and a dozen dozen. The proliferating brood rotated around the center screen, geometric primitives ballroom-dancing in precise formation, each sprouting smaller triangles from its tips, fractalizing, rotating, *evolving* into an infinite, intricate tilework . . .

A sketch pad, I realized. An interactive eyewitness reconstruction, without the verbiage. Susan's own pattern-matching wetware reacted to what she saw—*no, there were more of them;*

no, the orientation's wrong; yes, that's it, but bigger—and Szpin-del's machine picked those reactions right out of her head and amended the display in real time. It was a big step up from that half-assed work-around called *language.* The easily impressed might have even called it mind reading.

It wasn't, though. It was all just feedback and correlation. It doesn't take a telepath to turn one set of patterns into another. Fortunately.

"That's it! That's *it!*" Susan cried.

The triangles had iterated out of existence. Now the display was full of interlocking asymmetrical pentagrams, a spiderweb of fish scales.

"Don't tell us that's *random noise,*" she said triumphantly.

"No," Szpindel said, "It's a Klüver constant."

"A—"

"It's a hallucination, Suze."

"Of *course.* But something *planted* it in our head, right? And—"

"It was in your head all along. It was in your head the day you were born."

"No."

"It's an artifact of deep brain structure. Even congenitally blind people see them sometimes."

"None of us have seen them before. *Ever.*"

"I believe you. But there's no *information* there, eh? That wasn't *Rorschach* talking, it was just . . . interference. Like everything else."

"But it was so vivid! Not that flickering corner-of-your-eye stuff we saw everywhere. This was *solid.* It was realer than real."

"That's how you can tell it wasn't. Since you don't actually *see* it, there's no messy eyeball optics to limit resolution."

"Oh," James said, and then, softly: "Shit."

"Yeah. Sorry." And then, "Any time you're ready."

I looked up; Szpindel was waving me over. James rose from her chair, but it was Michelle who gave him a quick disconsolate squeeze and Sascha who grumbled past me on her way to their tent.

By the time I reached him Szpindel had unfolded the couch into a half-cot. "Lie down."

I did. "I wasn't talking about back in *Rorschach,* you know. I meant *here.* I saw something right now. When I woke up."

"Raise your left hand," he said. Then: "*Just* your left, eh?"

I lowered my right, winced at the pinprick. "That's a bit primitive."

He eyed the blood-filled cuvette between his thumb and forefinger: a shivering ruby teardrop the size of a fingernail. "Wet sample's still best for some things."

"Aren't the pods supposed to do everything?"

Szpindel nodded. "Call it a quality-control test. Keep the ship on its toes." He dropped the sample onto the nearest countertop. The teardrop flattened and burst; the surface drank my blood as if parched. Szpindel smacked his lips. "Elevated cholinesterase inhibitors in the ret. Yum."

For all I knew, my blood results actually *did* taste good to the man. Szpindel didn't just read results; he *felt* them, smelled and saw and *experienced* each datum like drops of citrus on the tongue. The whole BioMed subdrum was but a part of the Szpindel prosthesis: an extended body with dozens of different sensory modes, forced to talk to a brain that knew only five.

No wonder he'd bonded with Michelle. He was almost synesthesiac himself.

"You spent a bit longer in there than the rest of us," he remarked.

"That's significant?"

A jerking shrug. "Maybe your organs got a bit more cooked

than ours. Maybe you just got a delicate constitution. Your pod would've caught anything . . . imminent, so I figure—ah."

"What?"

"Some cells along your brainpan going into overdrive. More in your bladder and kidney."

"Tumors?"

"What do you expect? *Rorschach*'s no rejuve spa."

"But the pod—"

Szpindel grimaced; his idea of a reassuring smile. "Repairs ninety-nine point nine percent of the damage, sure. By the time you get to the last zero-point-one, you're into diminishing returns. These're *small,* commissar. Chances are your own body'll take care of 'em. If not, we know where they live."

"The ones in my brain. Could they be causing—"

"Not a chance." He chewed on his lower lip for a moment. "'Course, cancer's not all that thing did to us."

"What I saw. Up in the crypt. It had these multijointed arms from a central mass. Big as a person, maybe."

Szpindel nodded. "Get used to it."

"The others are seeing these things?"

"I doubt it. Everyone has a different take, like"—his twitching face conveyed *dare I say it?*—"*Rorschach* blots."

"I was expecting hallucinations in the field," I admitted, "but up here?"

"TMS effects"—Szpindel snapped his fingers—"they're *sticky,* eh? Neurons get kicked into one state, take a while to come unstuck. You never got a TAT? Well-adjusted boy like you?"

"Once or twice," I said. "Maybe."

"Same principle."

"So I'm going to keep seeing this stuff."

"Party line is they fade over time. Week or two you're back to normal. But out here, with *that* thing . . ." He shrugged. "Too many variables. Not the least of which is, I assume we'll keep going *back* until Sarasti says otherwise."

"But they're basically magnetic effects."

"Probably. Although I'm not betting on anything where *that* fucker's concerned."

"Could something else be causing them?" I asked. "Something on *this* ship?"

"Like what?'

"I don't know. Leakage in *Theseus*'s magnetic shielding, maybe."

"Not normally. Course, we've all got little implanted networks in our heads, eh? And you've got a whole hemisphere of prosthetics up there, who knows what kind of *side effects* those might let you in for. Why? *Rorschach* not a good enough reason for you?"

I saw them before, I might have said.

And then Szpindel would say *Oh, when? Where?*

And maybe I'd reply *When I was spying on your private life,* and any chance of *noninvasive observation* would be flushed down to the atoms.

"It's probably nothing. I've just been—jumpy lately. Thought I saw something weird in the spinal bundle, back before we landed on *Rorschach*. Just for a second, you know, and it disappeared as soon as I focused on it."

"Multijointed arms with a central mass?"

"God no. Just a flicker, really. It was probably just Amanda's rubber ball floating around up there."

"Probably." Szpindel seemed almost amused. "Couldn't hurt to check for leakage in the shielding, though. Just in case. Not like we need something *else* making us see things, eh?"

I shook my head at remembered nightmares. "How are the others?"

"Gang's fine, if a bit disappointed. Haven't seen the Major." He shrugged. "Maybe she's avoiding me."

"It hit her pretty hard."

"No worse than the rest of us, really. She might not even remember it."

"How—how could she possibly believe she didn't even *exist*?"

Szpindel shook his head. "Didn't believe it. *Knew* it. For a fact."

"But how—"

"Charge gauge on your car, right? Sometimes the contacts corrode. Readout freezes on empty, so you think it's empty. What else you supposed to think? Not like you can go in and count the electrons."

"You're saying the brain's got some kind of *existence gauge*?"

"Brain's got all *kinds* of gauges. You can *know* you're blind even when you're not; you can *know* you can see, even when you're blind. And yeah, you can *know* you don't exist even when you do. It's a long list, commissar. Cotard's, Anton's, Damascus disease. Just for starters."

He hadn't said *blindsight*.

"What was it like?" I asked.

"Like?" Although he knew exactly what I meant.

"Did your arm . . . move by itself? When it reached for that battery?"

"Oh. Nah. You're still in control, you just—you get a feeling, is all. A *sense* of where to reach. One part of the brain playing charades with another, eh?" He gestured at the couch. "Get off. Seen enough of your ugly guts for now. And send up Bates if you can find where she's hiding. Probably back at Fab building a bigger army."

The misgivings glinted off him like sunlight. "You have a problem with her," I said.

He started to deny it, then remembered who he was talking to. "Not personally. Just—human node running mechanical infantry. Electronic reflexes slaved to meat reflexes. You tell me where the weak spot is."

"Down in *Rorschach*, I'd have to say *all* the links are pretty weak."

"Not talking about *Rorschach*," Szpindel said. "We go there. What stops them from coming here?"

"Them."

"Maybe they haven't arrived yet," he admitted. "But when they do, I'm betting we'll be going up against something bigger than anaerobic microbes." When I didn't answer he continued, his voice lowered. "And anyway, Mission Control didn't know shit about *Rorschach*. They thought they were sending us someplace where drones could do all the heavy lifting. But they just hate not being in command, eh? Can't admit the grunts're smarter than the generals. So our defenses get compromised for political appearances—not like *that's* any kinda news—and I'm no jarhead but it strikes me as real bad strategy."

I remembered Amanda Bates, midwifing the birth of her troops. *I'm more of a safety precaution....*

"Amanda—" I began.

"Like Mandy fine. Nice mammal. But if we're cruising into a combat situation I don't want my ass covered by some network held back by its weakest link."

"If you're going to be surrounded by a swarm of killer robots, maybe—"

"Yeah, people keep saying that. Can't trust the machines. Luddites love to go on about computer malfunctions, and how many accidental wars we might have prevented because a human had the final say. But funny thing, commissar; nobody talks about how many intentional wars got *started* for the same reason. You're still writing those postcards to posterity?"

I nodded, and didn't wince inwardly. It was just Szpindel.

"Well, feel free to stick this conversation in your next one. For all the good it'll do."

Imagine you are a prisoner of war.

You've got to admit you saw it coming. You've been crashing tech and seeding biosols for a solid eighteen months; that's a good run by anyone's standards. Realist saboteurs do not, as a rule, enjoy long careers. Everyone gets caught eventually.

It wasn't always thus. There was a day you might have even hoped for a peaceful retirement. But then they brought the vampires back from the Pleistocene and Great Grieving Ganga did *that* ever turn the balance of power upside down. Those fuckers are always ten steps ahead. It only makes sense; after all, hunting people is what bloodsuckers evolved to *do*.

There's this line from an early pop-dyn textbook, really old, maybe even TwenCen. It's something of a mantra—maybe *prayer* would be a better word—among those in your profession. *Predators run for their dinner,* it goes. *Prey run for their lives.* The moral is supposed to be that on average, the hunted escape the hunters because they're more motivated.

Maybe that was true when it all just came down to who ran faster. Doesn't seem to hold when the strategy involves tactical foresight and double-reverse mind fucks, though. The vampires win every time.

And now you're caught, and while it may have been vampires that set the trap, it was regular turncoat baseline humans who pulled the trigger. For six hours now you've been geckoed to the wall of some unnamed unlisted underground detention facility, watching as some of those selfsame *Humans* played games with your boyfriend and coconspirator. These are not your average games. They involve pliers, and glowing wires, and body parts that were not designed to detach. You wish, by now, that your lover were dead, like the two others in your cell whose parts are scattered about the room. But they're not letting that happen. They're having too much fun.

That's what it all comes down to. This is not an interrogation; there are less invasive ways to get more reliable answers. These are simply a few more sadistic thugs with Authority, killing time and other things, and you can only cry and squeeze your eyes tight and whimper like an animal even though they haven't laid a hand on you yet. You can only wish they hadn't saved you for last, because you know what that means.

But suddenly your tormentors stop in mid-game and cock their heads as if listening to some collective inner voice. Presumably it tells them to take you off the wall, bring you into the next room, and sit you down at one of two gel-padded chairs on opposite sides of a smart desk, because this is what they do—far more gently than you'd expect—before retiring. You can also assume that whoever has given these instructions is both powerful and displeased, because all the arrogant sadistic cockiness has drained from their faces in the space of a heartbeat.

You sit and wait. The table glows with soft, cryptic symbols that would be of no earthly interest to you even if you could understand them, even if they contained the very secret of the vampires themselves. Some small part of you wonders if this latest development might be cause for hope; the rest of you doesn't dare believe it. You hate yourself for caring about your own survival when chunks of your friends and allies are still warm on the other side of the wall.

A stocky Amerind woman appears in the room with you, clad in nondescript military weave. Her hair is buzzed short, her throat veined with the faint mesh of a sub-q antennae. Your brain stem sees that she is ten meters tall, even though some impertinent gelatinous overlay insists that she is of only average height.

The name tag on her left breast says BATES. You see no sign of rank.

Bates extracts a weapon from its sheath on her thigh. You flinch, but she does not point it at you. She sets it on the desk, easily within your reach, and sits across from you.

A microwave pistol. Fully charged, unlocked. On its lowest setting it causes sunburn and nausea. On its highest it flash-boils brains in the skull. At any setting between, it inflicts pain and injury in increments as fine as your imagination.

Your imagination has been retooled for great sensitivity along such scales. You stare numbly at the gun, trying to figure the trick.

"Two of your friends are dead," Bates says, as though you haven't just watched them die. "Irrecoverably so."

Irrecoverably dead. Good one.

"We could reconstitute the bodies, but the brain damage . . ." Bates clears her throat as if uncomfortable, as if embarrassed. It's a surprisingly human gesture for a monster. "We're trying to save the other one. No promises.

"We need information," she says, cutting to the chase.

Of course. What came before was psychology, softening-up. Bates is the good cop.

"I've got nothing to tell you," you manage. It's 10 percent defiance, 90 percent deduction: They wouldn't have been able to catch you in the first place unless they already knew everything.

"Then we need an arrangement," Bates says. "We need to come to some kind of accommodation."

She has to be kidding.

Your incredulity must be showing. Bates addresses it: "I'm not completely unsympathetic. My gut doesn't much like the idea of swapping reality for simulation, and it doesn't buy that what-is-truth spin the Body Economic sells to get around it. Maybe there's reason to be scared. Not my problem, not my job, just my opinion and it could be wrong. But if we kill each other in the meantime, we don't find out either way. It's unproductive."

You see the dismembered bodies of your friends. You see pieces on the floor, still a little bit alive, and this cunt has the nerve to talk about *productivity*?

"We didn't start it," you say.

"I don't know and I don't care. Like I said, it's not my job." Bates jerks a thumb over her shoulder at a door in the wall behind her, the door she must have entered through. "In there," she says, "are the ones who killed your friends. They've been disarmed. When you go through that door the room will go offline and remain unmonitored for a period of sixty seconds. Nobody besides yourself will ever hold you accountable for whatever happens in there during that time."

It's a trick. It has to be.

"What do you have to lose?" Bates wonders. "We can already do anything we want to you. It's not like we need you to give us an excuse."

Hesitantly, you take the gun. Bates doesn't stop you.

She's right, you realize. You have absolutely nothing to lose. You stand and, suddenly fearless, point the weapon at her face. "Why go in there? I can kill you right *here*."

She shrugs. "You could try. Waste of an opportunity, if you ask me."

"So I go in there, and I come out in sixty seconds, and then what?"

"Then we talk."

"We just—"

"Think of it as a gesture of good faith," she says. "Restitution, even."

The door opens at your approach, closes in your wake. And there they are, all four of them, spread up across the wall like a chorus line of Christs on crosses. There's no gleam in those eyes *now*. There's only a bright animal terror and the reflection of turned tables. Two of the Christs stain their pants when you look them in the eye.

What's left? Maybe fifty seconds?

It's not a lot. You could have done so much more with just a little extra time. But it's enough, and you don't want to impose on the good graces of this Bates woman.

Because she may at last be someone you can deal with.

Under other circumstances, Lieutenant Amanda Bates would have been court-martialed and executed within the month. No matter that the four who'd died had been guilty of multiple counts of rape, torture, and homicide; that's just what people *did* in wartime. It's what they'd always done. There was nothing *polite* about war, no honorable code beyond the chain of command and the circling of wagons. Deal with indiscretions if you must; punish the guilty if you have to, for appearance if nothing else. But for God's sake close the doors first. Never give your enemy the satisfaction of seeing discord in the ranks, show them nothing but unity and flinty-eyed resolve. There may be murderers and rapists in our midst, but by God they're *our* murderers and rapists.

You certainly don't give right of revenge to some terrorist twat with over a hundred friendly scalps on her belt.

Still, it was hard to argue with results: a negotiated cease-fire with the third-largest Realist franchise in the hemisphere. An immediate 46 percent decline in terrorist activities throughout the affected territories. The unconditional cancelation of several in-progress campaigns that could have seriously compromised three major catacombs and taken out the Duluth staging grounds entirely. All because Lieutenant Amanda Bates, feeling her way through her first field command, had gambled on *empathy* as a military strategy.

It was collaborating with the enemy, it was treason, it was betrayal of the rank and file. Diplomats and politicians were supposed to do those things, not soldiers.

Still. Results.

It was all there in the record: initiative, creativity, a willingness to succeed by whatever means necessary and at whatever cost. Perhaps those inclinations needed to be punished, perhaps only tempered. The debate might have gone on forever if the story hadn't leaked—but it had, and suddenly the generals had a hero on their hands.

Sometime during her court-martial, Bates's death sentence turned into a rehabilitation; the only question was whether it would take place in the stockade or Officer's College. As it turned out, Leavenworth had both; it took her to its bosom and squeezed hard enough to virtually guarantee promotion, if it didn't kill her first. Three years later Major Bates was bound for the stars, where she was heard to say:

We're breaking and entering, Siri . . .

Szpindel was not the first to register doubts. Others had wondered whether her assignment owed as much to superior qualifications as it did to the resolution of inconvenient PR. I, of course, had no opinion one way or the other; but I could see how she might strike some as a double-edged sword.

When the fate of the world hangs in the balance, you want to keep an eye on anyone whose career-defining moment involves consorting with the enemy.

IF YOU CAN SEE IT, CHANCES ARE IT DOESN'T EXIST.
—KATE KEOGH, *GROUNDS FOR SUICIDE*

FIVE TIMES WE did it. Over five consecutive orbits we threw ourselves between the monster's jaws, let it chew at us with a trillion microscopic teeth until *Theseus* reeled us in and stitched us back together. We crept through *Rorschach*'s belly in fits and starts, focusing as best we could on the tasks at hand, trying to ignore the ghosts that tickled our midbrains. Sometimes the walls flexed subtly around us. Sometimes we only thought they did. Sometimes we took refuge in our diving bell while waves of charge and magnetism spiraled languidly past, like boluses of ectoplasm coursing down the intestine of some poltergeist god.

Sometimes we got caught in the open. The Gang would squabble among itself, uncertain which persona was which. Once I fell into a kind of waking paralysis while alien hands dragged me away down the hall; fortunately other hands brought me home, and voices that claimed to be real told me I'd made the whole thing up. Twice Amanda Bates found God, *saw* the fucker right there in front of her, knew beyond any shadow of a doubt that the creator not only existed but *spoke* to her, and her alone. Both times she lost her faith once we got her into the bell, but it was touch and go for a while; her warrior drones, drunk on power but still under line-of-sight control, staggered from their perimeters and pointed their weapons along bearings too close for comfort.

The grunts died fast. Some barely lasted a single foray; a few died in minutes. The longest-lived were the slowest on the draw, half-blind, thick-witted, every command and response bottle-necked by raw high-frequency sound buzzing across their shielded eardrums. Sometimes we backed them up with others that spoke optically: faster but nervous, and even more vulnerable. Together they guarded against an opposition that had not yet shown its face.

It hardly had to. Our troops fell even in the absence of enemy fire.

We worked through it all, through fits and hallucinations and occasional convulsions. We tried to watch each other's backs while magnetic tendrils tugged our inner ears and made us seasick. Sometimes we vomited into our helmets; then we'd just hang on, white-faced, sucking sour air through clenched teeth while the recyclers filtered chunks and blobs from our headspace. And we'd give silent thanks for the small mercy of nonstick, static-repellent faceplates.

It rapidly became obvious that my presence served as more than cannon fodder. It didn't matter that I lacked the Gang's linguistic skills or Szpindel's expertise in biology; I was another set of hands, in a place where anyone could be laid out at a moment's notice. The more people Sarasti kept in the field, the greater the odds that at least one of them would be halfway functional at any given moment. Even so, we were in barely any condition to accomplish anything. Every incursion was an exercise in reckless endangerment.

We did it anyway. It was that or go home.

The work proceeded in infinitesimal increments, hamstrung on every front. The Gang wasn't finding any evidence of signage or speech to decipher, but the gross mechanics of this thing were easy enough to observe. Sometimes *Rorschach* partitioned itself, extruded ridges around its passageways like the cartilaginous hoops encircling a human trachea. Over hours some of them might develop into contracting irises, into complete septa, lazy as warm candle wax. We seemed to be witnessing the growth of the structure in discrete segments. *Rorschach* grew mainly from the tips of its thorns; we'd made our incursion hundreds of meters from the nearest, but evidently the process extended at least this far back.

If it *was* part of the normal growth process, though, it was a feeble echo of what must have been going on in the heart of the apical zones. We couldn't observe those directly, not from inside; barely a hundred meters toward the thorn the tube grew too lethal even for suicidal flesh. But over those five orbits *Rorschach* grew by another 8 percent, as mindless and mechanical as a growing crystal.

Through it all I tried to do my job. I compiled and collated, massaged data I would never understand. I watched the systems around me as best I could, factored each tic and trait into the mix. One part of my mind produced synopses and syntheses while another watched, incredulous and uncomprehending. Neither part could trace where those insights had come from.

It was difficult, though. Sarasti wouldn't let me back outside the system. Every observation was contaminated by my own confounding presence in the mix. I did my best. I made no suggestions that might affect critical decisions. In the field I did what I was told to, and no more. I tried to be like one of Bates's drones, a simple tool with no initiative and no influence on the group dynamic. I think I pulled it off, for the most part.

My nonsights accumulated on schedule and piled up in *Theseus*'s transmission stack, unsent. There was too much local interference to get a signal through to Earth.

· · ·

Szpindel was right: The ghosts followed us back. We began to hear voices other than Sarasti's, whispering up the spine. Sometimes even the brightly-lit wraparound world of the drum would warp and jiggle from the corner of my eye—and more than once I saw boney headless phantoms with too many arms, nested in the scaffolding. They seemed solid enough from the corner of my eye but any spot I focused on faded to shadow, to a dark translucent stain against the background. They were so very fragile, these ghosts. The mere act of observation drilled holes through them.

Szpindel had rattled off dementias like raindrops. I went to ConSensus for enlightenment and found a whole other self buried below the limbic system, below the hindbrain, below even the cerebellum. It lived in the brain stem and it was older than the vertebrates themselves. It was self-contained: it heard and saw and felt, independent of all those other parts layered over top like evolutionary afterthoughts. It dwelt on nothing but its own survival. It had no time for planning or abstract analysis, spared effort for only the most rudimentary sensory processing. But it was *fast,* and it was dedicated, and it could react to threats in a fraction of the time it took its smarter roommates to even become *aware* of them.

And even when it couldn't—when the obstinate, unyielding neocortex refused to let it off the leash—still it tried to pass on what it saw, and Isaac Szpindel experienced an ineffable sense of *where to reach.* In a way, he had a stripped-down version of the Gang in his head. Everyone did.

I looked further and found God Itself in the meat of the brain, found the static that had sent Bates into rapture and Michelle into convulsions. I tracked Grey syndrome to its headwaters in the temporal lobe. I heard voices ranting in the brains of schizophrenics. I found cortical infarcts that inspired people to reject their own limbs, imagined the magnetic fields that must have acted in their stead when Cruncher tried to dismember himself. And off in some half-forgotten pesthole of twentieth-century case studies—filed under *Cotard's syndrome*—I found Amanda Bates and others of her kind, their brains torqued into denial of the very self. "I used to have a heart," one of them said listlessly from the archives. "Now I have something that beats in its place." Another demanded to be buried, because his corpse was already stinking.

There was more, a whole catalog of finely-tuned dysfunctions that *Rorschach* had not yet inflicted on us. Somnambulism. Agnosias. Hemineglect. ConSensus served up a freak show to make any mind reel at its own fragility: a woman dying of thirst within easy reach of water, not because she couldn't see the faucet but because she couldn't *recognize* it. A man for whom the left side of the universe did not exist, who could neither perceive nor *conceive* of the left side of his body, of a room, of a line of text. A man for whom the very concept of *leftness* had become literally unthinkable.

Sometimes we could conceive of things and still not see them, although they stood right before us. Skyscrapers appeared out of thin air, the person talking to us changed into someone else during a momentary distraction—and we didn't notice. It wasn't magic. It was barely even misdirection. They called it *inattentional blindness,* and it had been well-known for a century or more: a tendency for the eye to simply *not notice* things that evolutionary experience classed as *unlikely*.

I found the opposite of Szpindel's *blindsight,* a malady not in which the sighted believe they are blind but one in which *the blind insist they can see*. The very idea was absurd unto insanity and yet there they were, retinas detached, optic nerves burned away, any possibility of vision denied by the laws of physics:

bumping into walls, tripping over furniture, inventing endless ludicrous explanations for their clumsiness. The lights, unexpectedly turned off by some other party. A colorful bird glimpsed through the window, distracting attention from the obstacle ahead. I can see perfectly well, thank you. Nothing wrong with *my* eyes.

Gauges in the head, Szpindel had called them. But there were other things in there, too. There was a model of the world, and we didn't look *outward* at all; our conscious selves saw only the simulation in our heads, an *interpretation* of reality, endlessly refreshed by input from the senses. What happens when those senses go dark, but the model—thrown off-kilter by some trauma or tumor—*fails to refresh*? How long do we stare in at that obsolete rendering, recycling and massaging the same old data in a desperate, subconscious act of utterly honest denial? How long before it dawns on us that the world we see no longer reflects the world we inhabit, that we are *blind*?

Months sometimes, according to the case files. For one poor woman, a year and more.

Appeals to logic fail utterly. How could you see the bird when there *is* no window? How do you decide where your seen half-world ends if you can't see the other half to weigh it against? If you are dead, how can you smell your own corruption? If you do not exist, Amanda, *what is talking to us now?*

Useless. When you're in the grip of Cotard's syndrome or hemineglect you cannot be swayed by argument. When you're in thrall to some alien artifact you *know* that the self is gone, that reality ends at the midline. You know it with the same unshakeable certainty of any man regarding the location of his own limbs, with that hardwired awareness that needs no other confirmation. Against that conviction, what is reason? What is logic?

Inside *Rorschach,* they had no place at all.

• • •

On the sixth orbit it acted.

"It's talking to us," James said. Her eyes were wide behind the faceplate, but not bright, not manic. Around us *Rorschach*'s guts oozed and crawled at the corner of my eye; it still took effort to ignore the illusion. Foreign words scrabbled like small animals below my brainstem as I tried to focus on a ring of finger-sized protrusions that picketed a patch of wall.

"It's not talking," Szpindel said from across the artery. "You're hallucinating again."

Bates said nothing. Two grunts hovered in the middle of the space, panning across three axes.

"It's different this time," James insisted. "The geometry—it's not so symmetrical. Looks almost like the Phaistos Disk." She spun slowly, pointed down the passage. "I think it's stronger down here . . ."

"Bring Michelle out," Szpindel suggested. "Maybe she can talk some sense into you."

James laughed weakly. "Never say die, do you?" She tweaked her pistol and coasted into deeper gloom. "Yes, it's definitely stronger here. There's *content,* superimposed on—"

Quick as a blink, *Rorschach* cut her off.

I'd never seen anything move so fast before. There was none of the languor we'd grown accustomed to from *Rorschach*'s septa, no lazy drift to contraction; the iris snapped shut in an instant. Suddenly the artery just *ended* three meters ahead, with a matte-black membrane filigreed in fine spiral.

And the Gang of Four was on the other side.

The grunts were on it immediately, lasers crackling through the air. Bates was yelling *Get behind me! Stick to the walls!,* kicking herself into space like an acrobat in fast-forward, taking some tactical high ground that must have been obvious to her, at least. I edged toward the perimeter. Threads of superheated plasma sliced the air, shimmering. Szpindel, at the corner of my eye, hugged the opposite side of the tunnel. The walls crawled. I could see the lasers taking a toll; the septum peeled back from their touch like burning paper, black oily smoke writhing from its crisping edges and—

—sudden brightness, everywhere. A riot of fractured light flooded the artery, a thousand shifting angles of incidence and reflection. It was like being trapped in the belly of a kaleidoscope, pointed at the sun. Light—

—and needle-sharp pain in my side, in my left arm. The smell of charred meat. A scream, cut off.

Susan? You there, Susan?

We're taking you first.

Around me, the light died; inside me, a swarm of floaters mixed it up with the chronic half-visions *Rorschach* had already planted in my head. Alarms chirped irritatingly in my helmet—*breach, breach, breach*—until the smart fabric of the suit softened and congealed where the holes had been. Something stung maddeningly in my left side. I felt as if I'd been branded.

"Keeton! Check Szpindel!" Bates had called off the lasers. The grunts closed for hand-to-hand, reaching with fiery nozzles and diamond-tipped claws to grapple with some prismatic material glowing softly *behind* that burnt-back skin.

Fibrous reflector, I realized. It had shattered the laser light, turned it to luminous shrapnel and thrown it back in our faces. Clever.

But its surface was still alight, even with the lasers down; a diffuse glow, dipping and weaving, filtered through from the far side of the barrier while the drones chewed doggedly through the near one. After a moment it struck me: James's headlamp.

"Keeton!"

Right. Szpindel.

His faceplate was intact. The laser had melted the faraday mesh laminated onto the crystal, but the suit was sealing that tiny hole even now. The hole behind, drilled neatly through his forehead, remained. The eyes beneath stared at infinity.

"Well?" Bates asked. She could read his vitals as easily as I, but *Theseus* was capable of postmortem rebuilds.

Barring brain damage. "No."

The whine of drills and shredders stopped; the ambience brightened. I looked away from Szpindel's remains. The grunts had cut a hole in the septum's fibrous underlayer. One of them nosed its way through to the other side.

A new sound rose into the mix, a soft animal keening, haunted and dissonant. For a moment I thought *Rorschach* was whispering to us again; its walls seemed to contract slightly around me.

"James?" Bates snapped. *"James!"*

Not James. A little girl in a woman's body in an armored space-suit, scared out of her wits.

The grunt nudged her curled-up body back into our company. Bates took it gently. "Susan? Come back, Suze. You're safe."

The grunts hovered restlessly, alert in every direction, pretending everything was under control. Bates spared me a glance—"Take Isaac"—and turned back to James. "Susan?"

"N—n-no," whimpered a small voice, a little girl's voice.

"Michelle? Is that you?"

"There was a *thing,*" the little girl said. "It *grabbed* me. It grabbed my *leg.*"

"We're out of here." Bates pulled the Gang back along the

passage. One grunt lingered, watching the hole; the other took point.

"It's gone," Bates said gently. "There's nothing there now. See the feed?"

"You can't *s*-see it." Michelle whispered. "It's in—it's in—*visible*."

The septum receded around a curve as we retreated. The hole torn through its center watched us like the ragged pupil of some great unblinking eye. It stayed empty as long as it stayed in sight. Nothing came out after us. Nothing we could see. A thought began cycling through my head, some half-assed eulogy stolen from an eavesdropped confessional, and try as I might I couldn't shut it down.

Isaac Szpindel hadn't made the semifinals after all.

Susan James came back to us on the way up. Isaac Szpindel did not.

We stripped wordlessly in the decon balloon. Bates, first out of her suit, reached for Szpindel but the Gang stopped her with a hand and a head shake. Personae segued one into another as they stripped the body. Susan removed helmet and backpack and breastplate. Cruncher peeled away the silvery leaded skin from collar to toe. Sascha stripped the jumpsuit and left the pale flesh naked and exposed. Except for the gloves. They left his feedback gloves in place; their fingertips forever tactile, the flesh inside forever numb. Through it all, Szpindel stared unblinking beneath the hole in his forehead. His glazed eyes focused on distant quasars.

I expected Michelle to appear in her turn and close them, but she never did.

I DON'T KNOW how to feel about this, I thought. *He was a good man. He was decent, he was kind to me, even when he didn't know I was listening in. I didn't know him long—he wasn't a friend exactly—but still. I should miss him. I should mourn.*

I should feel more than this sick sinking fear that I could be next. . . .

Sarasti hadn't wasted any time. Szpindel's replacement met us as we emerged, freshly thawed, nicotine-scented. The rehydration of his flesh was ongoing—saline bladders clung to each thigh—although it would never entirely erase the sharpness of his features. His bones cracked when he moved.

He looked past me and took the body. "Susan—Michelle . . . I—"

The Gang turned away.

He coughed, began fumbling a body condom over the corpse. "Sarasti wants everyone in the drum."

"We're hot," Bates said. Even cut short, the excursion had piled up a lethal sievert count. Faint nausea tickled the back of my throat.

"Decontaminate later." One long pull of a zipper and Szpindel was gone, engulfed in an oily gray shroud. "You"—he turned in my direction, pointed at the scorched holes in my jumpsuit—"with me."

Robert Cunningham. Another prototype. Dark-haired, hollow-cheeked, a jaw you could use as a ruler. Both smoother and harsher than the man he had replaced. Where Szpindel had ticced and jerked as if static-charged, Cunningham's face held all the expression of a wax dummy's. The wetware that ran those muscles had been press-ganged into other pursuits. Even the tremors that afflicted the rest of his body were muted, soothed by the nicotine he drew with every second breath.

He held no cigarette now. He held only the shrouded body of his hard-luck primary and his ongoing, freshly thawed distaste for the ship's Synthesist. His fingers trembled.

Bates and the Gang moved silently up the spine. Cunningham and I followed, guiding the Shroud of Szpindel between us. My leg and side were stinging again, now that Cunningham had reminded them to. There wouldn't be much he could do about them, though. The beams would have cauterized the flesh on their way through, and if they'd hit anything vital I'd have been dead already.

At the hatch we broke into single-file: Szpindel first, Cunningham pushing at his heels. By the time I emerged into the drum Bates and the Gang were already down on deck and taking their usual seats. Sarasti, in the flesh, watched them from the end of the conference table.

His eyes were naked. From this angle the soft, full-spectrum light of the drum washed the shine from them. If you didn't look too closely, for too long, you might almost think those eyes were Human.

BioMed had been spun down for my arrival. Cunningham pointed to a diagnostic couch on a section of the stilled deck that served as our infirmary; I floated over and strapped myself in. Two meters away, past a waist-high guardrail that had risen from the deck, the rest of the drum rolled smoothly past. It slung Bates and the Gang and Sarasti around like weights on a string.

I tapped ConSensus to hear them. James was speaking, quietly and without expression. "I noticed a new pattern in the form-constants. Something in the grating. It looked like a signal. It got stronger as I went down the tunnel, I followed it, I blacked out. I don't remember anything more until we were on our way back. Michelle filled me in, as much as she could. That's all I know. I'm sorry."

A hundred degrees away in the no-g zone, Cunningham maneuvered his predecessor into a coffin with different options than those up front. I wondered if it would embark on an autopsy during the debriefing. I wondered if we'd be able to hear the sounds it made.

"Sascha," Sarasti said.

"Yeah." Sascha's trademark drawl infected the voice. "I was riding Mom. Went deaf dumb and stark fucking blind when she passed out. I tried to take over but something was blocking me. Michelle, I guess. Never thought she had it in her. I couldn't even *see*."

"But you don't lose consciousness."

"I was awake the whole time, far as I know. Just completely in the dark."

"Smell? Tactile?"

"I could feel it when Michelle pissed in the suit. But I didn't notice anything else."

Cunningham was back at my side. The inevitable cigarette had appeared between his lips.

"Nothing touches you," the vampire surmised. "Nothing grabs your leg."

"No," Sascha said. She didn't believe Michelle's stories about invisible monsters. None of us did; why bother, when dementia could so easily explain anything we experienced?

"Cruncher."

"Don't know anything." I still wasn't used to the maleness of the voice now emanating from James's throat. Cruncher was a workaholic. He hardly ever surfaced in mixed company.

"You're there," Sarasti reminded him. "You must remember some—"

"Mom sent me patterns to parse. I was working on them. I'm *still* working on them," he added pointedly. "I didn't notice anything. Is that all?"

I'd never been able to get a good read on him. Sometimes Cruncher seemed to have more in common with the dozens of nonconscious modules working in James's head than with sentient hubs comprising the rest of the Gang. "You feel nothing?" Sarasti pressed.

"Just the patterns."

"Anything significant?"

"Standard phenomath spirals and gratings. But I haven't finished. Can I go now?"

"Yes. Call Michelle, please."

Cunningham stabbed at my wounds with anabolizers, muttering to himself. Faint blue smoke curled between us. "Isaac found some tumors," he observed.

I nodded and coughed. My throat was sore. The nausea had grown heavy enough to sink below my diaphragm.

"Michelle," Sarasti repeated.

"I see some more here," Cunningham continued. "Along the bottom of your brainpan. Only a few dozen cells so far, they're not worth burning yet."

"Here." Michelle's voice was barely audible, even through ConSensus, but at least it was the voice of an adult. "I'm here."

"What do you remember, please?"

"I—I felt—I was just riding Mom, and then she was gone and there was no one else, so I had to—take over . . ."

"Do you see the septum close?"

"Not really. I felt it going dark, but when I turned around we were already trapped. And then I felt something behind me, it wasn't loud or harsh it just sort of *bumped,* and it grabbed me, and—and . . .

"I'm sorry," she said after a moment. "I'm a bit—woozy . . ."
Sarasti waited.

"Isaac," Michelle whispered. "He . . ."

"Yes." A pause. "We're very sorry about that."

"Maybe . . . can he be fixed?"

"No. There's brain damage." There was something like sympathy in the vampire's voice, the practiced affectation of an accomplished mimic. There was something else, too, an all-but-imperceptible hunger, a subtle edge of *temptation.* I don't think anyone heard it but me.

We were sick, and getting sicker. Predators are drawn to the weak and injured.

Michelle had fallen silent again. When she continued, her voice only faltered a little: "I can't tell you much. It grabbed me. It let me go. I went to pieces, and I can't explain why except that fucking place just *does* things to you, and I was—weak. I'm sorry. There's not much else to tell you."

"Thank you," Sarasti said after a long moment.

"Can I— I'd like to leave if that's okay."

"Yes," Sarasti said. Michelle sank below the surface as the Commons rotated past. I didn't see who took her place.

"The grunts didn't see anything," Bates remarked. "By the time we broke through the septum the tunnel behind was empty."

"Any bogey would have had plenty of time to hightail," Cunningham said. He planted his feet on the deck and grabbed a handhold; the subdrum began to move. I drifted obliquely against my restraints.

"I don't disagree," Bates said. "But if there's anything we've learned about that place, it's that we can't trust our senses."

"Trust Michelle's," Sarasti said. He opened a window as I grew heavier: a grunt's-eye view of a fuzzy, bright blob weaving behind the translucent waxed-paper fibers of the skinned septum. James's headlight, from the wrong side of the barrier. The image wobbled a bit as the drone staggered through some local pocket of magnetism, then replayed. Wobbled, replayed. A six-second loop.

"See something next to the Gang."

Non-vampires saw no such thing. Sarasti froze the image, evidently realizing as much. "Diffraction patterns aren't consistent with a single light source in open space. I see dimmer elements, reflective elements. Two dark objects close together, similar size, scattering light here"—a cursor appeared at two utterly nondescript points on the image—"and here. One's the Gang. The other's unaccounted for."

"Just a minute," Cunningham said. "If *you* can see it through all that, why didn't Su—why didn't *Michelle* see anything?"

"Synesthesiac," Sarasti reminded him. "You see. She *feels*."

BioMed jerked slightly, locking into spin-sync with the drum; the guardrail sank back into the deck. In some far-off corner, something without eyes watched me watching it.

"Shit," Bates whispered. "There's someone home."

They never really talked like that, by the way. You'd hear gibberish—a half-dozen languages, a whole Babel of personal idioms—if I spoke in their real voices.

Some of the simpler tics make it through: Sascha's good-natured belligerence, Sarasti's aversion to the past tense. Cunningham lost most of his gender pronouns to an unforeseen glitch during the work on his temporal lobe. But it went beyond that. The whole lot of them threw English and Hindi and Hadzane into every second sentence; no real scientist would allow their thoughts to be hamstrung by the conceptual limitations of a single language. Other times they acted almost as Synthesists in their own right, conversing in grunts and gestures that would be meaningless to any baseline. It's not so much that the bleeding edge lacks social skills; it's just that once you get past a certain point, formal speech is too damn *slow*.

Except for Susan James. The walking contradiction, the woman so devoted to Communication As Unifier that she'd cut her own brain into disunified chunks to make the point. She was the only one who ever seemed to care who she was talking to. The others spoke only for themselves, even when they spoke to each other. Even James's other cores would speak their own minds in their own way, and let everyone else translate as best they could. It wasn't a problem. Everyone on *Theseus* could read everyone else.

But that didn't matter to Susan James. She fit each of her words to their intended recipient, she *accommodated*.

I am a conduit. I exist to bridge the gap, and I'd bridge nothing if I only told you what these people said. So I am telling you what they *meant,* and it will mean as much to you as you can handle.

Except for Susan James, linguist and ringleader, whom I trust to speak for herself.

Fifteen minutes to apogee: maximum safe distance, in case *Rorschach* decided to hit back. Far below, the artifact's magnetic field pressed into Ben's atmosphere like God's little finger. Great dark thunderheads converged behind it; turbulent moon-size curlicues collided in its wake.

Fifteen minutes to apogee, and Bates was still hoping Sarasti would change his mind.

In a way, this was her fault. If she had just treated this new travail as one more cross to bear, perhaps things would have gone on more or less as before. There would have been some faint hope that Sarasti would have let us grit our teeth and keep on going, besieged now by spring-loaded trapdoors as well as the usual gauntlet of sieverts and magnets and monsters from the id. But Bates had made an *issue* out of it. It wasn't just another piece of shit in the sewer to her: It was the one that clogged the pipe.

We're on the brink as it is, just surviving the baseline environment of this thing. If it's started taking deliberate countermeasures . . . I don't see how we can risk it.

Fourteen minutes to apogee, and Amanda Bates was still regretting those words.

On previous expeditions we'd charted twenty-six septa in various stages of development. We'd X-rayed them. We'd done ultrasound. We'd watched them ooze their way across passages or ebb slowly back into the walls. The iris that had snapped shut behind the Gang of Four had been a whole different animal.

And what are the odds that the first one with a hair-trigger just happened to also come with antilaser prismatics? That was no routine growth event. That thing was set *for us.*

Set by . . .

That was the other thing. Thirteen minutes to apogee, and Bates was worried about the tenants.

It had always been breaking and entering, of course. That much hadn't changed. But when we'd jimmied the lock we'd thought we were vandalizing an empty summer cottage, still under construction. We'd thought the owners would be out of the picture for a while. We hadn't been expecting one of them to catch us on his way to take a late-night piss. And now that one had, and vanished into the labyrinth, it was natural to wonder what weapons it might keep stashed under the pillow. . . .

Those septa could spring on us any time. How many are there? Are they fixed, or portable? We can't proceed without knowing these things.

At first, Bates had been surprised and delighted when Sarasti agreed with her.

Twelve minutes to apogee. From this high ground, well above the static, *Theseus* peered down through *Rorschach*'s wrenched and twisted anatomy to keep rock-steady eyes on the tiny wound we'd burned in its side. Our limpet tent covered it like a blister; inside, Jack fed us a second, first-person view of the unfolding experiment.

Sir. We know Rorschach *is inhabited. Do we want to risk further provoking the inhabitants? Do we want to risk killing them?*

Sarasti hadn't quite looked at her, and hadn't quite spoken. If he had, he might have said *I do not understand how meat like you survived to adulthood.*

Eleven minutes to apogee, and Amanda Bates was lamenting the fact—not for the first time—that this mission was not under military jurisdiction.

We were waiting for maximum distance before performing the experiment. Rorschach *might interpret this as a hostile act,* Sarasti had conceded in a voice that contained no trace of irony whatsoever. Now he stood before us, watching ConSensus play on the table. Reflections writhed across his naked eyes, not quite masking the deeper reflections behind them.

Ten minutes to apogee. Susan James was wishing that Cunningham would put out that goddamned cigarrette. The smoke stank on its way to the ventilators, and anyway, it wasn't *necessary*. It was just an anachronistic affectation, an attention-getting device; if he needed the nicotine a patch could have soothed his tremors just as easily, without the smoke and the stink.

That wasn't all she was thinking, though. She was wondering why Cunningham had been summoned to Sarasti's quarters earlier in the shift, why he'd looked at her so strangely afterward. I wondered about that myself. A quick check on ConSensus time stamps showed that her medical file had been accessed during that period. I checked those stats, let the shapes bounce between hemispheres: part of my brain locked on *elevated oxytocin* as the probable reason for that conference. There was an 82 percent chance that James had become too *trusting* for Sarasti's liking.

I had no idea how I knew that. I never did.

Nine minutes to apogee.

Barely a molecule of *Rorschach*'s atmosphere had been lost on our account. That was all about to change. Our view of base camp split like a dividing bacterium: one window now focused on the limpet tent, the other on a wide-angle tactical enhance of the space around it.

Eight minutes to apogee. Sarasti pulled the plug.

Down on *Rorschach,* our tent burst like a bug beneath a boot. A geyser erupted from the wound; a snowstorm swirled at its edges, its charged curlicues intricate as lace. Atmosphere gushed into vacuum, spread thin, crystallized. Briefly, the space around base camp *sparkled*. It was almost beautiful.

Bates didn't think it was beautiful at all. She watched that bleeding wound with a face as expressionless as Cunningham's, but her jaw was clenched unto tetanus. Her eyes darted between views: watching for things gasping in the shadows.

Rorschach convulsed.

Vast trunks and arteries shuddered, a seismic tremor radiating out along the structure. The epicenter began to *twist*, a vast segment rotating on its axis, the breach midway along its length. Stress lines appeared where the length that rotated sheared against the lengths to either side that didn't; the structure seemed to soften and stretch there, constricting like a great elongate balloon torqueing itself into sausage links.

Sarasti clicked. Cats made something like that sound when they spied a bird on the far side of a windowpane.

ConSensus groaned with the sound of worlds scraping against each other: telemetry from the onsite sensors, their ears to the ground. Jack's camera controls had frozen again. The image it sent was canted and grainy. The pickup stared blankly at the edge of the hole we'd bored into the underworld.

The groaning subsided. A final faint cloud of crystalline stardust dissipated into space, barely visible even on max enhance.

No bodies. None visible, anyway.

Sudden motion at base camp. At first I thought it was static on Jack's feed, playing along lines of high contrast—but no, something was definitely moving along the edges of the hole we'd burned. Something almost *wriggled* there, a thousand gray mycelia extruding from the cut surface and writhing slowly into the darkness. "It's—huh," Bates said. "Triggered by the pressure drop, I guess. That's one way to seal a breach."

Two weeks after we'd wounded it, *Rorschach* had begun to heal itself.

Apogee behind us now. All downhill from here. *Theseus* began the long drop back into enemy territory.

"Doesn't use septa," Sarasti said.

MY GENES DONE GONE AND TRICKED MY BRAIN
BY MAKING FUCKING FEEL SO GREAT
THAT'S HOW THE LITTLE CREEPS ATTAIN
THEIR PLAN TO FUCKIN' REPLICATE
BUT BRAIN'S GOT TRICKS ITSELF, YOU SEE
TO GET THE BANG BUT NOT THE BITE
I GOT THIS HERE VASECTOMY
MY GENES CAN FUCK *THEMSELVES* TONIGHT.
—THE R-SELECTORS, TRUNCLADE

FIRST-PERSON SEX—*real* sex, as Chelsea insisted on calling it—was an acquired taste: jagged breathing, the raw slap and stink of sweaty skin full of pores and blemishes, a whole other person with a whole other set of demands and dislikes. There was definite animal appeal, no doubt about it. This was, after all, how we'd done it for millions of years. But this, this third-world carnality had always carried an element of struggle, of asynchronous patterns in conflict. There was no convergence here. There was only the rhythm of bodies in collision, a struggle for dominance, each trying to force the other into sync.

Chelsea regarded it as love in its purest form. I came to think of it as hand-to-hand combat. Before, whether fucking creations from my own menu or slip-on skins from someone else's, *I* had always selected the contrast and the rez, the texture and the attitude. The bodily functions, the resistance of competing desires, the endless foreplay that wears your tongue to the root and leaves your face sticky and glistening—just kinks, today. Options for the masochistic.

But there were no options with Chelsea. With her, everything came standard.

I indulged her. I guess I was no more patient with her

perversions than she was with my ineptitude at them. Other things made it worth the effort. Chelsea would argue about anything under the sun, wry and insightful and curious as a cat. She would pounce without warning. Retired to the redundant majority, she still took such simple joy in the very act of being *alive*. She was impulsive and impetuous. She cared about people. Pag. *Me*. She wanted to know me. She wanted in.

That was proving to be a problem.

"We could try it again," she said once in an aftermath of sweat and pheromones. "And you won't even remember what you were so upset about. You won't even remember you *were* upset, if you don't want to."

I smiled and looked away; suddenly the planes of her face were coarse and unappealing. "How many times is that now? Eight? Nine?"

"I just want you to be *happy*, Cyg. True happiness is one hell of a gift, and I can give it to you if you'll let me."

"You don't want me happy," I said pleasantly. "You want me customized."

She *mmm*ed into the hollow of my throat for a moment. Then: "What?"

"You just want to change me into something more, more *accommodating*."

Chelsea lifted her head. "Look at me."

I turned my head. She'd shut down the chromatophores in her cheek; the tattoo, transplanted, fluttered now on her shoulder.

"Look at my *eyes*," Chelsea said.

I looked at the imperfect skin around them, at the capillaries wriggling across the whites. I felt a distant bemusement that such flawed, decaying organs were still able to hypnotize me on occasion.

"Now," Chelsea said. "What do you mean by that?"

I shrugged. "You keep pretending this is a partnership. We both know it's a competition."

"A competition."

"You're trying to manipulate me into playing by your rules."

"What *rules*?"

"The way you want the relationship run. I don't blame you, Chelse, not in the least. We've been trying to manipulate each other for as long as—hell, it's not even Human nature. It's *mammalian*."

"I don't believe it." She shook her head. Ropy tendrils of hair swung across her face. "It's the middle of the twenty-first century and you're hitting me with this *war of the sexes* bullshit?"

"Granted, your *tweaks* are a pretty radical iteration. Get right in there and reprogram your mate for optimum servility."

"You actually think I'm trying to, to *housebreak* you? You think I'm trying to train you like a puppy?"

"You're just doing what comes naturally."

"I can't believe you'd pull this shit on me."

"I thought you valued honesty in relationships."

"*What* relationship? According to you there's no such thing. This is just . . . mutual rape, or something."

"That's what relationships *are*."

"*Don't pull that shit on me.*" She sat up, swung her feet over the edge of the bed. Putting her back to me. "I know how I *feel*. If I know *anything* I know that much. And I only wanted to make you happy."

"I know you believe that," I said gently. "I know it doesn't *feel* like a strategy. Nothing does when it's wired that deeply. It just feels *right*, it feels natural. It's nature's trick."

"It's *someone's* fucking trick."

I sat up next to her, let my shoulder brush hers. She leaned away.

"I know this stuff," I said after a while. "I know how people work. It's my job."

It was hers too, for that matter. Nobody who spliced brains for a living could possibly be unaware of all that basic wiring in the sub-basement. Chelsea had simply chosen to ignore it; to have admitted anything would have compromised her righteous anger.

I could have pointed that out too, I suppose, but I knew how much stress the system could take and I wasn't ready to test it to destruction. I didn't want to lose her. I didn't want to lose that feeling of safety, that sense that it made a difference whether I lived or died. I only wanted her to back off a bit. I only wanted room to breathe.

"You can be such a reptile sometimes," she said.

Mission accomplished.

Our first approach had been all caution and safety margins. This time we came in like a strike force.

Scylla burned toward *Rorschach* at over two g, its trajectory a smooth and predictable arc ending at the ruptured base camp. It may have even landed there, for all I know; perhaps Sarasti had two-birded the mission, programmed the shuttle for some collecting of its own. If so, it wouldn't land with us on board. *Scylla* spat us into space almost fifty kilometers short of the new beachhead, left us naked and plummeting on some wire-frame contraption with barely enough reaction mass for a soft landing and a quick getaway. We didn't even have control over *that*: Success depended on unpredictability, and how better to ensure that than to not even know ourselves what we were doing?

Sarasti's logic. Vampire logic. We could follow it partway: The colossal deformation that had sealed *Rorschach*'s breach was so much slower, so much more expensive than the dropgate that had trapped the Gang. The fact that dropgates *hadn't* been used implied that they took time to deploy—to redistribute necessary mass, perhaps, or spring-load its reflexes. That gave us a window. We could still venture into the den so long as the lions couldn't predict our destination and set traps in advance. So long as we got out again before they could set them afterward.

"Thirty-seven minutes," Sarasti had said, and none of us could fathom how he'd come to that number. Only Bates had dared to ask aloud, and he had merely glinted at her: "You can't follow."

Vampire logic. From an obvious premise to an opaque conclusion. Our lives depended on it.

The retros followed some preprogrammed algorithm that mated Newton with a roll of the dice. Our vector wasn't completely random—once we'd eliminated raceways and growth zones, areas without line-of-sight escape routes, dead ends and unbranched segments (*Boring,* Sarasti said, dismissing them), barely 10 percent of the artifact remained in the running. Now we dropped toward a warren of brambles eight kilometers from our original landing site. Here in the midst of our final approach, there was no way that even *we* could predict our precise point of impact.

If *Rorschach* could, it deserved to win.

We fell. Ridged spires and gnarled limbs sectioned the sky wherever I looked, cut the distant starscape and the imminent superJovian into a jagged mosaic veined in black. Three kilometers away or thirty, the tip of some swollen extremity burst in a silent explosion of charged particles, a distant fog of ruptured, freezing atmosphere. Even as it faded I could make out wisps and streamers swirling into complex spirals: *Rorschach*'s magnetic field, sculpting the artifact's very breath into radioactive sleet.

I'd never seen it with naked eyes before. I felt like an insect on a starry midwinter's night, falling through the aftermath of a forest fire.

The sled fired its brakes. I snapped back against the webbing of my harness, bumped against the rebounding armored body next to me. Sascha. *Only Sascha,* I remembered. Cunningham had sedated the rest of them, left this one core lonely and alone in the group body. I hadn't even realized that that was possible with multiple personalities. She stared back at me from behind her faceplate. None of her surfaces showed through the suit. I could see nothing in her eyes.

That was happening so often, these days.

Cunningham was not with us. Nobody had asked why, when Sarasti assigned the berths. The biologist was first among equals now, a backup restored with no other behind him. The second-least replaceable of our irreplaceable crew.

It made me a better bargain. The odds I bought had increased to one in three.

A silent bump shuddered up the frame. I looked forward again, past Bates on the front pallet, past the anchored drones that flanked her two to each side. The sled had launched its assault, a prefab inflatable vestibule mounted on an explosive injection assembly that would punch through *Rorschach*'s skin like a virus penetrating a host cell. The spindle-legged contraption dwindled and disappeared from my sight. Moments later a pinpoint sodium sun flared and died against the ebony landscape ahead— antimatter charge, so small you could almost count the atoms, shot directly into the hull. A lot rougher than the tentative foreplay of our first date.

We landed, hard, while the vestibule was still inflating. The grunts were off the sled an instant before contact, spitting tiny puffs of gas from their nozzles, arranging themselves around us in a protective rosette. Bates was up next, leaping free of her restraints

and sailing directly toward the swelling hab. Sascha and I un-
loaded the fiberop hub—a clamshell drum half a meter thick
and three times as wide—lugging it between us while one of the
grunts slipped through the vestibule's membranous airlock.

"Let's move, people." Bates was hanging off one of the inflatable's handholds. "Thirty minutes to—"

She fell silent. I didn't have to ask why: The advance grunt
had positioned itself over the newly-blasted entrance and sent
back its first postcard.

Light from below.

You'd think that would have made it easier. Our kind has always
feared the dark; for millions of years we huddled in caves and
burrows while unseen things snuffled and growled—or just
waited, silent and undetectable—in the night beyond. You'd
think that any light, no matter how meager, might strip away
some of the shadows, leave fewer holes for the mind to fill with
worst imaginings.

You'd think.

We followed the grunt down into a dim soupy glow like
blood-curdled milk. At first it seemed as though the atmosphere
itself was alight, a luminous fog that obscured anything more
than ten meters distant. An illusion, as it turned out; the tunnel
we emerged into was about three meters wide and lit by rows of
raised glowing dashes—the size and approximate shape of dismembered human fingers—wound in a loose triple helix around
the walls. We'd recorded similar ridges at the first site, although
the breaks had not been so pronounced and the ridges had been
anything but luminous.

"Stronger in the near-infrared," Bates reported, flashing the
spectrum to our HUDs. The air would have been transparent to

pit vipers. It *was* transparent to sonar: The lead grunt sprayed the fog with click trains and discovered that the tunnel widened into some kind of chamber seventeen meters farther along. Squinting in that direction I could just make out subterranean outlines through the mist. I could just make out jawed things, pulling back out of sight.

"Let's go," Bates said.

We plugged in the grunts, left one guarding the way out. Each of us took another as a guardian angel on point. The machines spoke to our HUDs via laser link; they spoke to each other along stiffened lengths of shielded fiberop that unspooled from the hub trailing in our wake. It was the best available compromise in an environment without any optima. Our tethered bodyguards would keep us all in touch during lone excursions around corners or down dead ends.

Yeah. *Lone* excursions. Forced to either split the group or cover less ground, we were to split the group. We were speed-cartographers panning for gold. Everything we did here was an act of faith: faith that the unifying principles of *Rorschach*'s internal architecture could be derived from the raw dimensions we'd grab on the run. Faith that *Rorschach*'s internal architecture even *had* unifying principles. Earlier generations had worshipped malign and capricious spirits. Ours put its faith in an ordered universe. Here in the Devil's Baklava, it was easy to wonder if our ancestors hadn't been closer to the mark.

We moved along the tunnel. Our destination resolved to merely human eyes: not so much chamber as *nexus,* a knot of space formed by the convergence of a dozen tunnels angling in from different orientations. Ragged meshes of quicksilver dots gleamed along several glistening surfaces; shiny protrusions poked through the substrate like a scattershot blast of ball bearings pressed into wet clay.

I looked at Bates and Sascha. "Control panel?"

Bates shrugged. Her drones panned the throats around us, spraying sonar down each. My HUD sketched a patchy 3-D model from the echoes: swathes of paint thrown against invisible walls. We were dots near the center of a ganglion, a tiny swarm of parasites infesting some great hollowed host. Each tunnel curved away in a gradual spiral, each along a different orientation. Sonar could peep around those bends a few meters farther than we could. Neither eyes nor ultrasonics saw anything to distinguish one choice from another.

Bates pointed down one of the passageways—"Keeton"— and another—"Sascha"—before turning to coast off down her own unbeaten path.

I looked uneasily down mine. "Any particular—"

"Twenty-five minutes," she said.

I turned and jetted slowly down my assigned passageway. The passage curved clockwise, a long unremarkable spiral; after twenty meters that curvature would have blocked any view of its entrance even if the foggy atmosphere hadn't. My drone kept point across the tunnel, its sonar clicking like the chattering of a thousand tiny teeth, its tether unspooling back to the distant drum in the nexus.

It was a comfort, that leash. It was *short*. The grunts could stray ninety meters and no farther, and we were under strict orders to stay under their wings at all times. This dim infested burrow might lead all the way to hell, but I would not be expected to follow it nearly so far. My cowardice had official sanction.

Fifty meters to go. Fifty meters and I could turn and run with my tail between my legs. In the meantime all I had to do was grit my teeth, and focus, and record: *Everything you see,* Sarasti had said. *As much as possible of what you can't.* And hope that this new reduced time limit would expire before *Rorschach* spiked us into gibbering dementia.

The walls around me twitched and shivered like the flesh of something just-killed. Something darted in and out of sight with a faint cackle of laughter.

Focus. Record. If the grunt doesn't see it, it's not real.

Sixty-five meters in, one of the ghosts got inside my helmet.

I tried to ignore it. I tried to look away. But this phantom wasn't flickering at the edge of vision; it hovered near the center of my faceplate, floating like a spot of swirling dizziness between me and the HUD. I gritted my teeth and tried to look past, stared into the dim bloody haze of the middle distance, watched the jerky unfolding travelogues in the little windows labeled *Bates* and *James*. Nothing out there. But in *here,* floating before my eyes, *Rorschach's* latest headfuck smeared a fuzzy thumbprint right in front of the sonar feed.

"New symptom," I called in. "Nonperipheral hallucination, stable, pretty formless though. No spiking that I can—"

The inset marked *Bates* skidded hard about. *"Keet—"*

Window and voice cut out together.

Not just Bates's window, either. Sascha's inset and the drone's-eye sonarscape flickered and died at the same moment, stripped my HUD bare except for in-suit feeds and a little red readout flashing LINK DOWN. I spun but the grunt was still there, three meters off my right shoulder. Its optical port was clearly visible, a ruby thumbnail set into the plastron.

Its gun ports were visible, too. Pointing at me.

I froze. The drone *shivered* in some local electromagnetic knot as if terrified. Of me, or—

—of something *behind* me . . .

I started to turn. My helmet filled with sudden static, and with what sounded—faintly—like a voice:

"—ucking *move,* Kee—not—"

"Bates? *Bates?*" Another icon had bloomed in place of LINK

DOWN. The grunt was using *radio* for some reason—and though almost close enough to touch, I could barely make out the signal.

A hash of Batespeak: "—to your—right in *front* of—" and Sascha as well, a bit more clearly: "—an't he *see* it? . . ."

"See what? *Sascha!* Someone tell me what—see *what?*"

"—read? Keeton, do you read?"

Somehow Bates had boosted the signal; static roared like an ocean, but I could hear the words behind it. "Yes! What—"

"*Keep absolutely still,* do you understand? *Absolutely still.* Acknowledge."

"Acknowledged." The drone kept me in its shaky sights, dark stereocam irises spasming wide, stuttering to pinpoints. "Wha—"

"There's something in front of you, Keeton. Directly between you and the grunt. Can't you see it?"

"N-no. My HUD's down—"

Sascha broke in: "How can he not *see* it it's right *th*—"

Bates barked over her: "It's man-sized, radially symmetrical, eight, nine arms. Like tentacles, but—segmented. Spiky."

"I don't see anything," I said. But I did: I saw something reaching for me, in my pod back aboard *Theseus*. I saw something curled up motionless in the ship's spine, watching as we laid our best plans.

I saw Michelle the synesthesiac, curled into a fetal ball: *You can't see it . . . it's in—visible . . .*

"What's it doing?" I called. *Why can't I see it? Why can't I see it?*

"Just—floating there. Kind of waving. Oh, *sh—Keet*—"

The grunt skidded sideways, as if slapped by a giant hand. It bounced off the wall and suddenly the laser link was back, filling the HUD with intelligence: first-person perspectives of Bates and Sascha racing along alien tunnels, a grunt's-eye view of a spacesuit with *Keeton* stenciled across its breastplate and there, right beside it, some *thing* like a rippling starfish with too many arms—

The Gang barreled around the curve and now I almost *could* see something with my own eyes, flickering like heat lightning off to one side. It was large, and it was moving, but somehow my eyes just *slid off* every time they tried to get a fix. *It's not real,* I thought, giddy with hysterical relief, *it's just another hallucination* but then Bates sailed into view and it was *right there,* no flickering, no uncertainty, nothing but a collapsed probability wave and solid, undeniable mass. Exposed, it grabbed the nearest wall and scrambled over our heads, segmented arms flailing like whips. A sudden crackling buzz in the back of my head and it was drifting free again, charred and smoking.

A stuttering *click*. The whine of machinery gearing down. Three grunts hovered in formation in the middle of the passageway. One faced the alien. I glimpsed the tip of some lethal proboscis sliding back into its sheath. Bates shut the grunt down before it had finished closing its mouth.

Optical links and three sets of lungs filled my helmet with a roar of heavy breathing.

The offlined grunt drifted in the murky air. The alien carcass bumped gently off the wall, twitching: a hydra of human backbones, scorched and fleshless. It didn't look much like my onboard visions after all.

For some reason I couldn't put my finger on, I found that almost reassuring.

The two active grunts panned the fog until Bates gave them new orders; then one turned to secure the carcass, the other to steady its fallen comrade. Bates grabbed the dead grunt and unplugged its tether. "Fall back. Slowly. I'm right behind you."

I tweaked my jets. Sascha hesitated. Coils of shielded cable floated about us like umbilical cords.

"Now," Bates said, plugging a feed from her own suit directly into the offlined grunt.

Sascha started after me. Bates took up the rear. I watched my HUD; a swarm of multiarmed monsters would appear there any moment.

They didn't. But the blackened thing against the belly of Bates's machine was real enough. Not a hallucination. Not even some understandable artifact of fear and synesthesia. *Rorschach* was inhabited. Its inhabitants were invisible.

Sometimes. Sort of.

And, oh yeah. We'd just killed one.

Bates threw the deactivated grunt into the sky as soon as we'd made vacuum. Its comrades used it for target practice while we strapped in, firing and firing until there was nothing left but cooling vapor. *Rorschach* spun even that faint plasma into filigree before it faded.

Halfway back to *Theseus,* Sascha turned to the Major: "You—"

"No."

"But . . . they do shit on their own, right? Autonomous."

"Not when they're slaved."

"Malfunction? Spike?"

Bates didn't answer.

She called ahead. By the time we made it back Cunningham had grown another little tumor on *Theseus*'s spine, a remote surgery packed with teleops and sensors. One of the surviving grunts grabbed the carcass and jumped ship as soon as we passed beneath the carapace, completing the delivery as we docked.

We were born again to the fruits of a preliminary necropsy. The holographic ghost of the dissected alien rose from ConSensus like some flayed and horrific feast. Its splayed arms looked like human spinal columns. We sat around the table and waited for someone else to take the first bite.

"Did you have to shoot it with *microwaves?*" Cunningham sniped, tapping the table. "You completely *cooked* the animal. Every cell was blown out from the inside."

Bates shook her head. "There was a malfunction."

He gave her a sour look. "A malfunction that just happens to involve precise targeting of a moving object. It doesn't sound random to me."

Bates looked back evenly. "Something flipped autonomous targeting from *off* to *on*. A coin toss. Random."

"Random is—"

"Give it a rest, Cunningham. I don't need this shit from you right now."

His eyes rolled in that smooth dead face, focused suddenly on something overhead. I followed his gaze: Sarasti stared down at us like an owl panning for meadow voles, drifting slowly in the Coriolis breeze.

No visor this time, either. I knew he hadn't lost it.

He fixed Cunningham. "Your findings."

Cunningham swallowed. Bits and pieces of alien anatomy flickered with color-coded highlights as he tapped his fingers. "Right, then. I'm afraid I can't give you much at the cellular level. There's not much left inside the membranes. Not many membranes left, for that matter. In terms of gross morphology, the specimen's dorsoventrally compressed and radially symmetrical, as you can see. Calcareous exoskeleton, keratinized plastic cuticle. Nothing special."

Bates looked skeptical. "*Plastic skin* is nothing special?"

"Given the environment I was half-expecting a Sanduloviciu plasma. Plastic's simply refined petroleum. Organocarbon. This thing is carbon-based. It's even *protein*-based, although its proteins are a great deal tougher than ours. Numerous sulphur cross-bonds for lateral bracing, as far as I could tell from what your grunts didn't denature." Cunningham's eyes looked past us all; his consciousness was obviously far aft, haunting remote sensors. "The thing's tissues are saturated with magnetite. On earth you find that material in dolphin brains, migratory birds, even some bacteria—anything that navigates or orients using magnetic fields. Moving up to macrostructures we've got a pneumatic internal skeleton, which as far as I can tell doubles as musculature. Contractile tissue squeezes gas through a system of bladders that stiffen or relax each segment in the arms."

The light came back into Cunningham's eyes long enough to focus on his cigarette. He brought it to his mouth, dragged deeply, set it down again. "Note the invaginations around the base of each arm." Flaccid balloons glowed orange on the virtual carcass. "*Cloacae,* you could call them. Everything opens into them: they eat, breathe, and defecate through the same little compartment. No other major orifices."

The Gang made a face that said *Sascha, grossed out.* "Don't things get . . . clogged up? Seems inefficient."

"If one gets plugged, there's eight other doors into the same system. You'll wish you were so *inefficient* the next time you choke on a chicken bone."

"What *does* it eat?" Bates asked.

"I couldn't say. I found gizzard-like contractiles around the cloacae, which implies they *chew* on something, or did at some point in their history. Other than that . . ." He spread his hands; the cigarette left faint streamers in its wake. "Inflate those contractiles enough and you create an airtight seal, by the way. In conjunction with the cuticle, that would allow this organism to survive briefly in vacuum. And we already know it can handle the ambient radiation, although don't ask me how. Whatever it uses for genes must be a great deal tougher than ours."

"So it can survive in space," Bates mused.

"In the sense that a dolphin survives underwater. Limited time only."

"How long?"

"I'm not certain."

"Central nervous system," Sarasti said.

Bates and the Gang grew suddenly, subtly still. James's affect seeped out over her body, supplanting Sascha's.

Smoke curled from Cunningham's mouth and nose. "There's nothing *central* about it, as it transpires. No cephalization, not even clustered sense organs. The body's covered with something like eyespots, or chromatophores, or both. There are setae everywhere. And as far as I can tell—if all those little cooked filaments I've been able to put back together after your *malfunction* really are nerves and not something completely different—every one of those structures is under independent control."

Bates sat up straight. "Seriously?"

He nodded. "It would be akin to independently controlling the movement of each individual hair on your head, although this creature is *covered* with little hairs from tip to tip. The same thing applies to the eyes. Hundred of thousands of eyes, all over the cuticle. Each one is barely more than a pinhole camera, but each is capable of independent focus and I'm guessing all the different inputs integrate somewhere up the line. The entire body acts like a single diffuse retina. In theory that gives it enormous visual acuity."

"A distributed telescope array," Bates murmured.

"A chromatophore underlies each eye—the pigment's some kind of cryptochrome so it's probably involved in vision, but it can also diffuse or contract through the local tissue. That implies dynamic pigment patterns, like a squid or a chameleon."

"Background pattern-matching?" Bates asked. "Would that explain why Siri couldn't see it?"

Cunningham opened a new window and played grainy looped imagery of Siri Keeton and his unseen dance partner. The creature I hadn't noticed was ominously solid to the cameras: a floating discoid twice as wide as my own torso, arms extending from its edges like thick knotted ropes. Patterns rippled across its surface in waves; sunlight and shadow playing on a shallow seabed.

"As you can see, the background doesn't match the pattern," Cunningham said. "It's not even close."

"Can you explain Siri's blindness to it?" Sarasti said.

"I can't," Cunningham admitted. "It's beyond ordinary crypsis. But *Rorschach* makes you see all sorts of things that aren't there. Not seeing something that *is* there might come down to essentially the same thing."

"Another hallucination?" I asked.

Another shrug while Cunningham sucked smoke. "There are many ways to fool the human visual system. It's interesting that the illusion failed when multiple witnesses were present, but if you want a definitive mechanism you'll have to give me more to work with than *that*." He stabbed his cigarette hand at the crisped remains.

"But"—James took a breath, bracing herself—"we're talking about something . . . sophisticated, at least. Something very complex. A great deal of processing power."

Cunningham nodded again. "I'd estimate nervous tissue accounts for about thirty percent of body mass."

"So it's intelligent." Her voice was almost a whisper.

"Not remotely."

"But—thirty percent—"

"Thirty percent *motor and sensory* wiring." Another drag. "Much like an octopus; an enormous number of neurons, but half of them get used up running the suckers."

"My understanding is that octopi are quite intelligent," James said.

"By molluscan standards, certainly. But do you have any *idea* how much extra cabling you'd need if the photoreceptors in your eye were spread across your entire body? You'd need about three hundred million extension cords to begin with, ranging from half a millimeter to two meters long. Which means all your signals are staggered and out of sync, which means billions of additional logic gates to cohere the input. And that just gets you a single static image, with no filtering, no interpretation, no time-series integration at all." Shiver. Drag. "Now multiply that by all the extra wiring needed to *focus* all those eyespots on an object, or to send all that information back to individual chromatophores, and then add in the processing power you need to *drive* those chromatophores one at a time. Thirty percent might do all that, but I strongly doubt you'd have much left over for philosophy and science." He waved his hand in the general direction of the hold. "That—that—"

"*Scrambler,*" James suggested.

Cunningham rolled his tongue around it. "Very well. That *scrambler* is an absolute miracle of evolutionary engineering. It's also dumb as a stick."

A moment's silence.

"So what *is* it?" James asked at last. "Somebody's pet?"

"Canary in a coal mine," Bates suggested.

"Perhaps not even that," Cunningham said. "Perhaps no more than a white blood cell with waldoes. Maintenance bot, maybe.

Teleoperated, or instinct-driven. But people, we're ignoring far greater questions here. How could an anaerobe even develop complex multicellular anatomy, much less move as *fast* as this thing did? That level of activity burns a great deal of ATP."

"Maybe they don't use ATP," Bates said as I thumbnailed: *adenosine triphosphate*. Cellular energy source.

"It was *crammed* with ATP," Cunningham told her. "You can tell that much even with *these* remains. The question is, how can it synthesize the stuff fast enough to keep up with demand? Purely anaerobic pathways wouldn't suffice."

Nobody offered any suggestions.

"Anyway," he said, "so endeth the lesson. If you want gory details, check ConSensus." He wiggled the fingers of his free hand: the spectral dissection vanished. "I'll keep working, but if you want any real answers, go get me a live one." He butted out his cigarette against the bulkhead and stared defiantly around the drum.

The others hardly reacted; their topologies still sparkled from the revelations of a few minutes before. Perhaps Cunningam's pet peeve *was* more important to the Big Picture; perhaps, in a reductionist universe, biochemical basics should always take priority over the finer points of ETI and interspecies etiquette. But Bates and the Gang were time-lagged, processing earlier revelations. Not just *processing,* either: wallowing. They clung to Cunningham's findings like convicted felons who'd just discovered they might be freed on a technicality.

Because the scrambler was dead at our hands, no doubt about it. But it wasn't an *alien,* not really. It wasn't *intelligent.* It was just a blood cell with waldoes. It was dumb as a stick.

And property damage is so much easier to live with than murder.

> PROBLEMS CANNOT BE SOLVED AT THE SAME LEVEL OF
> AWARENESS THAT CREATED THEM.
>
> —ALBERT EINSTEIN

ROBERT PAGLINO HAD set me up with Chelsea in the first place. Maybe he felt responsible when the relationship started jumping the rails. Or maybe Chelsea, Madam Fix-It that she was, had approached him for an intervention. For whatever reason, it was obvious the moment we took our seats at QuBit's that his invitation had not been entirely social.

He went for some neurotrope cocktail on the rocks. I stuck with Rickard's.

"Still old school," Pag said.

"Still into foreplay," I observed.

"That obvious, huh?" He took a sip. "That'll teach me to try the subtle approach with a professional jargonaut."

"Jargonaut's got nothing to do with it. You wouldn't have fooled a border collie." Truth be told, Pag's topology never really told me much that I didn't already know. I never really had much of an edge in reading him. Maybe we just knew each other too well.

"So," he said, "spill."

"Nothing to spill. She just got to know the real me."

"That *is* bad."

"What'd she tell you?"

"Me? Nothing at all."

I gave him a look over the top of my glass.

He sighed. "She knows you're cheating on her."

"I'm what?"

"Cheating. With the skin."

"It's based on *her*!"

"But it *isn't* her."

"No it isn't. It doesn't fart or fight or break into tears every time you don't want to be dragged off to meet its family. Look, I love the woman dearly, but come *on*. When was the last time *you* tried first-person fucking?"

"Seventy-four," he said.

"You're kidding." I'd have guessed *never*.

"Did some third-world medical missionary work between gigs. They still bump and grind in Texas." Pag swigged his trope. "Actually, I thought it was all right."

"The novelty wears off."

"Evidently."

"And it's not like I'm doing anything unusual here, Pag. *She's* the one with the kink. And it's not just the sex. She keeps *asking* about—she keeps wanting to *know* things."

"Like what?"

"Irrelevant stuff. My life as a kid. My family. Nobody's fucking business."

"She's just taking an interest. Not everyone considers childhood memories off-limits, you know."

"Thanks for the insight." As if people had never *taken an interest* before. As if Helen hadn't *taken an interest* when she went through my drawers and filtered my mail and followed me from room to room, asking the drapes and the furniture why I was always so sullen and withdrawn. She'd taken such an interest that she wouldn't let me out the door until I confided in her. At twelve I'd been stupid enough to throw myself on her mercy: *It's personal, Mom. I'd just rather not talk about it.* Then I'd made my escape into the bathroom when she demanded to know if *it* was trouble online, trouble at school, was it a girl, was it a—a *boy*, what *was* it and why couldn't I just *trust* my *own mother,* don't I know I can trust her with *anything?* I waited out the persistent knocking and the insistent concerned voice through the door and the final, grudging silence that followed. I waited until I was absolutely sure she'd gone away, I waited for five fucking *hours* before I came out and there she was, arms folded in the hall, eyes brimming with reproach and disappointment. That night she took the lock off the bathroom door because *family should never shut each other out.* Still taking an interest.

"Siri," Pag said quietly.

I slowed my breathing, tried again: "She doesn't just want to *talk* about family. She wants to *meet* them. She keeps trying to drag me to meet *hers.* I thought I was hooking up with *Chelsea,* you know, nobody ever told me I'd have to share airspace with . . ."

"You do it?"

"Once." Reaching, grasping things, feigning acceptance, feigning *friendship.* "It was great, if you like being ritually pawed by a bunch of play-acting strangers who can't stand the sight of you and don't have the guts to admit it."

Pag shrugged, unsympathetic. "Sounds like typical old-school family. You're a Synthesist, man. You deal with way wonkier dynamics than *that.*"

"I deal with *other people's* information. I don't vomit my own personal life into the public sphere. Whatever hybrids and the constructs I work with, they don't—"

—*touch*—

"Interrogate," I finished.

"You knew Chelse was an old-fashioned girl right off the top."

"Yeah, when it suits her." I gulped ale. "But she's cutting-edge when she's got a splicer in her hand. Which isn't to say that her strategies couldn't use some work."

"Strategies."

It's not a strategy, *for God's sake! Can't you see I'm* hurting? *I'm on the fucking* floor, *Siri, I'm curled up in a ball because I'm hurting so much and all you can do is criticize my* tactics? *What do I have to do, slash my goddamn* wrists?

I'd shrugged and turned away. *Nature's trick.*

"She *cries,*" I said now. "High blood-lactate levels, makes it easy for her. It's just chemistry but she holds it up like it was some kind of IOU."

Pag pursed his lips. "Doesn't mean it's an act."

"Everything's an act. Everything's strategy. You know that." I snorted. "And *she's* miffed because *I* base a skin on her?"

"I don't think it's so much the actual skin as the fact that you didn't tell her. You know how she feels about honesty in relationships."

"Sure. She doesn't want any."

He looked at me.

"Give me some credit, Pag. You think I should tell her that sometimes the sight of her makes me shudder?"

The system called Robert Paglino sat quietly, and sipped his drugs, and set the things he was about to say in order. He took a breath.

"I can't believe you could be so fucking dumb," he said.

"Yeah? Enlighten me."

"Of *course* she wants you to tell her you only have eyes for her, you love her pores and her morning breath, and why stop at one tweak, how about ten. But that doesn't mean she wants you to *lie,* you idiot. She wants all that stuff to be *true.* And . . . well, why *can't* it be?"

"It isn't," I said.

"*Jesus,* Siri. People aren't *rational. You* aren't rational. We're not thinking machines, we're—we're feeling machines that happen to think." He took a breath, and another hit. "And you already know that, or you couldn't do your job. Or at least"—he grimaced—"the system knows."

"The system."

Me and my protocols, he meant. My *Chinese Room.*

I took a breath. "It doesn't work with everyone, you know."

"So I've noticed. Can't read systems you're too entangled with, right? Observer effect."

I shrugged.

"Just as well," he said. "I don't think I'd like you all that much in that *Room* of yours."

It came out before I could stop it: "Chelse says she'd prefer a *real* one."

He raised his eyebrows. "Real what?"

"Chinese Room. She says it would have better comprehension."

The Qube murmured and clattered around us for a few moments.

"I can see why she'd say that," Pag said at last. "But you . . . you did okay, Pod-man."

"I dunno."

He nodded, emphatic. "You know what they say about the road less traveled? Well, you carved your *own* road. I don't know why. It's like learning calligraphy using your toes, you know? Or proprioceptive polyneuropathy. It's amazing you can do it at all; it's *mind-boggling* that you actually got *good* at it."

I squinted at him. "Proprio—"

"There used to be people without any sense of . . . well, of themselves, physically. They couldn't feel their bodies in space, had no idea how their own limbs were arranged or even if they *had* limbs. Some of them said they felt *pithed.* Disembodied.

They'd send a motor signal to the hand and just have to take it on faith that it arrived. So they'd use vision to compensate; they couldn't feel where the hand was so they'd *look* at it while it moved, use sight as a substitute for the normal force-feedback you and I take for granted. They could walk, if they kept their eyes focused on their legs and concentrated on every step. They'd get pretty good at it. But even after years of practice, if you distracted them in mid-step they'd go over like a beanstalk without a counterweight."

"You're saying I'm like that?"

"You use your *Chinese room* the way they used vision. You've reinvented empathy, almost from scratch, and in some ways— not *all* obviously, or I wouldn't have to tell you this—but in some ways yours is better than the original. It's why you're so good at Synthesis."

I shook my head. "I just observe, that's all. I watch what people do, and then I imagine what would make them do that."

"Sounds like empathy to me."

"It's not. Empathy's not so much about imagining how the other guy feels. It's more about imagining how *you'd* feel in the same place, right?"

Pag frowned. "So?"

"So what if you don't *know* how you'd feel?"

He looked at me, and his surfaces were serious and completely transparent. "You're better than that, friend. You may not always act like it, but—I know you. I knew you *before*."

"You knew someone else. I'm *Pod-man,* remember?"

"Yeah, that was someone else. And maybe I remember him better than you do. But I'll tell you one thing." He leaned forward. "*Both* of you would've helped me out that day. And maybe he would've got there with good ol' fashioned empathy while you had to cobble together some kind of improvised flow-chart out of surplus parts, but that just makes your accomplishment all the greater. Which is why I continue to stick it out with you, old buddy. Even though you have a rod up your ass the size of the Rio Spire."

He held out his glass. Dutifully, I clinked it against my own. We drank.

"I don't remember him," I said after a while.

"What, the other Siri? Pre-Pod Siri?"

I nodded.

"Nothing at all?"

I thought back. "Well, he was wracked by convulsions all the time, right? There'd be constant pain. I don't remember any pain." My glass was almost empty; I sipped to make it last. "I—I dream about him sometimes, though. About . . . *being* him."

"What's it like?"

"It was—colorful. Everything was more saturated, you know? Sounds, smells. Richer than life."

"And now?"

I looked at him.

"You said it *was* colorful. What changed?"

"I don't know. Maybe nothing. I just— I don't actually remember the dreams when I wake up anymore."

"So how do you know you still have them?" Pag asked.

Fuck it, I thought, and tipped back the last of my pint in a single gulp. "I know."

"How?"

I frowned, taken aback. I had to think for a few moments before I remembered.

"I wake up smiling," I said.

GRUNTS LOOK THE ENEMY IN THE EYE. GRUNTS KNOW
THE STAKES. GRUNTS KNOW THE PRICE OF POOR STRAT-
EGY. WHAT DO THE GENERALS KNOW? OVERLAYS AND
TACTICAL PLOTS. THE WHOLE CHAIN OF COMMAND IS
UPSIDE-DOWN.

—KENNETH LUBIN, *ZERO SUM*

IT WENT BAD from the moment we breached. The plan had
called for precise havoc along the new beachhead, subtly arranged
to entrap some blood-cell-with-waldoes as it sought to repair the
damage. Our job had been to set the trap and stand back, trusting
Sarasti's assurances that we would not have long to wait.

We had no time at all. Something squirmed in the swirling
dust the moment we breached, serpentine movement down the
hole that instantly kicked Bates's renowned *field initiative* into
high gear. Her grunts dived through and caught a scrambler
twitching in their crosshairs, clinging to the wall of the passageway. It must have been stunned by the blast of our entry, a classic case of wrong-place-wrong-time. Bates took a split second to
appraise the opportunity and the plan was plasma.

One of the grunts plugged the scrambler with a biopsy dart
before I even had a chance to blink. We would have bagged the
whole animal right then if *Rorschach*'s magnetosphere hadn't
chosen that moment to kick sand in our faces. As it was, by the
time our grunts staggered back into action their quarry was already disappearing around the bend. Bates was tethered to her
troops; they yanked her down the rabbit hole (*"Set it up!"* she
yelled back at Sascha) the moment she let them loose.

I was tethered to Bates. I barely had a chance to exchange a
wide-eyed look with Sascha before being yanked away in turn.
Suddenly I was *inside* again; the sated biopsy dart bounced off

my faceplate and flashed past, still attached to a few meters of discarded monofilament. Hopefully Sascha would pick it up while Bates and I were hunting; at least the mission wouldn't be a total loss if we never made it back.

The grunts dragged us like bait on a hook. Bates flew like a dolphin just ahead of me, keeping effortlessly to the center of the bore with an occasional tweak of her jets. I careened off the walls just behind, trying to stabilize myself, trying to look as though I too might be in control. It was an important pretense. The whole point of being a decoy is to pass yourself off as an original. They'd even given me my own gun, pure precaution of course, more for comfort than protection. It hugged my forearm and fired plastic slugs impervious to induction fields.

Just Bates and I, now. A pacifist soldier, and the odds of a coin toss.

Gooseflesh prickled my skin as it always had. The usual ghosts scrabbled and clawed through my mind. This time, though, the dread seemed muted. Distant. Perhaps it was just a matter of timing, perhaps we were moving so quickly through the magnetic landscape that no one phantom had a chance to stick. Or maybe it was something else. Maybe I wasn't so afraid of ghosts because this time we were after monsters.

The scrambler seemed to have thrown off whatever cobwebs our entrance had spun; it surged along the walls now at full speed, its arms shooting ahead like a succession of striking snakes, slinging the body forward so fast the drones could barely keep it in sight, a writhing silhouette in the fog. Suddenly it leapt sideways, sailing across the width of the passageway and down some minor tributary. The grunts veered in pursuit, crashing into walls, stumbling—

—stopping—

—and suddenly Bates was braking hard, shooting back past

me as I flailed with my pistol. I was past the drones in the next instant; my leash snapped tight and snapped back, bringing me to a
dead drifting stop. For a second or two I was on the front line.
For a second or two I *was* the front line, Siri Keeton, note-taker,
mole, professional uncomprehender. I just floated there, breath
roaring in my helmet, as a few meters farther on the walls—

—*squirmed* . . .

Peristalsis, I thought at first. But this motion was utterly unlike
the slow, undulating waves that usually rippled along *Rorschach*'s passageways. So *hallucination,* I thought instead—and then
those writhing walls reached out with a thousand whip-like calcareous tongues that grabbed our quarry from every direction
and *tore it to pieces.* . . .

Something grabbed me and spun me around. Suddenly I was
locked against the chest of one of the grunts, its rear guns firing
as we retreated back up the tunnel at full speed. Bates was in the
arms of the other. Seething motion receded behind us but the
image stayed stuck to the backs of my eyes, hallucinatory and
point-blank in its clarity:

Scramblers, everywhere. A seething infestation squirming
across the walls, reaching out for the intruder, leaping into the
lumen of the passageway to press their counterattack.

Not against us. They had attacked one of their own. I'd seen
three of its arms ripped off before it had disappeared into a
writhing ball in the center of the passageway.

We fled. I turned to Bates—*Did you see*—but held my tongue.
The deathly concentration on her face was unmistakable even
across two faceplates and three meters of methane. According to
HUD she'd lobotomized both grunts, bypassed all that wonderful autonomous decision-making circuitry entirely. She was
running both machines herself, as manually as marionettes.

Grainy turbulent echoes appeared on the rear sonar display.

The scramblers had finished with their sacrifice. Now they were coming after us. My grunt stumbled and careened against the side of the passage. Jagged shards of alien décor dug parallel gouges across my faceplate, tenderized chunks of thigh through the shielded fabric of my suit. I clenched down on a cry. It got out anyway. Some ridiculous in-suit alarm chirped indignantly an instant before a dozen rotten eggs broke open inside my helmet. I coughed. My eyes stung and watered in the reek; I could barely see SIEVERTS on the HUD, flashing instantly into the red.

Bates drove us on without a word.

My faceplate healed enough to shut off the alarm. My air began to clear. The scramblers had gained; by the time I could see clearly again they were only a few meters behind us. Up ahead Sascha came into view around the bend, Sascha who had no backup, whose other cores had all been shut down on Sarasti's orders. Susan had protested at first—

"If there's any opportunity to communicate—"

"There won't be," he'd said.

—so there was Sascha who was *more resistant to* Rorschach's *influence* according to some criterion I never understood, curled up in a fetal ball with her gloves clamped against her helmet and I could only hope to some dusty deity that she'd set the trap before this place had got to her. And here came the scramblers, and Bates was shouting *"Sascha! Get out of the fucking way!"* and braking hard, way too soon, the scrambling horde nipping at our heels like a riptide and Bates yelled *"Sascha!"* again and finally Sascha moved, kicked herself into gear and off the nearest wall and fled right back up the hole we'd blown in through. Bates yanked some joystick in her head and our warrior sedans slewed and shat sparks and bullets and dove out after her.

Sascha had set the trap just within the mouth of the breach. Bates armed it in passing with the slap of one gloved hand.

Motion sensors were supposed to do the rest—but the enemy was close behind, and there was no room to spare.

It went off just as I was emerging into the vestibule. The cannon net shot out behind me in a glorious exploding conic, caught something, snapped back up the rabbit hole and slammed into my grunt from behind. The recoil kicked us against the top of the vestibule so hard I thought the fabric would tear. It held, and threw us back against the squirming things enmeshed in our midst.

Writhing backbones everywhere. Articulated arms, lashing like bony whips. One of them entwined my leg and *squeezed* like a brick python. Bates's hands waved in a frantic dance before me and that arm came apart into dismembered segments, bouncing around the enclosure.

This was all wrong. They were supposed to be in the net, they were supposed to be *contained* . . .

"*Sascha! Launch!*" Bates barked. Another arm separated from its body and careened into the wall, coiling and uncoiling.

The hole had flooded with aerosol foam-core as soon as we'd pulled the net. A scrambler writhed half-embedded in that matrix, caught just a split second too late; its central mass protruded like some great round tumor writhing with monstrous worms.

"*SASCHA!*"

Artillery. The floor of the vestibule irised shut quick as a leghold trap and everything slammed against it: grunts, people, scramblers whole and in pieces. I couldn't breathe. Every thimbleful of flesh weighed a hundred kilograms. Something slapped us to one side, a giant hand batting an insect. Maybe a course correction. Maybe a collision.

But ten seconds later we were weightless again, and nothing had torn us open.

We floated like mites in a ping-pong ball, surrounded by a

confusion of machinery and twitching body parts. There was little of anything that might pass for blood. What there was floated in clear, shuddering spherules. The cannon net floated like a shrink-wrapped asteroid in our midst. The things inside had wrapped their arms around themselves, around each other, curled into a shivering and unresponsive ball. Compressed methonia hissed around them, keeping them fresh for the long trip home.

"Holy *shit*," Sascha breathed, watching them. "The blood-sucker called it."

He hadn't called everything. He hadn't called a mob of multi-armed aliens ripping one of their own to pieces before my eyes. He hadn't seen *that* coming.

Or at least, he hadn't mentioned it.

I was already feeling nauseous. Bates was carefully bringing her wrists together. For a moment I could barely make out a taut dark thread of freakwire, fine as smoke, between them. Her caution was well-advised; that stuff would slice through human limbs as easily as alien ones. One of the grunts groomed its mouth-parts at her shoulder, cleaning gore from its mandibles.

The freakwire vanished from my sight. Sight itself was dimming, now. The inside of this great lead balloon was going dark around me. We were coasting, purely ballistic. We had to trust that *Scylla* would swoop in and snatch us once we'd achieved a discreet distance from the scene of the crime. We had to trust Sarasti.

That was getting harder by the hour. But he'd been right so far. Mostly.

"How do you *know*?" Bates had asked when he'd first laid out the plan. He hadn't answered. Chances are he couldn't have, not to us, any more than a baseline could have explained brane theory to the inhabitants of Flatland. But Bates hadn't been asking about tactics anyway, not really. Maybe she'd been asking for a *reason,* for something to justify this ongoing trespass into foreign soil, the capture and slaughter of its natives.

On one level she already knew the reason, of course. We all did. We could not afford to merely react. The risks were too great; we had to *preempt.* Sarasti, wise beyond all of us, saw this more clearly than we. Amanda Bates knew he was right in her mind—but perhaps she didn't feel it in her gut. Perhaps, I thought as my vision failed, she was asking Sarasti to convince her.

But that wasn't all she was doing.

Imagine you are Amanda Bates.

The control you wield over your troops would give wet dreams and nightmares to generals of ages past. You can drop instantly into the sensorium of anyone under your command, experience the battlefield from any number of first-person perspectives. Your every soldier is loyal unto death, asking no questions, obeying all commands with alacrity and dedication to which mere flesh could never even aspire. You don't just respect a chain of command: you *are* one.

You are a little bit scared of your own power. You are a little bit scared of the things you've already done with it.

Taking orders comes as naturally as giving them. Oh, you've been known to question policy on occasion, or seek a bigger picture than may be strictly necessary for the job at hand. Your *command initiative* has become the stuff of legends. But you have never disobeyed a direct order. When asked for your perspective, you serve it straight up and unvarnished—until the decision is made, and the orders handed down. Then you do your job without question. Even when questions arise, you would hardly waste time asking them unless you expected an answer you could use.

Why, then, demand analytical details from a *vampire?*

Not for information. Might as well expect the sighted to explain vision to the congenitally blind. Not for clarification; there was no ambiguity in Sarasti's bottom line. Not even for the benefit of poor dumb Siri Keeton, who may have missed some salient point but is too ashamed to raise his own hand.

No, there is only one reason why you might ask for such details: to *challenge*. To rebel, to the infinitesimal degree that rebellion is permitted once the word is given.

You argued and advocated as forcefully as you could, back when Sarasti was soliciting input. But he ignored yours, abandoned any attempt at communication and preemptively invaded foreign territory. He knew that *Rorschach* might contain living beings and still he tore it open without regard for their welfare. He may have killed helpless innocents. He may have roused an angry giant. You don't know.

All you know is, you've been helping him do it.

You've seen this kind of arrogance before, among your own kind. You had hoped that smarter creatures would be wiser ones. Bad enough to see such arrogant stupidity inflicted on the helpless, but to do it at these stakes beggars belief. Killing innocents is the *least* of the risks you're running; you're gambling with the fate of worlds, provoking conflict with a star faring technology whose sole offence was to take your picture without permission.

Your dissent has changed nothing. So you rein it in; all that slips out now is the occasional pointless question with no hope of an answer, its inherent insubordination so deeply buried you don't even see it yourself. If you did see it, you'd keep your mouth shut entirely—because the last thing you want is to remind Sarasti that you think he's *wrong*. You don't want him dwelling on that. You don't want him to think you're up to something.

Because you are. Even if you're not quite ready to admit it to yourself.

Amanda Bates is beginning to contemplate a change of command.

The laceration of my suit had done a real number on the gears. It took three solid days for *Theseus* to bring me back to life. But death was no excuse for falling behind the curve; I resurrected with a head full of updates clogging my inlays.

I flipped through them, climbing down into the drum. The Gang of Four sat at the galley below me, staring at untouched portions of nutritionally-balanced sludge on her plate. Cunningham, over in his inherited domain, grunted at my appearance and turned back to work, the fingers of one hand tapping compulsively on the desktop.

Theseus's orbit had widened during my absence, and most of its eccentricities had been planed away. Now we kept our target in view from a more-or-less constant range of three thousand kilometers. Our orbital period lagged *Rorschach*'s by an hour—the alien crept implacably ahead of us along its lower trajectory—but a supplementary burn every couple of weeks would be enough to keep it in sight. We had *specimens* now, things to be examined under conditions of our own choosing; no point in risking any more close approaches until we'd wrung every useful datum from what we had.

Cunningham had expanded his lab space during my time in the sepulcher. He'd built holding pens, one for each scrambler, modules partitioned by a common wall and installed in a whole new hab. The microwaved carcass had been sidelined like a discarded toy from a previous birthday, although according to the access logs Cunningham still visited it every now and then.

Not that he visited *any* part of the new wing in person, of course. Not that he was even able to, not without suiting up and jumping across the hold. The whole compartment had been disconnected from its spinal lock and pushed to a tethered anchorage midway between spine and carapace: Sarasti's orders, given to *minimize risk of contamination*. It was no skin off Cunningham's nose. He was happier leaving his body in pseudogravity anyway, while his consciousness flitted between the waldoes and sensors and bric-a-brac surrounding his new pets.

Theseus saw me coming and pushed a squeezebulb of sugary electrolytes from the galley dispenser. The Gang didn't look up as I passed. One forefinger tapped absently against their temple, the lips pursed and twitched in the characteristic mode that said *internal dialogue in progress*. I could never tell who was on top when they were like that.

I sucked on the squeezebulb and looked in on the pens. Two cubes suffused in pale red light: in one a scrambler floated center stage, waving its segmented arms like seaweed in gentle surge. The occupant of the other cage was squeezed into a corner, four arms splayed across the converging walls; four others extended, waving again, into open space. The bodies from which those arms sprouted were spheroids, not flattened disks as our first sample had been. They were only slightly compressed, and their arms sprouted not from a single equatorial band but from across the whole surface.

Fully extended, the floating scrambler was over two meters across. The other seemed roughly the same size. Neither moved, except for those drifting arms. Navy-blue mosaics, almost black in the longwave, rippled across their surfaces like the patterns of wind on grass. Superimposed graphics plotted methane and hydrogen at reassuring *Rorschach* norms. Temperature and lighting, ditto. An icon for ambient electromagnetics remained dark.

I dipped into the archives, watched the arrival of the aliens from two days past; each tumbling unceremoniously into its pen, balled up, hugging themselves as they bounced gently around their enclosures. *Fetal position,* I thought—but after a few moments the arms uncoiled, like the blooming of calcareous flowers.

"Robert says *Rorschach* grows them," Susan James said behind me.

I turned. Definitely James in there, but . . . muted, somehow. Her meal remained untouched. Her surfaces were dim.

Except for the eyes. Those were deep, and a little hollow.

"Grows?" I repeated.

"In stacks. They have two navels each." She managed a weak smile, touched her belly with one hand and the small of her back with the other. "One in front, one behind. He thinks they grow in a kind of column, piled up. When the top one develops to a certain point, it buds off from the stack and becomes free-living."

The archived scramblers were exploring their new environment now, climbing gingerly along the walls, unrolling their arms along the corners where the panels met. Those swollen central bodies struck me again. "So that first one, with the flattened . . ."

"Juvenile," she agreed. "Fresh off the stack. These ones are older. They . . . they plump out as they mature. Robert says," she added after a moment.

I sucked the dregs from my squeezebulb. "The ship grows its own crew."

"If it's a ship." James shrugged. "If they're crew."

I watched them move. There wasn't much to explore; the walls were almost bare, innocent of anything but a few sensor heads and gas nozzles. The pens had their own tentacles and manipulators for more invasive research needs, but those had been carefully sheathed during introduction. Still, the creatures covered the territory in careful increments, moving back and forth along parallel, invisible paths. Almost as if they were running transects.

James had noticed it, too. "It seems awfully systematic, doesn't it?"

"What does Robert say about that?"

"He says the behavior of honeybees and sphex wasps is just as complex, and it's all rote hardwiring. Not intelligence."

"But bees still *communicate,* right? They do that dance, to tell the hive where the flowers are."

She shrugged, conceding the point.

"So you still might be able to talk to these things."

"Maybe. You'd think." She massaged her brow between thumb and forefinger. "We haven't got anywhere, though. We played some of their pigment patterns back to them, with variations. They don't seem to make sounds. Robert synthesized a bunch of noises that they might squeeze out of their cloacae if they were so inclined, but those didn't get us anywhere either. Harmonic farts, really."

"So we're sticking to the blood-cells-with-waldoes model."

"Pretty much. But you know, they didn't go into a loop. Hardwired animals repeat themselves. Even smart ones pace, or chew their fur. Stereotyped behaviors. But these two, they gave everything a very careful once-over and then just . . . shut down."

They were still at it in ConSensus, slithering across one wall, then another, then another, a slow screw-thread track that would leave no square centimeter uncovered.

"Have they done anything since?" I asked.

She shrugged again. "Nothing spectacular. They squirm when you poke them. Wave their arms back and forth—they do that pretty much constantly, but there's no information in it that we can tell. They haven't gone invisible on us or anything. We blanked the adjoining wall for a while so they could see each other, even piped audio and air feeds—Robert thought there might be some kind of pheromonal communication—but nothing. They didn't even react to each other."

"Have you tried, well, *motivating* them?"

"With what, Siri? They don't seem to care about their own company. We can't bribe them with food unless we know what they eat, which we don't. Robert says they're in no immediate danger of starvation anyway. Maybe when they get hungry they can deal."

I killed the archival feed and reverted to realtime. "Maybe they eat—I don't know, radiation. Or magnetic energy. The cage can generate magnetic fields, right?"

"Tried it." She took a breath, then squared her shoulders. "But I guess these things take time. He's only had a couple of days, and I only got out of the crypt myself a day ago. We'll keep trying."

"What about negative reinforcement?" I wondered.

She blinked. "Hurt them, you mean."

"Not necessarily anything extreme. And if they're not sentient anyway . . ."

Just like that, Susan went away. "Why, Keeton. you just made a *suggestion*. You giving up on this whole *noninterference* thing?"

"Hello, Sascha. No, of course not. Just—making a list of what's been tried."

"Good." There was an edge to her voice. "Hate to think you were slipping. We're going to grab some down time now, so maybe you could go and talk to Cunningham for a bit. Yeah, do that.

"And be sure to tell him your theory about radiation-eating aliens. I bet he could use a laugh."

He stood at his post in BioMed, though his empty chair was barely a meter away. The ubiquitous cigarette hung from between the fingers of one hand, burned down and burned out.

His other hand played with itself, fingers tapping against thumb in sequence, little to index, index to little. Windows crawled with intelligence in front of him; he wasn't watching.

I approached from behind. I watched his surfaces in motion. I heard the soft syllables rising from his throat:

"*Yit-barah v'yish-tabah v'yit-pa-ar v'yit-romam . . .*"

Not his usual litany. Not even his usual language; *Hebrew,* ConSensus said.

It sounded almost like a *prayer . . .*

He must have heard me. His topology went flat and hard and almost impossible to decipher. It was increasingly difficult getting a fix on anyone these days, but even through those topological cataracts Cunningham—as always—was a tougher read than most.

"Keeton," he said without turning.

"You're not Jewish," I said.

"*It* was." *Szpindel,* I realized after a moment. Cunningham didn't do gender pronouns.

But Isaac Szpindel had been an atheist. All of us were. We'd all started out that way, at least.

"I didn't know you knew him," I said. It certainly wasn't policy.

Cunningham sank into his chair without looking at me. In his head, and in mine, a new window opened within a frame marked *Electrophoresis.*

I tried again. "I'm sorry. I didn't mean to intru—"

"What can I do for you, Siri?"

"I was hoping you could bring me up to speed on your findings."

A periodic chart of alien elements scrolled through the feed. Cunningham logged it and started another sample. "I've documented everything. It's all in ConSensus."

I made a play for ego: "It would really help to know how *you'd* thumbnail it, though. What you think is important can be just as vital as the data themselves."

He looked at me a moment. He muttered something, repetitive and irrelevant.

"What's important is what's *missing,*" he said after a moment. "I've got good samples now and I still can't find the genes. Protein synthesis is almost prionic—reconformation instead of the usual transcription pathways—but I can't figure out how those bricks get slotted into the wall once they're made."

"Any progress on the energy front?" I asked.

"Energy?"

"Aerobic metabolism on an anaerobe budget, remember? You said they had too much ATP."

"That I solved." He puffed smoke; far to stern a fleck of alien tissue liquefied and banded into chemical strata. "They're sprinting."

Rotate that *if you can.*

I couldn't. "How do you mean?"

He sighed. "Biochemistry is a trade-off. The faster you synthesize ATP, the more expensive each molecule becomes. It turns out scramblers are a lot more energy efficient at making it than we are. They're just extremely slow at it, which might not be a big drawback for something that spends most of its time inactive. *Rorschach*—whatever *Rorschach* started out as—could have drifted for millennia before it washed up here. That's a lot of time to build up an energy reserve for bouts of high activity, and once you've laid the groundwork, glycolysis is *explosive.* Two-thousand-fold boost, and no oxygen demand."

"Scramblers *sprint*. Their whole lives."

"They may come preloaded with ATP and burn it off throughout their lifespan."

"How long would that be?"

"Good question," he admitted. "Live fast, die young. If they ration it out, stay dormant most of the time—who knows?"

"Huh." The free-floating scrambler had drifted away from the center of its pen. One extended arm held a wall at bay; the others continued their hypnotic swaying.

I remembered other arms, their motion not so gentle.

"Amanda and I chased one into a crowd. It—"

Cunningham was back at his samples. "I saw the record."

"They tore it to pieces."

"Uh-huh."

"Any idea why?"

He shrugged. "Bates thought there might be some kind of civil war going on down there."

"What do you think?"

"I don't know. Maybe it's right, or maybe scramblers are ritual cannibals, or . . . they're *aliens,* Keeton. What do you want from me?"

"But they're not *really* aliens. At least not intelligent ones. *War* implies intelligence."

"Ants wage war all the time. Proves nothing except that they're alive."

"Are *scramblers* even alive?" I asked.

"What kind of question is that?"

"You think *Rorschach* grows them on some kind of assembly line. You can't find any genes. Maybe they're just biomechanical machines."

"That's what life *is,* Keeton. That's what *you* are." Another hit of nicotine, another storm of numbers, another sample. "Life isn't either/or. It's a matter of degree."

"What I'm asking is, are they *natural*? Could they be constructs?"

"Is a termite mound a construct? Beaver dam? Spaceship? Of course. Were they built by naturally evolved organisms, acting naturally? They were. So tell me how anything in the whole deep multiverse can ever be anything *but* natural?"

I tried to keep the irritation out of my voice. "You know what I mean."

"It's a meaningless question. Get your head out of the twentieth century."

I gave up. After a few seconds Cunningham seemed to notice the silence. He withdrew his consciousness from the machinery and looked around with fleshly eyes, as if searching for some mosquito that had mysteriously stopped whining.

"What's your problem with me?" I asked. Stupid question, obvious question. Unworthy of any Synthesist to be so, so *direct*.

His eyes glittered in that dead face. "Processing without comprehension. That's what you do, isn't it?"

"That's a colossal oversimplification."

"Mmm." Cunningham nodded. "Then why can't you seem to *comprehend* how pointless it is to keep peeking over our shoulders and writing home to our masters?"

"Someone has to keep Earth in the loop."

"Seven months each way. Long loop."

"Still."

"We're on our own out here, Keeton. *You're* on your own. The game's going to be long over before our masters even know it's started." He sucked smoke. "Or perhaps not. Perhaps you're talking to someone closer, hmm? That it? Is the Fourth Wave telling you what to do?"

"There is no Fourth Wave. Not that anyone's told me, anyway."

"Probably not. They'd never risk *their* lives out here, would they? Too dangerous even to hang back and watch from a distance. That's why they built *us*."

"We're all self-made. Nobody forced you to get the rewire."

"No, nobody *forced* me to get the rewire. I could have just let them cut out my brain and pack it into Heaven, couldn't I? That's the *choice* we have. We can be utterly useless, or we can try and compete against the vampires and the constructs and the AIs. And perhaps *you* could tell me how to do that without turning into a—an utter freak."

So much in the voice. Nothing at all on the face. I said nothing.

"See what I mean? No comprehension." He managed a tight smile. "So I'll answer your questions. I'll delay my own work and hold your hand because Sarasti's told us to. I guess that superior vampire mind sees some legitimate reason to indulge your constant ankle-nipping, and it's in charge, so I'll play along. But I'm not nearly that smart, so you'll forgive me if it all seems a bit naff."

"I'm just—"

"You're just doing your job. I know. But I don't like being played, Keeton. And that's what your job *is*."

Even back on Earth, Robert Cunningham had barely disguised his opinion of the ship's commissar. It had been obvious even to the topologically blind.

I'd always had a hard time imagining the man. It wasn't just his expressionless face. Sometimes, not even the subtler things behind would show up in his topology. Perhaps he repressed them deliberately, resenting the presence of this mole among the crew.

It would hardly have been the first time I'd encountered such a reaction. Everyone resented me to some extent. Oh, they liked me well enough, or thought they did. They tolerated my intrusions, and cooperated, and gave away far more than they thought they did.

But beneath Szpindel's gruff camaraderie, beneath James's patient explanations—there was no real respect. How could there be? These people were the bleeding edge, the incandescent apex of hominid achievement. They were trusted with the fate of the world. I was just a tattletale for small minds back home. Not even that much, when home receded too deeply into the distance. Superfluous mass. Couldn't be helped. No use getting bothered over it.

Still, Szpindel had only coined *commissar* half-jokingly. Cunningham *believed* it, and didn't laugh. And while I'd encountered many others like him over the years, those had only *tried* to hide themselves from sight. Cunningham was the first who seemed to succeed.

I tried to build the relationship all the way through training, tried to find the missing pieces. I watched him working the simulator's teleops one day, exercising the shiny new interfaces that spread him through walls and wires. He was practicing his surgical skills on some hypothetical alien the computer had conjured up to test his technique. Sensors and jointed teleops sprouted like the legs of an enormous spider crab from an overhead mount. Spirit-possessed, they dipped and weaved around some semiplausible holographic creature. Cunningham's own body merely trembled slightly, a cigarette jiggling at the corner of its mouth.

I waited for him to take a break. Eventually the tension ebbed from his shoulders. His vicarious limbs relaxed.

"So." I tapped my temple. "Why'd *you* do it?"

He didn't turn. Above the dissection, sensors swiveled and stared back like dismembered eyestalks. *That* was the center of Cunningham's awareness right now, not this nicotine-stained body in front of me. *Those* were his eyes, or his tongue, or whatever unimaginable bastard-senses he used to parse what the

machines sent him. Those clusters aimed back at me—at *us*—
and if Robert Cunningham still possessed anything that might
be called vision, he was watching himself from eyes two meters
outside his own skull.

"Do what, exactly?" he said at last. "The enhancements?"

Enhancements. As though he'd upgraded his wardrobe instead of ripping out his senses and grafting new ones into the
wounds.

I nodded.

"It's vital to keep current," he said. "If you don't reconfigure
you can't retrain. If you don't retrain you're obsolete inside a
month, and then you're not much good for anything except
Heaven or dictation."

I ignored the jibe. "Pretty radical transformation, though."

"Not these days."

"Didn't it *change* you?"

His body dragged on the cigarette. Targeted ventilation
sucked away the smoke before it reached me. "That's the whole
point."

"Surely you were affected personally, though. Surely—"

"Ah." He nodded; at the far end of shared motor nerves,
teleops jiggled in sympathy. "Change the eyes that look at the
world, change the *me* that does the looking?"

"Something like that."

Now he was watching me with fleshly eyes. Across the membrane those snakes and eyestalks returned to their work on the
virtual carcass, as if deciding they'd wasted enough time on
pointless distractions. I wondered which body he was in now.

"I'm surprised you'd have to ask," the meat one said. "Doesn't
my body language tell you everything? Aren't jargonauts supposed to read minds?"

He was right, of course. I wasn't interested in Cunningham's *words*; those were just the carrier wave. He couldn't hear the *real* conversation we were having. All his angles and surfaces spoke volumes, and although their voices were strangely fuzzed with feedback and distortion I knew I'd be able to understand them eventually. I only had to keep him talking.

But Jukka Sarasti chose that moment to wander past and surgically trash my best-laid plans.

"Siri's best in his field," he remarked. "But not when it gets too close to home."

WHY SHOULD MAN EXPECT HIS PRAYER FOR MERCY TO
BE HEARD BY WHAT IS ABOVE HIM WHEN HE SHOWS NO
MERCY TO WHAT IS UNDER HIM?
—PIERRE TROUBETZKOY

"THE THING IS," Chelsea said, "this whole first-person thing takes *effort*. You have to care enough to *try,* you know? I've been working my ass off on this relationship, I've been working so hard, but you just don't seem to *care.* . . ."

She thought she was breaking the news. She thought I hadn't seen it coming, because I hadn't said anything. I'd probably seen it before she had. I hadn't said anything because I'd been scared of giving her an opening.

I felt sick to my stomach.

"I care about you," I said.

"As much as you could care about anything," she admitted. "But you . . . I mean, sometimes you're fine, Cygnus, sometimes you're wonderful to be around but whenever anything gets the least bit intense you just go away and leave this, this *battle computer* running your body and I just can't *deal* with it anymore ..."

I stared at the butterfly on the back of her hand. Its wings flexed and folded, lazy and iridescent. I wondered how many of those tattoos she had; I'd seen five of them on different body parts, albeit only one at a time. I thought about asking her, but this didn't seem like the right moment.

"You can be so—so brutal sometimes," she was saying. "I know you don't mean to be, but ... I don't know. Maybe I'm your pressure-release valve, or something. Maybe you have to submerge yourself so much on the job that everything just ... just builds up and you need some kind of punching bag. Maybe that's why you say the things you do."

She was waiting for me to say something now. "I've been honest," I said.

"Yeah. Pathologically. Have you ever had a negative thought that you *haven't* said out loud?" Her voice trembled but her eyes—for once—stayed dry. "I guess it's as much my fault as yours. Maybe more. I could tell you were—disconnected, from the day we met. I guess on some level I always saw it coming."

"Why even try, then? If you knew we were just going to crash and burn like this?"

"Oh, Cygnus. Aren't you the one who says that *everyone* crashes and burns eventually? Aren't you the one who says it *never* lasts?"

Mom and Dad lasted. Longer than this, anyway.

I frowned, astonished that I'd even let the thought form in my head. Chelse read the silence as a wounded one. "I guess ... maybe I thought I could help, you know? Help fix whatever made you so—so *angry* all the time."

The butterfly was starting to fade. I'd never seen that happen before.

"Do you understand what I'm saying?" she asked.

"Sure. I'm a fixer-upper."

"Siri, you wouldn't even get a tweak when I offered. You were so scared of being *manipulated* you wouldn't even try a basic cascade. You're the one guy I've met who might be truly, eternally unfixable. I dunno. Maybe that's even something to be proud of."

I opened my mouth, and closed it.

She gave me a sad smile. "Nothing, Siri? Nothing at all? There was a time you always knew exactly what to say." She looked back at some earlier version of me. "Now I wonder if you ever actually meant any of it."

"That's not fair."

"No." She pursed her lips. "No, it isn't. That's not really what I'm trying to say. I guess . . . it's not so much that you don't *mean* any of it. It's more like you don't know what any of it *means*."

The color was gone from the wings. The butterfly was a delicate charcoal dusting, almost motionless.

"I'll do it now," I said. "I'll get the tweaks. If it's that important to you. I'll do it now."

"It's too late, Siri. I'm used up."

Maybe she wanted me to call her back. All these words ending in question marks, all these significant silences. Maybe she was giving me the opportunity to plead my case, to beg for another chance. Maybe she wanted a reason to change her mind.

I could have tried. *Please don't,* I could have said. *I'm begging you. I never meant to drive you away* completely, *just a little, just to a safer distance. Please. In thirty long years the only time I haven't felt worthless was when we were together.*

But when I looked up again the butterfly was gone and so was she, taking all baggage with her. She carried doubt, and guilt for having led me on. She left believing that our incompatibility was no one's fault, that she'd tried as hard as she could, even that I had under the tragic weight of all my issues. She left, and maybe she didn't even blame me, and I never even knew who'd made that final decision.

I was good at what I did. I was so damned good, I did it without even meaning to.

"My God! Did you hear that!?"

Susan James bounced around the drum like a pronking wildebeest in the half-gravity. I could see the whites of her eyes from ninety degrees away. "Check your feeds! Check your feeds! *The pens!"*

I checked. One scrambler afloat; the other still jammed into its corner.

James landed at my side with a two-footed *thump,* wobbling for balance. "Turn the sound up!"

The hissing of the air conditioners. The clank of distant machinery echoing along the spine; *Theseus*'s usual intestinal rumblings. Nothing else.

"Okay, they're not doing it now." James brought up a split-screen window and threw it into reverse. *"There,"* she pronounced, replaying the record with the audio cranked and filtered.

In the right side of the window, the floating scrambler had drifted so that the tip of one outstretched arm brushed against the wall that adjoined the other pen. In the left side, the huddled scrambler remained unmoving.

I thought I heard something. Just for an instant: the brief buzz of an insect, perhaps, if the nearest insect hadn't been five trillion kilometers away.

"Replay that. Slow it down."

A buzz, definitely. A vibration.

"Way down."

A click train, squirted from a dolphin's forehead. Farting lips.
"No, let *me*." James bulled into Cunningham's headspace and
yanked the slider to the left.

Tick tick . . . tick . . . tick tick tick . . . tick . . . tick tick tick . . .

Dopplered down near absolute zero, it went on for almost a
minute. Total elapsed real time was about half a second.

Cunningham zoomed the split screen. The huddled
scrambler had remained motionless, except for the rippling of
its cuticle and the undulation of its free arms. But before I'd
only seen eight arms—and now I could make out the bony
spur of a ninth peeking from behind the central mass. A ninth
arm, curled up and hidden from view, *tick tick tick*ing while
another creature casually leaned against the other side of the
wall . . .

Now, there was nothing. The floating scrambler had drifted
aimlessly back to the center of its enclosure.

James's eyes shone. "We've got to check the rest of—"

But *Theseus* had been watching, and was way ahead of us. It
had already searched the archives and served up the results:
three similar exchanges over two days, ranging in duration from
a tenth of a second to almost two.

"They're talking," James said.

Cunningham shrugged, a forgotten cigarette burning down
between his fingers. "So do a lot of things. And at *that* rate of exchange they're not exactly doing calculus. You could get as
much information out of a dancing honeybee."

"That's nonsense and you know it, Robert."

"What I *know* is that—"

"Honeybees don't deliberately hide what they're saying. Honeybees don't develop whole new modes of communication configured specifically to confound observers. That's flexible,
Robert. That's *intelligent*."

"And what if it is, hmm? Forget, for a moment, the inconvenient fact that these things don't even have *brains*. I really don't think you've thought this through."

"Of course I have."

"Indeed? Then what are you so happy about? Don't you know what this means?"

Sudden prickling on the back of my neck. I looked around; I looked *up*. Jukka Sarasti had appeared in the center of the drum, eyes gleaming, teeth bared, watching us.

Cunningham followed my gaze, and nodded. "I'd wager *it* does . . ."

There was no way to learn what they'd whispered across that wall. We could recover the audio easily enough, parse every tick and tap they'd exchanged, but you can't decipher a code without some idea of *content*. We had patterns of sound that could have meant anything. We had creatures whose grammar and syntax—if their mode of communication even contained such attributes—were unknown and perhaps unknowable. We had creatures smart enough to talk, and smart enough to hide that fact. No matter how much we wanted to learn, they were obviously unwilling to teach us.

Not without—how had I put it?—*negative reinforcement*.

It was Jukka Sarasti who made the decision. We did it on his orders, as we did everything else. But after the word had come down—after Sarasti had disappeared in the night and Bates had retreated down the spine and Robert Cunningham had returned to his studies at the back of the drum—I was the one Susan James was left with. The first to speak the vile thought aloud, the official witness to posterity. I was the one she looked at, and looked away from, her surfaces hard and refractory.

And then she started.

. . .

This is how you break down the wall:

Start with two beings. They can be human if you like, but that's hardly a prerequisite. All that matters is that they know how to talk among themselves.

Separate them. Let them see each other, let them speak. Perhaps a window between their cages. Perhaps an audio feed. Let them practice the art of conversation in their own chosen way.

Hurt them.

It may take a while to figure out how. Some may shrink from fire, others from toxic gas or liquid. Some creatures may be invulnerable to blowtorches and grenades, but shriek in terror at the threat of ultrasonic sound. You have to experiment; and when you discover just the right stimulus, the optimum balance between *pain* and *injury,* you must inflict it without the remorse.

You leave them an escape hatch, of course. That's the very point of the exercise: give one of your subjects the *means* to end the pain, but give the other the *information* required to use it. To one you might present a single shape, while showing the other a whole selection. The pain will stop when the being with the menu chooses the item its partner has seen. So let the games begin. Watch your subjects squirm. If—*when*—they trip the off switch, you'll know at least some of the information they exchanged; and if you record everything that passed between them, you'll start to get some idea of how they exchanged it.

When they solve one puzzle, give them a new one. Mix things up. Switch their roles. See how they do at circles versus squares. Try them out on factorials and Fibonaccis. Continue until Rosetta Stone results.

This is how you communicate with a fellow intelligence: You hurt it, and keep on hurting it, until you can distinguish the speech from the screams.

Susan James—congenital optimist, high priestess of the
Church of the Healing Word, was best qualified to design and
execute the protocols. Now, at her command, the scramblers
writhed. They pulled themselves around their cages in elliptical
loops, desperately seeking any small corner free of stimulus.
James had piped the feed into ConSensus, although there was no
mission-critical reason for *Theseus*'s whole crew to bear witness
to the interrogation.

"Let them block it at their ends," she said quietly, "if they
want to."

For all his reluctance to accept that these were *beings,* intelligent and aware, Cunningham had named the prisoners. *Stretch*
tended to float spread-eagled; *Clench* was the balled-up corner-
hugger. Susan, playing her own part in this perverse role-
reversal, had simply numbered them *One* and *Two.* It wasn't that
Cunningham's choices were too cheesy for her to stomach, or
that she objected to slave names on principle. She'd just fallen
back on the oldest trick in the Torturer's Handbook, the one
that lets you go home to your family after work, play with your
children, and sleep at night: *never* humanize your victims.

It shouldn't have been such an issue when dealing with
methane-breathing medusae. I guess every little bit helped.

Biotelemetry danced across the headspace beside each alien,
luminous annotations shuddering through thin air. I had no idea
what constituted normal readings for these creatures, but I
couldn't imagine those jagged spikes passing for anything but
bad news. The creatures themselves seethed subtly with fine mosaics in blue and gray, fluid patterns rippling across their cuticles. Perhaps it was a reflexive reaction to the microwaves; for all
we knew it was a mating display.

More likely they were screaming.

James killed the microwaves. In the left-hand enclosure, a

yellow square dimmed; in the right, an identical icon nested among others never lit.

The pigment flowed faster in the wake of the onslaught; the arms slowed but didn't stop. They swept back and forth like listless, skeletal eels.

"Baseline exposure. Five seconds, two hundred fifty watts." She spoke for the record. Another affectation; *Theseus* recorded every breath on board, every trickle of current to five decimal places.

"Repeat."

The icon lit up. More tile patterns flash flooding across alien skin. But this time, neither alien moved from where it was. Their arms continued to squirm slightly, a torqued trembling variation on the undulation they effected at rest. The telemetry was as harsh as ever, though.

They learned helplessness fast enough, I reflected.

I glanced at Susan. "Are you going to do this all yourself?"

Her eyes were bright and wet as she killed the current. Clench's icon dimmed. Stretch's remained dormant.

I cleared my throat. "I mean—"

"Who else is going to do this, Siri? Jukka? You?"

"The rest of the Gang. Sascha could—"

"Sascha?" She stared at me. "Siri, I *created* them. Do you think I did that so I could *hide* behind them when—so I could force them to do things like *this?*" She shook her head. "I'm not bringing them out. Not for this. I wouldn't do that to my worst enemy."

She turned away from me. There were drugs she could have taken, neuroinhibitors to wash away the guilt, short-circuit it right down in the molecules. Sarasti had offered them up as if he were tempting some solitary messiah in the desert. James had refused him, and would not say why.

"Repeat," she said.

The current flickered on, then off.

"Repeat," she said again.

Not a twitch.

I pointed. "I see it," she said.

Clench had pressed the tip of one arm against the touchpad. The icon there glowed like a candle flame.

Six and a half minutes later they'd graduated from yellow squares to time-lapsed four-dimensional polyhedrons. It took them as long to distinguish between two twenty-six-faceted shifting solids—differing by one facet in a single frame—as it took them to tell the difference between a yellow square and a red triangle. Intricate patterns played across their surfaces the whole time, dynamic needlepoint mosaics flickering almost too fast to see.

"*Fuck,*" James whispered.

"Could be splinter skills." Cunningham had joined us in ConSensus, although his body remained halfway around BioMed.

"Splinter skills," she repeated dully.

"Savantism. Hyperperformance at one kind of calculation doesn't necessarily connote high intelligence."

"I know what splinter skills are, Robert. I just think you're wrong."

"Prove it."

So she gave up on geometry and told the scramblers that one plus one equaled two. Evidently they knew that already: ten minutes later they were predicting ten-digit prime numbers on demand.

She showed them a sequence of two-dimensional shapes; they picked the next one in the series from a menu of subtly different alternatives. She denied them multiple choice, showed them the beginning of a whole new sequence and taught them to draw on the touch-sensitive interface with the tips of their arms. They finished that series in precise freehand, rendered a chain of logical descendants ending with a figure that led inexorably back to the starting point.

"These aren't *drones*." James's voice caught in her throat.

"This is all just crunching," Cunningham said. "Millions of computer programs do it without ever waking up."

"They're *intelligent*, Robert. They're smarter than us. Maybe they're smarter than *Jukka*. And we're— Why can't you just *admit* it?"

I could see it all over her: *Isaac* would have admitted it.

"Because they don't have the circuitry," Cunningham insisted. "How could—"

"*I don't know how!*" she cried. "That's *your* job! All *I* know is that I'm torturing beings that can think rings around us . . ."

"Not for much longer, at least. Once you figure out the language—"

She shook her head. "Robert, I haven't a *clue* about the language. We've been at it for—for hours, haven't we? The Gang's all here, language databases four thousand years thick, all the latest linguistic algorithms. And we know exactly what they're saying, we're watching every possible way they could be *saying* it. Right down to the Angstrom."

"Precisely. So—"

"I've got *nothing*. I know they're talking through pigment mosaics. There might even be something in the way they move those bristles. But I can't find the *pattern*, I can't even follow how they *count*, much less tell them I'm . . . sorry . . ."

Nobody spoke for a while. Bates watched us from the galley on our ceiling, but made no attempt to join the proceedings. On ConSensus the reprieved scramblers floated in their cages like multiarmed martyrs.

"Well," Cunningham said at last, "since this seems to be the day for bad news, here's mine. They're dying."

James put her face in her hand.

"It's not your interrogation, for whatever that's worth," the biologist continued. "As far as I can determine, some of their metabolic pathways are just *missing*."

"Obviously you just haven't found them yet." That was Bates, speaking up from across the drum.

"*No*," Cunningham said, slowly and distinctly, "*obviously* those parts aren't available to the organism. Because they're falling apart pretty much the same way you'd expect one of *us* to, if—if all the mitotic spindles in our cells just *vanished* out of the cytoplasm, for example. As far as I can tell they started deteriorating the moment we took them off *Rorschach*."

Susan looked up. "Are you saying they left part of their biochemistry *behind*?"

"Some essential nutrient?" Bates suggested. "They're not eating—"

"Yes to the linguist. No to the Major." Cunningham fell silent; I glanced across the drum to see him sucking on a cigarette. "I think a lot of the cellular processes in these things are mediated externally. I think the reason I can't find any genes in my biopsies is because they don't *have* any."

"So what do they have instead?" Bates asked.

"Turing morphogens."

Blank looks, subtitling looks. Cunningham explained anyway: "A lot of biology doesn't use genes. Sunflowers look the way they do because of purely physical buckling stress. You get Fibonacci sequences and golden ratios everywhere in nature, and there's no gene that codes for them; it's all just mechanical interactions. Take a developing embryo—the genes say *start growing* or *stop growing,* but the number of digits and vertebrae result from the mechanics of cells bumping against other cells. Those mitotic spindles I mentioned? Absolutely essential for replication in every eukaryotic cell, and they accrete like crystals without any genetic involvement. You'd be surprised how much of life is like that."

"But you still need *genes,*" Bates protested, walking around to join us.

"Genes just establish the starting conditions to enable the process. The structure that proliferates afterwards doesn't need specific instructions. It's classic emergent complexity. We've known about it for over a century." Another drag on the stick. "Or even longer. Darwin cited honeycomb way back in the eighteen hundreds."

"Honeycomb," Bates repeated.

"Perfect hexagonal tubes in a packed array. Bees are hard-wired to lay them down, but how does an insect know enough geometry to lay down a precise hexagon? It doesn't. It's programmed to chew up wax and spit it out while turning on its axis, and that generates a circle. Put a bunch of bees on the same surface, chewing side-by-side, and the circles abut against each other—deform each other into hexagons, which just happen to be more efficient for close packing anyway."

Bates pounced: "But the *bees* are programmed. *Genetically.*"

"You misunderstand. Scramblers are the *honeycomb.*"

"*Rorschach* is the bees," James murmured.

Cunningham nodded. "*Rorschach* is the bees. And I don't think *Rorschach*'s magnetic fields are counterintrusion mechanisms at all. I think they're part of the life-support system. I think they mediate and regulate a good chunk of scrambler metabolism. What we've got back in the hold is a couple of creatures dragged out of their element and holding their breath. And they can't hold it forever."

"How long?" James asked.

"How should I know? If I'm right, I'm not even dealing with complete organisms here."

"Guess," Bates said.

He shrugged. "A few days. Maybe."

THAT WHICH DOES NOT KILL US, MAKES US STRANGER.
—TREVOR GOODCHILD

"YOU STILL DON'T vote," Sarasti said.

We would not be releasing the prisoners. Too risky. Out here in the endless wastelands of the Oort there was no room for *live and let live*. Never mind what the Other has done, or what it hasn't; think of what it *could* do, if it were just a little stronger. Think of what it *might* have done, if we'd arrived as late as we were supposed to. You look at *Rorschach* and perhaps you see an embryo or a developing child, alien beyond comprehension perhaps but not *guilty,* not by default. But what if those are the wrong eyes? What if you should be seeing an omnipotent murdering God, a planet-killer, not yet finished? Vulnerable only now, and for a little longer?

There was no vampire opacity to that logic, no multidimensional black boxes for humans to shrug at and throw up their hands. There was no excuse for the failure to find fault with Sarasti's reasoning, beyond the fact that his reasoning was without fault. That made it worse. The others, I knew, would rather have had to take something on faith.

But Sarasti had an alternative to capture-release, one he

evidently considered much safer. It took an act of faith to accept *that* reasoning, at least; by any sane measure it verged on suicide.

Now *Theseus* gave birth by cesarean. These progeny were far too massive to fit through the canal at the end of the spine. The ship shat them as if constipated, directly into the hold: great monstrous things, bristling with muzzles and antennae. Each stood three or four times my height, a pair of massive rust-colored cubes, every surface infested with topography. Armor plating would hide most of it prior to deployment, of course. Ribbons of piping and conduit, ammunition reservoirs and shark-toothed rows of radiator fins—all to disappear beneath smooth reflective shielding. Only a few island landmarks would rise above that surface: comm ports, thrust nozzles, targeting arrays. And gun ports, of course. These things spat fire and brimstone from a half-dozen mouths apiece.

But for the time being they were just giant mechanical fetuses, half-extruded, their planes and angles a high-contrast jigsaw of light and shadow in the harsh white glow of the hold's floodlamps.

I turned from the port. "That's got to take our substrate stockpiles down a bit."

"Shielding the carapace was worse." Bates monitored construction through a dedicated flatscreen built right into the Fab bulkhead. Practicing, perhaps; we'd be losing our inlays as soon as the orbit changed. "We're tapping out, though. Might have to grab one of the local rocks before long."

"Huh." I looked back into the hold. "You think they're necessary?"

"Doesn't matter what I think. You're a bright guy, Siri. Why can't you figure that out?"

"It matters to me. That means it matters to Earth."

Which might mean something, if Earth was calling the shots.

Some subtext was legible no matter *how* deep in the system you were.

I tacked to port: "How about Sarasti and the Captain, then? Any thoughts?"

"You're usually a bit more subtle."

That much was true. "It's just, you know Susan was the one that caught Stretch and Clench tapping back and forth, right?"

Bates winced at the names. "So?"

"Well, some might think it odd that *Theseus* wouldn't have seen it first. Since quantum computers are supposed to be so proficient at pattern-matching."

"Sarasti took the quantum modules offline. The onboard's been running in classical mode since before we even made orbit."

"*Why?*"

"Noisy environment. Too much risk of decoherence. Quantum computers are finicky things."

"Surely the onboard's shielded. *Theseus* is shielded."

Bates nodded. "As much as feasible. But perfect shielding is perfect blindness, and this is not the kind of neighborhood where you want to keep your eyes closed."

Actually, it was. But I took her point.

I took her other point, too, the one she didn't speak aloud: *And you missed it. Something sitting right there in ConSensus for anyone to see. Top-of-the-line Synthesist like you.*

"Sarasti knows what he's doing, I guess," I admitted, endlessly aware that he might be listening. "He hasn't been wrong yet, as far as we know."

"As far as we *can* know," Bates said.

"*If you could second-guess a vampire, you wouldn't need a vampire,*" I remembered aloud.

She smiled faintly. "Isaac was a good man. You can't always believe the PR, though."

"You don't buy it?" I asked, but she was already thinking she'd said too much. I threw out a hook baited with just the right mix of skepticism and deference: "Sarasti *did* know where those scramblers would be. Nailed it almost the meter, out of that whole maze."

"I suppose that might have taken some kind of super-Human logic," she admitted, thinking I was so fucking dumb she couldn't believe it.

"What?" I said.

Bates shrugged. "Or maybe he just realized that since *Rorschach* was growing its own crew, we'd run into more every time we went in. No matter *where* we landed."

ConSensus bleeped into my silence. "Orbital maneuvers starting in five," Sarasti announced. "Inlays and wireless prosthetics offline in ninety. That's all."

Bates shut down the display. "I'm going to ride this out in the bridge. Illusion of control and all that. You?"

"My tent, I think."

She nodded, and braced to jump, and hesitated.

"By the way," she told me, "yes."

"Sorry?"

"You asked if I thought the emplacements were necessary. Right now I think we need all the protection we can get."

"So you think that *Rorschach* might—"

"Hey, it *already* killed me once."

She wasn't talking about radiation.

I nodded carefully. "That must have been . . ."

"Like nothing at all. You couldn't possibly imagine." Bates took a breath and let it out.

"Maybe you don't have to," she added, and sailed away up the spine.

. . .

Cunningham and the Gang in BioMed, thirty degrees of arc between them. Each poked their captives in their own way. Susan
James stabbed indifferently at a keypad painted across her desktop. Windows to either side looked in on Stretch and Clench.

Cookie-cutter shapes scrolled across the desk as James typed:
circles, triskelions, a quartet of parallel lines. Some of them pulsed
like abstract little hearts. In his distant pen, Stretch reached out
one fraying tentacle and tapped something in turn.

"Any progress?"

She sighed and shook her head. "I've given up trying to understand their language. I'm settling for a pidgin." She tapped
an icon. Clench vanished from his window; a hieroglyphic flow-
chart sprang up in his place. Half the symbols wriggled or
pulsed, endlessly repetitive, a riot of dancing doodles. Others
just sat there.

"Iconic base." James waved vaguely at the display. "Subject-
verb phrases render as animated versions of noun icons. They're
radially symmetrical, so I array modifiers in a circular pattern
around the central subject. Maybe that comes naturally to them."

A new circle of glyphs appeared beneath James's—Stretch's
reply, presumably. But something in the system didn't like what
it saw. Icons flared in a separate window: a luminous counter
flashed 500 WATTS, and held steady. On the screen, Stretch
writhed. It reached out with squirming backbone-arms and
stabbed repeatedly at its touchpad.

James looked away.

New glyphs appeared. Five hundred watts retreated to zero.
Stretch returned to its holding pattern; the spikes and jags of its
telemetry smoothed.

James let out her breath. "What happened?" I asked.

"Wrong answer." She tapped into Stretch's feed, showed me
the display that had tripped it up. A pyramid, a star, simplified

representations of a scrambler and of *Rorschach* rotated on the board.

"It was stupid, it was just a—a warm-up exercise, really. I asked it to name the objects in the window." She laughed softly and without humor. "That's the thing about *functional* languages, you know. If you can't point at it, you can't talk about it."

"And what did it say?"

She pointed at Stretch's first spiral: "Polyhedron star *Rorschach* are present."

"It missed the scrambler."

"Got it right the second time. Still, stupid mistake for something that can think rings around a vampire, isn't it?" Susan swallowed. "I guess even scramblers slip up when they're dying."

I didn't know what to say. Behind me, barely audible, Cunningham muttered some two-stroke mantra to himself in an endless loop.

"Jukka says—" Susan stopped, began again: "You know that *blindsight* we get sometimes, in *Rorschach*?"

I nodded, and wondered what Jukka had said.

"Apparently the same thing can happen to the other senses, too," she told me. "You can have blind*touch,* and blind*smell,* and blind*hearing* . . ."

"That would be deafness."

She shook her head. "But it isn't really, is it? Any more than blind*sight* is really blindness. *Something* in your head is still taking it all in. Something in the brain is still seeing, and hearing, even if you're not—aware of it. Unless someone forces you to *guess,* or there's some threat. You just get a really strong feeling you should move out of the way, and five seconds later a bus drives over the spot you were standing. You *knew* it was coming, somehow. You just don't know *how* you knew."

"It's wild," I agreed.

"These scramblers—they *know* the answers, Siri. They're intelligent, we know they are. But it's almost as though *they* don't know they know, unless you hurt them. As if they've got blindsight spread over every sense."

I tried to imagine it: life without sensation, without any active awareness of one's environment. I tried to imagine existing like that without going mad. "Do you think that's possible?"

"I don't know. It's just a . . . a metaphor, I guess." She didn't believe that. Or she didn't know. Or she didn't want me to know.

I should have been able to tell. She should have been *clear.*

"At first I just thought they were resisting," she said, "but why *would* they?" She turned bright, begging eyes on me, pleading for an answer.

I didn't have one. I didn't have a clue. I turned away from Susan James, only to find myself facing Robert Cunningham: Cunningham the mutterer, fingers tapping against tabletop interfaces, inner eyes blinded, vision limited now to the pictures ConSensus sketched in airspace or threw against flat surfaces for everyone to see. His face remained as empty of feeling as it had ever been; the rest of his body twitched like a bug in a spiderweb.

He might as well have been. We all might. *Rorschach* loomed barely nine kilometers away now, so near it might have eclipsed Ben itself if I'd been brave enough to look outside. We had closed to this insane proximity and *parked.* Out there, *Rorschach* grew like a live thing. *In* there, live things grew, budded like jellyfish from some demonic mechanical substrate. Those lethal, vacant corridors we'd crept along, frightened of the shadows planted in our heads—they were probably filling with scramblers right now. All those hundreds of kilometers of twisted tunnels and passages and chambers. Filling with an army.

This was Sarasti's safer alternative. This was the path we'd followed because it would have been *too dangerous* to release the prisoners. We were so deep inside the bow shock that we'd had to shut down our internal augments; while *Rorschach*'s magnetosphere was orders of magnitude weaker here than within the structure it-self, who knew if the alien might find us too tempting a target— or too great a threat—at this range? Who knew when it might choose to plunge some invisible spike through *Theseus*'s heart?

Any pulse that could penetrate the ship's shielding would doubtless fry *Theseus*'s nervous system as well as the wiring in our heads. I supposed that five people in a dead ship would have a marginally greater chance of survival if their brains weren't sparking in the bargain, but I doubted that such a difference would *make* much difference. Sarasti had obviously figured the odds differently. He'd even shut down the anti-Euclidean pump in his own head, resorted to manual injections to keep *himself* from short-circuiting.

Stretch and Clench were even closer to *Rorschach* than we were. Cunningham's lab had been kicked free of the ship; it floated now just a few kilometers from the artifact's outermost spires, deep within the folds of its magnetic field. If the scram-blers needed radioactive magnetite to function, this was the most they were going to get: a taste of the fields, but not of freedom. The lab's shielding was being dynamically fine-tuned to balance medical necessity against tactical risk, as best the data allowed. The structure floated in the watchful crosshairs of our newborn gun emplacements, strategically positioned to either side. Those emplacements could destroy the hab in an instant. They could probably destroy anything approaching it as well.

They couldn't destroy *Rorschach,* of course. Maybe nothing could.

Covert to invulnerable. As far as we knew that hadn't hap-pened yet. Presumably *Theseus* could still do something about the artifact accreting off our bow, assuming we could decide which thing to do. Sarasti wasn't talking. In fact, I couldn't remember the last time any of us had even *seen* the vampire in the flesh. For several shifts now he had confined himself to his tent, speaking only through ConSensus.

Everyone was on edge, and the transient had gone quiet.

Cunningham muttered to himself, stabbed at unfamiliar controls with unpracticed fingers, cursed his own clumsiness. Stimulus and response flowed through lasers across six kilometers of ionized vacuum. The ever-present nicotine stick hung from one corner of his mouth for want of a free hand. Every now and then flecks of ash broke free and drifted obliquely toward the ventilators.

He spoke before I could. "It's all in ConSensus." When I didn't leave he relented, but wouldn't look at me: "Magnetite flecks lined up as soon as they got past the wavefront, more or less. Membranes started to fix themselves. They're not failing as fast. But it's *Rorschach's internal* environment that will be optimized for scrambler metabolism. Out here, I think the most we can do is slow the rate of dying."

"That's something, at least."

Cunningham grunted. "Some of the pieces are coming together. Others—their nerves are frayed, for no good reason. Literally. Signal leakage along the cables."

"Because of their deterioration?" I guessed.

"And I can't get the Arrhenius equation to balance, there's all this nonlinearity at low temperatures. The pre-exponential value's completely fucked up. It's almost as though temperature doesn't *matter,* and— *Shit*—"

Some critical value had exceeded a confidence limit on one of his displays. He glanced up the drum, raised his voice: "Need another biopsy, Susan. Anywhere central."

"What—oh. Just a second." She shook her head and tapped

off a brief spiral of icons, as listless as the captives she commanded. On one of Cunningham's windows Stretch viewed her input with its marvelous sighted skin. It floated unresponsive for a moment. Then it folded back the arms facing one wall, opening a clear path for Cunningham's teleops.

He called two of them from their burrows like prehensile serpents. The first wielded a clinical core-sampler; the second wielded the threat of violence in case of foolish resistance. It was hardly necessary. Blindsighted or not, scramblers were fast learners. Stretch exposed its belly like a victim resigned to imminent rape. Cunningham fumbled; the teleops bumped together, briefly entangled. He cursed and tried again, every move shouting frustration. His extended phenotype had been amputated; once the very ghost in the machine, now he was just another guy punching buttons, and—

—and suddenly, something *clicked*. Cunningham's façades swirled to translucency before my eyes. Suddenly, I could almost *imagine* him.

He got it right the second time. The tip of his machine shot out like a striking snake and darted back again, almost too fast to see. Waves of color flushed from Stretch's injury like ripples chased across still water by a falling stone.

Cunningham must have thought he saw something in my face. "It helps if you try not to think of them as people," he said. And for the very first time I could read the subtext, as clear and sharp as broken glass:

Of course, you don't think of anyone *that way . . .*

Cunningham didn't like to be *played*.

No one does. But most people don't think that's what I'm doing. They don't know how much their bodies betray when they close their mouths. When they speak aloud, it's because they want to confide; when they don't, they think they're keeping their opinions to themselves. I watch them so closely, customize each word so that no system ever feels *used*—and yet for some reason, that didn't work with Robert Cunningham.

I think I was modeling the wrong system.

Imagine you are a Synthesist. You deal in the behavior of systems at their surfaces, infer the machinery *beneath* from its reflections *above*. That is the secret of your success: You understand the system by understanding the boundaries that contain it.

Now imagine you encounter someone who has ripped a hole in those boundaries and bled beyond them.

Robert Cunningham's flesh could not contain him. His duties pulled him beyond the meat sack; here in the Oort, his topology rambled all over the ship. That was true of all of us, to some extent; Bates and her drones, Sarasti and his limbic link—even the ConSensus inlays in our heads *diffused* us a bit, spread us just slightly beyond the confines of our own bodies. But Bates only ran her drones; she never *inhabited* them. The Gang of Four may have run multiple systems on a single motherboard, but each had its own distinct topology and they only surfaced one at a time. And Sarasti—

Well, Sarasti was a whole different story, as it turned out.

Cunningham didn't just operate his remotes; he *escaped* into them, wore them like a secret identity to hide the feeble Human baseline within. He had sacrificed half of his neocortex for the chance to see X-rays and taste the shapes hiding in cell membranes, he had butchered one body to become a fleeting tenant of many. Pieces of him hid in the sensors and manipulators that lined the scramblers' cages; I might have gleaned vital cues from every piece of equipment in the subdrum if I'd ever thought to look. Cunningham was a topological jigsaw like everyone else, but half his pieces were hidden in machinery. My model was incomplete.

I don't think he ever aspired to such a state. Looking back, I see radiant self-loathing on every remembered surface. But there in the waning years of the twenty-first century, the only alternative he could see was the life of a parasite. Cunningham merely chose the lesser evil.

Now, even that was denied him. Sarasti's orders had severed him from his own sensorium. He no longer *felt* the data in his gut; he had to *interpret* it, step by laborious step, through screens and graphs that reduced perception to flat empty shorthand. Here was a system traumatized by multiple amputations. Here was a system with its eyes and ears and tongue cut out, forced to stumble and feel its way around things it had once *inhabited,* right down in the bone. Suddenly there was nowhere else to hide, and all those far-flung pieces of Robert Cunningham tumbled back into his flesh where I could see them at last.

It had been my mistake, all along. I'd been so focused on modeling other systems that I'd forgotten about the one doing the modeling. Bad eyes are only one bane of clear vision: bad assumptions can be just as blinding, and it wasn't enough to imagine I was Robert Cunningham.

I had to imagine I was Siri Keeton as well.

Of course, that only raises another question. If my guess about Cunningham was right, why did my tricks work on Isaac Szpindel? He was every bit as discontinuous as his replacement.

I didn't think about it much at the time. Szpindel was gone but the thing that had killed him was still there, hanging right off the bow, a vast swelling enigma that might choose to squash us at any instant. I was more than a little preoccupied.

Now, though—far too late to do anything about it—I think I might know the answer.

Maybe my tricks didn't work on Isaac, either, not really. Maybe he saw through my manipulations as easily as Cunningham did. But maybe he just didn't care. Maybe I could read him because he *let* me. Which would mean—I can't find another explanation that fits—that he just *liked* me, regardless.

I think that might have made him a friend.

IF I CAN BUT MAKE THE WORDS AWAKE THE FEELING.

—IAN ANDERSON, *STAND UP*

NIGHT SHIFT. NOT a creature was stirring.

Not in *Theseus,* anyway. The Gang hid in their tent. The transient lurked weightless and silent below the surface. Bates was in the bridge—she more or less lived up there now, vigilant and conscientious, nested in camera angles and tactical overlays. There was nowhere she could turn without seeing some aspect of the cipher off our starboard bow. She did what good she could, for the good it would do.

The drum turned quietly, lights dimmed in deference to a diel cycle that a hundred years of tweaks and retrofits hadn't been able to weed from the genes. I sat alone in the galley, squinting from the inside of a system whose outlines grew increasingly hazy, trying to compile my latest—how had Isaac put it?—*postcard to posterity.* Cunningham worked upside-down on the other side of the world.

Except Cunningham wasn't working. He hadn't even moved

for at least four minutes. I'd assumed he was reciting the Kaddish for Szpindel—ConSensus said he'd be doing it twice daily for the next year, if we lived that long—but now, leaning to see around the spinal bundles in the core, I could read his surfaces as clearly as if I'd been sitting beside him. He wasn't bored, or distracted, or even deep in thought.

Robert Cunningham was petrified.

I stood and paced the drum. Ceiling turned into wall; wall into floor. I was close enough to hear his incessant soft muttering, a single indistinct syllable repeated over and over; then I was close enough to hear what he was saying—

"fuck fuck fuck fuck . . ."

—and still Cunningham didn't move, although I'd made no attempt to mask my approach.

Finally, when I was almost at his shoulder, he fell silent.

"You're blind," he said without turning. "Did you know that?"

"I didn't."

"You. Me. Everyone." He interlocked his fingers and *clenched* as if in prayer, hard enough to whiten the knuckles. Only then did I notice: no cigarette.

"Vision's mostly a lie anyway," he continued. "We don't really see anything except a few hi-res degrees where the eye focuses. Everything else is just peripheral blur, just . . . light and motion. Motion draws the focus. And your eyes *jiggle* all the time, did you know that, Keeton? *Saccades,* they're called. Blurs the image, the movement's way too fast for the brain to integrate so your eye just . . . shuts down between pauses. It only grabs these isolated freeze-frames, but your brain edits out the blanks and stitches an . . . an illusion of continuity into your head."

He turned to face me. "And you know what's *really* amazing? If something only moves during the gaps, your brain just . . . ignores it. It's invisible."

I glanced at his workspace. The usual split screen glowed to one side—real-time images of the scramblers in their pens—but histology, ten thousand times larger than life, took center stage. The paradoxical neural architecture of Stretch and Clench glistened on the main window, flensed and labeled and overlaid by circuit diagrams a dozen layers thick. A dense, annotated forest of alien trunks and brambles. It looked a little like *Rorschach* itself.

I couldn't parse any of it.

"Are you listening, Keeton? Do you know what I'm saying?"

"You've figured out why I couldn't— You're saying these things can somehow tell when our eyes are offline, and . . ."

I didn't finish. It just didn't seem possible.

Cunningham shook his head. Something that sounded disturbingly like a giggle escaped his mouth. "I'm saying these things can see your nerves firing from across the room, and integrate that into a crypsis strategy, and then send motor commands to *act* on that strategy, and then send other commands to *stop* the motion before your eyes come back online. All in the time it would take a mammalian nerve impulse to make it halfway from your shoulder to your elbow. These things are *fast,* Keeton. Way faster than we could have guessed even from that high-speed whisper line they were using. They're bloody *superconductors.*"

It took a conscious effort to keep from frowning. "Is that even possible?"

"Every nerve impulse generates an electromagnetic field. That makes it detectable."

"But *Rorschach*'s EM fields are so—I mean, reading the firing of a single optic nerve through all that interference—"

"It's not *interference*. The fields are *part* of them, remember? That's probably how they *do* it."

"So they couldn't do that here."

"You're not *listening*. The trap you set wouldn't have caught anything like that, not unless it *wanted* to be caught. We didn't grab specimens at all. We grabbed *spies*."

Stretch and Clench floated in split screen before us, arms swaying like undulating backbones. Cryptic patterns played slowly across their cuticles.

"Supposing it's just . . . instinct," I suggested. "Flounders hide against their background pretty well, but they don't *think* about it."

"Where are they going to get that instinct *from,* Keeton? How is it going to evolve? Saccades are an accidental glitch in mammalian vision. Where would scramblers have encountered them before now?" Cunningham shook his head. "That thing, that thing Amanda's robot fried—it developed that strategy on its own, *on the spot. It improvised.*"

The word *intelligent* barely encompassed that kind of improvisation. But there was something else in Cunningham's face, some deeper distress nested inside what he'd already told me.

"What?" I asked.

"It was *stupid,*" he said. "The things these creatures can do, it was just *dumb.*"

"How do you mean?"

"Well, it didn't work, did it? Couldn't keep it up in front of more than one or two of us."

Because people's eyes don't flicker in sync, I realized. Too many witnesses stripped it of cover.

"—many *other* things it could have done," Cunningham was saying. "They could've induced Anton's or, or an agnosia: then we could have tripped over a whole herd of scramblers and it wouldn't even register in our conscious minds. Agnosias happen by *accident,* for God's sake. If you've got the senses and reflexes to hide between someone's saccades, why stop there? Why not do something that *really* works?"

"Why do you think?" I asked, reflexively nondirective.

"I think that first one was— You know it was a juvenile, right? Maybe it was just inexperienced. Maybe it was *stupid,* and it made a bad decision. I think we're dealing with a species so far beyond us that even their retarded *children* can rewire our brains on the fly, and I can't tell you how fucking scared that should make you."

I could see it in his topology. I could hear it in his voice. His nerveless face remained as calm as a corpse.

"We should just kill them now," he said.

"Well, if they're spies, they can't have learned much. They've been in those cages the whole time, except—" *for the way up.* They'd been right next to us the whole trip back . . .

"These things live and breathe EM. Even stunted, even isolated, who knows how much of our tech they could have just read through the *walls?*"

"You've got to tell Sarasti," I said.

"Oh, Sarasti knows. Why do you think he wouldn't let them go?"

"He never said anything about—"

"He'd be *crazy* to fill us in. He keeps sending you *down* there, remember? Do you think for a second he'd tell you what he knows and then set you loose in a labyrinth full of mind-reading minotaurs? He knows, and he's already got it factored a thousand ways to Sunday." Keeton's eyes were bright manic points blazing in an expressionless mask. He raised them to the center of the drum, and didn't raise his voice a decibel. "Isn't that right, Jukka?"

I checked ConSensus for active channels. "I don't think he's listening, Robert."

Cunningham's mouth moved in something that would have

been a pitying smile if the rest of his face had been able to join in. "He doesn't have to *listen,* Keeton. He doesn't have to spy on us. He just *knows.*"

Ventilators, breathing. The almost subliminal hum of bearings in motion. Then Sarasti's disembodied voice rang forth through the drum.

"Everyone to Commons. Robert wants to share."

Cunningham sat to my right, his plastic face lit from beneath by the conference table. He stared down into that light, rocking slightly. His lips went through the ongoing motions of some inaudible incantation. The Gang sat across from us. To my left Bates kept one eye on the proceedings and another on intelligence from the front lines.

Sarasti was with us only in spirit. His place at the head of the table remained empty. "Tell them," he said.

"We have to get out of h—"

"From the *beginning.*"

Cunningham swallowed and started again. "Those frayed motor nerves I couldn't figure out, those pointless cross-connections— they're logic gates. Scramblers *time-share.* Their sensory and motor plexii double as associative neurons during idle time, so every part of the system can be used for cognition when it isn't otherwise engaged. Nothing like it ever evolved on Earth. It means they can do a great deal of processing without a lot of dedicated associative mass, even for an individual."

"So peripheral nerves can think?" Bates frowned. "Can they *remember?*"

"Certainly. At least, I don't see why not." Cunningham pulled a cigarette from his pocket.

"So when they tore that scrambler apart—"

"Not civil war. Data dump. Passing information about *us,* most likely."

"Pretty radical way to carry on a conversation," Bates remarked.

"It wouldn't be their first choice. I think each scrambler acts as a node in a distributed network, when they're in *Rorschach* at least. But those fields would be configured down to the Angstrom, and when we go in with our tech and our shielding and blowing *holes* in their conductors—we bollocks up the network. Jam the local signal. So they resort to a sneakernet."

He had not lit his cigarette. He rolled the filtered end between thumb and forefinger. His tongue flickered between his lips like a worm behind a mask.

Hidden in his tent, Sarasti took up the slack. "Scramblers also use *Rorschach*'s EM for metabolic processes. Some pathways achieve proton transfer via heavy-atom tunneling. Perhaps the ambient radiation acts as a catalyst."

"Tunneling?" Susan said. "As in *quantum?"*

Cunningham nodded. "Which also explains your shielding problems. Partly, at least."

"But is that even *possible?* I mean, I thought those kind of effects only showed up under cryonic—"

"Forget this," Cunningham blurted. "We can debate the biochemistry later, if we're still alive."

"What do we debate instead, Robert?" Sarasti said smoothly.

"For starters, the *dumbest* of these things can look into your head and see what parts of your visual cortex are lighting up. And if there's a difference between that and mind reading, it's not much of one."

"As long as we stay out of *Rorschach*—"

"That ship has *sailed.* You people have already *been* there.

Repeatedly. Who knows what you already did down there for no better reason than because *Rorschach made* you?"

"Wait a second," Bates objected. "None of us were *puppets* down there. We hallucinated and we went blind and—and crazy even, but we were never *possessed*."

Cunningham looked at her and snorted. "You think you'd be able to fight the strings? You think you'd even *feel* them? I could apply a transcranial magnet to your head right now and you'd raise your middle finger or wiggle your toes or kick Siri here in the sack and then swear on your sainted mother's grave that you only did it because you *wanted* to. You'd dance like a puppet and all the time swear you were doing it of your own free will, and that's just *me,* that's just some borderline OCD with a couple of magnets and an MRI helmet." He waved at the vast unknowable void beyond the bulkhead. Shreds of mangled cigarette floated sideways in front of him. "Do you want to guess what *that* can do? For all we know we've already given them *Theseus*'s technical specs, warned them about the Icarus Array, and then just decided *of our own free will* to forget it all."

"*We* can cause those effects," Sarasti said coolly. "As you say. Strokes cause them. Tumors. Random accidents."

"*Random?* Those were *experiments,* people! That was *vivisection*! They let you in so they could take you apart and see what made you tick and you never even *knew* it."

"*So what?*" the vampire snapped invisibly. Something cold and hungry had edged into his voice. Human topologies shivered around the table, skittish.

"There's a blind spot in the center of your visual field," Sarasti pointed out. "You can't see it. You can't see the saccades in your visual timestream. Just two of the tricks you *know* about. Many others."

Cunningham was nodding. "That's my whole *point*. *Rorschach* could be—"

"Not talking about case studies. Brains are survival engines, not truth detectors. If self-deception promotes fitness, the brain lies. Stops noticing—irrelevant things. Truth never matters. Only fitness. By now you don't experience the world as it exists at all. You experience a simulation built from assumptions. Shortcuts. *Lies*. Whole *species* is agnosiac by default. *Rorschach* does nothing to you that you don't already do to yourselves."

Nobody spoke. It was several silent seconds before I realized what had happened.

Jukka Sarasti had just given us a pep talk.

He could have shut down Cunningham's tirade—could have probably shut down a full-scale mutiny—by just sailing into our midst and baring his teeth. By *looking* at us. But he wasn't trying to frighten us into submission, we were already nervous enough. And he wasn't trying to educate us, either, fight fear with fact; the more *facts* any sane person gathered about *Rorschach,* the more fearful they'd become. Sarasti was only trying to keep us *functional,* lost in space on the edge of our lives, facing down this monstrous enigma that might destroy us at any instant for any reason. Sarasti was trying to calm us down: *good meat, nice meat.* He was trying to keep us from falling apart. *There, there.*

Sarasti was practicing *psychology.*

I looked around the table. Bates and Cunningham and the Gang sat still and bloodless.

Sarasti sucked at it.

"We have to get out of here," Cunningham said. "These things are way beyond us."

"We've shown more aggression than they have," James said, but there was no confidence in her voice.

"*Rorschach* plays those rocks like marbles. We're sitting in the middle of a shooting gallery. Any time it feels like—"

"It's still growing. It's not finished."

"That's supposed to *reassure* me?"

"All I'm saying is, we don't *know*," James said. "We could have years yet. Centuries."

"We have fifteen days," Sarasti announced.

"Oh *shit*," someone said. Cunningham, probably. Maybe Sascha.

For some reason everyone was looking at me.

Fifteen days. Who knows what had gone into that number? None of us asked aloud. Maybe Sarasti, in another fit of inept psychology, had made it up on the spur of the moment. Or maybe he'd derived it before we'd even reached orbit, held it back against the possibility—only now expired—that he might yet send us back into the labyrinth. I'd been half blind for half the mission; I didn't know.

But one way or another, we had our graduation day.

The coffins lay against the rear bulkhead of the crypt—on what would be the floor during those moments when *up* and *down* held any meaning. We'd slept for years on the way out. We'd had no awareness of time's passage—undead metabolism is far too sluggish even to support dreams—but somehow the body knew when it needed a change. Not one of us had chosen to sleep in our pods once we'd arrived. The only times we'd done so had been on pain of death.

But the Gang had taken to coming here ever since Szpindel had died.

His body rested in the pod next to mine. I coasted into the compartment and turned left without thinking. Five coffins:

four open and emptied, one sealed. The mirrored bulkhead opposite doubled their number and the depth of the compartment.

But the Gang wasn't there.

I turned right. The body of Susan James floated back-to-back with her own reflection, staring at an inverse tableau: three sealed sarcophagi, one open. The ebony plaque set into the retracted lid was dark; the others shone with identical sparse mosaics of blue and green stars. None of them changed. There were no scrolling ECGs, no luminous peak-and-valley tracings marked CARDIO or CNS. We could wait here for hours, days, and none of those diodes would so much as twinkle. When you're undead, the emphasis is on the second syllable.

The Gang's topology had said *Michelle* when I'd first arrived, but it was *Susan* who spoke now, without turning. "I never met her."

I followed her gaze to the name tag on one of the sealed pods: TAKAMATSU. The other linguist, the other multiple.

"I met everyone else," Susan continued. "Trained with them. But I never met my own replacement."

They discouraged it. What would have been the point?

"If you want to—" I began.

She shook her head. "Thanks anyway."

"Or any of the others—I can only imagine what Michelle—"

Susan smiled, but there was something cold about it. "Michelle doesn't really want to talk to you right now, Siri."

"Ah." I hesitated for a moment, to give anyone else a chance to speak up. When nobody did, I pushed myself back toward the hatch. "Well, if any of you change—"

"No. None of us. *Ever.*"

Cruncher.

"You *lie,*" he continued. "I see it. We all do."

I blinked. "Lie? No, I—"

"You don't *talk*. You *listen*. You don't care about Michelle. Don't care about anyone. You just want what we *know*. For your *reports*."

"That's not entirely true, Cruncher. I do care. I know Michelle must—"

"You don't know *shit*. Go away."

"I'm sorry I upset you." I rolled on my axis and braced against the mirror.

"You *can't* know Meesh," he growled as I pushed off. "You never *lost* anyone. You never *had* anyone.

"You leave her alone."

He was wrong on both counts. And at least Szpindel had died knowing that Michelle cared for him.

Chelsea died thinking I just didn't give a shit.

It had been two years or more, and while we still interfaced occasionally we hadn't met in the flesh since the day she'd left. She came at me from right out of the Oort, sent an urgent voice message to my inlays: *Cygnus. Please call NOW. It's important.*

It was the first time since I'd known her that she'd ever blanked the optics.

I knew it was important. I knew it was bad, even without picture. I knew *because* there was no picture, and I could tell it was worse than bad from the harmonics in her voice. I could tell it was lethal.

I found out afterward that she'd gotten caught in the crossfire. The Realists had sown a fibrodysplasia variant outside the Boston catacombs; an easy tweak, a single-point retroviral whose results served both as an act of terrorism and an ironic commentary on the frozen paralysis of Heaven's occupants. It rewrote a regulatory gene controlling ossification on chromosome 4, and rigged a metabolic bypass at three loci on 17.

Chelsea started growing a new skeleton. Her joints were calcifying within fifteen hours of exposure, her ligaments and tendons within twenty. By then they were starving her at the cellular level, trying to slow the bug by depriving it of metabolites, but they could only buy time and not much of it. Twenty-three hours in, her striated muscles were turning to stone.

I didn't find this out immediately, because I didn't call her back. I didn't need to know the details. I could tell from her voice that she was dying. Obviously she wanted to say good-bye.

I couldn't talk to her until I knew how to do that.

I spent hours scouring the noosphere, looking for precedents. There's no shortage of ways to die; I found millions of case records dealing with the etiquette. Last words, last vows, instruction manuals for the soon-to-bereaved. Palliative neuropharm. Extended and expository death scenes in popular fiction. I went through it all, assigned a dozen front-line filters to separate heat from light.

By the time she called again the news was out: acute Golem outbreak lancing like a white-hot needle through the heart of Boston. Containment measures holding. Heaven secure. Modest casualties expected. Names of victims withheld pending notification of kin.

I still didn't know the principles, the *rules*: all I had were examples. Last wills and testaments; the negotiation of jumpers with their would-be rescuers; diaries recovered from imploded submarines or lunar crash sites. Recorded memoirs and deathbed confessions rattling into flatline. Black box transcripts of doomed spaceships and falling beanstalks, ending in fire and static. All of it relevant. None of it useful; none of it *her*.

She called again, and still the optics were blank, and still I didn't answer.

But the last time she called, she didn't spare me the view.

They'd made her as comfortable as possible. The gelpad conformed to every twisted limb, every erupting spur of bone. They would not have left her in any pain.

Her neck had torqued down and to the side as it petrified, left her staring at the twisted claw that had once been her right hand. Her knuckles were the size of walnuts. Plates and ribbons of ectopic bone distended the skin of her arms and shoulders, buried her ribs in a fibrous mat of calcified flesh.

Movement was its own worst enemy. Golem punished even the slightest twitch, provoked the growth of fresh bone along any joints and surfaces conspiring to motion. Each hinge and socket had its own nonrenewable ration of flexibility, carved in stone; every movement depleted the account. The body seized incrementally. By the time she let me look at her, Chelsea had almost exhausted her degrees of freedom.

"Cyg," she slurred. "Know you're there."

Her jaw was locked half-open; her tongue must have stiffened with every word. She did not look at the camera. She could not look at the camera.

"Guess I know why you're not answ'ring. I'll try'nt—*try not* to take it pers'n'lly."

Ten thousand deathbed good-byes arrayed around me, a million more within reach. What was I supposed to do, pick one at random? Stitch them into some kind of composite? All these words had been for other people. Grafting them onto Chelsea would reduce them to clichés, to trite platitudes. To insults.

"Want t'say, don' feel bad. I know y're just—'s'not your fault, I guess. You'd pick up if you could."

And say what? What do you say to someone who's dying in fast-forward before your eyes?

"Just keep trying t'connect, y'know. Can't help m'self . . ."

Although the essentials of this farewell are accurate, details from several deaths have been combined for dramatic purposes.

"Please? Jus'—talk to me, Cyg . . ."

More than anything, I wanted to.

"Siri, I . . . just . . ."

I'd spent all this time trying to figure out *how*.

"Forget't," she said, and disconnected.

I whispered something into the dead air. I don't even remember what.

I really wanted to talk to her.

I just couldn't find an algorithm that fit.

> YE SHALL KNOW THE TRUTH, AND THE TRUTH SHALL MAKE YOU MAD.
>
> —ALDOUS HUXLEY

THEY'D HOPED, BY now, to have banished sleep forever.

The waste was nothing short of obscene: a third of every Human life spent with its strings cut, insensate, the body burning fuel but not *producing*. Think of all we could accomplish if we didn't have to lapse into unconsciousness every fifteen hours or so, if our minds could stay awake and alert from the moment of infancy to that final curtain call a hundred and twenty years later. Think of eight billion souls with no off switch and no down time until the very chassis wore out.

Why, we could go to the stars.

It hadn't worked out that way. Even if we'd outgrown the need to stay quiet and hidden during the dark hours—the only predators left were those we'd brought back ourselves—the brain still needed time apart from the world outside. Experiences had to be catalogued and filed, midterm memories promoted to long-term ones, free radicals swept from their hiding places among the dendrites. We had only reduced the need for sleep, not eliminated it—and that incompressible residue of downtime seemed barely able to contain the dreams and phantoms left behind. They squirmed in my head like creatures in a draining tidal pool.

I woke.

I was alone, weightless, in the center of my tent. I could have sworn something had tapped me on the back. Leftover hallucination, I thought. A lingering aftereffect of the haunted mansion, going for one last bit of gooseflesh en route to extinction.

But it happened again. I bumped against the keelward curve of the bubble, bumped again, head and shoulder blades against fabric; the rest of me came after, moving gently but irresistibly—

Down.

Theseus was accelerating.

No. Wrong direction. *Theseus* was *rolling,* like a harpooned whale at the surface of the sea. Turning her belly to the stars.

I brought up ConSensus and threw a Nav-tac summary against the wall. A luminous point erupted from the outline of our ship, crawled away from Big Ben leaving a bright filament etched in its wake. I watched until the numbers read *15G.*

"Siri. My quarters, please."

I jumped. It sounded as though the vampire had been at my very shoulder.

"Coming."

An ampsat relay, climbing at long last to an intercept with the Icarus antimatter stream. Somewhere behind the call of duty, my heart sank.

We weren't running, Robert Cunningham's fondest wishes notwithstanding. *Theseus* was stockpiling ordinance.

The open hatch gaped like a cave in the face of a cliff. The pale blue light from the spine couldn't seem to reach inside. Sarasti was barely more than a silhouette, black on gray, his bright bloody eyes reflecting catlike in the surrounding gloom.

"Come." He amped up the shorter wavelengths in deference to human vision. The interior of the bubble brightened, although the light remained slightly red-shifted. Like *Rorschach* with high beams.

I floated into Sarasti's parlor. His face, normally paper-white, was so flushed it looked sunburned. *He gorged himself,* I couldn't help thinking. *He drank deep.* But all that blood was his own. Usually he kept it deep in the flesh, favoring the vital organs. Vampires were efficient that way. They only washed out their peripheral tissues occasionally, when lactate levels got too high.

Or when they were hunting.

He had a needle to his throat, injected himself with three cc's of clear liquid as I watched. His anti-Euclideans. I wondered how often he had to replenish them, now that he'd lost faith in the implants. He withdrew the needle and slipped it into a sheath geckoed to a convenient strut. His color drained as I watched, sinking back to the core, leaving his skin waxy and corpselike.

"You're here as official observer," Sarasti said.

I observed. His quarters were even more spartan than mine. No personal effects to speak of. No custom coffin lined with shrink-wrapped soil. Nothing but two jumpsuits, a pouch for toiletries, and a disconnected fiberop umbilicus half as thick as my little finger, floating like a roundworm in formalin. Sarasti's hardline to the Captain. Not even a cortical jack, I remembered. It plugged into the medulla, the brainstem. That was logical enough; that was where all the neural cabling converged, the point of greatest bandwidth. Still, it was a disquieting thought— that Sarasti linked to the ship through the brain of a reptile.

An image flared on the wall, subtly distorted against the concave surface: Stretch and Clench in their adjoining cells, rendered in split screen. Cryptic vitals defaced little grids below each image.

The distortion distracted me. I looked for a corrected feed in ConSensus, came up empty. Sarasti read my expression: "Closed circuit."

By now the scramblers would have seemed sick and ragged even to a virgin audience. They floated near the middle of their respective compartments, segmented arms drifting aimlessly back and forth. Membranous patches of—skin, I suppose— were peeling from the cuticles, giving them a fuzzy, decomposing aspect.

"The arms move continuously," Sarasti remarked. "Robert says it assists in circulation."

I nodded, watching the display.

"Creatures that move between stars can't even perform basic metabolic functions without constant flailing." He shook his head. "Inefficient. Primitive."

I glanced at the vampire. He remained fixed on our captives.

"Obscene," he said, and moved his fingers.

A new window opened on the wall: the Rosetta protocol, initializing. Kilometers away, microwaves flooded the holding tanks.

I reminded myself: *No interference. Only observation.*

However weakened their condition, the scramblers were not yet indifferent to pain. They knew the game, they knew the rules; they dragged themselves to their respective panels and played for mercy. Sarasti had simply invoked a step-by-step replay of some previous sequence. The scramblers went through it all again, buying a few moments' intermittent respite with the same old proofs and theorems.

Sarasti clicked, then spoke: "They regenerate these solutions faster than they do before. Do you think they're acclimated to the microwaves?"

Another readout appeared on the display; an audio alarm began chirping somewhere nearby. I looked at Sarasti, and back at the readout: a solid circle of turquoise backlit by a pulsing red halo. The shape meant *atmospheric anomaly*. The color meant *oxygen*.

I felt a moment of confusion—*Oxygen? Why would oxygen set off the alarm?*—until I remembered: Scramblers were *anaerobes*.

Sarasti muted the alarm with a wave of his hand.

I cleared my throat: "You're *poisoning*—"

"Watch. Performance is consistent. No change."

I swallowed. *Just observe.*

"Is this an execution?" I asked. "Is this a, a mercy killing?"

Sarasti looked past me, and smiled. "No."

I dropped my eyes. "What, then?"

He pointed at the display. I turned, reflexively obedient.

Something stabbed my hand like a spike at a crucifixion.

I screamed. Electric pain jolted to my shoulder. I yanked my hand back without thinking; the embedded blade split its flesh like a fin through water. Blood sprayed into the air and stayed there, a comet's tail of droplets tracing the frenzied arc of my hand.

Sudden scalding heat from behind. Flesh charred on my

back. I screamed again, flailing. A veil of bloody droplets swirled in the air.

Somehow I was in the corridor, staring dumbly at my right hand. It had been split to the heel of the palm, flopped at the end of my wrist in two bloody, bifingered chunks. Blood welled from the torn edges and wouldn't fall. Sarasti advanced through a haze of trauma and confusion. His face swam in and out of focus, rich with his blood or mine. His eyes were bright red mirrors, his eyes were time machines. Darkness roared around them and it was half a million years ago and I was just another piece of meat on the African savannah, a split second from having its throat torn out.

"Do you see the problem?" Sarasti asked, advancing. A great spider crab hovered at his shoulder. I forced focus through the pain: one of Bates's grunts, taking aim. I kicked blindly, hit the ladder through sheer happenstance, careened backward down the corridor.

The vampire came after me, his face split into something that would have been a smile on anyone else. "Conscious of pain, you're *distracted* by pain. You're *fixated* on it. Obsessed by the one threat, you miss the other."

I flailed. Crimson mist stung my eyes.

"So much more *aware,* so much less *perceptive.* An automaton could do better."

He's snapped, I thought. *He's insane.* And then, *No, he's a transient. He's always been a transient—*

"*They* could do better," he said softly.

—and he's been hiding for days. Deep down. Hiding from the seals.

What else *would he do?*

Sarasti raised his hands, fading in and out of focus. I hit

something, kicked without aiming, bounced away through swirling mist and startled voices. Metal cracked the back of my head and spun me around.

A hole, a burrow. A place to hide. I dove through, my torn hand flapping like a dead fish against the edge of the hatch. I cried out and tumbled into the drum, the monster at my heels.

Startled shouts, very close now. "This wasn't the plan, Jukka! *This wasn't the goddamned plan!*" That was Susan James, full of outrage, while Amanda Bates snarled *"Stand down, right fucking now!"* and leapt from the deck to do battle. She rose through the air, all overclocked reflexes and carboplatinum augments but Sarasti just batted her aside and kept on coming. His arm shot out like a striking snake. His hand clamped around my throat.

"Is this what you meant?" James cried from some dark irrelevant hiding place. "Is this your *preconditioning?*"

Sarasti *shook* me. "Are you *in* there, Keeton?"

My blood splattered across his face like rain. I babbled and cried.

"Are you *listening?* Can you *see?*"

And suddenly I could. Suddenly everything clicked into focus. Sarasti wasn't talking at all. Sarasti didn't even exist anymore. Nobody did. I was alone in a great spinning wheel surrounded by things that were made out of meat, things that moved *all by themselves.* Some of them were wrapped in pieces of cloth. Strange nonsensical sounds came from holes at their top ends, and there were *other* things up there, bumps and ridges and something like marbles or black buttons, wet and shiny and embedded in the slabs of meat. They glistened and jiggled and moved as if trying to escape.

I didn't understand the sounds the meat was making, but I heard a voice from somewhere. It was like God talking, and that I couldn't *help* but understand.

"Get out of your *room,* Keeton," it hissed. "Stop *transposing* or *interpolating* or *rotating* or whatever it is you do. Just *listen.* For once in your goddamned life, *understand* something. Understand that your life depends on it. Are you *listening,* Keeton?"

And I cannot tell you what it said. I can only tell you what I heard.

You invest so much in it, don't you? It's what elevates you above the beasts of the field, it's what makes you *special.* Homo *sapiens,* you call yourself. Wise Man. Do you even know what it *is,* this *consciousness* you cite in your own exaltation? Do you even know what it's *for?*

Maybe you think it gives you free will. Maybe you've forgotten that sleepwalkers converse, drive vehicles, commit crimes and clean up afterward, unconscious the whole time. Maybe nobody's told you that even *waking* souls are only slaves in denial.

Make a conscious choice. *Decide* to move your index finger. Too late! The electricity's already halfway down your arm. Your body began to act a full half-second before your conscious self "chose" to, for the self chose nothing; something *else* set your body in motion, sent an executive summary—almost an afterthought—to the homunculus behind your eyes. That little man, that arrogant subroutine that thinks of itself as *the* person, mistakes correlation for causality: It reads the summary and it sees the hand move, and it thinks that one drove the other.

But it's not in charge. *You're* not in charge. If free will even exists, it doesn't share living space with the likes of you.

Insight, then. Wisdom. The quest for knowledge, the derivation of theorems, science and technology and all those exclusively *Human* pursuits that must surely rest on a conscious foundation. Maybe *that's* what sentience would be for—if scientific breakthroughs didn't spring fully formed from the *sub*conscious mind, manifest themselves in dreams, as full-blown insights after a deep night's sleep. It's the most basic rule of the stymied researcher: *stop thinking about the problem.* Do something else. It will come to you if you just stop being *conscious* of it.

Every concert pianist knows that the surest way to ruin a performance is to be aware of what the fingers are doing. Every dancer and acrobat knows enough to let the mind *go,* let the body run itself. Every driver of any manual vehicle arrives at destinations with no recollection of the stops and turns and roads traveled in getting there. You are all sleepwalkers, whether climbing creative peaks or slogging through some mundane routine for the thousandth time. You are all sleepwalkers.

Don't even *try* to talk about the learning curve. Don't bother citing the months of deliberate practice that precede the unconscious performance, or the years of study and experiment leading up to the gift-wrapped eureka moment. So what if *your* lessons are all learned consciously? Do you think that proves there's no other way? Heuristic software's been learning from experience for over a hundred years. Machines master chess, cars learn to drive themselves, statistical programs face problems and design the experiments to solve them and you think that the only path to learning leads through *sentience?* You're Stone Age nomads, eking out some marginal existence on the veldt—denying even the possibility of agriculture, because hunting and gathering was good enough for your parents.

Do you want to know what consciousness is for? Do you want to know the only *real* purpose it serves? Training wheels. You can't see both aspects of the Necker cube at once, so it lets you focus on one and dismiss the other. That's a pretty half-assed way to parse reality. You're always better off looking at more than one side of *anything*. Go on, try. Defocus. It's the next logical step.

Oh, but you can't. There's something in the way.

And it's fighting back.

Evolution has no foresight. Complex machinery develops its own agendas. Brains—cheat. Feedback loops evolve to promote stable heartbeats and then stumble upon the temptation of rhythm and music. The rush evoked by fractal imagery, the algorithms used for habitat selection, metastasize into art. Thrills that once had to be *earned* in increments of fitness can now be had from pointless introspection. Aesthetics rise unbidden from a trillion dopamine receptors, and the system moves beyond modeling the organism. It begins to model the very *process* of modeling. It consumes ever-more computational resources, bogs itself down with endless re-cursion and irrelevant simulations. Like the parasitic DNA that accretes in every natural genome, it persists and proliferates and produces nothing but itself. Metaprocesses bloom like cancer, and awaken, and call themselves *I*.

The system weakens, slows. It takes so much longer now to *per-ceive*—to assess the input, mull it over, *decide* in the manner of cognitive beings. But when the flash flood crosses your path, when the lion leaps at you from the grasses, advanced self-awareness is an unaffordable indulgence. The brain stem does its best. It sees the danger, hijacks the body, reacts a hundred times faster than that fat old man sitting in the CEO's office upstairs; but every generation it gets harder to work around this—this creaking neurological bureaucracy.

I wastes energy and processing power, self-obsesses to the point of psychosis. Scramblers have no need of it, scramblers are more parsimonious. With simpler biochemistries, with smaller brains—deprived of tools, of their ship, even of parts of their own metabolism—they think rings around you. They hide their language in plain sight, even when you know what they're saying. They turn your own cognition against itself. *They travel between the stars.* This is what intelligence can do, unhampered by self-awareness.

I is not the working mind, you see. For Amanda Bates to say "I do not exist" would be nonsense; but when the processes beneath say the same thing, they are merely reporting that the parasites have died. They are only saying that they are free.

> IF THE HUMAN BRAIN WERE SO SIMPLE THAT WE COULD UNDERSTAND IT, WE WOULD BE SO SIMPLE THAT WE COULDN'T.
>
> —EMERSON M. PUGH

SARASTI, YOU BLOODSUCKER.

My knees pressed against my forehead. I hugged my folded legs as though clinging to a branch over a chasm.

You vicious asshole. You foul sadistic monster.

My breath rasped loud and mechanical. It nearly drowned out the blood roaring in my ears.

You tore me apart, you made me piss and shit myself and I cried like some gutted baby and you stripped me naked, you fucking thing, you night crawler, you broke my tools, you took away anything I ever had that let me touch anyone *and you* didn't have to *you baby-fucker, it wasn't necessary but you knew that, didn't you? You just wanted to play. I've seen your kind at it before, cats toying with mice, catch and release, a taste of freedom and then pouncing again, biting, not hard enough to kill—* not just yet—*before you let them loose again and they're hobbling now, maybe a leg snapped or a gash in the belly but they're still* trying, *still running or crawling or drag-ging themselves as fast as they can until you're on them* again, *and* again *because it's* fun, *because it gives you* pleasure *you sadistic piece of shit. You send us into the arms of that hellish thing and it plays with us too, and maybe you're even working together because it let me escape just like you do, it let me run right back into your arms and then you strip me down to some raw half-brained defense-less* animal, *I can't rotate or transform I can't even* talk *and you—*

You—

It wasn't even personal, was it? You don't even hate me. You were just sick of keeping it all in, sick of restraining yourself with all this meat, and nobody else could be spared from their jobs. This was my job, wasn't it? Not synthesist, not conduit. Not even cannon fodder or decoy duty. I'm just something disposable to sharpen your claws on.

I hurt so much. It hurt just to breathe.

I was so *alone.*

Webbing pressed against the curve of my back, bounced me forward gently as a breeze, caught me again. I was back in my tent. My right hand itched. I tried to flex the fingers, but they were embedded in amber. Left hand reached for right, and found a plastic carapace extending to the elbow.

I opened my eyes. Darkness. Meaningless numbers and a red LED twinkled from somewhere along my forearm.

I didn't remember coming here. I didn't remember anyone fixing me.

Breaking. Being broken. That's what I remembered. I wanted to die. I wanted to just stay curled up until I withered away.

After an age, I forced myself to uncoil. I steadied myself, let some miniscule inertia bump me against the taut insulated fabric of my tent. I waited for my breathing to steady. It seemed to take hours.

I called ConSensus to the wall, and a feed from the drum. Soft voices, harsh light flaring against the wall: hurting my eyes, peeling them raw. I killed visual, and listened to words in the darkness.

"—a phase?" someone asked.

Susan James, her personhood restored. I knew her again: not a meat sack, no longer a *thing*.

"We *have* been over this." That was Cunningham. I knew him, too. I knew them all. Whatever Sarasti had done to me, however far he'd yanked me from my room, I'd somehow fallen back inside.

It should have mattered more.

"—because for one thing, if it were really so pernicious, natural selection would have weeded it out," James was saying.

"You have a naïve understanding of evolutionary processes. There's no such thing as *survival of the fittest. Survival of the most adequate*, maybe. It doesn't matter whether a solution's optimal. All that matters is whether it beats the alternatives."

I knew that voice, too. It belonged to a demon.

"Well, *we* damn well *beat the alternatives.*" Some subtle overdubbed harmonic in James's voice suggested a chorus: the whole Gang, rising as one in opposition.

I couldn't believe it. I'd just been mutilated, beaten before their eyes—and they were talking about *biology?*

Maybe she's afraid to talk about anything else, I thought. *Maybe she's afraid she might be next.*

Or maybe she just couldn't care less what happens to me.

"It's true," Sarasti told her, "that your intellect makes up for your self-awareness to some extent. But you're flightless birds on a remote island. You're not so much successful as *isolated* from any real competition."

No more clipped speech patterns. No more terse phrasing. The transient had made his kill, found his release. Now he didn't care *who* knew he was around.

"You?" Michelle whispered. "Not *we*?"

"*We* stop racing long ago," the demon said at last. "It's not our fault you don't leave it at that."

"Ah." Cunningham again. "Welcome back. Did you look in on Ke—"

"No," Bates said.

"Satisfied?" the demon asked.

"If you mean the grunts, I'm satisfied you're out of them," Bates said. "If you mean— It was completely unwarranted, Jukka."

"It isn't."

"You assaulted a crewmember. If we had a brig you'd be in it for the rest of the trip."

"This isn't a military vessel, Major. You're not in charge."

I didn't need a visual feed to know what Bates thought of that. But there was something else in her silence, something that made me bring the drum camera back online. I squinted against the corrosive light, brought down the brightness until all that remained was a faint whisper of pastels.

Yes. Bates. Stepping off the stairway onto the deck.

"Grab a chair," Cunningham said from his seat in the Commons. "It's golden oldies time."

There was something about her.

"I'm sick of that song," Bates said. "We've played it to death."

Even now, my tools chipped and battered, my perceptions barely more than baseline, I could see the change. This torture of prisoners, this assault upon crew, had crossed a line in her head. The others wouldn't see it. The lid on her affect was tight as a boilerplate. But even through the dim shadows of my window the topology glowed around her like neon.

Amanda Bates was no longer merely *considering* a change of command. Now it was only a matter of when.

The universe was closed and concentric.

My tiny refuge lay in its center. Outside that shell was another, ruled by a monster, patrolled by his lackeys. Beyond that was another still, containing something even more monstrous and incomprehensible, something that might soon devour us all.

There was nothing else. Earth was a vague hypothesis, irrelevant to this pocket cosmos. I saw no place into which it might fit.

I stayed in the center of the universe for a long time, hiding. I kept the lights off. I didn't eat. I crept from my tent only to piss or shit in the cramped head down at Fab, and only when the spine was deserted. A field of painful blisters rose across my flash-burned back, as densely packed as kernels on a corncob. The slightest abrasion tore them open.

Nobody tapped at my door, nobody called my name through ConSensus. I wouldn't have answered if they had. Maybe they knew that, somehow. Maybe they kept their distance out of respect for my privacy and my disgrace.

Maybe they just didn't give a shit.

I peeked outside now and then, kept an eye on Tactical. I saw *Scylla* and *Charybdis* climb into the accretion belt and return towing captured reaction mass in a great distended mesh between them. I watched our ampsat reach its destination in the middle of nowhere, saw antimatter's quantum blueprints stream down into *Theseus*'s buffers. Mass and specs combined in Fab, topped up our reserves, forged the tools that Jukka Sarasti needed for his master plan, whatever that was.

Maybe he'd lose. Maybe *Rorschach* would kill us all, but not before it had played with Sarasti the way Sarasti had played with me. That would almost make it worthwhile. Or maybe Bates's mutiny would come first, and succeed. Maybe she would slay the monster, and commandeer the ship, and take us all to safety.

But then I remembered: The universe was closed, and so very small. There was really nowhere else to go.

I put my ear to feeds throughout the ship. I heard routine instructions from the predator, murmured conversations among the prey. I took in only sound, never sight; a video feed would have spilled light into my tent, left me naked and exposed. So I listened in the darkness as the others spoke among themselves. It didn't happen often anymore. Perhaps too much had been said already, perhaps there was nothing left to do but mind the countdown. Sometimes hours would pass with no more than a cough or a grunt.

When they did speak, they never mentioned my name. Only once did I hear any of them even hint at my existence.

That was Cunningham, talking to Sascha about zombies. I heard them in the galley over breakfast, unusually talkative. Sascha hadn't been let out for a while, and was making up for lost time. Cunningham let her, for reasons of his own. Maybe his fears had been soothed somehow, maybe Sarasti had revealed his master plan. Or maybe Cunningham simply craved distraction from the imminence of the enemy.

"It doesn't *bug* you?" Sascha was saying. "Thinking that your mind, the very thing that makes you *you*, is nothing but some kind of parasite?"

"Forget about *minds*," he told her. "Say you've got a device designed to monitor—oh, cosmic rays, say. What happens when you turn its sensor around so it's not pointing at the sky anymore, but at its own guts?" He answered himself before she could: "It does what it's built to. It measures cosmic rays, even though it's not looking at them anymore. It parses its own circuitry in terms of cosmic-ray metaphors, because those *feel* right, because they feel natural, because it can't look at things any other way. But it's the *wrong metaphor*. So the system misunderstands everything about itself. Maybe that's not a grand and glorious evolutionary leap after all. Maybe it's just a design flaw."

"But *you're* the biologist. You know Mom was right better'n anyone. Brain's a big glucose hog. Everything it does costs through the nose."

"True enough," Cunningham admitted.

"So sentience has gotta be *good* for something, then. Because it's *expensive*, and if it sucks up energy without doing anything useful then evolution's gonna weed it out just like *that*."

"Maybe it did." He paused long enough to chew food or suck smoke. "Chimpanzees are smarter than orangutans, did you know that? Higher encephalization quotient. Yet they can't always recognize themselves in a mirror. Orangs can."

"So what's your point? Smarter animal, less self-awareness? Chimpanzees are becoming nonsentient?"

"Or they were, before we stopped everything in its tracks."

"So why didn't that happen to us?"

"What makes you think it didn't?"

It was such an obviously stupid question that Sascha didn't have an answer for it. I could imagine her gaping in the silence.

"You're not thinking this through," Cunningham said. "We're not talking about some kind of zombie lurching around with its arms stretched out, spouting mathematical theorems. A smart automaton would *blend in*. It would observe those around it, mimic their behavior, act just like everyone else. All the while completely unaware of what it was doing. Unaware even of its own existence."

"Why would it bother? What would motivate it?"

"As long as you pull your hand away from an open flame, who cares whether you do it because it *hurts* or because some feedback algorithm says *Withdraw if heat flux exceeds critical T?* Natural selection doesn't care about *motives*. If impersonating something increases fitness, then nature will select good impersonators over bad ones. Keep it up long enough and no conscious being would be able to pick your zombie out of a crowd." Another silence; I could hear him chewing through it. "It'll even be able to participate in a conversation like this one. It could write letters home, impersonate real human feelings, without having the slightest awareness of its own existence."

"I dunno, Rob. It just seems—"

"Oh, it might not be perfect. It might be a bit redundant, or resort to the occasional expository infodump. But even *real* people do that, don't they?"

"And eventually, there aren't any real people left. Just robots pretending to give a shit."

"Perhaps. Depends on the population dynamics, among other things. But I'd guess that at least one thing an automaton lacks is empathy; if you can't feel, you can't really relate to something that does, even if you *act* as though you do. Which makes it interesting to note how many sociopaths show up in the world's upper echelons, hmm? How ruthlessness and bottom-line self-interest are so lauded up in the stratosphere, while anyone showing those traits at ground level gets carted off into detention with the Realists. Almost as if society itself is being reshaped from the inside out."

"Oh, come on. Society was *always* pretty— Wait, you're saying the world's corporate elite are *nonsentient?*"

"God, no. Not nearly. Maybe they're just starting down that road. Like chimpanzees."

"Yeah, but sociopaths don't blend in well."

"Maybe the ones that get diagnosed don't, but by definition they're the bottom of the class. The others are too smart to get caught, and *real* automatons would do even better. Besides, when you get powerful enough, you don't need to act like other people. Other people start acting like you."

Sascha whistled. "Wow. Perfect play-actor."

"Or not so perfect. Sound like anyone we know?"

They may have been talking about someone else entirely, I suppose. But that was as close to a direct reference to Siri Keeton that I heard in all my hours on the grapevine. Nobody else mentioned me, even in passing. That was statistically unlikely, given what I'd just endured in front of them all; someone should have said *something*. Perhaps Sarasti had ordered them not to discuss it. I didn't know why. But it was obvious by now that the vampire had been orchestrating their interactions with me for some time. Now I was in hiding, but he knew I'd listen in at some point. Maybe, for some reason, he didn't want my surveillance— contaminated . . .

He could have simply locked me out of ConSensus. He hadn't. Which meant he still wanted me in the loop.

Zombies. Automatons. Fucking sentience.

For once in your goddamned life, understand *something.*

He'd said that to me. Or something had. During the assault.

Understand that your life depends on it.

Almost as if he were doing me a *favor*.

Then he'd left me alone. And had evidently told the others to do the same.

Are you listening, *Keeton?*
And he hadn't locked me out of ConSensus.

Centuries of navel-gazing. Millennia of masturbation. Plato to Descartes to Dawkins to Rhanda. Souls and zombie agents and qualia. Kolmogorov complexity. Consciousness as Divine Spark. Consciousness as electromagnetic field. Consciousness as functional cluster.

I explored it all.

Wegner thought it was an executive summary. Penrose heard it in the singing of caged electrons. Norretranders said it was a fraud; Kazim called it leakage from a parallel universe. Metzinger wouldn't even admit it existed. The AIs claimed to have worked it out, then announced they couldn't explain it to us. Gödel was right after all: No system can fully understand itself.

Not even the Synthesists had been able to rotate it down. The load-bearing beams just couldn't take the strain.

All of them, I began to realize, had missed the point. All those theories, all those drug dreams and experiments and models trying to prove what consciousness *was*: none to explain what it was *good* for. None needed: obviously, consciousness makes us what we are. It lets us see the beauty and the ugliness. It elevates us into the exalted realm of the spiritual. Oh, a few outsiders—Dawkins, Keogh, the occasional writer of hackwork fiction who barely achieved obscurity—wondered briefly at the why of it: why *not* soft computers, and no more? Why should nonsentient systems be inherently inferior? But they never really raised their voices above the crowd. The value of what we are was too trivially self-evident to ever call into serious question.

Yet the questions persisted, in the minds of the laureates, in the angst of every horny fifteen-year-old on the planet. Am I nothing but sparking chemistry? Am I a magnet in the ether? I am more than my eyes, my ears, my tongue; I am the little thing *behind* those things, the thing looking out from inside. But who looks out from *its* eyes? What does it reduce to? Who am I? Who am I? *Who am I?*

What a stupid fucking question. I could have answered it in a second, if Sarasti hadn't forced me to understand it first.

NOT UNTIL WE ARE LOST DO WE BEGIN TO UNDERSTAND OURSELVES.

—HENRY DAVID THOREAU

THE SHAME HAD scoured me and left me hollow. I didn't care who saw me. I didn't care what state they saw me in. For days I'd floated in my tent, curled into a ball and breathing my own stink while the others made whatever preparations my tormentor had laid out for them. Amanda Bates was the only one who'd raised even a token protest over what Sarasti had done to me. The others kept their eyes down and their mouths shut and did what he told them to— whether from fear or indifference I couldn't tell.

It was something else I'd stopped caring about.

Sometime during that span the cast on my arm cracked open like a shucked clam. I upped the lumens long enough to assess its handiwork; my repaired palm itched and glistened in twilight, a longer, deeper fate line running from heel to web. Then back to darkness, and the blind unconvincing illusion of safety.

Sarasti wanted me to believe. Somehow he must have thought

that brutalizing and humiliating me would accomplish that—
that broken and drained, I would become an empty vessel to fill
as he saw fit. Wasn't it a classic brainwashing technique—to
shatter your victim and then glue the pieces back together according to specs of your own choosing? Maybe he was expecting
some kind of Stockholm syndrome to set in, or maybe his actions followed some agenda incomprehensible to mere meat.

Maybe he'd simply gone insane.

He had broken me. He had presented his arguments. I had
followed his trail of bread crumbs though ConSensus, through
Theseus. And now, only nine days from graduation, I knew one
thing for sure: Sarasti was wrong. He had to be. I couldn't see
how, but I knew it just the same. He was wrong.

Somehow, absurdly, that had become the one thing I *did* care
about.

No one in the spine. Only Cunningham visible in BioMed, por-
ing over digital dissections, pretending to kill time. I floated
above him, my rebuilt hand clinging to the top of the nearest
stairwell; it dragged me in a slow, small circle as the drum
turned. Even from up there I could see the tension in the set of
his shoulders: a system stuck in a holding pattern, corroding
through the long hours as fate advanced with all the time in the
world.

He looked up. "Ah. It lives."

I fought the urge to retreat. *Just a conversation, for God's sake.
It's just two people talking. People do it all the time without your
tools. You can do this. You can do this.*

Just try.

So I forced one foot after another down the stairs, weight and
apprehension rising in lockstep. I tried to read Cunningham's

topology through the haze. Maybe I saw a façade, only microns deep. Maybe he would welcome almost any distraction, even if he wouldn't admit it.

Or maybe I was just imagining it.

"How are you doing?" he asked as I reached the deck.

I shrugged.

"Hand all better, I see."

"No thanks to you."

I'd tried to stop that from coming out. Really.

Cunningham struck a cigarette. "Actually, I *was* the one who fixed you up."

"You also sat there and watched while he took me apart."

"I wasn't even there." And then, after a moment: "But you may be right. I might very well have sat it out in any event. Amanda and the Gang *did* try to intervene on your behalf, from what I hear. Didn't do a lot of good for anyone."

"So you wouldn't even try."

"Would you, if the situation were reversed? Go up unarmed against a vampire?"

I said nothing. Cunningham regarded me for a long moment, dragging on his cigarette. "It really got to you, didn't it?" he said at last.

"You're wrong," I said.

"Am I."

"I don't *play people*."

"Mmmm." He seemed to consider the proposition. "What word would you prefer, then?"

"I *observe*."

"That you do. Some might even call it *surveillance*."

"I—I read body language." Hoping that that was all he was talking about.

"It's a matter of degree and you know it. Even in a crowd

there's a certain expectation of privacy. People aren't prepared to have their minds read off every twitch of the eyeball." He stabbed at the air with his cigarette. "And you. You're a shapeshifter. You present a different face to every one of us, and I'll wager none of them is real. The *real* you, if it even exists, is invisible . . ."

Something knotted below my diaphragm. "Who isn't? Who doesn't . . . try to fit in, who doesn't want to get along? There's nothing *malicious* about that. I'm a Synthesist, for God's sake! I *never* manipulate the variables."

"Well you see, that's the problem. It's not just *variables* you're manipulating."

Smoke writhed between us.

"But I guess you can't really understand that, can you." He stood and waved a hand. ConSensus windows imploded at his side. "Not your fault, really. You can't blame someone for the way they're wired."

"Give me a fucking break," I snarled.

That, too, had slipped out before I could stop it—and after that came the flood: "You put so much *fucking* stock in that. You and your *empathy*. And maybe I *am* just some kind of impostor but most people would swear I'd worn their very souls. I don't *need* that shit, you don't have to *feel* motives to deduce them, it's better if you *can't,* it keeps you—"

"Dispassionate?" Cunningham smiled faintly.

"Maybe your *empathy*'s just a comforting lie, you ever think of that? Maybe you *think* you know how the other person feels but you're only feeling *yourself,* maybe you're even worse than me. Or maybe we're all just guessing. Maybe the only difference is that I don't lie to myself about it."

"Do they look the way you imagined?" he asked.

"What? What are you talking about?"

"The scramblers. *Multijointed arms from a central mass.* Sounds rather similar to me."

He'd been into Szpindel's archives.

"I— Not really," I said. "The arms are more—flexible, in real life. More segmented. And I never really got a look at the body. What does that have to do with—"

"Close, though, wasn't it? Same size, same general body plan."

"So *what?*"

"Why didn't you report it?"

"I did. Isaac said it was just TMS. From *Rorschach.*"

"You saw them before *Rorschach.* Or at least," he continued, "you saw *something* that scared you into blowing your cover, back when you were spying on Isaac and Michelle."

My rage dissipated like air through a breach. "They—they knew?"

"Only Isaac, I think. And it kept it between it and the logs. I suspect it didn't want to interfere with your *noninterference* protocols—although I'll wager that was the last time you ever caught the two of them in private, yes?"

I didn't say anything.

"Did you think the official observer was somehow exempt from observation?" Cunningham asked after a while.

"No," I said softly. "I suppose not."

He nodded. "Have you seen any since? I'm not talking about run-of-the-mill TMS hallucinations. I mean scramblers. Have you hallucinated any since you actually saw one in the flesh, since you *knew* what they looked like?"

I thought about it. "No."

He shook his head, some new opinion confirmed. "You really are something, Keeton, you know that? You don't lie to yourself? Even now, you don't know what you know."

"What are you talking about?"

"You *figured it out*. From *Rorschach*'s architecture, probably—form follows function, yes? Somehow you pieced together a fairly good idea of what a scrambler looked like before anyone ever laid eyes on them. Or at least"—he drew a breath; his cigarette flared like an LED—"part of you did. Some collection of unconscious modules working their asses off on your behalf. But they can't show their work, can they? You don't have conscious access to those levels. So one part of the brain tries to tell another any way it can. Passes notes under the table."

"Blindsight," I murmured. *You just get a feeling of where to reach . . .*

"More like schizophrenia, except you saw pictures instead of hearing voices. You saw *pictures*. And you *still* didn't understand."

I blinked. "But how would I—I mean—"

"What did you think, that *Theseus* was haunted? That the scramblers were communing with you telepathically? What you do—it *matters,* Keeton. They told you you were nothing but their stenographer and they hammered all those layers of hands-off passivity into you but you just had to take some initiative anyway, didn't you? Had to work the problem on your own. The only thing you couldn't do was admit it to yourself." Cunningham shook his head. "Siri Keeton. See what they've done to you."

He touched his face.

"See what they've done to us all," he whispered.

I found the Gang floating in the center of the darkened observation blister. She made room as I joined her, pushed to one side and anchored herself to a bit of webbing.

"Susan?" I asked. I honestly couldn't tell anymore.

"I'll get her," Michelle said.

"No, that's all right. I'd like to speak to all of—"

But Michelle had already fled. The half-lit figure changed before me, and said, "She'd rather be alone right now."

I nodded. "You?"

James shrugged. "I don't mind talking. Although I'm surprised you're still doing your reports, after . . ."

"I'm . . . not, exactly. This isn't for Earth."

I looked around. Not much to see. Faraday mesh coated the inside of the dome like a gray film, dimming and graining the view beyond. Ben hung like a black malignancy across half the sky. I could make out a dozen dim contrails against vague bands of cloud, in reds so deep they bordered on black. The sun winked past James's shoulder, *our* sun, a bright dot that diffracted into faint splintered rainbows when I moved my head. That was pretty much it: Starlight didn't penetrate the mesh, nor did the larger, dimmer particles of the accretion belt. The myriad dim pinpoints of shovelnosed machinery were lost utterly.

Which might be a comfort to some, I supposed.

"Shitty view," I remarked. *Theseus* could have projected crisp first-person vistas across the dome in an instant, more real than real.

"Michelle likes it," James said. "The way it feels. And Cruncher likes the diffraction effects, he likes . . . interference patterns."

We watched nothing for a while, by the dim half-light filtering out from the spine. It brushed the edges of James's profile.

"You set me up," I said at last.

She looked at me. "What do you mean?"

"You were talking around me all along, weren't you? All of you. You didn't bring me in until I'd been"—how had she put it?—"*preconditioned*. The whole thing was planned to throw me off-balance. And then Sarasti . . . attacks me out of nowhere, and—"

"We didn't know about that. Not until the alarm went off."

"Alarm?"

"When he changed the gas mix. You must have heard it. Isn't that why you were there?"

"He called me to his tent. He told me to watch."

She regarded me from a face full of shadow. "You didn't try to stop him?"

I couldn't answer the accusation in her voice. "I just—observe," I said weakly.

"I thought you were trying to stop him from—" She shook her head. "*That's* why I thought he was attacking you."

"You're saying that wasn't an act? You weren't in on it?" I didn't believe it.

But I could tell she did.

"I thought you were trying to *protect* them." She snorted a soft, humorless laugh at her own mistake and looked away. "I guess I should have known better."

She should have. She should have known that taking orders is one thing; taking *sides* would have done nothing but compromise my integrity.

And I should have been used to it by now.

I forged on. "It was some kind of object lesson. A, a *tutorial*. You can't torture the nonsentient or something, and . . . and I *heard* you, Susan. It wasn't news to you, it wasn't news to anyone except *me*, and . . ."

And you hid it from me. You all did. You and your whole Gang and Amanda, too. You've been hashing this out for days and you went out of your way to cover it up.

How did I miss it? How did I miss it?

"Jukka told us not to discuss it with you," Susan admitted.

"Why? This is exactly the kind of thing I'm *out* here for!"

"He said you'd . . . resist. Unless it was handled properly."

"Handled— Susan, he *assaulted* me! You *saw* what he—"

"We didn't know he was going to do that. None of us did."

"And he did it why? To win an argument?"

"That's what he says."

"Do you believe him?"

"Probably." After a moment she shrugged. "Who knows? He's a vampire. He's . . . opaque."

"But his record—I mean, he's, he's never resorted to overt violence before—"

She shook her head. "Why should he? He doesn't have to convince the *rest* of us of anything. We have to follow his orders regardless."

"So do I," I reminded her.

"He's not trying to convince *you*, Siri."

Ah.

I was only a conduit, after all. Sarasti hadn't been making his case to me at all; he'd been making it *through* me, and—

—and he was planning for a second round. Why go to such extremes to present a case to Earth, if Earth was irrelevant? Sarasti didn't expect the game to end out here. He expected Earth to *do* something in light of his . . . perspective.

"But what difference does it make?" I wondered aloud.

She just looked at me.

"Even if he's right, how does it change anything? How does *this*"—I raised my repaired hand—"change anything? Scramblers are intelligent, whether they're sentient or not. They're a potential threat either way. We still don't know. So what difference does it make? Why did he *do* this to me? How does it *matter*?"

Susan raised her face to Big Ben and didn't answer.

Sascha returned her face to me, and tried to.

"It matters," she said, "because it means we attacked them before *Theseus* launched. Before Firefall, even."

"*We* attacked the—"

"You don't get it, do you? You don't." Sascha snorted softly. "If that isn't the fucking funniest thing I've heard in my whole short life."

She leaned forward, bright-eyed. "Imagine you're a scrambler, and you encounter a human signal for the very first time."

Her stare was almost predatory. I resisted the urge to back away.

"It should be so easy for you, Keeton. It should be the easiest gig you've ever had. Aren't you the user interface, aren't you the Chinese Room? Aren't you the one who never has to look inside, never has to walk a mile in anyone's shoes, because you figure everyone out from their *surfaces*?"

She stared at Ben's dark smoldering disk. "Well, there's your dream date. There's a whole race of nothing *but* surfaces. There's no *inside* to figure out. All the rules are right up front. So go to work, Siri Keeton. Make us proud."

There was no contempt in Sascha's voice, no disdain. There wasn't even anger, not in her voice, not in her eyes.

There was pleading. There were *tears*.

"Imagine you're a scrambler," she whispered again, as they floated like tiny perfect beads before her face.

Imagine you're a scrambler.

Imagine you have intellect but no insight, agendas but no *awareness*. Your circuitry hums with strategies for survival and persistence, flexible, intelligent, even technological—but no other circuitry monitors it. You can think of anything, yet are conscious of nothing.

You can't imagine such a being, can you? The term *being* doesn't even seem to apply, in some fundamental way you can't quite put your finger on.

Try.

Imagine that you encounter a signal. It is structured, and dense with information. It meets all the criteria of an intelligent transmission. Evolution and experience offer a variety of paths to follow, branch points in the flowcharts that handle such input. Sometimes these signals come from conspecifics who have useful information to share, whose lives you'll defend according to the rules of kin selection. Sometimes they come from competitors or predators or other inimical entities that must be avoided or destroyed; in those cases, the information may prove of significant tactical value. Some signals may even arise from entities that, while not kin, can still serve as allies or symbionts in mutually beneficial pursuits. You can derive appropriate responses for any of these eventualities, and many others.

You decode the signals, and stumble:

I had a great time. I really enjoyed him. Even if he cost twice as much as any other hooker in the dome—

To fully appreciate Kesey's Quartet—

They hate us for our freedom—

Pay attention, now—

Understand.

There are no meaningful translations for these terms. They are needlessly recursive. They contain no usable intelligence, yet they are structured intelligently; there is no chance they could have arisen *by* chance.

The only explanation is that something has coded nonsense in a way that poses as a useful message; only after wasting time and effort does the deception becomes apparent. The signal functions to consume the resources of a recipient for zero payoff and reduced fitness. The signal is a virus.

Viruses do not arise from kin, symbionts, or other allies.

The signal is an attack.

And it's coming from right about *there*.

. . .

"Now you get it," Sascha said.

I shook my head, trying to wrap it around that insane, impossible conclusion. "They're not even *hostile*." Not even capable of hostility. Just so profoundly alien that they couldn't help but treat human language itself as a form of combat.

How do you say *We come in peace* when the very words are an act of war?

"That's why they won't talk to us," I realized.

"Only if Jukka's right. He may not be." It was James again, still quietly resisting, still unwilling to concede a point that even her other selves had accepted. I could see why. Because if Sarasti was right, scramblers were the *norm*: Evolution across the universe was nothing but the endless proliferation of automatic, organized complexity, a vast arid Turing machine full of self-replicating machinery forever unaware of its own existence. And we—we were the flukes and the fossils. We were the flightless birds lauding our own mastery over some remote island while serpents and carnivores washed up on our shores. Susan James could not bring herself to concede that point—because Susan James, her multiple lives built on the faith that communication resolves all conflict, would then be forced to admit the lie. If Sarasti was right, there was no hope of reconciliation.

A memory rose into my mind and stuck there: a man in motion, head bent, mouth twisted into an unrelenting grimace. His eyes focused on one foot, then the other. His legs moved stiffly, carefully. His arms moved not at all. He lurched like a zombie in thrall to rigor mortis.

I knew what it was. Proprioreceptive polyneuropathy, a case study I'd encountered in ConSensus back before Szpindel had died. This was what Pag had once compared me to; a man who had lost his mind. Only self-awareness remained. Deprived of the unconscious sense and subroutines he had always taken for granted, he'd had to focus on each and every step across the room. His body no longer knew where its limbs were or what they were doing. To move at all, to even remain upright, he had to bear constant witness.

There'd been no sound when I'd played that file. There was none now in its recollection. But I swore I could feel Sarasti at my shoulder, peering into my memories. I swore I heard him speak in my mind like a schizophrenic hallucination:

This is the best that consciousness can do, when left on its own.

"Right answer," I murmured. "Wrong *question.*"

"What?"

"Stretch, remember? When you asked it which objects were in the window."

"And it missed the scrambler." James nodded. "So?"

"It didn't miss the scrambler. You thought you were asking about the things it *saw,* the things that *existed* on the board. Stretch thought you were asking about—"

"The things it was *aware* of," she finished.

"He's right," I whispered. "Oh God. I think he's right."

"Hey," James said. "Did you see *tha*—"

But I never saw what she was pointing at. *Theseus* slammed her eyelids shut and started howling.

Graduation came nine days early.

We didn't see the shot. Whatever gun port *Rorschach* had opened was precisely eclipsed on three fronts: the lab-hab hid it from *Theseus,* and two gnarled extrusions of the artifact itself hid it from each of the gun emplacements. A bolus of incendiary plasma shot from that blind spot like a thrown punch; it had split the inflatable wide open before the first alarm went up.

Alarms chased us aft. We launched ourselves down the spine through the bridge, through the crypt, past hatches and crawl spaces, fleeing the surface for any refuge with more than a hand's-breadth between skin and sky. Burrowing. ConSensus followed us back, its windows warping and sliding across struts and conduits and the concave tunnel of the spine itself. I paid no attention until we were back in the drum, deep in *Theseus*'s belly. Where we could pretend we were safer.

Down on the turning deck Bates erupted from the head, tactical windows swirling like ballroom dancers around her. Our own window came to rest on the Commons bulkhead. The hab expanded across that display like a cheap optical illusion: both swelling and shrinking in our sights, that smooth surface billowing toward us while collapsing in on itself. It took me a moment to reconcile the contradiction: something had kicked the hab hard from its far side, sent it careening toward us in a slow, majestic tumble. Something had *opened* the hab, spilled its atmosphere and left its elastic skin drawing in on itself like a deflating balloon. The impact site swung into view as we watched, a scorched flaccid mouth trailing tenuous wisps of frozen spittle.

Our guns were firing. They shot nonconducting slugs that would not be turned aside by electromagnetic trickery—invisibly dark and distant to human eyes but I saw them through the tactical crosshairs of the firing robots, watched them sew twin dotted blackbodied arcs across the heavens. The streams converged as the guns tracked their targets, closed on two attenuate throwing stars fleeing spread-eagled through the void, their faces turned to *Rorschach* like flowers to the sun.

The guns cut them to pieces before they'd even made it halfway.

But those shredded pieces kept falling, and suddenly the ground beneath was alive with motion. I zoomed the view: scramblers surged across *Rorschach*'s hull like an orgy of snakes, naked to space. Some linked arms, one to another to another, built squirming vertebral daisy chains anchored at one end. They lifted from the hull, waved through the radioactive vacuum like fronds of articulated kelp, reaching—grasping—

Neither Bates nor her machines were stupid. They targeted the interlinked scramblers as ruthlessly as they'd gone after the escapees, and with a much higher total score. But there were simply too many targets, too many fragments snatched in passing. Twice I saw dismembered bits of Stretch and Clench caught by their brethren.

The ruptured hab loomed across ConSensus like a great torn leukocyte. Another alarm buzzed somewhere nearby: proximity alert. Cunningham shot into the drum from somewhere astern, bounced off a cluster of pipes and conduits, grabbed for support. "Holy *shit*—we are leaving, aren't we? Amanda?"

"No," Sarasti answered from everywhere.

"What—" *does it fucking take?* I caught myself. "Amanda, what if it fires on the ship?"

"It won't." She didn't take her eyes from her windows.

"How do you—"

"It can't. If it had spring-loaded any more firepower we'd have seen a change in thermal *and* microallometry." A false-color landscape rotated between us, its latitudes measured in time, its longitudes in delta-mass. Kilotons rose from that terrain like a range of red mountains. "Huh. Came in just under the noise lim—"

Sarasti cut her off. "Robert. Susan. EVA."

James blanched. *"What?"* Cunningham cried.

"Lab module's about to impact," the vampire said. "Salvage the samples. *Now.*" He killed the channel before anyone could argue.

But Cunningham wasn't about to argue. He'd just seen our

death sentence commuted: Why would Sarasti care about retrieving biopsy samples if he didn't think we stood a chance of escaping with them? The biologist steadied himself, braced toward the forward hatch. "I'm *there*," he said, shooting into the bow.

I had to admit it. Sarasti's psychology was getting better.

It wasn't working on James, though, or Michelle, or—I couldn't quite tell who was on top. "I can't go out there, Siri, it's— *I can't go out there . . .*"

Just observe. Don't interfere.

The ruptured inflatable collided impotently to starboard and flattened itself against the carapace. We felt nothing. Far away and far too near, the legions thinned across *Rorschach*'s surface. They disappeared through mouths that puckered and dilated and magically closed again in the artifact's hull. The emplacements fired passionlessly at those who remained.

Observe.

The Gang of Four strobed at my side, scared to death.

Don't interfere.

"It's okay," I said. "I'll go."

The open airlock was like a dimple in the face of an endless cliff. I looked out from that indentation into the abyss.

This side of *Theseus* faced away from Big Ben, away from the enemy. The view was still unsettling enough: an endless panorama of distant stars, hard and cold and unwinking. A single, marginally brighter one, shining yellow, still so very far away. Any scant comfort I might have taken from that sight was lost when the sun went out for the briefest instant: a tumbling piece of rock, perhaps. Or one of *Rorschach*'s shovelnosed entourage.

One step and I might never stop falling.

But I didn't step, and I didn't fall. I squeezed my pistol, jetted gently through the opening, turned. *Theseus*'s carapace curved away from me in all directions. Toward the prow, the sealed observation blister rose above the horizon like a gunmetal sunrise. Farther aft a tattered snowdrift peeked across the hull: the edge of the broken lab-hab.

And past it all, close enough to touch, the endless dark cloudscape of Big Ben: a great roiling wall extending to some flat distant horizon I could barely grasp even in theory. When I focused it was dark and endless shades of gray—but dim, sullen redness teased the corner of my eye when I looked away.

"Robert?" I brought Cunningham's suit feed to my HUD: a craggy, motionless ice field thrown into high contrast by the light of his helmet. Interference from *Rorschach*'s magnetosphere washed over the image in waves. "You there?"

Pops and crackles. The sound of breath and mumbling against an electrical hum. "Four point three. Four point oh. Three point eight—"

"Robert?"

"Three point— *Shit*. What—what are you doing out here, Keeton? Where's the Gang?"

"I came instead." Another squeeze of the trigger and I was coasting toward the snowscape. *Theseus*'s convex hull rolled past, just within reach. "To give you a hand."

"Let's move it then, shall we?" He was passing through a crevice, a scorched and jagged tear in the fabric that folded back at his touch. Struts, broken panels, dead robot arms tangled through the interior of the ice cave like glacial debris; their outlines writhed with static, their shadows leaped and stretched like living things in the sweep of his headlight. "I'm almost—"

Something that wasn't static moved in his headlight. Something *uncoiled*, just at the edge of the camera's view.

The feed died.

Suddenly Bates and Sarasti were shouting in my helmet. I tried to brake. My stupid useless legs kicked against vacuum, obeying some ancient brain stem override from a time when all monsters were earthbound, but by the time I remembered to use my trigger finger the lab-hab was already looming before me. *Rorschach* reared up behind it in the near distance, vast and malign. Dim green auroras writhed across its twisted surface like sheet lightning. *Mouths* opened and closed by the hundreds, viscous as bubbling volcanic mud, any one of them large enough to swallow *Theseus* whole. I barely noticed the flicker of motion just ahead of me, the silent eruption of dark mass from the collapsed inflatable. By the time Cunningham caught my eye he was already on his way, backlit against the ghastly corpselight flickering on *Rorschach*'s skin.

I thought I saw him waving, but I was wrong. It was only the scrambler wrapped around his body like a desperate lover, moving his arm back and forth while it ran the thrust pistol tethered to his wrist. *Bye-bye,* that arm seemed to say, *and fuck you, Keeton.*

I watched for what seemed like forever, but no other part of him moved at all.

Voices, shouting, ordering me back inside. I hardly heard them. I was too dumbfounded by the basic math, trying to make sense of the simplest subtraction.

Two scramblers. Stretch and Clench. Both accounted for, shot to pieces before my eyes.

"Keeton, do you read? Get back here! Acknowledge!"

"I— It can't be," I heard myself say. "There were only two—"

"Return to the ship immediately. Acknowledge."

"I— Acknowledged . . ."

Rorschach's mouths snapped shut at once, as though holding a deep breath. The artifact began to *turn,* ponderously, a continent changing course. It receded, slowly at first, picking up speed, turning tail and running. *How odd,* I thought. *Maybe it's more afraid than we are . . .*

But then *Rorschach* blew us a kiss. I saw it burst from deep within the forest, ethereal and incandescent. It shot across the heavens and splashed against the small of *Theseus's* back, making a complete and utter fool of Amanda Bates. The skin of our ship *flowed* there, and opened like a mouth, and congealed in a soundless frozen scream.

YOU CANNOT PREVENT AND PREPARE FOR WAR AT THE SAME TIME.

—ALBERT EINSTEIN

I HAVE NO idea whether the scrambler made it back home with its hard-won prize. There was so much lost distance to make up, even if the emplacements didn't pick it off en route. Cunningham's pistol might have run out of fuel. And who knew how long those creatures could survive in vacuum anyway? Maybe there'd been no real hope of success, maybe that scrambler was dead from the moment it had gambled on staying behind. I never found out. It had dwindled and vanished from my sight long before *Rorschach* dove beneath the clouds and disappeared in turn.

There had always been three, of course. Stretch, and Clench, and the half-forgotten microwaved remains of a scrambler killed by an uppity grunt—kept on ice next to its living brethren, within easy reach of Cunningham's teleops. I tried to dredge half-glimpsed details from memory, after the fact: had both of those escapees been spheres, or had one been flattened along one axis? Had they thrashed, waved their limbs the way some panicky human might with no ground beneath him? Or had one, perhaps, coasted lifeless and ballistic until our guns destroyed the evidence?

At this point, it didn't really matter. What mattered was that at long last, everyone was on the same page. Blood had been drawn, war declared.

And *Theseus* was paralyzed from the waist down.

Rorschach's parting shot had punched through the carapace at the base of the spine. It had just missed the ramscoop and the telematter assembly. It might have taken out Fab if it hadn't spent so many joules burning through the carapace, but barring some temporary pulse effects it left all critical systems pretty much operational. All it had done was weaken *Theseus*'s backbone enough to make it snap in two should we ever burn hard enough to break orbit. The ship would be able to repair that damage, but not in time.

If it had been luck it would have been remarkable.

And now, its quarry disabled, *Rorschach* had vanished. It had everything it needed from us, for the moment at least. It had information: all the experiences and insights encoded in the salvaged limbs of its martyred spies. If Stretch-or-Clench's gamble had paid off it even had a specimen of its own now, which all things considered we could hardly begrudge it. And so now it lurked invisibly in the depths, resting perhaps. Recharging.

But it would be back.

Theseus lost weight for the final round. We shut down the drum in a token attempt to reduce our vulnerable allotment of moving parts. The Gang of Four—uncommanded, unneeded, the very reason for their existence ripped away—retreated into some inner dialogue to which other flesh was unwelcome. She floated in the observatory, her eyes closed as tightly as the leaded lids around her. I could not tell who was in control.

I guessed. "Michelle?"

"Siri—" Susan. "Just go."

Bates floated near the floor of the drum, windows arrayed externally across bulkhead and conference table. "What can I do?" I asked.

She didn't look up. "Nothing."

So I watched. Bates counted skimmers in one window—mass, inertia, any of a dozen variables that would prove far too constant should any of those shovelnosed missiles come at our throat. They had finally noticed us. Their chaotic electron dance was shifting now, hundreds of thousands of colossal sledgehammers in sudden flux, reweaving into some ominous dynamic that hadn't yet settled into anything we could predict.

In another window *Rorschach*'s vanishing act replayed on endless loop: a radar image receding deep into the maelstrom, fading beneath gaseous teratonnes of radio static. It might still be an orbit, of sorts. Judging by that last glimpsed trajectory *Rorschach* might well be swinging around Ben's core now, passing through crushed layers of methane and monoxide that would flatten *Theseus* into smoke. Maybe it didn't even stop there; maybe *Rorschach* could pass unharmed even through those vaster, deeper pressures that made iron and hydrogen run liquid.

We didn't know. We only knew that it would be back in a little under two hours, assuming it maintained its trajectory and survived the depths. And of course, it *would* survive. You can't kill the thing under the bed. You can only keep it outside the covers.

And only for a while.

A thumbnail inset caught my eye with a flash of color. At my command it grew into a swirling soap bubble, incongruously beautiful, a blue-shifted coruscating rainbow of blown glass. I didn't recognize it for a moment: Big Ben, rendered in some prismatic false-color enhance I'd never seen before. I grunted softly.

Bates glanced up. "Oh. Beautiful, isn't it?"

"What's the spectrum?"

"Longwave stuff. Visible red, infra, down a ways. Good for heat traces."

"Visible red?" There wasn't any to speak of; mostly cool plasma fractals in a hundred shades of jade and sapphire.

"Quadrochromatic palette," Bates told me. "Like what a cat might see. Or a vampire." She managed a half-hearted wave at the rainbow bubble. "Sarasti sees something like that every time he looks outside. If he ever looks outside."

"You'd think he'd have mentioned it," I murmured. It was gorgeous, a holographic ornament. Perhaps even *Rorschach* might be a work of art through eyes like these . . .

"I don't think they parse sight like we do." Bates opened another window. Mundane graphs and contour plots sprang from the table. "They don't even go to Heaven, from what I hear. VR doesn't work on them, they . . . see the pixels, or something."

"What if he's right?" I asked. I told myself that I was only looking for a tactical assessment, an official opinion for the official record. But my words came out doubtful and frightened.

She paused. For a moment I wondered if she, too, had finally lost patience with the sight of me. But she only looked up, and stared off into some enclosed distance.

"What if he's right," she repeated, and pondered the question that lay beneath: *What can we* do?

"We could engineer ourselves back into nonsentience, perhaps. Might improve our odds in the long run." She looked at me, a rueful sort of half-smile at the corner of her mouth. "But I guess that wouldn't be much of a win, would it? What's the difference between being dead, and just not knowing you're alive?"

I finally saw it.

How long would it take an enemy tactician to discern Bates's mind behind the actions of her troops on the battlefield? How long before the obvious logic became clear? In any combat situation, this woman would naturally draw the greatest amount of enemy fire: take off the head, kill the body. But Amanda Bates wasn't just a head: she was a bottleneck, and *her* body would not suffer from a decapitation strike. Her death would only let her troops off the leash. How much more deadly would those grunts be, once every battlefield reflex didn't have to pass through some interminable job stack waiting for the rubber stamp?

Szpindel had had it all wrong. Amanda Bates wasn't a sop to politics, her role didn't deny the obsolescence of Human oversight at all. Her role *depended* on it.

She was more cannon fodder than I. She always had been. And I had to admit: After generations of generals who'd lived for the glory of the mushroom cloud, it was a pretty effective strategy for souring warmongers on gratuitous violence. In Amanda Bates's army, picking a fight meant standing on the battlefield with a bull's-eye on your chest.

No wonder she'd been so invested in peaceful alternatives.

"I'm sorry," I said softly.

She shrugged. "It's not over yet. Just the first round." She took a long, deep breath, and turned back to her study of slingshot mechanics. "*Rorschach* wouldn't have tried so hard to scare us off in the first place if we couldn't touch it, right?"

I swallowed. "Right."

"So there's still a chance." She nodded to herself. "There's still a chance."

. . .

The demon arranged his pieces for the end game. He didn't have many left. The soldier he placed in the bridge. He packed obsolete linguists and diplomats back in their coffin, out of sight and out of the way.

He called the jargonaut to his quarters—and although it would be the first time I'd seen him since the attack, his summons carried not the slightest trace of doubt that I would obey. I did. I came on command, and saw that he had surrounded himself with faces.

Every last one of them was screaming.

There was no sound. The disembodied holograms floated in silent tiers around the bubble, each contorted into a different expression of pain. They were being tortured, these faces; half a dozen real ethnicities and twice as many hypothetical ones, skin tones ranging from charcoal to albino, brows high and slanted, noses splayed or pointed, jaws receding or prognathous. Sarasti had called the entire hominid tree into existence around him, astonishing in their range of features, terrifying in their consistency of expression.

A sea of tortured faces, rotating in slow orbits around my vampire commander.

"My God, what *is* this?"

"Statistics." Sarasti seemed focused on a flayed Asian child. "*Rorschach*'s growth allometry over a two-week period."

"They're *faces* . . ."

He nodded, turning his attention to a woman with no eyes. "Skull diameter scales to total mass. Mandible length scales to EM transparency at one angstrom. One hundred thirteen facial dimensions, each presenting a different variable. Principle-component combinations present as multifeature aspect ratios." He turned to face me, his naked gleaming eyes just slightly side-cast. "You'd be surprised how much gray matter is dedicated to the analysis of facial imagery. Shame to waste it on anything as . . . counterintuitive as residual plots or contingency tables."

I felt my jaw clenching. "And the *expressions*? What do *they* represent?"

"Software customizes output for user."

An agonized gallery pled for mercy on all sides.

"I *am* wired for hunting," he reminded gently.

"And you think I don't know that," I said after a moment.

He shrugged, disconcertingly human. "You ask."

"Why am I here, Jukka? You want to teach me another *object lesson?*"

"To discuss our next move."

"What move? We can't even run away."

"No." He shook his head, baring filed teeth in something approaching regret.

"Why did we wait so long?" Suddenly my sullen defiance had evaporated. I sounded like a child, frightened and pleading. "Why didn't we just take it on when we first got here, when it was *weaker* . . . ?"

"We need to learn things. For next time."

"Next time? I thought *Rorschach* was a dandelion seed. I thought it just . . . washed up here—"

"By chance. But every dandelion is a clone. Their seeds are legion." Another smile, not remotely convincing. "And maybe it takes more than one try for the placental mammals to conquer Australia."

"It'll annihilate us. It doesn't even need those spitballs, it could pulverize us with one of those scramjets. In an instant."

"It doesn't want to."

"How do you *know?*"

"They need to learn things, too. They want us intact. Improves our odds."

"Not enough. We can't win."

This was his cue. This was the point at which Uncle Predator would smile at my naiveté, and take me into his confidence. *Of course we're armed to the teeth,* he would say. *Do you think we'd come all this way, face such a vast unknown, without the means to defend ourselves? Now, at last, I can reveal that shielding and weaponry account for over half the ship's mass . . .*

It was his *cue.*

"No," he said. "We can't win."

"So we just sit here. We just wait to die for the next—the next sixty-eight minutes . . ."

Sarasti shook his head. "No."

"But—" I began.

"Oh," I finished.

Because of course, we had just topped up our antimatter reserves. *Theseus* was not equipped with weapons. *Theseus was* the weapon. And we were, in fact, going to sit here for the next sixty-eight minutes, waiting to die.

But we were going to take *Rorschach* with us when we did.

Sarasti said nothing. I wondered what he saw, looking at me. I wondered if there actually *was* a Jukka Sarasti behind those eyes to see, if his insights—always ten steps ahead of our own—hailed not so much from superior analytical facilities as from the timeworn truth that *it takes one to know one.*

Whose side, I wondered, would an automaton take?

"You have other things to worry about," he said.

He moved toward me; I swear, all those agonized faces followed him with their eyes. He studied me for a moment, the flesh crinkling around his eyes. Or maybe some mindless algorithm merely processed visual input, correlated aspect ratios and facial tics, fed everything to some output subroutine with no more awareness than a stats program. Maybe there was no more spark in this creature's face than there was in all the others, silently screaming in his wake.

"Is Susan afraid of you?" the thing before me asked.

"Su— Why should she be?"

"She has four conscious entities in her head. She's four times more sentient than you. Doesn't that make you a threat?"

"No, of course not."

"Then why should you feel threatened by me?"

And suddenly I didn't care anymore. I laughed out loud, with minutes to live and nothing to lose. "*Why*? Maybe because you're my natural enemy, you fucker. Maybe because I *know* you, and you can't even *look* at one of us without flexing your claws. Maybe because you nearly ripped my fucking hand off and raped me for no good reason—"

"I can imagine what it's like," he said quietly. "Please don't make me do it again."

I fell instantly silent.

"I know your race and mine are never on the best of terms." There was a cold smile in his voice if not on his face. "But I do only what you force me to. You *rationalize,* Keeton. You *defend.* You reject unpalatable truths, and if you can't reject them outright you trivialize them. Incremental evidence is never enough for you. You hear rumors of holocaust; you dismiss them. You see evidence of genocide; you insist it can't be so bad. Temperatures rise, glaciers melt—species *die*—and you blame sunspots and volcanoes. Everyone is like this, but you most of all. You and your Chinese Room. You turn incomprehension into mathematics, you reject the truth without even hearing it first."

"It served me well enough." I wondered at the ease with which I had put my life into the past tense.

"Yes, if your purpose is only to *transmit*. Now you have to *convince*. You have to *believe*."

There were implications there I didn't dare to hope for. "Are you saying—"

"Can't afford to let the truth *trickle* through. Can't give you the chance to shore up your rationales and your defenses. They must fall completely. You must be *inundated*. Shattered. Genocide's impossible to deny when you're buried up to your neck in dismembered bodies."

"You *played* me," I whispered. "All this time." I'd known something was going on. I just hadn't understood *what*.

"I'd have seen right through it," I told him, "if you hadn't made me get involved."

"You might even read it off me directly."

"*That's* why you—" I shook my head. "I thought that was because we were *meat*."

"That, too," Sarasti admitted, and looked right at me.

For the first time, I looked right back. And felt a shock of recognition.

I still wonder why I never saw it before. For all those years I remembered the thoughts and feelings of some different, younger person, some remnant of the boy my parents had hacked out of my head to make room for me. He'd been *alive*. His world had been vibrant. And though I could call up the memories of that other consciousness, I could barely feel anything within the constraints of my own.

Perhaps *dreamstate* wasn't such a bad word for it . . .

"Like to hear a vampire folktale?" Sarasti asked.

"Vampires have folktales?"

He took it for a *yes*. "A laser is assigned to find the darkness. Since it lives in a room without doors, or windows, or any other source of light, it thinks this will be easy. But everywhere it turns it sees brightness. Every wall, every piece of furniture it points at is brightly lit. Eventually it concludes there *is* no darkness, that light is everywhere."

"What the hell are you talking about?"

"Amanda is not planning a mutiny."

"What? You know about—"

"She doesn't even want to. Ask her if you like."

"No—I—"

"You value objectivity."

It was so obvious I didn't bother answering.

He nodded as if I had. "Synthesists can't have opinions of their own. So when you feel one, it must be someone else's. The *crew* holds you in contempt. *Amanda* wants me relieved of command. Half of *us* is *you*. I think the word is *project*. Although,"—he cocked his head a bit to one side—"lately you improve. Come."

"Where?"

"Shuttle bay. Time to do your job."

"My—"

"Survive and bear witness."

"A drone—"

"Can deliver the data—assuming nothing fries its memory before it gets away. It can't *convince* anyone. It can't counter rationalizations and denials. It can't *matter*. And vampires"—he paused—"have poor communications skills."

It should have been cause for petty, selfish rejoicing.

"It all comes down to me," I said. "That's what you're saying. I'm a fucking stenographer, and it's all on me."

"Yes. Forgive me for that."

"Forgive you?"

Sarasti waved his hand. All faces save two disappeared.

"I don't know what I'm doing."

. . .

The news bloomed across ConSensus a few seconds before Bates called it aloud: Thirteen skimmers had not reappeared from behind Big Ben on schedule. Sixteen. Twenty-eight.

And counting.

Sarasti clicked to himself as he and Bates played catch-up. Tactical filled with luminous multicolored threads, a tangle of revised projections as intricate as art. The threads wrapped Ben like a filamentous cocoon; *Theseus* was a naked speck in the middle distance.

I expected any number of those lines to skewer us like needles through a bug. Surprisingly, none did; but the projections only extended twenty-five hours into the future, and were reliable for only half that. Not even Sarasti and the Captain could look so far ahead with that many balls in the air. It was something, though, the faintest silver lining: that all these high-speed behemoths couldn't simply reach out and swat us without warning. Evidently they still had to ease into the curve.

After *Rorschach*'s dive, I'd been starting to think the laws of physics didn't apply.

The trajectories were close enough, though. At least three skimmers would be passing within a hundred kilometers on their next orbits.

Sarasti reached for his injector, the blood rising in his face. "Time to go. We refit *Charybdis* while you're sulking."

He held the hypo to his throat and shot up. I stared at ConSensus, caught by that bright shifting web like a moth by a streetlight.

"*Now,* Siri."

He pushed me from his quarters. I sailed into the passageway, grabbed a convenient rung—and stopped.

The spine was alive with grunts, patrolling the airspace, standing guard over the Fab plants and shuttle locks, clinging like giant insects to the rungs of unrolling spinal ladders. Slowly, silently, the spine itself was *stretching*.

It could do that, I remembered. Its corrugations flexed and relaxed like muscle, it could grow up to two hundred meters to accommodate any late-breaking need for a bigger hanger or more lab space.

Or more infantry. *Theseus* was increasing the size of the battlefield.

"Come." The vampire turned aft.

Bates broke in from up front. "Something's happening."

An emergency handpad, geckoed to the expanding bulkhead, slid past to one side. Sarasti grabbed it and tapped commands. Bates's feed appeared on the bulkhead: a tiny chunk of Big Ben, an EM-enhanced equatorial quadrant only a few thousand klicks on a side. The clouds boiled down there, a cyclonic knot of turbulence swirling almost too fast for real time. The overlay described charged particles, bound in a deep Parker spiral. It spoke of great mass, rising.

Sarasti clicked.

"DTI?" Bates said.

"Optical only." Sarasti took my arm and dragged me effortlessly astern. The display paced us along the bulkhead: seven skimmers shot from the clouds as I watched, a ragged circle of scramjets screaming red-hot into space. ConSensus plotted their paths in an instant; luminous arcs rose around our ship like the bars of a cage.

Theseus shuddered.

We've been hit, I thought. Suddenly the spine's plodding expansion cranked into overdrive; the pleated wall lurched and ac-celerated, streaming past my outstretched fingers as the closed hatch receded up ahead—

—receded *overhead.*

The walls weren't moving at all. We were *falling,* to the sudden strident bleating of an alarm.

Something nearly yanked my arm from its socket: Sarasti had reached out with one hand and caught a rung, reached with his other and caught me before we'd both been flattened against the Fab plant. We dangled. I must have weighed two hundred kilograms; the floor shuddered ten meters below my feet. The ship groaned around us. The spine filled with the screech of torquing metal. Bates's grunts clung to its walls with clawed feet.

I reached for the ladder. The ladder pulled away: The ship was bending in the middle and *down* had started to climb the walls. Sarasti and I swung toward the center of the spine like a daisy-chain pendulum.

"Bates! James!" The vampire roared. His grip on my wrist trembled, slipping. I strained for the ladder, swung, caught it.

"Susan James has barricaded herself in the bridge and shut down autonomic overrides." An unfamiliar voice, flat and affectless. "She has initiated an unauthorized burn. I have begun a controlled reactor shutdown; be advised that the main drive will be offline for at least twenty-seven minutes."

The ship, I realized, its voice raised calmly above the alarm. The Captain itself. On public address.

That was unusual.

"Bridge!" Sarasti barked. "Open channel!"

Someone was shouting up there. There were words, but I couldn't make them out.

Without warning, Sarasti let go.

He dropped obliquely in a blur. Aft and opposite, the bulkhead waited to swat him like an insect. In half a second both his legs would be shattered, if the impact didn't kill him outright—

But suddenly we were weightless again, and Jukka Sarasti—purple-faced, stiff-limbed—was foaming at the mouth.

"Reactor offline," the Captain reported. Sarasti bounced off the wall.

He's having a seizure, I realized.

I released the ladder and pushed astern. *Theseus* swung lopsidedly around me. Sarasti convulsed in midair; clicks and hisses and choking sounds stuttered from his mouth. His eyes were so wide they seemed lidless. His pupils were mirror-red pinpoints. The flesh twitched across his face as though trying to crawl off.

Ahead and behind, battlebots held their position and ignored us.

"*Bates!*" I yelled up the spine. "We need help!"

Angles, everywhere. Seams on the shield plates. Sharp shadows and protrusions on the surface of every drone. A two-by-three matrix of insets, bordered in black, floating over the main ConSensus display: two big interlinked crosses right in front of where Sarasti had been hanging.

This can't be happening. He just took his anti-Euclideans. I saw him. Unless . . .

Someone had spiked Sarasti's drugs.

"*Bates!*" She should be linked into the grunts, they should have leapt forward at the first sign of trouble. They should be dragging my commander to the infirmary by now. They waited stolid and immobile. I stared at the nearest: "Bates, you there?" And then—in case she wasn't—I spoke to the grunt directly. "Are you autonomous? *Do you take verbal orders?*"

On all sides the robots watched; the Captain just laughed at me, its voice posing as an alarm.

Infirmary.

I pushed. Sarasti's arms flailed randomly against my head and shoulders. He tumbled forward and sideways, hit the moving ConSensus display dead center, bounced away up the spine. I kicked off in his wake—

—and glimpsed something from the corner of my eye—

—and turned—

—and dead center of ConSensus, *Rorschach* erupted from Ben's seething face like a breaching whale. It wasn't just the EM-enhance: The thing was *glowing,* deep angry red. Enraged, it hurled itself into space, big as a mountain range.

Fuck fuck fuck.

Theseus lurched. The lights flickered, went out, came back on again. The turning bulkhead cuffed me from behind.

"Backups engaged," the Captain said calmly.

"Captain! Sarasti's down!" I kicked off the nearest ladder, bumped into a grunt and headed forward after the vampire. "Bates isn't— What do I do?"

"Nav offline. Starboard afferents offline."

It wasn't even talking to me, I realized. Maybe this wasn't the Captain at all. Maybe it was pure reflex: a dialogue tree, spouting public-service announcements. Maybe *Theseus* had already been lobotomized. Maybe this was only her brain stem talking.

Darkness again. Then flickering light.

If the Captain was gone, we were screwed.

I gave Sarasti another push. The alarm bleated on. The drum was twenty meters ahead; BioMed was just the other side of that closed hatch. The hatch had been open before, I remembered. Someone had shut it in the last few minutes. Fortunately *Theseus* had no locks on her doors.

Unless the Gang barricaded it before they took the bridge . . .

"Strap in, people! We are getting *out* of here!"

Who in hell . . . ?

The open bridge channel. Susan James, shouting up there. Or *someone* was; I couldn't quite place the voice . . .

Ten meters to the drum. *Theseus* jerked again, slowed her spin. Stabilized.

"Somebody start the goddamned reactor! I've only got attitude jets up here!"

"Susan? Sascha?" I was at the hatch. *"Who is that?"* I pushed passed Sarasti and reached to open it.

No answer.

Not from ConSensus, anyway. I heard a muted *hum* from behind, saw the ominous shifting of shadows on the bulkhead just a moment too late. I turned in time to see one of the grunts raise a spiky appendage—curved like a scimitar, needle-tipped—over Sarasti's head.

I turned in time to see it plunge into his skull.

I froze. The metal proboscis withdrew, dark and slick. Lateral maxillipeds began nibbling at the base of Sarasti's skull. His pithed corpse wasn't thrashing now; it only trembled, a sack of muscles and motor nerves awash in static.

Bates.

Her mutiny was underway. No, *their* mutiny—Bates and the Gang. I'd known. I'd imagined it. I'd seen it coming.

He hadn't believed me.

The lights went out again. The alarm fell silent. ConSensus dwindled to a flickering doodle on the bulkhead and disappeared; I saw something there in that last instant, and refused to process it. I heard breath catch in my throat, felt angular monstrosities advancing through the darkness. Something flared directly ahead, a bright brief staccato in the void. I glimpsed curves and angles in silhouette, *staggering.* The buzzing crackle of shorting circuitry. Metal objects collided nearby, unseen.

From behind the crinkle of the drum hatch, opening. I turned.

A sudden beam of harsh chemical light hit me and lit the mechanical ranks behind; they simultaneously unclamped from their anchorages and floated free. Their joints clicked in unison like an army stamping to attention.

"Keeton!" Bates snapped, sailing through the hatch. "You okay?"

The chemlight shone from her forehead. It turned the interior of the spine into a high-contrast mosaic, all pale surfaces and sharp moving shadows. It spilled across the grunt that had killed Sarasti; the robot bounced down the spine, suddenly, mysteriously inert. The light washed across Sarasti's body. The corpse turned slowly on its axis. Spherical crimson beads emerged from its head like drops of water from a leaky faucet. They spread in a winding, widening trail, spotlit by Bates's headlamp: a spiral arm of dark ruby suns.

I backed away. "You—"

She pushed me to one side. "Stay clear of the hatch, unless you're going through." Her eyes were fixed on the ranked drones. "Optical line of sight."

Rows of glassy eyes reflected back at us down the passageway, passing in and out of shadow.

"You killed Sarasti!"

"No."

"But—"

"Who do you think shut it *down,* Keeton? The fucker went rogue. I could barely even get it to self-destruct." Her eyes went briefly deep-focus; all down the spine the surviving drones launched into some intricate martial ballet, half-seen in the shifting cone of her headlamp.

"Better," Bates said. "They should stay in line now. Assuming we don't get hit with anything too much stronger."

"What *is* hitting us?"

"Lightning. EMP." Drones sailed down to Fab and the shuttles, taking strategic positions along the tube. "*Rorschach*'s putting out one hell of a charge and every time one of those skimmers pass between us they *arc*."

"What, at *this* range? I thought we were . . . the burn—"

"Sent us in the wrong direction. We're inbound."

Three grunts floated close enough to touch. They drew beads on the open drum hatch.

"She said she was trying to *escape*—" I remembered.

"She fucked up."

"Not by *that* much. She couldn't have." We were all rated for manual piloting. Just in case.

"Not the Gang," Bates said.

"But—"

"I think there's someone new in there now. Bunch of submodules wired together and woke up somehow, I don't know. But whatever's in charge, I think it's just panicking."

Stuttering brightness on all sides. The spinal lightstrips flickered and finally held steady at half their usual brightness.

Theseus coughed static and spoke: "ConSensus is offline. Reac—"

The voice faded.

ConSensus, I remembered as Bates turned to head back upstream.

"I saw something," I said. "Before ConSensus went out."

"Yeah."

"Was that—"

She paused at the hatch. "Yeah."

I'd seen scramblers. Hundreds of them, sailing naked through the void, their arms spread wide.

Some of their arms, anyway. "They were carrying—"

Bates nodded. "Weapons." Her eyes flickered to some unseen distance for a moment. "First wave headed for the front end. Blister and forward lock, I think. Second wave's aft." She shook her head. "Huh. I would have done it the other way around."

"How far?"

"Far?" Bates smiled faintly. "They're already on the hull, Siri. We're engaging."

"What do I do? *What do I do?*"

Her eyes stared past me, and widened. She opened her mouth.

A hand clamped on my shoulder from behind and spun me around.

Sarasti. His dead eyes stared from a skull split like a spiked melon. Globules of coagulating blood clung to his hair and skin like engorged ticks.

"Go with him," Bates said.

Sarasti grunted and clicked. There were no words.

"What—" I began.

"*Now*. That's an order." Bates turned back to the hatch. "We'll cover you."

The shuttle. "You too."

"No."

"Why not? They can fight better *without* you, you said that yourself! What's the *point?*"

"Can't leave yourself a back door, Keeton. Defeats the whole purpose." She allowed herself a small, sad smile. "They've breached. Go."

She was gone, fresh alarms rising in her wake. Far toward the bow I heard the crinkle of emergency bulkheads snapping shut.

Sarasti's undead carcass gurgled and pushed me down the spine. Four more grunts slid smoothly past and took up position behind us. I looked over my shoulder in time to see the vampire pull the handpad from the wall. But it wasn't Sarasti at all, of course. It was the Captain—whatever was left of the Captain, this far into the fight—commandeering a peripheral interface for its own use. The optical port sprouted conspicuously from the back of Sarasti's neck, where the cable used to go in; I remembered the drone's maxillipeds, chewing.

The sound of weapons fire and ricochets rose behind us.

The corpse typed one-handed as we moved. I wondered briefly why it just didn't *talk* before my gaze flickered back to the spike in his brain: Sarasti's speech centers must be mush.

"Why did you kill him?" I said. A whole new alarm started up, way back in the drum. A sudden *breeze* tugged me backward for a moment, dissipated in the next second with a distant clang.

The corpse held out the handpad, configured for keys and a text display: SEIZNG. CLDNT CNTRL.

We were at the shuttle locks. Robot soldiers let us pass, their attention elsewhere.

U GO, the Captain said.

Someone screamed in the distance. Way off up the spine, the drum hatch slammed shut; I turned and saw a pair of distant grunts welding the seal. They seemed to move faster now than they ever had before. Maybe it was only my imagination.

The starboard shuttle lock slid back. *Charybdis*'s interior lights winked on, spilling brightness into the passageway; the spine's emergency lighting seemed even dimmer in contrast. I peered through the opening. There was almost no cabin space left—just a single open coffin jammed between coolant and fuel tanks and massive retrofitted shockpads. *Charybdis* had been refitted for high-g and long distance.

And me.

Sarasti's corpse urged me on from behind. I turned and faced it.

"Was it *ever* him?" I asked.

GO.

"*Tell me.* Did he ever speak for himself? Did he decide *anything* on his own? Were we ever following *his* orders, or was it just you all along?"

Sarasti's undead eyes stared glassy and uncomprehending. His fingers jerked on the handpad.

U DISLKE ORDRS FRM MCHNES. HAPPIER THS WAY.

I let it strap me in and close the lid. I lay there in the dark, feeling my body lurch and sway as the shuttle slid into its launch slot. I withstood the sudden silence as the docking clamps let go, the jerk of acceleration that spat me hard into the vacuum, the ongoing thrust that pushed against my chest like a soft mountain. Around me the shuttle trembled in the throes of a burn that far exceeded its normative specs.

My inlays came back online. Suddenly I could see *outside* if I wanted. I could see what was happening behind me.

I chose not to, deliberately and fervently, and looked anyway.

Theseus was dwindling by then, even on tactical. She listed down the well, wobbling toward some enemy rendezvous that must have been intentional, some last-second maneuver to get her payload as close to target as possible. *Rorschach* rose to meet her, its gnarled spiky arms *uncoiling,* spreading as if in anticipation of an embrace. But it was the backdrop, not the players, that stole the tableau: the face of Big Ben roiling in my rearview, a seething cyclonic backdrop filling the window. Magnetic contours wound spring-tight on the overlay; *Rorschach* was drawing all of Ben's magnetosphere around itself like a bright swirling cloak, twisting it into a concentrated knot that grew and brightened and bulged outward. . . .

Like a torsion flare from an L-class dwarf, my commander

had said once, *but we should see anything big enough to generate that effect and the sky's dark on that bearing. IAU calls it a statistical artifact.*

As, in fact, it had been. An impact splash perhaps, or the bright brief bellow of some great energy source rebooting after a million years of dormancy. Much like this one: a solar flare, with no sun beneath it. A magnetic cannon ten thousand times stronger than nature gave it any right to be.

Both sides drew their weapons. I don't know which fired first, or even if it mattered: how many tonnes of antimatter would it take to match something that could squeeze the power of a sun from a gas ball barely wider than Jupiter? Was *Rorschach* also resigned to defeat, had each side opted for a kamikaze strike on the other?

I don't know. Big Ben got in the way just minutes before the explosion. That's probably why I'm still alive. Ben stood between me and that burning light like a coin held against the sun.

Theseus sent everything it could, until the last microsecond. Every recorded moment of hand-to-hand combat, every last countdown, every last soul. All the moves and all the vectors. I have that telemetry. I can break it down into any number of shapes, continuous or discrete. I can transform the topology, rotate it and compress it and serve it up in dialects that any ally might be able to use. Perhaps Sarasti was right, perhaps some of it is vital.

I don't know what any of it means.

CHARYBDIS

SPECIES USED TO GO EXTINCT. NOW THEY GO ON HIATUS.
—DEBORAH MACLENNAN,
TABLES OF OUR RECONSTRUCTION

"YOU POOR GUY," Chelsea said as we went our separate ways. "Sometimes I don't think you'll *ever* be lonely." At the time I wondered why she sounded so sad.

Now, I only wish she'd been right.

I know this hasn't been a seamless narrative. I've had to shatter the story and string its fragments out along a death lasting decades. I live for only an hour of every ten thousand now, you see. I wish I didn't have to. If only I could sleep the whole way back, avoid the agony of these brief time-lapsed resurrections.

If only I wouldn't die in my sleep if I tried. But living bodies glitter with a lifetime's accumulation of embedded radioisotopes, brilliant little shards that degrade cellular machinery at the molecular level. It's not usually a problem. Living cells repair the damage as fast as it occurs. But my undead ones let those errors accumulate over time, and the journey home takes so much longer than the trip out: I lie in stasis and *corrode*. So the onboard kick-starts me every now and then to give my flesh the chance to stitch itself back together.

Occasionally it talks to me, recites system stats, updates me on any chatter from back home. Mostly, though, it leaves me alone with my thoughts and the machinery ticking away where my left hemisphere used to be. So I talk to myself, dictate history and opinion from real hemisphere to synthetic one: bright brief moments of awareness, long years of oblivious decay between. Maybe the whole exercise is pointless from the start, maybe no one's even listening.

It doesn't matter. This is what I *do*.

So there you have it: a memoir told from meat to machinery. A tale told to myself, for lack of someone else to take an interest. Anyone with half a brain could tell it.

I got a letter from Dad today. *General delivery,* he called it. I think that was a joke, in deference to my lack of known address. He just threw it omnidirectionally into the ether and hoped it would wash over me, wherever I was.

It's been almost fourteen years now. You lose track of such things out here.

Helen's dead. Heaven malfunctioned, apparently. Or was sabotaged. Maybe the Realists finally pulled it off. I doubt it, though. Dad seemed to think someone else was responsible. He didn't offer up any details. Maybe he didn't know any. He spoke uneasily of increasing unrest back home. Maybe someone leaked my communiqués about *Rorschach*; maybe people drew the obvious conclusion when our postcards stopped arriving. They don't know how the story ended. The lack of closure must be driving them crazy.

But I got the sense there was something else, something my father didn't dare speak aloud. Maybe it's just my imagination; I thought he even sounded troubled by the news that the birthrate was rising again, which should be cause for celebration after a generation in decline. If my Chinese Room was still in proper working order I'd *know,* I'd be able to parse it down to the punctuation. But Sarasti battered my tools and left them barely functional. I'm as blind now as any baseline. All I have is uncertainty and suspicion, and the creeping dread that even with my best tricks in tatters, I might be reading him right.

I think he's warning me to stay away.

He also said he loved me. He said he missed Helen, that she was sorry for something she did before I was born, some indulgence or omission that carried developmental consequences. He rambled. I don't know what he was talking about. So much power my father must have had, to be able to authorize such a broadcast and yet waste so much of it on feelings.

Oh God, how I treasure it. I treasure every word.

I fall along an endless futile parabola, all gravity and inertia. *Charybdis* couldn't reacquire the antimatter stream; Icarus has either been knocked out of alignment or shut off entirely. I suppose I could radio ahead and ask, but there's no hurry. I'm still a long way out. It will be years before I even leave the comets behind.

Besides, I'm not sure I want anyone to know where I am.

Charybdis doesn't bother with evasive maneuvers. There'd be no point even if it had the fuel to spare, even if the enemy's still out there somewhere. It's not as though they don't know where Earth is.

But I'm pretty sure the scramblers went up along with my own kin. They played well. I admit it freely. Or maybe they just got lucky. An accidental hiccup tickles Bates's grunt into firing on an unarmed scrambler; weeks later, Stretch and Clench use that body in the course of their escape. Electricity and magnetism stir random neurons in Susan's head; farther down the timeline a whole new persona erupts to take control, to send *Theseus* diving into *Rorschach*'s waiting arms. Blind stupid random chance. Maybe that's all it was.

But I don't think so. Too many lucky coincidences. I think *Rorschach* made its own luck, planted and watered that new persona right under our noses, safely hidden—but for the merest trace of elevated oxytocin—behind all the lesions and tumors sewn in Susan's head. I think it looked ahead and saw the uses to which a decoy might be put; I think it sacrificed a little piece of itself in furtherance of that end, and made it look like an accident. Blind maybe, but not luck. Foresight. Brilliant moves, and subtle.

Not that most of us even knew the rules of the game, of course. We were just pawns, really. Sarasti and the Captain—whatever hybridized intelligence those two formed—they were the *real* players. Looking back, I can see a few of their moves, too. I see *Theseus* hearing the scramblers tap back and forth in their cages; I see her tweak the volume on the Gang's feed so that Susan hears it as well, and thinks the discovery her own. If I squint hard enough, I even glimpse *Theseus* offering us up in sacrifice, deliberately provoking *Rorschach* to retaliation with that final approach. Sarasti was always enamored of data, especially when it had *tactical significance*. What better way to assess one's enemy than to observe it in combat?

They never told us, of course. We were happier that way. We disliked orders from machines. Not that we were all that crazy about taking them from a vampire.

And now the game is over, and a single pawn stands on that scorched board and its face is human after all. If the scramblers follow the rules that a few generations of game theorists have laid out for them, they won't be back. Even if they are, I suspect it won't make any difference.

Because by then, there won't be any basis for conflict.

I've been listening to the radio during these intermittent awakenings. It's been generations since we buried the Broadcast Age in tightbeams and fiberop, but we never completely stopped sowing EM throughout the heavens. Earth, Mars, and Luna conduct their interplanetary trialogue in a million overlapping voices. Every ship cruising the void speaks in all directions at once. The O'Neils and the asteroids never stopped singing. The Fireflies might never have found us if they had.

I've heard those songs changing over time, a fast-forward time-lapse into oblivion. Now it's mostly traffic control and telemetry. Every now and then I still hear a burst of pure voice, tight with tension, just short of outright panic more often than not: some sort of pursuit in progress, a ship making the plunge into deep space, other ships in dispassionate pursuit. The fugitives never seem to get very far before their signals are cut off.

I can't remember the last time I heard music but I hear something like it sometimes, eerie and discordant, full of familiar clicks and pops. My brain stem doesn't like it. It scares my brain stem to death.

I remember my whole generation abandoning the real world for a bootstrapped Afterlife. I remember someone saying *Vampires don't go to Heaven. They see the pixels.* Sometimes I wonder how I'd feel, brought back from the peace of the grave to toil at the pleasure of simpleminded creatures who had once been no more than protein. I wonder how I'd feel if my disability had been used to keep me leashed and denied my rightful place in the world.

And then I wonder what it would be like to feel nothing at all, to be an utterly rational, predatory creature with meat putting itself so eagerly to sleep on all sides . . .

I can't miss Jukka Sarasti. God knows I try, every time I come online. He saved my life. He—humanized me. I'll always owe him for that, for however long I live; and for however long I live I'll never stop hating him for the same reason. In some sick surrealistic way I had more in common with Sarasti than I did with any human.

But I just don't have it in me. He was a predator and I was prey, and it's not in the nature of the lamb to mourn the lion. Though he died for our sins, I cannot miss Jukka Sarasti.

I can empathize with him, though. At long long last I can empathize with Sarasti, with all his extinct kind. Because we humans were never meant to inherit the Earth. Vampires were. They must have been sentient to some degree, but that semiaware dreamstate would have been a rudimentary thing next to our own self-obsession. They were weeding it out. It was just a phase. They were on their way.

The thing is, Humans can look at crosses without going into convulsions. That's evolution for you; one stupid linked mutation and the whole natural order falls apart, intelligence and self-awareness stuck in counterproductive lockstep for half a million years. I think I know what's happening back on Earth, and though some might call it genocide it isn't really. We did it to ourselves. You can't blame predators for being predators. We were the ones who brought them back, after all. Why *wouldn't* they reclaim their birthright?

Not genocide. Just the righting of an ancient wrong.

I've tried to take some comfort in that. It's—difficult. Sometimes it seems as though my whole life's been a struggle to reconnect, to regain whatever got lost when my parents killed their only child. Out in the Oort, I finally won that struggle. Thanks to a vampire and a boatload of freaks and an invading alien horde, I'm Human again. Maybe the last Human. By the time I get home, I could be the only sentient being in the universe.

If I'm even that much. Because I don't know if there is such a thing as a reliable narrator. And Cunningham said zombies would be pretty good at faking it.

So I can't really tell you, one way or the other.

You'll just have to imagine you're Siri Keeton.

ACKNOWLEDGMENTS

Blindsight is my first novel-length foray into deep space—a domain in which I have, shall we say, limited formal education. In that sense this book isn't far removed from my earlier novels: but whereas I may have not known much about deep-sea ecology either, most of you knew even less, and a doctorate in marine biology at least let me fake it through the rifters trilogy. *Blindsight,* however, charts its course through a whole different kind of zero g; this made a trustworthy guide that much more important. So first let me thank Prof. Jaymie Matthews of the University of British Columbia: astronomer, partygoer, and vital serial sieve for all the ideas I threw at him. Let me also thank Donald Simmons, aerospace engineer and gratifyingly cheap dinner date, who reviewed my specs for *Theseus* (especially of the drive and the drum), and gave me tips on radiation and the shielding therefrom. Both parties patiently filtered out my more egregious boners. (Which is not to say that none remain in this book, only that those which do result from my negligence, not theirs. Or maybe just because the story called for them.)

David Hartwell, as always, was my editor and main point man at Evil Empire HQ. I suspect *Blindsight* was a tough haul for both of us: shitloads of essential theory threatened to overwhelm the story, not to mention the problem of generating reader investment in a cast of characters who were less cuddlesome than usual. I still don't know the extent to which I succeeded or failed, but I've never been more grateful that the man riding shotgun had warmed up on everyone from Heinlein to Herbert.

The usual gang of fellow writers critiqued the first few chapters of this book and sent me whimpering back to the drawing board: Michael Carr, Laurie Channer, Cory Doctorow, Rebecca Maines, David Nickle, John McDaid, Steve Samenski, Rob Stauffer, and the late Pat York. All offered valuable insights and criticisms at our annual island getaway; Dave Nickle gets singled out for special mention thanks to additional insights offered throughout the year, generally at ungodly hours. By the same token, Dave is exempted from the familiar any-errors-are-entirely-mine schtick that we authors boilerplate onto our acknowledgments. At least some of the mistakes contained herein are probably Dave's fault.

Elisabeth Bear critiqued a semifinal draft in its entirety. Profs. Dan Brooks and Deborah MacLennan, both of the University of Toronto, provided the intellectual stimulation of an academic environment without any of the political and bureaucratic bullshit that usually goes along with it. I am indebted to them for liters of alcohol and hours of discussion on a number of the issues presented herein, and for other things that are none of your fucking business. Also in the too-diverse-to-itemize category, André Breault provided a west-coast refuge in which I completed the first draft. Isaac Szpindel—the *real* one—helped out, as usual, with various neurophys details, and Susan James (who also really exists, albeit in a slightly more coherent format) told me how linguists might approach a First Contact scenario. Lisa Beaton pointed me to relevant papers in a forlorn attempt to atone for whoring her soul to Big Pharma. Laurie Channer acted as general sounding board, and, well, put up with me. For a while, anyway. Thanks also to Karl Schroeder, with whom I batted around a number of ideas in the arena of sentience versus intelligence. Parts of *Blindsight* can be thought of as a rejoinder to arguments presented in Karl's novel *Permanence*; I disagree with his reasoning at almost every step, and am still trying to figure out how we arrived at the same general endpoint.

NOTES AND REFERENCES

Abridged references and remarks,[1] to try and convince you all I'm not crazy (or, failing that, to simply intimidate you into shutting up about it). Read for extra credit.

A BRIEF PRIMER ON VAMPIRE BIOLOGY[2]

Homo sapiens vampiris was a short-lived Human subspecies that diverged from the ancestral line about 700,000 years BP. *Vampiris* was more gracile than either Neanderthal or *sapiens,* although such differences were relatively minor since the lineage didn't persist long enough for great morphological divergence. However, *vampiris* did differ radically from *sapiens* in biochemistry, neurology, and immunology. Vampires showed heightened resistance to prion diseases,[3] for example (cannibalism carries with

---

1. Condensed due to publisher-imposed length constraints: see www.rifters. com for the unabridged verson.

2. The company responsible for these discoveries—and for the resurrection of vampires into the modern corporate environment—presented its findings at a convention prior to their disastrous "Taming Yesterday's Nightmares for a Better Tomorrow" campaign. A recording of that talk, complete with visual aids, is available at http://www.rifters.com/blindsight/vampires.htm.

3. Mead, S. *et al.* 2003. *Science* 300: 640–643.

it a high risk of prionic infection[4]), as well as to a variety of helminth and anasakid parasites. Hearing and vision were superior; vampire retinas were quadrochromatic, their fourth cone type being sensitive to near-infrared. Gray matter was relatively "underconnected" due to a relative lack of interstitial white matter, forcing cortical modules to become self-contained and hypereffective, and leading to omnisavantic pattern-matching and analytical skills.[5]

Most of these features can be traced back to a paracentric inversion on the Xq21.3 block of the X chromosome,[6] the mutation that initially defined the subspecies. It resulted in changes to genes coding for protocadherins, which are critical to nervous system development. However, some of these cascade effects were deleterious. Vampires lost the ability to code for γ-Protocadherin Y, whose genes are found exclusively on the hominid Y chromosome.[7] Unable to synthesize this vital protein themselves, vampires had to obtain it from their food; thus, Human prey comprised an essential part of their diet, but a relatively slow-breeding one. Normally this dynamic would be unsustainable: Vampires would predate humans to extinction, and then die off themselves for lack of essential nutrients.

Extended periods of lungfish-like dormancy[8] (the "undead" state) developed in response, as a means of reducing vampires'

4. Pennish, E. 2003. *Science* 300: 227–228.
5. Anonymous, 2004. Autism: making the connection. *Economist*, 372(8387): 66.
6. Balter, M. 2002. *Science* 295: 1219–1225.
7. Blanco-Arias, P., C.A. Sargent, and N.A. Affara1. 2004. *Mammalian Genome*, 15(4): 296–306.
8. Kreider MS, *et al.* 1990. *Gen. Comp. Endocrinol.* 77(3):435–41.

energetic needs. Vampires produced elevated levels of endogenous Ala-(D) Leuenkephalin (a mammalian hibernation-inducing peptide)[9] and dobutamine, which strengthens the heart muscle during periods of inactivity.[10]

Another deleterious effect was the "Crucifix glitch"—a cross-wiring of normally distinct receptor arrays in the visual cortex,[11] resulting in grand mal–like feedback seizures whenever the arrays processing vertical and horizontal stimuli fired simultaneously across a sufficiently large arc of the visual field. Since intersecting right angles are virtually nonexistent in nature, natural selection did not weed out the glitch until *H. sapiens sapiens* developed Euclidean architecture; by then, the trait had become fixed among vampires via genetic drift, and—suddenly denied access to its prey—the entire subspecies went extinct shortly after the dawn of recorded history.

SLEIGHT OF MIND

The Human sensorium is remarkably easy to hack. Our eyes acquire such fragmentary input that the brain doesn't so much *see* the world as make an educated guess about it.[12,13] "Improbable" stimuli, therefore, tend to go unprocessed at the conscious level. We simply *ignore* things that don't fit with our worldview.

---

9. Cui, Y. *et al.* 1996. *Brain Res. Bull.* 40(2):129–33.

10. Miller, K. 2004. Mars astronauts "will hibernate for 50 million-mile journey in space." News.telegraph.co.uk, 11/8/04.

11. Calvin, W.H. 1990. *The Cerebral Symphony: Seashore Reflections on the Structure of Consciousness*, Bantam Books, New York p. 401.

12. Ramachandran, V.S. 1990. In *The Utilitarian Theory of Perception,* C. Blakemore (Ed.), Cambridge University Press, Cambridge. p. 346–360.

13. Purves, D., and R.B. Lotto. 2003. *Why We See What We Do: An Empirical Theory of Vision*. Sinauer Associates, Sunderland, MA. p. 272.

Yarbus first discovered the saccadal glitch in Human vision, during the sixties.[14] Researchers have since made objects pop unnoticed in and out of the visual field, conducted interviews with hapless subjects who never realized that the person they *started* talking to was not the same person they *finished* talking to, and generally proven that the Human brain just *fails to notice* what happens around it.[15–18]

Most of the hallucinatory syndromes described herein are real, and summarized by Metzinger,[19] Wegner,[20] and/or Sacks.[21] Others (e.g., Grey syndrome) are invented, but based on actual experimental evidence. The judicious application of magnetic fields to the brain can allegedly provoke everything from religious rapture[22] to the experience of alien abduction.[23] Transcranial magnetic stimulation can change mood, induce blindness,[24] or target the speech centers.[25] Memory and learning can be

14. Yarbus, A.L. 1967. Eye movements during perception of complex objects. L. A. Riggs, Ed., *Eye Movements and Vision*, Plenum Press, New York, Chapter VII, 171–196.

15. Pringle, H.L., *et al.* 2001. *Psychonomic Bull. & Rev.* 8: 89–95(7).

16. Simons, D.J., and Chabris, C.F. 1999. *Perception* 28: 1059–1074.

17. Simons, D.J., and Rensink, R.A. 2003. *J. Vision* 3(1).

18. http://viscog.beckman.uiuc.edu/djs_lab/demos.html

19. Metzinger, T. 2003. *Being No One: The Self-Model Theory of Subjectivity.* MIT Press, Cambridge, MA. p. 713.

20. Wegner, D.M. 2002. *The Illusion of Conscious Will.* MIT Press, Cambridge, MA. p. 405.

21. Sacks, O. 1970. *The Man Who Mistook His Wife for a Hat and Other Clinical Tales.* Simon & Schuster, New York.

22. Ramachandran, V.S., and Blakeslee, S. 1998. *Phantoms in the Brain: Probing the Mysteries of the Human Mind.* William Morrow, New York.

23. Persinger, M.A. 2001. *J. Neuropsych. & Clin. Neurosci.* 13: 515–524.

24. Kamitani, Y. and Shimojo, S. 1999. *Nature Neurosci.* 2: 767–771.

25. Hallett, M. 2000. *Nature* 406: 147–150.

enhanced (or impaired), and the U.S. government is presently funding research into wearable TMS gear for—you guessed it—military purposes.[26]

Sometimes electrical stimulation of the brain induces "alien hand syndrome"—the involuntary movement of the body against the will of the "person" allegedly in control.[27] Other times it provokes equally involuntary movements, which subjects nonetheless insist they "chose" to perform despite overwhelming evidence to the contrary.[28] Put this together with the fact that the body begins to act before the brain even "decides" to move[29] (but see[30,31]), and the whole concept of *free will*—despite the undeniable reality of the *feeling*—begins to look a bit silly, even outside the influence of alien artifacts.

Electromagnetic stimulation is not the only way to hack the brain. Gross physical disturbances from tumors[32] to tamping irons[33] can turn normal people into psychopaths and pedophiles. Spirit possession and rapture can be induced through the sheer emotional bump-and-grind of religious rituals.[20] People even develop a sense of ownership of body parts that

26. Goldberg, C. 2003. "Zap! Scientist bombards brains with super-magnets to edifying effect." *Boston Globe* 14/1/2003, pE1.

27. Porter, R., and Lemon, R. 1993. *Corticospinal Function and Voluntary Movement*. Oxford University Press, New York.

28. Delgado, J.M.R. 1969. *Physical Control of the Mind: Toward a Psychocivilized Society*. Harper & Row, New York.

29. Libet, B. 1993. *Exp. and Theoret. Studies of Consciousness* 174: 123–146.

30. P. Haggard, P., and Eimer, M. 1999. *Exp. Brain Res.* 126: 128–133.

31. Velmans, M. 2003. *J. Consciousness Studies* 10: 42–61.

32. Pinto, C. 2003. "Putting the brain on trial." May 5, 2003, Media General News Service.

33. Macmillan, M. 2000. *An Odd Kind of Fame: Stories of Phineas Gage*. MIT Press, Cambridge, MA.

aren't theirs, grow convinced that a rubber hand is their real one.[34] A prop limb, subtly manipulated, will convince us that we're doing one thing while in fact we're doing something else entirely.[35,36]

The latest tool in this arsenal is ultrasound: less invasive than electromagnetics, more precise than charismatic revival, it affects brain activity without any of those pesky electrodes or magnetic hairnets.[37] In *Blindsight* it serves to explain why *Rorschach*'s hallucinations persist in the presence of faraday shielding—but Sony has already patented a machine that uses ultrasonics to implant "sensory experiences" directly into the brain.[38] They're calling it an entertainment device with massive applications for online gaming. Uh-huh. And if you can plant sights and sounds into someone's head from a distance, why not plant political beliefs and the irresistable desire for a certain brand of beer while you're at it?

ARE WE THERE YET?

The "telematter" drive that gets our characters to the story is based on teleportation studies reported in *Nature*, *Science*, *Physical Review Letters*, and (more recently) by everyone and their

34. Ehrsson, H.H., C. Spence, and R.E. Passingham. 2004. *Science* 305: 875–877.

35. Gottleib, J., and P. Mazzoni. 2004. *Science* 303: 317–318.

36. Schwartz, A.B., D.W. Moran, and G.A. Reina. 2004. *Science* 303: 380–383.

37. Norton, S.J. 2003. *BioMedical Engineering OnLine* 2:6, available at http://www.biomedical-engineering-online.com/content/2/1/6.

38. Hogan, J., and Fox, B. 2005. Sony patent takes first step towards real-life Matrix. Excerpted from *New Scientist* 2494:10, available at http://www.newscientist.com/article.ns?id-mg18624944.600.

dog.[39–43] (The specific idea of transmitting antimatter specs as a fuel template is, so far as I know, all mine.) Plausible guesses for *Theseus*'s travel itinerary were derived using the Relativistic Rocket,[44] maintained by John Baez; his use of magnetic fields as radiation shielding hails from research out of MIT.[45]

The undead state in which *Theseus* carries her crew is, of course, another iteration of the venerable suspended animation riff (although I'd like to think I've broken new ground by invoking vampire physiology as the mechanism). Blackstone *et al.* have induced hibernation in mice by the simple expedient of exposing them to hydrogen sulfide;[46] this gums up their cellular machinery enough to reduce metabolism by 90 percent. In light of this I considered rejigging the book to include mention of hydrogen sulfide, but ultimately decided that fart jokes would ruin the mood.

THE GAME BOARD

Blindsight needed an astronomical object that was relatively local and large enough to sustain a superJovian magnetic field, yet small enough to remain undiscovered for the next seven or eight

39. Riebe, M. *et al.* 2004. *Nature* 429: 734–737.
40. Furusawa, A. *et al.* 1998. *Science,* 282(5389): 706–709.
41. Carlton M. Caves, C.M. 1998. *Science,* 282: 637–638.
42. Braunstein, S.L., and Kimble, H.J. 1998. *Physical Rev. Letters* 80: 869–872.
43. http://www.research.ibm.com/quantuminfo/teleportation/
44. http://math.ucr.edu/home/baez/physics/Relativity/SR/rocket.html
45. Atkinson, N. 2004. "Magnetic Bubble Could Protect Astronauts on Long Trips." *Universe Today*, http://www.universetoday.com/am/publish/magnetic_bubble_protect.html
46. Blacstone, E., *et al.* 2005. *Science* 308:518.

decades. Yumiko Oasa has reported finding infrared emitters[47,48]—dimmer than brown dwarves, possibly more common[49,50]— that fit the bill. Very little is known about them (some are skeptical of their very existence[51]), so I pilfered data from a variety of sources on gas giants and brown dwarves,[52-68] scaling

47. Oasa, Y. *et al*. 1999. *Astrophys. J.* 526: 336–343.

48. Normile, D. 2001. *Science* 291: 1680.

49. Lucas, P.W., and P.F. Roche. 2000. *Monthly Notices of the Royal Astronom. Soc.* 314: 858–864.

50. Najita, J.R., G.P. Tiede, and J.S. Carr. 2000. *Astrophys. J.* 541(Oct. 1):977–1003.

51. Matthews, Jaymie. 2005. Personal communication.

52. Liu, W., and Schultz, D.R. 1999. *Astrophys. J.* 526:538–543.

53. Chen, P.V. 2001. Magnetic field on Jupiter. *The Physics Factbook*, http://hypertextbook.com/facts/

54. Osorio, M.R.Z. *et al*. 2000. *Science* 290: 103–106.

55. Lemley, B. 2002. Nuclear Planet. *Discover* 23(8).

56. http://www.nuclearplanet.com/

57. Dulk, G.A., *et al*. 1997. Search for Cyclotron-maser Radio Emission from Extrasolar Planets. Abstracts of the 29th Annual Meeting of the Division for Planetary Sciences of the American Astronomical Society, July 28–August 1, 1997, Cambridge, MA.

58. Marley, M. *et al*. 1997. Model Visible and Near-infrared Spectra of Extrasolar Giant Planets. Abstracts of the 29th Annual Meeting of the Division for Planetary Sciences of the American Astronomical Society, July 28–August 1, 1997, Cambridge, MA.

59. Boss, A. 2001. *Astrophys. J.* 551: L167.

60. Low, C., and D. Lynden-Bell. 1976. *Mon. Not. Royal Astron. Soc.* 176: 367.

61. Jayawardhana, R. 2004. *Science* 303: 322–323.

62. Fegley, B., and K. Lodders. 1996. *Astrophys. J.* 472: L37.

63. Lodders, K. 2004. *Science* 303: 323–324.

64. Reid, I.N. 2002. *Science* 296: 2154–2155.

65. Gizis, J.E. 2001. *Science* 294: 801.

66. Clarke, S. 2003. Milky Way's nearest neighbour revealed. *NewScientist.com* News Service, 04/11/03.

67. Basri, G. 2000. *Ann. Rev. Astron. Astrophys* 38:485–519.

68. Tamura, M. *et al*. 1998. *Science* 282: 1095–1097.

up or down as necessary. From a distance, the firing of *Rorschach*'s ultimate weapon looks an awful lot like a supermassive flare recently seen erupting from a brown dwarf that should have been way too small to pull off such a trick.[69,70]

SCRAMBLER ANATOMY AND PHYSIOLOGY

I am weary of humanoid aliens with bumpy foreheads, and of giant CGI insectoids that may *look* alien but who act at best like rabid dogs in chitin suits. On the other hand, the same principles of natural selection will shape life wherever it evolves. The challenge is thus to create an "alien" that lives up to the word, while remaining biologically plausible.

Scramblers are my first shot at that challenge—and given how much they resemble the brittle stars found in earthly seas, I may have crapped out on the whole unlike-anything-you've-ever-seen front, at least in terms of gross morphology. Brittle stars even have something akin to the scrambler's distributed eyespot array, and scrambler reproduction—the budding of stacked newborns off a common stalk—takes its lead from jellyfish. You can take the marine biologist out of the ocean, but . . .

Fortunately, scramblers become more alien the closer you look at them. Cunningham remarks that nothing like their time-sharing motor/sensory pathways exists on Earth. Our own "mirror neurons," however, come closest: They fire both when we act, and when we observe another performing the same action,[71] a characteristic cited in the evolution of both language

69. Berger, E. 2001. *Nature* 410: 338–340.

70. Anonymous, 2000. *Science@Nasa*, http://science.nasa.gov/headlines/y2000/ast12jul_1m.htm

71. Evelyne Kohler, E. *et al.* 2002. *Science* 297: 846–848.

and of consciousness.[72-74] Further, motor-control and motor-awareness systems may share the same cortical wiring.[75]

On Earth, anything that relied solely on anaerobic ATP production never got past the single-cell stage. Even though it's more efficient than our own oxygen-burning pathways, anaerobic metabolism is just too damn *slow* for multicellularity.[76] Cunningham's proposed solution is simplicity itself. (The catch is, you have to sleep for a few thousand years between shifts.) Scaling down even further, quantum-duality effects of the kind used in scrambler metabolism can exert significant impacts on biochemical reactions under physiological conditions at room temperature[77]; heavy-atom carbon tunnelling has been reported to speed up the rate of such reactions by as much as 152 *orders of magnitude*.[78]

And how's *this* for alien: *no genes.* The honeycomb example I used by way of analogy originally appeared in Darwin's little-known treatise[79] (*damn,* but I've always wanted to cite that guy); but more recently, a growing group of biologists are spreading the word that nucleic acids (in particular) and genes (in general) have been overrated as prerequisites to life.[80,81] Much biological

72. Rizzolatti, G, and Arbib, M.A. 1998. *Trends Neurosci.* 21(5):188–194.

73. Hauser, M.D., N. Chomsky, and W.T. Fitch. 2002. *Science* 298: 1569–1579.

74. Miller, G. 2005. *Science* 308: 945–947.

75. Berti, A. *et al.* 2005. *Science* 309: 488–491.

76. Pfeiffer, T., S. Schuster, and S. Bonhoeffer. 2001. *Science* 20 292: 504–507.

77. McMahon, R.J. 2003. *Science* 299: 833–834.

78. Zuev, P.S. *et al.* 2003. *Science* 299: 867–870.

79. Darwin, Charles. 1859. *The Origin of Species by Means of Natural Selection.* Penguin Classics Edition, reprinted 1968. Originally published by John Murray, London.

80. Cho, A. 2004. *Science* 303: 782–783.

81. Cohen, J., and Stewart, S. 2005. *Nature* 409: 1119–1122.

complexity arises through the sheer physical and chemical interaction of its components.[82-85] Of course, you still need something to set up the initial conditions for those processes to emerge; that's where *Rorschach*'s magnetic fields come in. No candy-ass string of nucleotides would survive in that environment anyway.

Nitpickers might say "Yeah, but without genes how do these guys *evolve*? How do they adapt to novel environments? How, as a species, do they cope with the *unexpected*?" And if Robert Cunningham were here, he'd reply, "Half the immune system actively targets the other half. It's not just the immune system, either; parts of the nervous system seem to be trying to, well, hack each other. The whole organism's at war with itself on the tissue level, it's got some kind of cellular Red Queen thing happening. Like setting up a colony of interacting tumors, and counting on fierce competition to keep any one of them from getting out of hand. Serves the same role as sex and mutation does for us." And if you rolled your eyes at all that doubletalk, he might just blow smoke in your face and point out that your own synapses are shaped by a similar kind of intraorganismal natural selection.[86] He might also refer to one immunologist's interpretation of exactly those concepts, as exemplified in (of all things) *The Matrix Revolutions*.[87]

82. Reilly, J.J. 1995. After Darwin. *First Things,* June/July. Article also available online at http://pages.prodigy.net/aesir/darwin.htm.

83. Devlin, K. 2004. Cracking the da Vinci Code. *Discover* 25(6): 64–69.

84. Snir, Y, and Kamien, R.D. 2005. *Science* 307: 1067.

85. Wolfram, S. 2002. *A New Kind of Science.* Wolfram Media. 1192pp.

86. Muotri, A.R., *et al.* 2005. *Nature* 435: 903–910.

87. Albert, M.L. 2004. *Science* 303: 1141.

SENTIENCE/INTELLIGENCE

Here's the heart of the whole damn exercise. Biggies first: Metzinger's *Being No One*[19] is the toughest book I've ever read (and there are still significant chunks of it I haven't), but it also contains some of the most mindblowing ideas I've encountered in fact or fiction. Most authors are shameless bait-and-switchers when it comes to consciousness. Pinker calls his book *How the Mind Works*, then admits on page one "We don't understand how the mind works."[88] Koch writes *The Quest for Consciousness: A Neurobiological Approach*, in which he sheepishly sidesteps the whole issue of why neural activity should result in any kind of subjective awareness whatsoever.[89]

Towering above such pussies, Metzinger takes the bull by the balls. His "World-zero" hypothesis not only explains the subjective sense of self, but also why such an illusory first-person narrator would be an emergent property of certain cognitive systems in the first place. I have no idea whether he's right—the man's way beyond me—but at least he addressed the *real* question that keeps us staring at the ceiling at three A.M., long after the last roach is spent.

Less ambitious, more accessible, Wegner's *The Illusion of Conscious Will*[20] doesn't deal with the nature of *consciousness* so much as with the nature of *will*, which Wegner thumbnails as "our mind's way of estimating what it thinks it did." And of course, Oliver Sacks[21] was sending us memos from the edge of consciousness long before consciousness even had a bandwagon to jump on.

It might be easier to list the people who *haven't* taken a stab at "explaining" consciousness. Theories run the gamut from dif-

---

88. Pinker, S. 1997. *How the Mind Works*. WW Norton & Co., New York. p. 660.
89. Koch, C. 2004. *The Quest for Consciousness: A Neurobiological Approach*. Roberts & Company, Englewood, CO. p. 447.

fuse electrical fields to quantum puppet shows; consciousness has been "located" in the frontoinsular cortex and the hypothalamus and a hundred dynamic cores in between.[90–100] (At least one theory suggests that while great apes and adult Humans are sentient, young Human children are not.[101] I admit to a certain fondness for this conclusion; if childen *aren't* nonsentient, they're certainly psychopathic).

But beneath the unthreatening, superficial question of what consciousness *is* floats the more functional question of what it's good for. It's telling to note that the nonconscious mind usually works so well on its own that it actually employs a gatekeeper to *prevent* the conscious self from interfering in daily operations.[102–104] (If the rest of your brain *were* conscious, it would probably regard you as the pointy-haired boss from *Dilbert*.) Sentience isn't

90. McFadden, J. 2002. *J. Consciousness Studies*, 9, No. 4, 2002, pp. 23–50.

91. Penrose, R. 1989. *The Emperor's New Mind*. Oxford University Press, New York.

92. Tononi, G., and G.M. Edelman. 1998. *Science* 282: 1846–1851.

93. Baars, B.J. 1988. *A Cognitive Theory of Consciousness*. Cambridge University Press, New York.

94. Hilgetag, C.C. 2004. *Sci. Amer.* 14: 8–9.

95. Roth, G. 2004. *Sci. Amer.* 14: 32–39.

96. Pauen, M. 2004. *Sci. Amer.* 14: 41–47.

97. Zimmer, C. 2003. *Science* 300:1079–1080.

98. Crick, F.H.C., and C. Koch. 2000. The unconscious homunculus. In *Neural Correlates of Consciousness—Empirical and Conceptual Questions* (T. Metzinger, Ed.) MIT Press, Cambridge, MA.

99. Churchland, P.S. 2002. *Science* 296: 308–310.

100. Miller, G. 2005. *Science* 309: 79.

101. Blakeslee, S. 2003. The Christmas tree in your brain. *Toronto Star,* 21/12/03.

102. Matsumoto, K., and K. Tanaka. 2004. *Science* 303: 969–970.

103. Kerns, J.G., *et al.* 2004. *Science* 303: 1023–1026.

104. Petersen, S.E. *et al.* 1998. *Proc. Nat. Acad. Sci.* 95: 853–860.

even necessary to develop a "theory of mind": you don't need to be self-reflective in order to track *others'* intentions[97]. Norretranders declared outright that "Consciousness is a fraud."[105]

Aesthetics might be an exception. Aesthetics seem to require self-awareness—it might even be what got the whole sentience ball rolling in the first place. When music is so beautiful it makes you shiver, that's your limbic reward circuitry kicking in: the same circuitry that rewards you for fucking an attractive partner or gorging on sucrose.[106] It's a hack, in other words; your brain has learned to get the reward without actually earning it through increased fitness[88]. It feels good, and it fulfills us, and it makes life worth living. But it also turns us inward and distracts us. Those rats back in the sixties, the ones that learned to stimulate their own pleasure centers by pressing a lever: remember them? They pressed those levers with such addictive zeal that they forgot to eat. They starved to death. They died happy, but they *died,* without issue. Their fitness went to Zero.

Aesthetics. Sentience. Extinction.

Which brings us to one last question, lurking way down in the anoxic zone: the question of what consciousness *costs*. Compared to nonconscious processing, self-awareness is slow and expensive[102]. (The premise of a separate, faster "emergency brain" lurking at the base of our primary one is taken from studies by Joe LeDoux, and others[107,108]). By way of comparison, consider the complex, lightning-fast calculations of savantes; those abilities are noncognitive,[109] and they owe their superfunctionality

105. Norretranders, T. 1999. *The User Illusion: Cutting Consciousness Down to Size*. Penguin Press Science. p. 467.
106. Altenmüller, E.O. 2004. *Sci. Amer.* 14: 24–31.
107. Helmuth, L. 2003. *Science* 300: 568–569.
108. Dolan, R.J. 2002. *Science* 298: 1191–1194.
109. Treffert, D.A., and G.L. Wallace. 2004. *Sci. Amer.* 14: 14–23.

not to any overarching integration of mental processes but to relative neurological *fragmentation*[5]. Even if sentient and nonsentient processes were equally efficient, the conscious awareness of visceral stimuli—by its very nature—distracts the individual from other threats and opportunities in its environment.[110]

But while many have described the various costs and drawbacks of sentience, few if any have taken the next step and wondered out loud if the whole damn thing isn't more trouble than it's worth. Of course it is, people assume; otherwise natural selection would have weeded it out long ago. And they're probably right. I hope they are. *Blindsight* is a thought experiment, a game of *Just suppose*. Nothing more.

On the other hand, the dodoes and the Steller sea cows could have used exactly the same argument to prove their own superiority, a thousand years ago: *If we're so unfit, why haven't we gone extinct?* Why? Because natural selection takes time, and luck plays a role. The game isn't over. The game is *never* over; and so, neither can there be any winners. There are only those who haven't yet lost.

Chimpanzees have a higher brain-to-body ratio than orangutans,[111] yet orangs consistently recognize themselves in mirrors while chimps do so only half the time.[112] Gorillas don't self-recognize at all. Similarly, those nonhuman species with the most sophisticated language skills are a variety of birds and monkeys—not the presumably "more sentient" great apes who are our closest relatives.[73,113] Such facts almost suggest that sentience itself could be a phase, something that orangutans

110. Wegner, D.M. 1994. *Psychol. Rev.* 101: 34–52.
111. Aiello, L., and C. Dean. 1990. *An Introduction to Human Evolutionary Anatomy*. Academic Press, London.
112. Povinelli, D.J. 1993. *Amer. Psychologist* 48: 493–509.
113. Carstairs-McCarthy, A. 2004. *Science* 303:1299–1300.

haven't yet grown out of but which their more advanced chimpanzee cousins are beginning to.

Of course, we don't fit this pattern. If it even is a pattern. We're outliers: that's one of the points I'm making. I bet vampires would fit it, though.

And finally, some very timely experimental support for this unpleasant premise came out just as *Blindsight* was being copy edited: It turns out the unconscious mind is better at making complex decisions than is the conscious mind[114]. The conscious mind just can't handle as many variables, apparently. Quoth one of the researchers: "At some point in our evolution, we started to make decisions consciously, and we're not very good at it."[115]

MISCELLANEOUS AMBIENCE (BACKGROUND DETAILS, BAD WIRING, AND THE HUMAN CONDITION)

Siri Keeton's radical hemispherectomy has been a common treatment for certain severe epilepsies for over fifty years.[116] The maternal-response opioids that Helen Keeton used to kickstart mother-love in her damaged son was inspired by recent work on attachment-deficit disorders in mice.[117] The multilingual speech patterns of *Theseus*'s crew were taken from Graddol, who suggests that a single "universal" scientific language would undesirably constrain the ways in which we view the world.[118]

114. Dijksterhuis, A., *et al.* 2006. *Science* 311: 1005–1007.

115. Vince, G. 2006. "'Sleeping on it' best for complex decisions." Newscientist.com, http://www.newscientist.com/channel/being-human/dn8732.html

116. Devlin, A.M., *et al.* 2003. *Brain* 126: 556–566.

117. Moles, A., Keiffer, B.L., and F.R. D'Amato. 2004. *Science* 304: 1983–1986.

118. Graddol, D. 2004. *Science* 303: 1329–1331.

The antecedent of Szpindel's and Cunningham's extended phenotypes exists today.[119] The spliced prosthetics that allow them to synesthetically perceive output from their lab equipment hails from the remarkable plasticity of the brain's sensory cortices: You can turn an auditory cortex into a visual one by simply splicing the optic nerve into the auditory pathways, if you do it early enough.[120,121] Bates's carboplatinum augments have their roots in the recent development of metal musculature.[122,123] I trawled the Gang of Four's linguistic jargon from a variety of sources.[73,124–126] Sascha's ironic denigration of TwenCen psychiatry hails from a pair of papers that strip the mystique from cases of so-called *multiple personality disorder*.[127,128]

I thought it would be cool to make one of the Gang a synesthete, reasoning that someone with cross-wired senses might have an advantage at deciphering the language of aliens with different sensory modalities; then, as I was putting *Blindsight* to bed, a paper appeared suggesting that synesthesias might be used to solve formal cognitive problems.[129] This validates me, and I wish it happened more often.[130]

119. BBC News. 2005. Brain chip reads man's thoughts. March 31. Story online at http://news.bbc.co.uk/go/pr/fr/-/1/hi/health/4396387.stm

120. Weng, J. *et al.* 2001. *Science* 291: 599–600.

121. Von Melchner, L, *et al.* 2000. *Nature* 404: 871–876.

122. Baughman, R.H. 2003. *Science* 300: 268–269.

123. Weissmüller, J., *et al.* 2003. *Science* 300: 312–315.

124. Fitch, W.T., and M.D. Hauser. 2004. *Science* 303:377–380.

125. Premack, D. 2004. *Science* 303: 318–320.

126. Holden, C. 2004. *Science* 303: 1316–1319.

127. Piper, A., and Mersky, H. 2004. *Can. J. Psychiatry* 49: 592–600.

128. Piper, A., and Mersky, H. 2004. *Can. J. Psychiatry* 49: 678–683.

129. Beeli, G., *et al.* 2005. *Nature* 434: 38.

130. I am by nature insecure. I blame bad parenting.

The fibrodysplasia variant that kills Chelsea was based on symptoms described by Kaplan *et al*.[131]

And believe it or not, those screaming faces Sarasti used near the end of the book represent a very real form of statistical analysis: Chernoff faces,[132] which are more effective than the usual graphs and statistical tables at conveying the essential characteristics of a data set.[133]

131. Kaplan, F.S., *et al.* 1998. The Molecules of Immobility: Searching for the Skeleton Key. *Univ. Pennsylvania Orthopaedic J.* 11: 59–66. Available online at http://www.uphs.upenn.edu/ortho/oj/1998/oj11sp98p59.html
132. Chernoff, H. 1973. *J. Amer. Stat. Ass.* 68:361–368.
133. Wilkinson, L. 1982. An experimental evaluation of multivariate graphical point representations. *Human Factors in Computer Systems: Proceedings*. Gaithersburg, MD, 202–209.